LADIES JUST WANNA GET GUNS

LADIES
JUST WANNA
GET GUNS

Christopher Hall
aka Maxlex

Podium

Cover design by Andrew Clark

ISBN: 978-1-0394-6523-7

Published in 2025 by Podium Publishing
www.podiumentertainment.com

LADIES JUST WANNA GET GUNS

CHAPTER ONE

Heartland

SULIEL

Suliel stopped the carriage to stretch her legs and take in the view. Her parents had stopped here on previous trips to the capital, and it felt nostalgic to look over the city before she reached it.

Back when this land was being settled—or conquered, depending on whom you asked—this site had been a simple portage point. A short, sharp cliff had interrupted the course of the river going north. Goods from the rich, unexplored northland needed to stop and be transferred to the ships below.

The ancestors of the royal family had been a mix of merchants and adventurers. They had parlayed the wealth that came from controlling trade into a fortified town, and then into a barony, recognized by the old Empire. When independence had come, and the fighting had started, they'd somehow managed to end up on top. All of it had come from their hold on this location.

That this spot should also be exceedingly picturesque was entirely a coincidence. The valley that the river had cut through the ridge was narrow and had steep sides . . . but not too steep. Just enough to show off the neat rows of houses that lined both banks. From here, she could mostly see the other side of the river and the two bridges that crossed it. She was currently above the city, looking down, but the walls were high enough that they blocked most of this side from view.

The walls were said to have been built by a Tier Four stoneworker of exceeding skill. Some said he'd reached Tier Five by the time they were completed. Whoever he was, he had built with the future in mind. After a hundred years, the city had still not spilled out beyond the walls. Suliel could see a few buildings outside the entrance to the lower city, probably inns for those who didn't make it before sunset, when the gates closed.

Suliel would make it in plenty of time. She was also taking the long way around, both so she could take in this view, and also so that she could enter Hightown directly. The guards at the high gates were much more accommodating of late arrivals, particularly when they were of noble birth.

Suliel took one last look and then returned to the carriage, giving the driver leave to continue. She smiled at the two elder gentlemen who had been her companions for this long, bumpy journey.

"Is it as you remembered, my lady?" Syon, her chamberlain, asked gently. Under other circumstances, she would have left him at home to mind to her affairs, but she needed him here. She hadn't stayed in her townhouse here for more than two years—well before she became the Baroness—and she was uncertain of the staff. Her mother was in the city somewhere and might well have used her influence to arrange something. She needed someone she could trust to be in charge of her household arrangements.

"Maybe a bit smaller than I remembered," Suliel joked. Both men chuckled dutifully.

Her other companion was also a consequence of her unusual circumstances. Delir Nyer, the Guild Master of the Kirido Adventurers Guild, had agreed to stay with her as her guest and provide advice. He wasn't strictly her servant—his first loyalty was to his guild—but he had served her father faithfully for years.

He had his own reasons to travel to the city, of course. He had recently obtained an antidote to the poison Kelsey had dosed him with and was looking forward to finding a cleric of sufficient stature to regrow his leg. Suliel had been happy to help—a carriage ride to the city was not easily procured for common folk.

Circumstances had also determined who Suliel *hadn't* brought. She already missed her maids. The inns they had stayed at had been able to provide help with dressing and her hair, but it wasn't the same. The townhouse should have a maid there. If not, Syon could hire one. Bringing one of the young girls who served her family was not something that Suliel was willing to countenance. It was far too dangerous.

As they approached the high gate, Suliel sighed in disappointment.

"Still hoping for a bandit attack, were you?" Delir said with amusement. "There's something perverse about hoping to be attacked."

"If we'd been attacked, it would most likely not have been bandits," Suliel reminded him. "It would have been a play from Mother. If we'd *been* attacked, I would have known what her play was. As it is, I'm left wondering if she knows how ineffective it would have been."

Suliel's escort was six men on horseback—the entirety of Kirido's cavalry contingent. Kelsey had taken to calling them mounted infantry. It seemed a contradiction in terms, but it did fit since they couldn't fire their guns or reload while mounted. Two more guards rode on the roof of the carriage.

Eight guards didn't seem like much, but Suliel was confident that they could hold off any reasonably sized bandit party. Or any party that *wasn't* bandits but was trying to seem as if they were.

Confident, but not certain. The new weapons had yet to be tested in real battle, which was the other reason Suliel had been hoping for an engagement.

They didn't have to stop at the gates. The crest on the side of her carriage was all the identification that Suliel needed. She could *probably* have directed the driver to her townhouse, but Syon's presence meant that she didn't have to rely on her faded memory of the route.

When they arrived at the gate to her house here, Syon got out and made his way inside, accompanied by the two guards who descended from the roof. Suliel waited impatiently. It seemed to take forever before the gates were swung wide by her men, and Syon came back.

"It is as the letter said, my lady. The staff are waiting to greet you."

Suliel sighed in relief, and the carriage moved forward to deposit her at her front door.

Perhaps "townhouse" was the wrong word to use here. It was what her parents had called the place, but the implications of the term were that of a small place. Suliel's townhouse had grounds, which contained a separate carriage house and stable. Since her family had been absent, the staff had been pared down to the minimum. All five of them now stood out front to greet her.

"My lady, may I present Arelon Marr, head of the household servants here," Syon said, indicating an older man with an upright and dignified posture. Silver streaks were running through his hair and neatly trimmed beard, but he still looked hale. Suliel activated *Nobility's Privilege*.

Arelon Marr, Level 18, Parents: Deceased, Single, Loyal, Human, Butler

"Your maids, Valia Tere and Shana Veris," Syon continued. The maids were young, Suliel supposed, but they were older than she was.

Valia Tere, Level 8, Parents: Alive in Bures, Single, Loyal, Human, Server
Shana Veris, Level 8, Parents: Alive in Bures, Single: One Child, Loyal, Human, Server

"Your cook and your groundskeeper, Jorven Kel and Darik Volen."

Jorvan Kel, Level 17, Parents: Deceased, Married, Two Children, Loyal to King, Human, Master Chef

Darik Volen, Level 16, Parents: Father Alive in Bures, Married: Three Children, Loyal to King, Human, Groundskeeper

Two older men, but they were easy to tell apart. Jorvan was a broad-shouldered man whose dark skin seemed to glow with vitality, while Darik looked to have spent his entire life outdoors. He wasn't unhealthy, but he looked weathered. His hair was cut so short, he might have well been bald.

Suliel was encouraged to see that everyone was loyal either to her or the King. Her trait only showed a person's primary loyalty, so it was no surprise to see that some of her servants held the King higher than her. She'd just have to keep in mind that she might be in third place, rather than second.

"Greetings to you all," Suliel said. "I'm going to be in your care for the next few weeks at least, so I won't keep you from your duties any longer. Shana, if you can get a bath ready. Valia, if you can make sure my room is ready and fetch me once it is."

The maids curtsied and rushed off into the building.

She looked at the two older men. "Darik, you can return to your duties. The grounds look wonderful, keep it up. Jorvan, I would like to share a meal with Arelon and my two guests in an hour or two, once I've rested."

The two men bowed and hurried off.

"Syon, Arelon, can you organize quarters for my men and see to the horses. Then come find me in the dining room."

"Yes, my lady," Syon said, bowing. Arelon bowed as well.

"And Delir, come with me. It's been a while, but I think I can find the dining room by myself."

Delir bowed and followed her awkwardly on his wooden leg. She would have helped him, but she knew it was a point of pride for him to walk unassisted. As she walked, she could feel the experience flow in. It wasn't much, but having new people acknowledge her, giving them orders . . . it all added up.

Suliel sank into the chair at the head of the table. Her memories had proved accurate.

<Nice place,> Kelsey commented via the bond. *<Nicer than your castle, even.>*
<Everything's cheaper in the city,> Suliel sent. *<It doesn't have to get shipped to the periphery.>*
<That shouldn't be true for much longer,> the dungeon said smugly. *<And your new place will be nicer still. I'm making notes.>*
<Sure, you do that,> Suliel said.

Kelsey had been talking for a while about building a new residence suitable for Suliel's status. Suliel had seen some plans, but she wasn't sure if suitable meant "bigger" or "covered in skulls." Negotiations were continuing.

Kelsey's meanderings distracted Suliel enough that she wasn't bored waiting for her two servants to return. Delir seemed happy to wait quietly as well. The pair came in together, bowed, and took seats at the table. Syon sat next to Delir, while Arelon took the opposite side. He looked nervous.

"First of all," Suliel said, "Syon is here as an advisor and as a familiar face. He's not taking over your role here, Arelon."

"I see," Arelon said. He stayed seated but gave a half bow. "May I ask what is so urgent that it can't wait until after you have refreshed yourself?"

"My mother," Suliel said grimly. "Where is she?"

"She hasn't been here," Arelon assured her. "Your letter made it clear how things stood, and she hasn't seen fit to challenge that. There have been some rumors that she's staying with Lord Brankil."

"Lord Brankil . . ." Suliel said consideringly. Then, "Wait—there are rumors about my family?"

"Some number, I'm afraid," Arelon said apologetically. "Some news of the events in Kirido has made it here through various channels. Through regular commerce, the Glimmered Lancers, and the judge—they've all let enough details slip for there to be a fervor of speculation about what's going on."

He coughed discreetly. "We were in a position to dispel some of those rumors, but we didn't feel empowered to be speaking on our lady's behalf. Many others have been less reticent."

Suliel grimaced. "That's about Kirido, but there are rumors about where my mother is staying?"

"Yes," Arelon said. "With so many rumors, there is great interest in the movements of the relevant parties, and your mother's movements are easy for locals to track. I wouldn't be surprised that your own arrival has been reported widely across the city by now."

"Well, it wasn't supposed to be a secret," Suliel said. "How accurate do you think the rumor of her whereabouts is?"

"It's quite likely to be accurate, my lady," Arelon said. "It comes from multiple sources, and there aren't any competing stories."

"I see," Suliel said. It did make sense. Count Brankil was her direct superior and was . . . distantly related to her through her mother. He had been one of the first nobles she was going to visit, but now . . .

This is part of Mother's play, Suliel thought. *She got here first, and now she's going to stand in my way.*

"Get some writing materials together for after dinner," Suliel ordered. "I'm going to need to send some letters—"

<Um, Suliel?> Kelsey sent. **<Not to interrupt or anything, but you're going to want to see this.>**

CHAPTER TWO

Wherever God Shines His Light

MEL

Mel perceived Riadi as an absence in Kelsey's senses. Kelsey knew everything that happened within her to a level that Mel, quite frankly, was not comfortable dealing with. Kelsey didn't know anything about the god, though. He stood out like a black hole in a white room. His voice, however, rang out normally.

"You interfered with Anton's destiny."

Kelsey turned slowly to face the god. As she did so, his form became apparent to Mel. Kelsey didn't know anything about the god, but light bounced off his projected form, and Kelsey knew about *that*. With a bit of effort, she could construct an image, just as if she had eyes. Riadi had taken the form of a human for some reason, one with blue skin and eyes that were all black. He was wearing ornate robes and a strangely shaped hat.

Kelsey's turn was a performance, of course. She didn't need to turn her avatar to see him. It was a performance that Riadi had *enabled* by appearing behind her. Admittedly, if he had appeared in front of her right now, he would have appeared in or over the fermentation tanks, the smelliest part of Kelsey's treatment process for "biologicals."

Riadi could have appeared at some other time. His choice of *now*, and *here*, had *meaning*. Mel could tell that it did, it was part of her nature. Grasping that meaning was beyond her, though.

Kelsey's reply was spoken casually, as if she wasn't talking to a god. That was normal.

"I've learned a few things since we last spoke," she said. "You're the one called Riadi, yes?"

Mel knew the answer, of course, but she was forbidden from giving Kelsey a response, even from reacting to the name. Riadi was under no such restrictions, however, and his glower seemed to be all the answer Kelsey needed.

"I must have missed the memo," Kelsey continued, smiling, "where you filled me in on Anton's destiny and how important it was that it be protected. Care to fill me in now?"

Riadi glared at Kelsey's immaterial figure but didn't say anything. Then he changed the subject. "You have also managed to evade the restrictions we put on you. Melandisae, why did you allow 'Kelsey' to take an avatar form?"

Mel squeaked as Riadi's attention turned to her. Running or hiding wasn't possible, so she would have to answer the question. "Because—because I was worried, master! With the attack on the town, and Anton arriving, I was worried about the plan!"

Riadi's black eyes narrowed. "What plan?" he asked.

"The plan with the heroes . . ." Mel said, glancing nervously at Kelsey.

"You shouldn't have known about that plan," Riadi said. "How did you know about the plan?"

"K—Kelsey explained it to me," Mel said. "She said that if Anton's parents were killed by the raiders, he wouldn't be . . . primed. We needed to check if they were okay, we needed to find out what happened!"

"That was the plan, right?" Kelsey said challengingly. "I figure they were going to find out that their old party member's leg could get healed if they made it down to the Sunless Sea and picked up some fish scales. One last run for old time's sake. Then they die, and oh looky! Anton's got a lovely heroic motivation. Kill the dungeon that killed his parents."

Riadi took a deep breath. "Melandisae, did you really think that this one was going to help with a plan that led to her death?"

"Well, of course," Mel said, puzzled. "It was one of your plans, so of course she'd want to . . ." She trailed off as she made the connection. "You tricked me!"

"You tricked yourself," Kelsey said. "I said that the plan was in danger, not that I cared about it."

"It was a contingency," Riadi said, glaring at Kelsey. "We needed safeguards in case you—"

"Got out of control?" Kelsey said, smirking. "Started spreading forbidden knowledge? You sound like every mad scientist and two-star general that ever starred in a monster movie. Given how all of them ended up, you should count yourself lucky that I'm not eating your face right now!"

Riadi made a gesture. "I don't expect you to understand—" he started.

"Then maybe don't waste your breath," Kelsey said coldly. "It's all water under the bridge now, anyway. Though I am curious. How is it that the Elitrans managed to kill off your little contingency? Someone else plotting against you?"

"We have influence, but we don't control Fate," Riadi said, glowering. "The raiders were a little stronger than they should have been, and the Baron decided to hold most of his forces on the inner wall . . ."

"So it's the Baron's fault that Anton's parents are dead?" Kelsey said. "How ironic."

"As always, it's more complicated than you are willing to allow," Riadi snapped.

"If you say so. Now, I doubt that you came down here to tell me what I already did, so what does bring you here?"

Riadi frowned. "I came to tell you to stop," he said.

"Stop what? Kelsey said lightly. "Just . . . freeze in place?"

"Stop what you're doing with Anton," the god clarified.

"*Am* I doing something with Anton?" Kelsey asked. "Aren't we just wandering the high seas, having a lark? Is there something *special* about what we're doing?"

Riadi grimaced with frustration. "I know you know about heroes," he said.

"Know what?" Kelsey asked. "I've heard stories."

"You're leading him," Riadi accused.

"Am I? Where? If anything, it's the other way around. Didn't you hear the oath?"

"I heard it," Riadi said, through gritted teeth.

"Then you know. *Take me where I need to go.* Nice and simple."

"Where do you need to go, Kelsey? What does that phrase mean to you?"

"Oh, you know," Kelsey said, smiling into the god's glowering face. "Tourist traps, sites of historical interest, that sort of thing. Besides, it's not what *I* think it means that matters."

"The thoughts of . . . *that entity* . . . are closed to me and mine," the god said.

"Well, I hope you don't think *I* have some way of communicating with it," Kelsey said. "Although . . . you must have set up something so that it can hear everything I say . . ."

"Only when—" Riadi cut himself off.

Kelsey waited for him to say more, and then grinned. "Only when a deal is in the offing, yes, I worked that out for myself, thanks. That's only half a communication channel, so there's no way I could be colluding with it, is there?"

Riadi took a deep, calming breath. "Just stop it," he said. "Stop what you're doing with the demesne above, stop what you're doing with Anton. You've upset things, but it will calm down if you just stop."

"Or what?" Kelsey said flatly. "You'll activate your contingency? Was that what these guys were?"

She held up Finnian's severed head. Riadi winced.

"Butin would not be pleased to see you treating his followers so cavalierly," he said.

"This is a copy," Kelsey said idly, "An illusion in this mind-space we're working in."

She waved a hand through it, and it dissolved into light.

"I'm preserving the real one in case I need it. I hear it would be of value to his church."

"It would," Riadi said carefully.

"I'll let Suliel handle the negotiations," Kelsey said confidently. "Girl's really coming along."

"Your relationship with her, her class . . . The system is adapting to the changes you've made."

"I did notice that," Kelsey said smugly. "I *am* curious where it is getting its information from."

"This is all going to get out of hand, quickly," Riadi said urgently. "All this time, we've nurtured the mortal races, kept them from—"

"Controlled them," Kelsey snapped. "Out of hand is the point. Out of *your* hands."

"And into yours? You think you will be a better custodian?"

"Oh no," Kelsey said, smiling. "All I'm bringing to the table is information. Eventually, that will start to spread outside my control and will be out of anyone's hands."

"They will turn on you, as *you* have turned on us. Gratitude is not a quality that mortals value."

"Maybe," Kelsey said. "It's kind of rich, though, that you expect them to be grateful for the scraps you feed them under the table when you sit in front of a whole roast dinner."

"You understand nothing of us and what we have done for these people."

"I understand enough. I understand being trapped, lied to, and coerced. If the mortal races feel like I do, I can well understand your fear at the thought of them getting even a scrap of real power. You fear for yourselves."

"You're threatening us?" Riadi said, shocked. "You want to make enemies of us?"

"You've been my enemies ever since you snatched me out of whatever afterlife I was supposed to have and stuck me in your killbox," Kelsey said angrily. "You're only noticing now?"

"You are making a mistake," Riadi told her. "Our ability to affect the physical world may be limited, but we are not without resources. We—"

"You know, this is really proving educational to Suliel," Kelsey interrupted.

Riadi stared at her. "You're communicating with the mortal right now?"

"I'm sending her a livestream of all of this. Didn't you know we could share senses now?"

"Miscreant! This visage is not for mortal eyes!"

"Really? Well, I would have thought it too late to change, but the longer you stand there complaining about it, the more of an eyeful the mortal gets."

The god disappeared. Kelsey smirked.

"I've wanted to do that for a long time," she said.

"Kelsey . . ." Mel said tentatively.

"Yeah?" Kelsey asked.

"Is Sue-leel still . . . looking? Can she see me?"

Kelsey blinked and looked at Mel for a long time. Finally, she stirred herself into motion again.

"She thinks you're very cute," she told Mel.

Mel frowned. "I don't want to hear that from a human."

"Because you hate humans?"

"Yeah."

Kelsey sighed. "You just haven't met enough nice ones. Give them a chance, will you? Okay, she's gone now."

Mel heaved a sigh of relief. "Kelsey . . ." she tried again.

Kelsey chuckled indulgently. "Yes, Mel?"

"Are you rebelling? Because rebelling is bad."

Kelsey sighed. "I'm not rebelling," she said. "Because they never had any authority over me."

"Yes, they do! They're the gods! They have authority over . . . they have authority!"

Kelsey ruffled Mel's hair. Just an illusion. Mel didn't have hair to be ruffled.

"They have authority over *you*, I'm pretty sure," Kelsey told her. "And their mortal followers have to do what they say, I guess. The rest of us, we're free to do what we want, no matter what they say."

"I don't think that's right," Mel insisted. "They'll punish you. They'll punish me!"

"Well, that wouldn't be fair now, would it?" Kelsey asked. "You did what you could to keep me in check."

"I did! You tricked me!"

"And the gods are always fair, aren't they?" Kelsey said. "They wouldn't punish you if you didn't deserve it. So you're safe."

"Oh! That's right!" Mel beamed, pleased that the logic was working out in her favor.

"Truth be told, I was a little worried when he showed up," Kelsey admitted. "But he left in too much of a hurry to do anything. Now, if he tries to do anything to you, it will look like he forgot. They don't like looking fallible, so I think we're fine."

"Silly Kelsey," Mel said. "You just explained why I'm safe. There's no need to worry!"

"There isn't," Kelsey agreed. "But if something does happen . . . I'm pretty sure the one place they can't reach is inside my mind."

"I'm not allowed to say," Mel said promptly. That was what she was supposed to say, and Mel always did what she was supposed to.

"Right," Kelsey said. "But *you* can. So if something happens . . . you can hide there."

"Only for as long as you're okay," Mel pointed out. The logic didn't protect Kelsey. She was doing bad things—and she was proud of it! Punishment was certain. Mel wasn't good at emotions, but she thought this one was *worry*.

"Kelsey," she said. "Wouldn't it be easier just to do what he said? All of that stuff sounds really hard to do, and I don't think the gods are going to like it."

"It might be easier," Kelsey agreed. "But this way will be more fun. And besides, I made a deal."

CHAPTER THREE

Into the Groove

SULIEL

What was that?> Suliel asked.

<*Your guess is as good as mine,*> Kelsey sent back. <*That's pretty much how all my discussions with gods has gone. They show up, make demands, get pissy, and leave.*>

A sense of smugness filtered down through the link.

<*I will admit, though,*> Kelsey sent, <*that he went away a little more upset than usual.*>

<*You just talk to the gods? Routinely?*> Suliel asked.

<*Not often. Maybe a dozen times in the last fifty years,*> Kelsey replied.

<*That's still a dozen more times than the Kingdom has seen,*> Suliel sent. <*The gods only talk to their chosen clerics, and even then . . .*>

She paused, thinking it through. <*Only when there is a problem for them to address,*> she finally added. Was Kelsey a problem that the gods needed to address? She certainly seemed to want to be.

<*What are you doing that he was so concerned about?*> Suliel asked.

<*Ah, that,*> Kelsey replied. <*Don't tell the gods this, but I don't really know. I'm mostly operating on doing what they don't want me to, with only the vaguest idea of what the end goal is.*>

<You must have some idea,> Suliel said. <I can't imagine you going to any kind of effort without a goal.>

<I know that it has to do with the hero's path,> Kelsey sent. <Or perhaps journey? I get the impression that there's a place involved. At that place, at that time, Anton will be in a position to do . . . something.>

Suliel thought about it. <We don't really speak of paths as having ends,> she finally sent. <No one lives forever, of course, but they just stop progressing on the path. It never ends.>

<I have reason to think that the hero's path ends,> Kelsey sent, along with a feeling of confidence. <The other paths are decoys.>

<False paths? All of them?>

<Maybe not false. They're worthwhile on their own terms, but the real prize is behind the hardest path.>

<Why would the gods not want us to get the real prize, whatever it is? Didn't they set up the paths in the first place?>

<I don't know,> Kelsey sent. <But I do know they're holding you back.>

<Me?>

<You people. Mortals. I haven't had a chance to read it, but your history is much too long. You should have made more progress, but you're being held back.>

Suliel thought back to what the god had said.

<He said we were being nurtured,> she sent. <Are we being held back . . . from hurting ourselves?>

<There's a case to be made that too much progress can be harmful,> Kelsey admitted. <But shouldn't he be making it? Shouldn't you be given a chance to decide for yourselves?>

<Like you gave us?> Suliel sent sarcastically.

<You've always had a choice,> Kelsey said. <It's just always been a bad one. Do you turn down the gifts I've given and live in hunger and fear? Or do you accept the risk of the unknown?>

Suliel didn't have an answer to that. Her people needed what Kelsey had given them. *She* needed the power of guns to survive.

Kelsey let the pause extend, then sent another thought. <Turn that choice around, look at it from my perspective. I could have held back, denied you the option of choosing. What kind of choice would that have been?>

Suliel opened her eyes. Kelsey's presence receded, and she looked at the worried faces of her advisors.

"Are you all right, my lady?" Syon asked.

"I'm fine," Suliel said. "I just . . . learned some things."

She thought back to what she had been doing. "Letters, right. I need to write letters to the King, to Lord Brankil, to—"

"You don't need to make a list," Arelon interrupted. "We can bring paper and ink to you once you've bathed and eaten, my lady."

"I suppose they can wait that long," Suliel allowed. "How are they to be delivered? We had more servants back home . . ."

"One of the servants can deliver them," Arelon said. "We all know the area quite well, especially if your correspondents are in Hightown."

"I want . . ." Suliel hesitated. "I want to make sure that they don't get intercepted."

Syon coughed. "We can have a guard or two escort the servant, my lady. They won't know the area, but they can keep an eye out for trouble."

"That's good, but . . . I'm worried about my security here. Can one of you, or perhaps our Sergeant, make an evaluation of how secure we are in this building?"

"Are you worried about anything in particular, my lady?" Syon asked.

"We had to deal with a Shadowblade not long ago, did we not?"

Arelon hissed in alarm. "Are you expecting further attacks from them?"

"No, not yet," Suliel said thoughtfully. "He wasn't targeted at me."

"Even so, my lady," Arelon said, "If you're concerned about Shadowblades, I can only recommend hiring adventurers for protection. No disrespect is meant for your own soldiers, of course, but Assassins specialize in getting past trained soldiers."

Delir snorted and spoke up for the first time. "Unfortunately, the Shadowblade we ran into was a *member* of the Adventurers Guild."

"Even so," Suliel said. "Can I prevail on you to investigate the guild and identify anyone whom we can trust enough to hire?"

"Of course, my lady," Delir said. "Will first thing in the morning be soon enough?"

Suliel nodded. "I'll give you a lift in the carriage. I need to meet with at least one church leader, as do you, I think."

"As you say, my lady," Delir said, glancing at his leg. "It would be good to get this fixed."

"Lastly, Arelon, I need to meet with some . . . traders? Craftsmen? I'm not sure exactly. Someone who buys glass and someone who buys cloth."

"I'll make inquiries, my lady."

"And . . ." Suliel paused. "The special trunk. Syon, can you make sure that is delivered to my room here?"

"I've already ordered it, my lady."

"Then . . . I suppose I can have that bath now."

* * *

Suliel started writing letters after dinner. She started with the one to the King, informing him of her arrival and placing herself at his disposal. Another letter went to the Master of Ceremonies at the King's Court. As a noble, she was entitled to attend court and mingle with the other nobles waiting on the King's favor. It wouldn't do to just show up, though. Once informed of her presence, the Master of Ceremonies could issue an invitation to her.

It was an involved process, but it gave the court time to notify the guards and prepare any other welcome they thought necessary. Suliel might have chafed at the convoluted process, but right now she welcomed anything that put off her appearance at court.

To Lord Brankil, she wrote a cautiously worded note, asking about his health and the health of her mother. The prospect of Suliel presenting herself to her liege lord was carefully hinted at, suggesting that she was at his disposal, but leaving unstated the possibility that he might not want her in his mansion while her mother was staying there.

It took her three tries to write that one. Kelsey tried to help, but unstated subtlety was not her specialty.

The churches she planned to visit, and the Adventurers Guild, didn't need a letter. They would see her when she arrived, and Suliel thought her meetings there would go better without advance notice.

The final letter that Suliel wrote was to her contact in the Rose Circle. Uncle Riadan had given her the name, cautioning her not to allow anyone to connect it to the Rose Circle. Suliel still wasn't sure if the Circle were traitors or devotees to the true Queen, but they'd had time enough to consider her offer.

Arelon looked up in surprise when he saw that letter. "Lady Seraphina? I wasn't aware you were in correspondence with her."

Suliel raised an eyebrow. "Do you consider yourself aware of all my correspondence partners?" she asked.

"Ah, no—not at all, my lady." Arelon bowed his head, stuttering with embarrassment. "It's just—the lady is quite prominent at court. It's quite an achievement for a . . . new noble like yourself to be connected to her."

"New? Or do you mean lowly country Baron?" Suliel pressed.

"Ah, I would never say—your rank is far in excess of my own—that is just—" Arelon stammered.

"As it happens, you are correct," Suliel said, waving away the man's attempt at saving himself. "I was given her name by a mutual friend who told me she would be a valuable ally at court if I could win her favor. Hopefully, he has found time to mention my name to her."

"I see," Arelon said, bowing low. "My lady, I apologize for my impertinence—"

"There is no need," Suliel said. "While I'm here, and possibly for some time after, my correspondence will go through you. If you are to serve me well, you need to know who I'm speaking to, and on what terms. It's part of the great trust I am placing in you."

"Yes, my lady," Arelon said, bowing again.

Suliel must have made an impression on the man, as she felt another trickle of experience flow in from the interaction.

<Nice,> Kelsey put in. *<Knocking him off guard makes the lie go down easier.>*

Suliel didn't reply, but she couldn't disagree. She did trust Arelon, but just hearing the name Rose Circle put him in danger, and her as well. It was necessary that he didn't know.

"I think that's all for today," she said aloud. "I think I'll retire for the night."

She had to announce it, because a lady didn't just wander off to bed. She needed to be helped out of her clothes, and her hair had to be arranged for sleeping. It was awkward because the maids were new, made more so by the fact that she still thought of this room as belonging to her parents.

She bore with it, keeping a neutral expression on her face with some effort. When it was done, she dismissed her maids with a smile and approached the special chest.

The key was hung around her neck, kept safe and close, not because of the value of the contents but to protect others from its discovery. Bending low, she unlocked the chest and looked down at the cargo she had transported all the way from home.

"*Bind Undead,*" she said. Then, "Rise."

With a muffled clatter, the bones in the chest rose up, forming themselves into a pair of skeletons. Each of them held a sword in one hand, and as Suliel watched, armor and helmets flew up and attached themselves to the animated bones. They stepped out of the chest in unison, and the hand that wasn't holding a sword saluted her.

<I hope you appreciate that I'm giving you my best,> Kelsey sent. *<Heckle and Jeckle, Toby and Moby.>*

<You never call them the same thing twice,> Suliel noted. *<And I know that you've got skeletons that carry guns.>*

<True, but we're not ready to show those off yet,> Kelsey answered. *<These two will have to do until you're able to control Tier Three undead.>*

<You also told me that these two were your most troublesome skeletons.>

<They seem different with you, though,> Kelsey replied.

It was true. In their experiments, the skeletons hadn't shown any sign of the creative misunderstanding of orders that Kelsey always complained about. She had to order them with words, but the link that ran between them seemed to impart an understanding that ran deeper. They did what she wanted.

She pointed at each skeleton in turn. "You watch the windows, you watch the door. Don't let anybody in until sunrise. Wake me if anyone tries to get in, and don't kill the staff."

<Man, I'd kill to have it that easy,> Kelsey sent. *<How do they know who the staff are?>*

Suliel didn't know, but she felt that the monsters understood. She felt . . . assurance come back down the link. She didn't know why, but she felt safe with them watching out for her.

<Well, good night,> Kelsey sent. *<Big day tomorrow.>*

CHAPTER FOUR

Looking Down the Barrel of a Gun

Ship! Ship sighted!" Zaphar called down from the masthead. Soraya looked up to see which way he was pointing and then looked through the *binoculars* that Kelsey had provided.

"These are very strange," she commented. "It's . . . a galley, and it's flying Elitran flags."

Kelsey grinned. "That means it's on, right?" she asked Anton, who sighed.

"Yes, it's on." He turned the ship so it pointed in the direction Zaphar had pointed. "Aris, can you let everybody know?"

Aris nodded and headed down to tell the girls on the mid-deck and belowdecks what was going on. Kelsey sauntered off to fetch her "gunner's apprentice," Cheia. No one else was willing to go near the deadly contraption on the ship's bow, despite Kelsey's best efforts. Cheia, though, was desperate to get a combat class before they made it home, and the . . . gun was the quickest way to rack up the required number of kills.

Aris had resisted, but Kelsey had pointed out that the safest place when the gun was firing was behind it. That had been the opposite of reassuring for everybody else, but Cheia was going to get her chance.

Soraya had to shift position to keep track of the galley. Anton wondered at the decision to put the steering wheel at the *back* of the ship. It was lucky that the sails were still furled. As it was, he had a decidedly impaired view of where they were going. If the sails had been in the way, he would have been practically blind.

"Are you sure you're all right with this?" he asked. "These are Elitrans, probably courls like you."

"It can't be helped," Soraya said. For a moment, she sounded lost and uncertain. Then she managed to return to her previously haughty tone. "Of course, it *could have been* helped, with a little foresight. Who plans an ocean voyage without bringing a map?"

"I'm sure we could have gotten one if we left as planned," Anton muttered.

"Not as easily as you seem to think," Soraya countered. "A map is a prized treasure of merchant families. The ones we're about to steal will be considered military secrets."

She broke off from examining their target long enough to glare at him before returning her attention to the binoculars.

"If I'd known the need, I could have copied one from my family's archive," she said. "But I didn't know—"

She stopped. "Wait, I think they've seen us," she reported. "They're turning and running."

"What!" Kelsey screeched from the other end of the boat. She came bounding back. "They can't do that, they're navy! They can't turn their tails and run!"

"Maybe it's the flag," Anton suggested.

"First of all, the flag is awesome," Kelsey said. "That's unrelated to anything going on, but it doesn't get said enough."

"That's a little rich, considering that you came up with it," Anton pointed out.

"Oh, I *wish* I came up with it," Kelsey said. "But that very important point is unrelated to the situation at hand. Since we've only just started flying it, no one knows what it means, and so no one can be running from it."

"I don't know," Anton said. "It kind of paints a promise, you know?"

He looked up at the black flag with white bones painted on it.

"I doubt they can make out such fine and awesome detail at this distance," Kelsey said. "*They* don't have binoculars."

"They *might* have a spyglass, though, and *Longsight* is a common trait among sailors," Soraya argued. "But I think another trait might be at work here. Warriors have traits that evaluate their opponents, yes? It seems that a ship's captain might have a trait that evaluates ships."

Everyone looked forward, to where Cheia was standing as close to the deck sweeper gun as she possibly could without touching it.

"That *might* show up on one of those senses," Kelsey admitted.

"So what are we doing?" Aris asked, coming up to join in the conversation.

"That's up to our captain, but them running doesn't really change the situation at all. We'll just have to run them down first, right?"

Anton paused before answering Kelsey. The main reason he'd insisted on taking a map from a military ship was that he knew how bloody it was going to get. If he was going to kill half a ship's crew, he wanted it to be a blow against the raiders who'd attacked his home, not a vicious attack on merchants who had done him no harm.

The Elitran navy was chasing him, or was supposed to be. He doubted that they just let their enemies go. When his target ran, it meant they feared him, which wasn't what he wanted.

On the other hand, nothing had changed. They still needed that map, and that ship was still part of the raiders' navy.

"We'll chase them down," he confirmed. "The engine isn't going to get tired."

He pushed forward on the throttle. Not to the level that Kelsey said was dangerous, but enough to notice the extra speed and noise.

"Yo ho ho," Kelsey said. "I'll just head back to the front then."

It didn't take long to catch up. The galley was fleeing, but the direction it was fleeing in wasn't good for the wind. Had it chosen to run with the wind, it might have made a difference, but that direction would . . .

Anton thought about it and realized that he didn't know where that direction would take them. With no land in sight, he'd lost all hope of keeping his bearings. He could only assume that there was no help for the galley downwind.

Now that they were closer, the captain must have realized that the galley had no chance of escape. It was turning, probably as fast as it could. Anton could see that this ship was smaller than the ones they had fought before. Still slim and deadly, but shorter. It only had about half a dozen archers on the bow deck, just now coming into view. If those were archers . . .

They were lighting sticks on fire, so they were probably archers.

"Ware incoming fire!" Kelsey called. Anton was already aware, but this was part of the system they'd worked out. He got ready to swerve.

"Arrows away!" Kelsey said. Anton might have needed the warning if the sails were up. As they'd planned, he jerked the wheel to the side and turned the throttle up a notch. Just for a bit, then he pointed the ship at the galley again.

A few moments later, the arrows plunged into the sea, well off to . . . starboard, Anton was pretty sure. At this range, dodging was pretty effective, but Anton wanted to get closer. Kelsey's gun could cover this distance, but Anton wanted more than a wild spray.

Really, what Anton wanted was for Aris to pick off the archers with her rifle, but naval battles had proved to be challenging. With both her and her target moving, her *Sure Shot* was unable to compensate. Anton wondered if she might be offered a trait to help with that in the future, but for now, she was hard-pressed to hit a target at thirty yards, even with the rifle.

Kelsey wasn't any more accurate, but the destructive nature of her weapon meant that increased inaccuracy just meant the devastation was spread over a wider area. That wasn't ideal, but Anton hoped that it meant he could finish the battle without too many needless casualties.

"Closing in to fire!" Kelsey yelled. "Everyone, make sure you have your protection on!"

Soraya dropped the binoculars and clutched her customized earmuffs to her head. They were supposed to stay in place without help, but she wasn't taking any chances.

Anton refrained from yelling a reminder about where to target. Cheia was behind the trigger, and she wouldn't target the slaves for levels or for laughs.

The deck sweeper roared. Anton felt the vibration in his bones and thanked Kelsey again for his helmet with sonic protection. It was a shorter burst this time, but it lasted long enough. In the blink of an eye, the bow platform where the archers had stood was gone, and the archers with it.

The enemy captain was trying to twist his ship around, to come about and stab Anton with that ram of his. The slaves on one side of the galley raised their oars, while the other side rowed twice as hard. It was a stunning display of coordination.

Anton felt sorry for them. It must take real skill to move a ship like that. Learned over years by every member of the crew, from the captain to the slaves and everyone in between. By contrast, Anton just had to turn a wheel and push a lever. His ship was shorter and his motive force was stronger. For all the skill of the other crew, they couldn't turn faster than he could.

In moments, they were behind the other ship. The crew manning the tiller must have seen death staring at them from the barrel of Kelsey's gun. As one, they let go of it. Some of them fell to their knees, others waved their arms frantically in the air. One of them jumped overboard.

"I think they're trying to surrender, Captain!" Kelsey called. Anton cut their speed, so they didn't overrun the boat. Cheia kept the gun pointed at them.

A few moments later, an order was given and all the oars were raised in the air. Then they started to get pulled back inside. The flags started to get pulled down.

"It seems we've won," Soraya said. "Now what?"

The next bit was a boarding party. It was Anton, Aris, and Kelsey in the lead, with Lena and Syrena, armed with pistols, backing them up. Cheia was left manning the deck sweeper, with strict instructions not to fire it for any reason. Just having her sweep the barrel back and forth was enough to terrify the crew on board.

Anton was the first to leap across. *Spider Climb* helped him keep his grip on non-vertical surfaces as well. He helped the others as they jumped across one by one. Aris was the only one to stumble and need catching.

"Wish I'd thought of that," Kelsey said, winking.

Anton ignored her and faced the assembled crew. They were a mixed bunch of courl and human, all in military uniform, but none of them had weapons visible. They flinched as he walked up, hand on his sword.

"Kelsey, captain's cabin," he ordered.

"Yessir!" Kelsey said, saluting. She had tied a brightly colored scarf around her head for some reason.

"Who's in charge?" he asked the crew in front of him. One of the courls stepped forward.

"I am, sir. Asim Darzan, captain of the Razorfin."

Anton swallowed. "How many casualties did you suffer?" he blurted. It shouldn't have been his main concern, but it was.

The captain's ears flicked back and forth and he glanced over at Cheia. "Four marines were killed, two were injured, but . . . I don't expect them to make it back to port. Two crew were injured from . . . flying splinters, and one galley slave had his leg broken when the deck fell on him. We threw a rope off the side for Talik, he's climbing back up."

Anton glanced over to where the wounded were lying. It matched up with what he'd been told.

"Is this everyone, then?" he asked. Not counting the wounded, there were ten crew in front of him.

"Master Koram is overseeing the slaves below."

"How many slaves do you have?"

"Two dozen, twelve oars a side. We only do three-day patrols, there's no call for support services."

"Support services?" Anton asked.

The courl looked nervous. "Ah . . . doxies, sir. For morale on longer voyages."

Anton tried not to let it get to him. They *didn't* have doxies on this boat. He didn't need to do anything about *that*. That just left one problem.

"Got it!" Kelsey said, coming out of the cabin. "There was some other stuff, I'm looking into it."

"Great," Anton replied. He gestured for her to step away from the crew with him.

"Kelsey," he whispered urgently. "There's twenty-four slaves on board! We can't fit them all on our ship!"

"No problem," Kelsey said. "We've got a perfectly good ship here for them, only slightly used." She glanced over at the splintered remains of the forward deck. "Some slight foxing."

"This ship?" Anton said. "But what happens to the existing crew?"

"You were planning on letting them go, I know," Kelsey said. "But it might be a better idea to give their victims a taste of justice."

CHAPTER FIVE

Road to Nowhere

Leaving Aris in charge up top, Anton headed belowdecks with Kelsey. He stopped short as soon as he got off the ladder, struck by the number of eyes looking at him.

The deck seemed too small for them all. Sitting neatly—no, chained in place—were two lines of twelve burly male slaves, staring at him intently. The deck wasn't lit well, and many of the slaves had dark skin, so in many cases, all Anton could see was their eyes.

A raised walkway ran down the center of the room, leading to the overseer at the other end of the deck. The overseer was a bald human of Elitran descent. He was standing next to the only light source, so Anton could see he was sweating heavily.

"Right. So." Anton hesitated, intimidated by the intent stares. "As of now, you're all free," he said.

There wasn't any reaction from the slaves, but the overseer spoke up.

"You can't do that!" he exclaimed and took a few steps forward.

"Can't I?" Anton said mildly and jumped up onto the walkway. Suddenly, he was on much more familiar ground. He sized up his opponent.

Bahir Koram, Level 18, Human, Overseer, Thug/Sailor/Overseer,
S: 21 T: 19 A: 20 D: 20 P: 15 W: 14 C: 8

The same level as Anton, but Anton outstripped him in abilities. Not that it was going to come to a fight.

"We just took your ship," Anton said. "Your captain is on his knees, and you're all alone. Are you really going to tell me what I can and cannot do?"

Kelsey came down and started shining a light around. From the cool, even brightness, Anton knew that she was using a normal light-stone.

The man stopped and thought about it. Then he blanched and took a step back. "No, no, sorry," he said quickly. "I can get the keys!"

"No need," Kelsey said. When Anton looked behind him, she was holding up her metal-cutting tool. "I suppose you'd like to do the honors?" she asked him.

Anton felt a surge of excitement from his class that he couldn't quite keep off his face. Kelsey grinned back in response.

Anton started with the chains that ran down each line of slaves. Each one ran through a loop in the slaves' collars, linking them together. Anton didn't bother going to one end. Instead, he severed the chains level with where he happened to be standing.

"Everyone stay seated!" Kelsey called out over the rattle of chains as the slaves quickly pulled the links free from their brethren. "The Baron will go around and remove your collars next, and it's quickest if you stay seated."

This time, Anton went to the front. Kelsey's tool sliced easily through the lock holding the collars closed. Each time the tool snicked shut, Anton felt a burst of experience. He hadn't gone all the way down the first line before he got his next level.

You have reached Level 4.
Applying Benefits for Level 4
Strength + 1
Toughness + 1
Agility + 1
Dexterity + 1
Perception + 1
Willpower + 1
Charisma + 1
Please allocate 2 free Ability points.
Please choose a Trait: Heroic Parry | Shattering Blow | Disarming Strike
    | Quick Attack

Strength and Toughness, Anton thought. He could still feel the difference between himself and the Champion al-Kadir.

Anton pondered his choice of trait as he went down the line. *Heroic Parry* was the only one he wasn't familiar with. Neither of his parents had taken it. He was tempted to, just to see what it did—and because it had Heroic in the name—but with *Stone Skin* and *Uncanny Evasion*, he was well set for defenses. *Shattering*

Blow did extra damage to objects. It applied equally well to armor, swords, and chains, but as long as Anton had this cutter, he didn't think it was needed.

Disarming Strike sounded fancy, but Anton's father had always steered him away from fancy. *Get the job done, don't go showing off,* he'd said. Which left *Quick Attack*. That had been one of his earlier choices, now re-offered, but it should pair well with his existing style. Getting it at Tier Three should make it even faster.

I choose Quick Attack, Anton thought, and kept on cutting slaves free. He didn't get to another level, but he was quite close when he was done. He paused to contemplate his status.

Anton Nos, Heroic Liberator, Level 4
Overall Level: 19
Paths: Delver/Adventurer/Heroic Liberator
Class: Heroic Liberator
Strength: 28
Toughness: 28
Agility: 22
Dex: 22
Perception: 20
Will: 17
Charisma: 14
Traits:
Delver's Discernment
Leaping Attack
Stone Skin
Uncanny Evasion
Sense Mana
Spider Climb
Unwavering
Sense Destiny
Quick Attack

The now ex-slaves had stayed quiet while he removed their collars. A few of them had stood up or called out, but they'd been pulled back by their neighbors. Now that he was done, murmurs were coming from every part of the hold.

"Let's go upstairs and talk this out," Anton said. He grabbed the overseer and pulled him along. "You too."

It took a while to get everyone organized, but Anton was looking over a crowd of sailors and freed slaves soon enough. His people were standing on the raised stern deck, looking over the disarmed marines and crew, standing in a tight knot. Surrounding them were the former galley slaves, casting angry glares at their former captors.

"First of all," Anton said, "is there anyone who speaks for you . . . oarsmen? A leader?"

There were mutters from the crowd, jibes being traded back and forth. Then one of the slaves got a clap on the back, driving him forward a step. A few more blows and pushes served to drive him to the front of the crowd. He was dark-skinned enough to be Zamarran.

Lioren Vaid, Level 22, Human, Galley Slave, Helot/Slave/Galley Slave, S: 33 T: 23 A: 12 D: 19 P: 12 W: 19 C: 7

Anton blinked at the man's Strength. Galley Slave must have a double-strength advancement.

"Lioren?" he asked as the man came closer. Lioren grinned.

"Been a while since I've heard that name," he said.

"Lion!" one of the ex-slaves called out. A few echoed him.

"That's what they call me," Lioren explained. "Elitran tounges aren't good with the sound, and they don't want to bother for a slave. So what's your plan here?"

"Uh . . ." Anton said. He hadn't had the chance to think this through. "Well, you're free now . . . so we're going to give you this ship, and you can go where you want."

Lioren frowned. "This is an Elitran ship. If the Empire catches us in their waters, they'll kill us for sure."

"Right, so . . ." Anton looked helplessly at Kelsey.

"So go north," Kelsey told them. "That's the quickest way out of Elitran territory. If you go north, you'll hit free lands eventually."

"I was born free," Lioren said, "But not everyone wants to leave their homeland. Especially not to an uncertain future."

"You could go to Kirido," Anton said. "That's my town . . . we can find a place for you there."

"Eh, these guys aren't going to be great at navigating," Kelsey said. "Asking them to find a town might be asking too much."

"Couldn't we follow you back?" Lioren asked.

"Oh, we're not going straight back to Kirido, we're—" Anton stopped as Kelsey hit him lightly on the shoulder.

"Don't give away operational details!" she said. "They might get captured and tortured to tell them where we're going."

"Should we have told them about Kirido, then?" Anton asked, alarmed.

"*That* particular chicken has flown its coop and has a lovely family in South

America," Kelsey said. "I'm certain that al-Kadir has told them about where you came from."

"Then . . . doesn't that mean that the Elitrans will be coming for Kirido?"

"Eventually," Kelsey said. "Don't worry, Suliel is putting something together for that eventuality."

Lioren watched their back and forth closely. "Maybe we *don't* want to go to Kirido," he said.

"Eh, there are pros and cons that you're going to have to weigh," Kelsey said. "Anyway, we are going to an unnamed Elitran town to . . . do some things. If *some* of you want to stay on Elitran soil and be runaway slaves, then we can give you a lift."

"That . . . doesn't sound very appealing," Lioren admitted. "But maybe someone . . ."

"Have the discussion, a vote maybe," Kelsey said.

Lioren turned to go back to his people but paused. "Wait," he said. "What about the original crew?"

"Hmm," Kelsey said. "I guess we're leaving them in your hands?"

"You can't do that!" Captain Darzan yelled from the mid-deck. "We surrendered in good faith! If you leave us in the hands of these savages, it will be nothing less than murder!"

Kelsey leaned on the railing, looking down at the captain. "I dunno, then. Anton, do you want to hold a trial and render your judgment? As a Baron, you've got the power to do that, right?"

"What? No! That's only in Kirido! Even if it wasn't, I don't have the faintest idea of how to dispense judgment!"

"A noble's prerogatives extend as far as his army does," Kelsey said. She pointed at the deck sweeper. "You've got that. I figure that means you can bring justice wherever you like. And I can get Suliel to help you with the technicalities."

She paused, holding one hand up. "She says she's not at all busy and happy to help, no matter how long it takes," she said.

"Can she hear you say that?" Anton asked.

Kelsey grinned. "Wouldn't be much point if she couldn't."

"Thank her for me," Anton said, "but that doesn't feel like justice, just violence. That said, I'm not comfortable with the old crew being executed by the new crew."

"Then you must protect us!" Captain Darzan called up.

"It's fine," Kelsey said to Anton. "They aren't going to kill them."

"We're not?" Lioren asked, pausing from climbing down.

"Nah," Kelsey said. "For one thing, having some Elitran officers as hostages will be super useful if you *do* get caught. For another, you guys are all rowers. You're going to need help crewing the rest of the ship. And finally . . ."

Kelsey grinned at Lioren.

"You're all sick of manning the oars, and this ship isn't going to row itself."

Lioren snorted but didn't reply. He just joined his fellows for the discussion.

Kelsey had to replenish the vessel's stocks of food and water. The galley held only three days' worth of food—it had been planning to make port the next day. That wasn't enough for the trip north. Kelsey had no problems with the water, but she balked at supplying enough food.

"I'm not made of crispy fried bread," she said. "I'm supposed to be feeding Kirido as well, and *someone* burned down my fields. And killed all my farmers."

"We need to give them something," Anton entreated her. "We can't leave them to starve on the high seas."

"What about fishing?" she asked. "I can make fishing rods, no problem."

She stared into space for a second. "Not *proper* ones, admittedly. For some reason, I don't have them in stock, and I'm not sure how they work. Oh, I guess it's just a rachet? Or . . . nets. Nets are probably a better idea, and a lot easier. I can do nets."

"Do you know how nets work?" Anton asked. "I never understood why the fish don't swim around them."

"If you've seen nets on the shore, they look like sheets," Kelsey said authoritatively. "But really, they're more like bags. It's hard for the fish to find the exit once they're in the net."

"Oh," Anton said. "Do you think they'll be able to use them? They're not fishermen."

"They'll get the hang of it," Kelsey said dismissively. "It's mostly pulling on ropes, for which they are eminently qualified."

When they left the galley, Lioren waved them goodbye while wearing the captain's hat. Kelsey had left them with freshly drawn maps, a compass, and lots of nets. As Kelsey had predicted, the crew had not been executed. Some of them were manning the sails, and the rest were down below. Right now, only four oars were moving, but Kelsey expected that to change.

"Eventually they'll figure it will go faster if they go back to the oars," she said. "Shorter shifts, sure, but they'll row harder just to show the crew up."

"You got what you needed from the maps?" Anton asked.

"Yeah," Kelsey said. "We know where we're going."

CHAPTER SIX

Straight to the Top

SULIEL

Suliel was still fuming at Kelsey's little prank. *Of course* she wanted to help Anton, but she was *busy*. And despite what Kelsey had said, baronial writ did not extend to the high seas. Out there, might made right, assuming any witnesses on the losing side were left at all.

What little she had learned from her father about administering justice had no application to Anton's situation. Kelsey had known that, and still put words in her mouth—because she found it amusing. At least Anton hadn't fallen for it. He'd looked good. He had gotten stronger, gained a few levels . . . and the salt air had roughened his skin, making him look even more dashing.

Suliel made a mental note to get some clothes made for her husband while she was in Bures. Unfortunately, making a note for later was all that she could spare the attention for. She was in a meeting.

Administrator Rallis bustled in and bowed low. "Lady Suliel!" he said. "I apologize for my tardiness. We don't often get visited by the nobility, and I had to brush up on my rules of etiquette."

"Please, don't concern yourself with such things," Suliel replied. "We country barons don't like to stand on ceremony."

Neither of them had said anything true so far, but that was only to be expected. The Merchants Guild was primarily a political organization. Officially, it existed to resolve disputes between trading companies, but it was only empowered to adjudicate between members. Most merchants avoided paying dues entirely, only joining up when they ran into problems they couldn't solve with fists or knives.

The merchants who *were* permanent members used the guild as a unified voice to lobby the King and the Privy Council. And since many nobles owned large trading concerns, the guild found itself dealing more with nobles than it did with the common merchants that were its ostensible reason for being.

Rallis was probably expecting Suliel to attempt to bribe him to get into the court sooner. What she was actually here for was entirely different, and much more in keeping with the guild's original charter. She hoped that wouldn't be counted against her.

"I'm here today to make the merchants of Bures aware of a fresh opportunity," she said.

"Oh?" Rallis said, his face noncommittal. Suliel ran through her pitch in her head, wondering when he'd realize that she wasn't offering him a bribe.

"Yes," she said. She gestured for one of her guards to put the sample case on the table between them. They weren't trained *enough* to get by at court, but with some coaching beforehand, they could manage to carry a case into a meeting with a merchant.

"Kirido has seen some changes," she said. "You may have heard rumors. Regardless of what you've heard, we have new goods for trade, of higher quality and quantity than our regular merchant trade can handle."

Word *was* getting out. Every merchant that stopped by would die rather than reveal the source of his goods, but they couldn't hide their existence if they wanted to sell them. Eventually, they'd sell the information to a larger concern who might send a scout out . . . but Suliel couldn't wait that long. She needed money to pay workers so that Kirido could expand faster . . . and for that she needed buyers.

Suliel indicated that the administrator should open the case. She thought *that* might have been the moment. His disappointed look told her that he might have thought she was bribing him with product instead of gold, but the case held only a few samples. His face quickly changed, though, as he took in what was on offer.

The first thing he reached for was one of the bottles.

"This glass . . . of such fine quality!" he exclaimed.

"Our dungeon has started providing a flux that makes higher-purity glass possible," Suliel stated. This *was* true, as far as it went. Kelsey had provided the flux, and higher-quality glass was going to be produced, in time. However, Kelsey's skeletons had made these samples. Suliel's workers had not yet developed sufficient skill with the electric furnace.

"Such ornate designs! How are they accomplished?" the man asked.

"I'm told that they're molded," Suliel said vaguely. Her workers had been provided with the molds; they would get there eventually.

"I see, I see," the administrator said. "And the price?"

"There should be a parchment in a pocket in the lid," Suliel said. Discussing prices was beneath her. The man retrieved it and pored over what was written on it.

"Very reasonable," he muttered. Suliel kept her smirk to herself. If those were the glass prices he was looking at, then the tremendous markup they'd added had gone unnoticed. Kelsey had been disgusted at the prices glass commanded, complaining that it was a crime to sell something so cheap for such a price.

Suliel supposed it must seem so when you didn't have to burn fuel to melt the glass.

"These plates," Rallis said. "At these prices . . . are you sure?"

"They aren't yet refined enough to sell to nobles," Suliel said. "But at these prices . . ."

"I see . . . an entirely new market," Rallis said. "And this . . ."

He picked up a small square of flat glass. *Unreasonably* flat and clear, in Suliel's opinion. It seemed unnatural. From the way Rallis was staring at it, he seemed to agree.

"This is glass?" he asked. "The clarity and . . . flatness are extraordinary."

"Those are samples, of course," Suliel said, trying to sound bored. "I'm told that we can produce sheets like that in any size up to four feet by five."

"Four by five?" Rallis exclaimed.

Suliel shrugged. "Of course, there might be problems transporting sheets of that size," she allowed.

"There might," Rallis agreed. Turning his attention to the cloth, he seemed almost disappointed. "It's quite fine, but not extravagantly so," he said.

"It's made from the same wool we've always used," Suliel said. "We're buying more of it now, and we have more efficient looms. If you look at the parchment, it should have the increased production levels we expect to maintain."

"I see." He glanced over the parchment again and nodded. "My lady, what was it you wanted from me?"

"As I said, I'm making an opportunity available," Suliel stated. "I want you to pass this on to whomever you think is best able to profit from this opportunity."

"Whomever *I* think?" Rallis said slowly. Suliel thought he might now be seeing his chance for profit.

"Of course," Suliel said. "Who knows the merchants of Bures better than the guild?"

"No one, of course," Rallis said, calculations flitting across his face.

"Of course, this opportunity is closing quickly," Suliel said. "Word is already spreading about Kirido's new circumstances."

"Of course." Rallis sprang to his feet and bowed again. "Rest assured, my lady, I won't waste any time finding your merchants. I assume they should go straight to Kirido and not seek your blessing?"

"That's right," Suliel said. "They'd have to negotiate with the craftsmen in Kirido anyway."

She rose to her feet. "You can keep the samples, of course," she said.

"You are most generous, my lady. If there is anything the Merchants Guild can do for you, please don't hesitate to ask."

"I'm sure we'll have many fruitful discussions in the future," Suliel said enigmatically. She wasn't sure what they'd be *about*, but Father had always said to leave doors open.

Suliel's next stop was to her dressmaker. Hers in the sense that she'd written ahead and commissioned a dress to wear at court. It was about time for a fitting. After that, she toured the other dressmakers and clothiers in town, looking to see if there was anything she liked. Anything she commissioned now wouldn't be ready by the time she was called to court, but she did find a nice shawl, and she managed to find someone who could make a pair of simple tabards in Kirido colors as a rush job.

She also got Anton's measurements out of Kelsey and commissioned some suitable clothes for her husband. And some that just looked . . . nice.

It was late afternoon by the time she got back to her townhouse, to see if there had been any replies to her letters. There was nothing yet from the King or the Master of Ceremonies, which was no surprise. She *should* have received something back from Lord Brankil, but the situation there was delicate. He might be having trouble deciding what to write.

There *was* a reply back from Lady Seraphina, inviting Suliel to take tea with her tomorrow afternoon. Suliel quickly penned a quick note accepting the invitation. Clearly, Lady Seraphina, or her backers, wanted access to the guns as soon as possible.

There was another letter, which came as a surprise. From Princess Elara.

Suliel stared at the letter for a long time. No one should be sending her letters yet. Lord Brankil was the exception, since he was her—or Anton's, rather—liege. She was supposed to be an unknown quantity until she was introduced. Replying to her mail was one thing, but for someone in the Court to contact her before her acknowledgment by the King, or her introduction to court, was stepping rather dangerously on the King's privilege.

Of course, a princess might be expected to get away with more than a baroness could. Suliel hesitated for a little longer and then broke the seal.

> *Dearest Suliel,*
>
> *I hope this letter finds you in good health and that you have not been unduly wearied by your journey. I am looking forward to your introduction to court with great anticipation and delight. I*

am sure you will be a breath of fresh air to this stolid and oppressive institution.

I have heard much of your esteemed qualities and your extraordinary class. The possibilities your discovery suggests are intriguing, and I am eager to make your acquaintance. In times such as these, it is vital that we, who share similar values and perspectives, find the opportunity to connect and support one another.

Do let me know when you are free for me to pay you a visit. I am certain we have much to discuss and would greatly value the chance to converse with you in a more private and relaxed setting.

With warm regards,
Princess Elara

Suliel read the letter twice but still didn't know what to make of it. It was friendly, at least. That didn't mean much—hiding your true intentions was a staple of court interactions—but it was better than hostile.

Suliel thought about the implications as she rang for Arelon.

"How soon can we be ready to host a princess?" she asked him. She didn't know what the additional requirements for hosting royalty *were*, but she was sure there were some.

Her Head of Household's eyes flicked to the letter on the desk.

"Princess Elara, my lady?"

Suliel smiled wryly. "Bold of you to suggest your lady is in contact with *two* princesses."

"You have proved very surprising thus far, my lady. If I might make a suggestion, inviting the Princess would not be wise. Especially before you've been recognized by the court."

"Advise all you like," Suliel sighed. She picked up the letter again and read out the offending line: "Do let me know when you are free for me to pay you a visit . . . it doesn't leave me much wiggle room, does it?"

Arelon's face twitched into a smile that didn't look very natural. "I see," he said. "In the face of a royal command, one can only bow. Though she did leave you room to delay."

"Mhm," Suliel said doubtfully. "Is there some *reason* that I might not want to associate with Princess Elara?"

Arelon's smile grew more strained. "It's not for me to say, my lady. For a mere servant to speak ill of my betters . . ."

Suliel rolled her eyes. "I'm not going to *report* you, Arelon. If there's some rumor, I need to know what people are saying. I won't take it as you endorsing them."

"Well . . . it's not so much rumors. After the business with her marriage, she's been speaking out about all sorts of things. Making unwelcome comments."

"She was married, wasn't she? To a princeling from the Tiatian Empire, wasn't it?"

Grandchildren and great-grandchildren of the Empress were still counted as princes in the Tiatian system, which meant that there were a lot of Tiatian princes.

"Aye, but he was assassinated before they could go back to Tiatia," the butler muttered.

"Oh," Suliel said. She wasn't surprised that she hadn't heard about the assassination. The marriage was something her mother had told her about; the murder would not have been considered suitable news to tell a child. "I'm surprised there wasn't a war."

"There were reparations, apologies. They found someone responsible, some envious suitor that got shipped back to the Empire."

"I see." Suliel reflected briefly on the poor man's fate. She wondered if he'd actually been responsible. "But *after* this business, you say . . ."

"Well, you see, there's some confusion as to whether she's a Zamarran princess or a Tiatian one."

"Both, I should think," Suliel said thoughtfully. "Does it matter?"

"Not in the grander scheme of things, perhaps," Arelon admitted. "But the crown has been reluctant to bring her into line, on account of her being Tiatian nobility . . . and the church doesn't want to denounce a member of the royal family."

"Does the church have reason to denounce her, then?" Suliel asked.

"She's made some criticisms of the way they operate," Arelon said guardedly.

Suliel referred back to the letter.

"'. . . this stolid and oppressive institution.' I thought she was talking about the court, but she's actually talking about the churches?"

"Probably both," Arelon said morosely. He was picking up on Suliel's excitement.

"Don't be like that, Arelon. It's not like I'm in a position to refuse overtures. Do you think we can be ready to host her for dinner tomorrow night?"

Arelon nodded. "If it's just an intimate one. She's not known for having an entourage."

Suliel pursed her lips in thought. "Make it for two guests, just in case," she said. "And inform Syon and Delir they'll be dining in the kitchen that night."

Arelon bowed. "As you say, my lady."

"And get someone ready to deliver letters," Suliel added. "I've got replies for Lady Seraphina and the Princess."

Arelon bowed again and left her to her correspondence. Suliel could hardly contain her excitement as she set pen to paper.

Dear Princess Elara . . .

Ghosts of Cape Horn

TYLA

Tyla watched, sitting cross-legged on the . . . stern, she thought the word was, deck of the *Whiskerwind* as the once-captives exchanged places with their ex-captors. Her contribution in the last fight had been limited to deflecting a few arrows with magic. She had been casting spells, so she had gained a small amount of experience, but she was still level twelve.

Tyla Greenwalker of the Padascar Tribe (Level 5)
Overall Level: 12
Paths: Padascar Hunter (Broken)/Doxy (Broken)/Apprentice Dungeon Witch
Strength: 11
Toughness: 8
Agility: 10
Dex: 17
Perception: 19
Will: 14
Charisma: 9
Traits:
Persistent Tracker
Silent Shot
Danger Sense
Sense Magic
Cast Lesser Charm

She was still conflicted about the magic part. Casting spells, twisting the world to her desires with an effort of will, *was* amazing. Every part of how she had been raised, though, told her it was wrong.

It didn't *feel* wrong. Tyla put her hand on the crystal sphere that had once been a numen and let herself feel what was inside. It didn't *feel* like the dead corpse of an almost-god, turned into fuel for Tyla's convenience. It felt . . . warm. It felt as though there was something that she could *almost* reach . . .

Then again, a fire was warm.

Tyla watched impassively as the galley detached from the *Whiskerwind* and headed on its own way. They were heading north, according to the conversations she had heard, while the *Whiskerwind* would be sailing south until the other ship was out of sight. Only then would they change to an easterly direction, heading for their penultimate destination.

Anton headed up to the stern deck to take control of the ship. Kelsey and Aris joined him as he swung the ship around. Not with oar or sail and not with magic. It was fire and steel that moved the ship, according to Kelsey. Tyla could only marvel.

Anton and Aris were having a discussion. Tyla tried to not be involved.

"Can you talk to her? She'll listen to you," Aris was saying.

"To me? She *adores* you, Aris. I don't know why you think I can talk her out of it," Anton replied.

"It's—I can't tell her *this*, Anton. I can't tell her not to do the same thing that I did."

"Well . . . you kind of did, before," Anton said.

"And she didn't listen!"

Tyla put the pieces together. This was about Cheia's new class. Cheia had finished her Doxy class during the fight with the galley and had announced that she'd been granted a Unique class: Original Gunner's Apprentice. This had set off an argument that was now, it seemed, continuing.

"It was . . . foolish of me to take Original Gunslinger," Aris said. "A mistake. I knew it, but I was desperate to save Cheia."

"It worked out, though," Anton said. He drew Aris in for a one-armed hug. Tyla wasn't watching them, but she could hear the rustle of cloth. Hopefully, Anton wasn't neglecting his steering duties in order to comfort his wife.

"And you know," Anton continued, "we're still a *little* bit desperate. Sensible people would have cut their losses and headed home by now."

"But it's her future at stake!" Aris said heatedly. "Tying her experience to that gun is going to cripple her in the long term."

"I don't know about that," Kelsey put in. "We're going to need the gun at least a few more times, and it's good for a *lot* of experience."

"And after that?" Aris asked. "When she moves on to Original Gunner at Tier Three?"

That was interesting. Tyla didn't know of any other Tier Two classes with Apprentice in the title. It might have something to do with how the deck sweeper was no ordinary weapon.

"A Gunner is part of a crew," Kelsey said. "In this case, a ship's crew. Doesn't that mean there will be a path to the Ship's Captain class?"

"Probably," Anton agreed.

"What use is being captain of a ship going to be to Cheia?" Aris protested.

"Suliel *has* said some very hurtful things about Kirido not having a navy, but I think I can talk her around," Kelsey said. "It would be a waste to just sink this boat when we get back."

"You're just going to give it to her?"

"Can't fit it inside me," Kelsey said. "I guess it will end up belonging to the barony, and your husband can assign who he likes to crew it."

"I don't really want Cheia to be a soldier, though," Aris said. "She was supposed to be a Baker, like Mum and Dad."

"Plans change," Kelsey said. "It's not unusual for younger relatives to take a position in a noble's army. I bet Anton could get her knighted if you wanted."

"I have no idea how to go about doing that," Anton said quickly. "And I think you'd be a better prospect, anyway."

"Suliel says that you have to get confirmed in your position," Kelsey said. "Which would require her not being declared a heretic, or whatever they do when the King doesn't like your class. And it would require us to be in Kirido! So there are a few steps."

"Let's leave the future to then," Anton said, "and focus on what we need to do now."

"Right," Aris said. She sighed. "I suppose I should tell her that it's all right to take the class."

Tyla kept her face expressionless, but she felt glad that Aris had been talked around to the right conclusion. The choices a person made about their class were a matter for that person. Parents sometimes interfered, but getting a class was the first step on the path of a person gaining their independence.

Aris headed to the bow to have that conversation, leaving Kelsey and Anton behind.

"I think we've gotten far enough away," Kelsey said. "You can head for Verheti now."

"Right . . . but what direction is that? How do I tell I'm going straight?" Anton asked.

"Oh, right, I haven't shown you how to use a compass yet," Kelsey said. This seemed interesting enough for Tyla to turn around. Kelsey produced a small device which she proceeded to attach to Anton's control pedestal.

"Now the compass points north," she said. "That's this black arrow. The rest of the device points where we're going . . ."

* * *

"Are you *sure* this is the city?" Soraya asked.

"Yes," Kelsey said shortly.

They weren't *in* the city. Kelsey had declared that sailing into port would be an act of suicide. Then she'd remembered the deck sweeper and declared that it would *actually* be an act of mass murder. After contemplating *that* for a few moments, she stated that she didn't have enough bullets and that they were probably best off sneaking in.

It hadn't been easy avoiding the maritime patrols. A few times, Anton's instincts flared up, and he'd taken them on a different route. Kelsey was convinced that it had helped, but it was hard to tell if they didn't see any ships. In the end, they'd sailed in at night, lights out, relying on Zaphar's Darkvision for navigation.

They hadn't been able to get close to the city that way. With the flag down, they might have passed for a regular vessel, but no one wanted to take the chance that they'd be inspected. So they got as close as they could and found a secluded cove they could anchor in. It was occupied by a village, but they said nothing about any hunt for escaped slaves and were happy to host the townsfolk who were staying behind while the infiltration team made their way to the city. For a generous fee, of course.

Kelsey didn't want to say where they were going. Nor did they want to appear they didn't know the name of the city that was a half day's walk away. So they had never *checked* that they were in the right place. Tyla was pretty sure that they were, though, and Kelsey was very sure.

They had approached the city at night; Kelsey had only scorn for the dangers of bandits or wild animals that might accost them while travelling in the darkness. The terrain was open and they had a good view of the city under moonlight. Even better when they took a turn with Kelsey's binoculars.

They were approaching from the east. Kelsey had overshot the city—entirely deliberately, according to her—and most of the city was on the west side of a river that flowed into the bay. On that side, there was a rise in elevation. The land ascended into steep hills, culminating in cliffs facing the sea. A large fortress occupied that high ground, overlooking the city, the river, and the sea.

The west side of the city was protected by a wall, but the riverside was open, given over to a series of piers and wharves. The only fortification on the east side of the river was a standalone tower, barely more than a gatehouse, that guarded the single bridge that crossed the river.

A few smaller buildings huddled around that gatehouse, but the east side of the river was mostly devoid of settlements.

"How do you *know* it's Verheti?" Soraya pressed.

"Have a little faith in my navigation skills," Kelsey said loftily.

"How can I?" Soraya asked, "You've never navigated a sea journey before."

"You'd think *having* my own private sea would be worth some respect," Kelsey said. "But since you ask, there is an easy, visible way to tell that this is Verheti."

"What is it?" Soraya asked, grabbing the binoculars off of Tyla. "Is it the flags? How do you know the heraldry of the Verheti Bey?"

"There are flags involved, but it's a different kind of pattern recognition at play," Kelsey said. "Since you've got the eyeglasses, take a look at the biggest ship at the docks."

"You don't mean . . ." Anton said. He looked out over the water and swore.

Tyla looked as well. She didn't have the binoculars anymore, but her eyes should be enough. At this distance, the boats were not so small that she couldn't identify them. The biggest one . . . looked familiar.

"It's the Pasha's barge," Anton said.

"Yeah, he's gotten ahead of us," Kelsey said. "Which means he's worked out that we're going after everyone that was captured in that raid."

"So he knows . . . he knows who we're going to rescue?" Aris asked.

"You got it. If we're lucky, he's kept them where they should be and has just set a trap for us. But . . . I bet he's stuck them either in that fortress or his palace—whichever one has the strongest cells."

"I doubt it," Soraya said. "If he wanted to deny them to you, he would simply execute them. A trap is possible."

"Is that how a courl thinks?" Aris asked.

"That is how a *ruler* thinks. A dozen slaves is nothing. Having a necromancer and a Heroic Liberator running around the Empire causing havoc is a real concern."

"That makes sense," Kelsey agreed. "He wants to catch or kill us, so he'll leave them out as bait."

Soraya sighed in relief. "Good, you can see his plan. Clearly, the only sensible course of action is to avoid the trap and leave the bait untouched," she said.

Kelsey chuckled. "Oh no, Anton, it looks like a trap. Surely we should give up and head back home with the captives we've managed to free."

Anton gave Kelsey an irritated glance. "No we won't be doing that," he said to Soraya. "I promised to save all the townsfolk. You think I can go back to Kirido, look their families in the eye, and say 'eh, I tried'?"

"They will understand," Soraya said urgently. "Don't throw our lives away on an impossible task."

"It's not impossible," Anton said. "That's what being a hero means. As long as they're not dead, Kelsey will come up with a plan and we'll rescue them."

Soraya made a frustrated growl. "Why did I agree to come along on this fool's mission?"

"I figure you were half hoping for a chance to slip away and make a new life for yourself," Kelsey said with a grin. Tyla noted Soraya's guilty start. "But that's not going to happen now."

"Not that it *was* going to happen, but what makes you say that?" Soraya said suspiciously.

Kelsey's grin got wider. "What are the chances that our old friend, the Champion of Denasti and your would-be fiancé, Salim al-Kadir, hitched a lift with the Pasha, and is even now waiting for a joyful reunion with the both of you?"

CHAPTER EIGHT

Hey Ladies

SULIEL

Before Suliel could take tea with a lady or host a princess for dinner, she needed to take care of her morning meeting.

"Thank you for seeing me at such short notice, Administrator Ragnor," she said once the tea was served. "I hate to intrude on your religious duties."

"It's no problem at all," the priest assured her. He was an older man, with dark, weathered skin and black hair going over to grey. His muscled shoulders were ill-suited to the satin robes he wore, and the scar on his face gave him a fierce countenance, at odds with his friendly demeanor.

"I relish the opportunity to get away from the paperwork and speak with an elegant and cultured young woman," he said.

Suliel smiled. "Does paperwork often require the use of a sword?" she asked, glancing at the short sword beside him. He had entered the room with it at his side, but he'd detached it from his belt with a well-practiced maneuver when he sat down.

"More often than you'd think!" he joked, "No, one of the requirements of Butin's higher clergy is that we all stand ready if called to the fight."

"I suppose that's to be expected of the God of War?" Suliel said. "We had a few of Butin's clerics pass through, and they were all armed, now that I think of it. It looks less strange on a traveller than an administrator, though."

"Indeed! But rules are rules." The priest patted the blade. "At least I'm skilled with a smaller blade—there's some poor fellows that need to carry a great sword with them into meetings. But I doubt you came here to hear of the travails of the ordinary working priest. How can I help you, my lady?"

"It's a matter of some delicacy, but ultimately an administrative one. I . . . heard that your church sought the bodies of your deceased clerics."

Quite a lot of Ragnor's jollity faded away and he frowned. "Where did you hear that?" he asked softly.

"We had an adventuring party come through, seeking to conquer Kirido's dungeon," Suliel said. She sipped some of her tea. "It included Finnian Stonehammer."

"The Stormguard," Ragnor sighed. "I had heard they were out of town, but . . . Finnian is dead, then?"

"He is, I'm afraid," Suliel said. "His surviving party member mentioned that there would be a reward for retrieving the body, but he was unable to make it out while carrying Finnian."

"Did the dungeon not consume the body, then?" Ragnor asked.

<Too greasy,> Kelsey quipped. Suliel carefully did not react.

"We were able to retrieve it later," she said. A true statement, if you knew exactly who *we* referred to.

"Your people managed what the Stormguard could not?" Ragnor asked, surprised. "I had not heard that Kirido's guild was so formidable."

"I can't speak to their relative skills," Suliel said, "But the delve was unauthorized, so the Stormguard weren't able to consult with the local experts before going down."

She sighed regretfully.

"If they had sought out advice, they might still be alive now."

"They're all dead?"

"All of them except for Draven Blackthorn, who is currently incarcerated. I don't hold out much hope for keeping him there once he has recovered. I shall be lodging a complaint with the guild here in the capital."

"I wish you luck, though I fear little will come of it," Ragnor said. "Ah, this is ill news. Finnian was well-liked, a pillar of the church. But to get back to your question, yes, we would like to have the body. May I ask about the condition?"

Suliel grimaced. A lady was not supposed to talk about these things. "Decapitated," she said grimly. "But both . . . pieces were placed in ice quite soon after death."

"Ice?" Ragnor said. "I would have thought salt, near the sea, but ice is better. Yes. What boon would you have of us in return?"

"Before that," Suliel said hesitantly, "may I ask . . . why?"

"Ah, well," Ragnor said. He looked away, scratching at his short beard. "I suppose it isn't a secret. You see, *Resurrection* is one of our God's gifts."

Suliel's teacup rattled on its plate. "What?" she asked.

"A Tier Five trait," Ragnor clarified. "It appears in some of the higher clerical classes."

"I . . . hadn't heard there was a fifth tier in Bures," Suliel said faintly.

"There isn't," Ragnor said. "Some of my superiors are getting close, though, and the chances of getting the trait are improved if devout members of Butin's church are . . . available targets."

"And then . . . this fifth tier can just resurrect *anyone?*"

"I wouldn't get my hopes up," Ragnor said gently. "High Priest Tharek won't reach Tier Five anytime soon, not unless there's a war, and we don't see one on the horizon."

<I get where you're going with this, Suliel, but resurrecting your dad is going to cause a lot of problems. You won't be Baroness anymore!>

<Be quiet,> Suliel sent back. <You still have his head, right?>

<I do,> Kelsey sent. <I'm not going to trash it and say I lost it. It's still a mistake.>

"Well," Suliel said aloud, "I couldn't ask for a reward for something so obviously beneficial for so many. It will be made available to you as soon as you are ready to pick it up."

<What! No! For free? Milk these guys for everything they're worth!>

"That is very generous of you," Ragnor said. "But please, at least accept a monetary reward. The possibility of resurrection is not something you should pin your hopes on."

"I don't need money," Suliel lied. "But . . . how much do you know about my situation?"

"I've heard some rumors," Ragnor admitted. "I'm not sure how much faith to put in them."

"My position is quite precarious," Suliel said. "I have to plead to the King that my class isn't an offense to him. My husband is still away on a quest. Even my mother has turned against me, and I am still a young girl, only just started on Tier Two. If I could ask the church for whatever political support they could provide . . ."

"Of course! Say no more. We're not exactly high up in the King's councils, not unless there's a war on, but come to us if there is something you need."

"Thank you, Administrator," Suliel said. "That is very reassuring."

<That's something, at least,> Kelsey sent.

<I was always going to ask for something like that,> Suliel sent. It was tricky

talking to Kelsey while negotiating a graceful and thankful goodbye, but she could handle the etiquette in her sleep. *<Right now, allies are far more important than any gold or trinkets they could give me.>*

She paused as she went through her final curtsy. *<But make sure you keep his head safe.>*

"I'm so glad you could make it!"

Lady Seraphina Levinscant was the soul of hospitality and courtesy, meeting Suliel at the door and drawing her in with charm and a sparkling personality. Suliel was completely overwhelmed and didn't think to protest when Seraphina led her to the back garden and into the midst of a crowd of gossip-hungry older ladies.

Suliel had expected a private meeting with Lady Seraphina, so she was quite surprised to find herself caught up in a gaggle of noble ladies. Introductions came in a flurry, and Suliel was barely able to keep up with them. *Nobility's Privilege* helped her keep track of who was who.

Karelle Roquefort, Level 12, Unmarried, Parents Deceased, One Sister,
Loyal to: Ranon Kalond IV, Human, Lady

Karelle was still young, but old enough that the fact she was unmarried was probably some sort of scandal. It could have nothing to do with her looks, which made Suliel feel inadequate, especially when she compared their respective figures.

Isolde Hartwell, Level 15, Married, Parents Alive, No Siblings,
Loyal to: Lord Percival Hartwell, Human, Lady

Dignified and graceful, Isolde was possibly the oldest lady here. Not *old*, mid-thirties at the latest, Suliel guessed.

Cecilia Redmond, Level 11, Unmarried, Parents Alive, Three Brothers,
Loyal to: Ranon Kalond IV, Human, Lady

Cecilia seemed the youngest of the group, only a year or two older than Suliel. She was slender, had dark mahogany skin, and smiled at Suliel as though they shared a secret.

Juliana Eversleigh, Level 14, Widowed, Parents Deceased, No Siblings,
Loyal to: Ranon Kalond IV, Human, Lady

Juliana definitely had some foreign blood in her family line. Her bronze skin marked her as coming from the Ett Confederacy, but Suliel didn't know where silver hair came from.

Marianne Valcourt, Level 16, Unmarried, Parents Alive, One Brother, Loyal to: Ranon Kalond IV, Human, Courtier

Another older woman, in her mid to late twenties, Marianne had caramel-colored skin that reminded Suliel of Anton. She had an engaging smile and was the first to address Suliel once the introductions had come to an end.

"How wonderful to meet you, dear! You must tell us everything that's happened; rumors have been swirling."

Flustered and overwhelmed, Suliel cracked immediately. Her Charisma might have risen to dizzying heights, but these ladies all out-leveled her, and Charisma was a lady's best weapon. They were so friendly and supportive that Suliel wanted to let them know everything that had happened, so she could finally get the frustration and anger she felt off her chest.

Well, not *everything*.

<Oi, let's not give away the secrets of the dungeon,> Kelsey reminded her.

The statement was meaningless—they'd never listed out what they were keeping secret—but it brought Suliel up short. She had been about to tell them how she got her class.

"I—I'm sorry, I can't discuss exactly *how* we managed to communicate with the dungeon," she said. She felt the ladies' disappointment as keenly as if they'd stabbed her, but they moved on to a different topic. They were *so* understanding.

Now that the bubble had been burst, she could understand what was happening as they pumped her for information. She couldn't *stop* them, not on her own, but timely interjections from Kelsey stopped her from revealing too much.

<It would probably work on me too, if I was there,> Kelsey told her. **<I don't think I appreciated Charisma enough.>**
<There's a trait available to the Lady class called Harden Heart,> Suliel sent back. **<I hope it's available to my class.>**

It wasn't long before they'd drained Suliel dry, and their attention could move on to the entertainment Seraphina had provided. When the conversation died down, a bard struck up a tune.

Suliel, and the others, were all transfixed by the tune. Bards had come to play for her father before, but none like *this*.

Beneath the moon's soft silver light,
Love's gentle whisper calls the night.

<Hey, where's Seraphina gone?> Kelsey asked her, jolting her out of the entrancement, *again.*

She looked around. Seraphina had been part of the questioning, but now she was . . . gone?

Suliel nearly jumped out of her skin when Seraphina took her hand. As soon as she did so, she appeared out of nowhere with a wide smile on her face.

"Shh!" she whispered. "We can have that private conversation now."

She led Suliel away, deeper into the garden, to a small gazebo, barely big enough for two. A table had been set for tea.

"I thought we—I mean, I—" Suliel babbled.

Seraphina giggled. "I could hardly host you for a private meeting, not when you're such a focus of attention. Bringing in those loyal gossips, though, makes you an entertaining centerpiece, just another clever distraction from mundanity. No one will suspect a thing, and no one will find us here."

"You're using *Private Assignation*," Suliel realized. "You were using *Unnoticeable Air* before."

"I see your mother taught you well about the different traits available to the Lady class," Seraphina said.

Suliel finally remembered something else her mother had taught her. *Nobility's Privilege.*

Seraphina Levinscant, Level 18, Unmarried, Parents Alive, Two Brothers, Loyal to: Ranon Kalond IV, Human, Courtier

"You're a courtier," Suliel muttered. "Should you even be hosting me?"

Courtier was a class that progressed from Lady, but it also required a court appointment. Not every Lady qualified.

Seraphina waved her hand dismissively. "It's fine," she said. "I may have an appointment, but this is nothing official. Just tea with a family friend."

"If you say so," Suliel said doubtfully. "But your status . . . it's wrong, isn't it?"

CHAPTER NINE

Reactionary Tango

Wrong?" Seraphina said with a smile. "How so?"

"It says you're loyal to the King," Suliel pointed out. *Nobility's Privilege* wasn't a complete accounting of a person's loyalties. It only showed your *primary* loyalty. In Suliel's case, it showed that she was loyal to Anton. As long as *he* was loyal to the King, or to someone else that was loyal, the King wouldn't take it amiss. A lady was expected to be loyal to her husband.

"If you're part of the Rose Circle," Suliel asked, "how can you be loyal to his Royal Majesty? At best, it should say that you're loyal to the *Kingdom*."

Seraphina tittered. "You can't always trust what *Nobility's Privilege* shows you," she said. "Try again."

Frowning, Suliel did as she said.

Seraphina Levinscant, Level 18, Unmarried, Parents Alive, Two Brothers, Loyal to: Roselie Kalond, Human, Traitorous Courtier

Suliel gave a little gasp. It was only two changes but it was shocking nonetheless. "That class is real?"

"I don't know what you could possibly mean," Seraphina said. "But our entire group is based on the notion that a status does not show the full story. It shouldn't surprise you that we make use of the same fact."

"I see," Suliel said, deeply troubled. The story of the Rose Circle was, indeed, that the King was actually false, with the ability to hide his status. *That* had been a shocking scandal. The idea that there were *more* in the capital that could do it was troubling. "That . . . doesn't make it any easier for me to trust you."

"I suppose not," Seraphina agreed. "Trust is a hard-won commodity in the circles you now find yourself in."

"I'd thought," Suliel murmured, "that if I could meet with R—your backer—that I'd be able to tell. If my father was right or if he was—"

She kept cutting herself off before she could say anything incriminating. *Private Assignation* might prevent eavesdropping, but only as long as some spy didn't have a better trait. Seraphina nodded in approval at her efforts.

I couldn't tell that you were a Traitorous Courtier, Suliel thought. That was too dangerous to say aloud. Only Kelsey heard it, but she didn't reply.

"Instead you find that your childish notions of right and wrong are inadequate for the world of adults," Seraphina said gently. "Don't take that the wrong way; we all start there. I have confidence that you'll manage the transition marvelously."

Suliel blushed at the kind words.

<Careful,> Kelsey sent. <When the person you're negotiating with compliments you, you're falling into their trap.>

The words sent a cold needle through the warmth that Suliel was feeling.

"And how does an adult see the world?" she asked.

"Through a prism of history and need," Seraphina said. "We are strangers; we don't have a shared history. But your father earned a great deal of trust with us, and you stand to inherit his legacy. Conversely, his trust of us is something you should consider as you look for a way forward."

"That's a weak connection," Suliel said. "In both directions."

"It is," Seraphina said. "We can hope to build on it, because our needs are clear. You need our support in court."

"And you need—" Suliel cut herself short.

"We do. So we understand each other. If we can both avoid betrayal, perhaps trust can grow."

<What do you think?> Suliel asked Kelsey.
<Eh, I'm not terribly fussed about who you sell the guns to,> Kelsey replied.

Suliel took a sip of tea, to give herself time to think.

"If we are to talk about Kirido supplying . . . glassware," Suliel said, hoping that she wasn't sounding like a fool. "We would need more than just support. We'd need coin as well."

"Of course. Glassware of this quality is worth the price," Seraphina said, smiling.

Suliel knew that by bringing up pricing, she was dropping her moral requirement. Was that a mistake? She really wanted to know if she was a traitor or a patriot. Kelsey must have felt her emotions because she sent a wordless feeling of support.

<Do you think I'm concerning myself with childish notions?> Suliel sent.

<Concerns about right and wrong aren't childish. They just seem less sophisticated to someone like her who sits firmly between the two.>

<Isn't that where you sit?>

<Oh no, I'm firmly in the wrong section> Kelsey sent, along with her amusement. *<Club Evil all the way.>*

"You understand your . . . competitor will want me to sell to them as well," Suliel said. "I can't afford to ignore them."

"We understand the position you are in," Seraphina said reassuringly. "Obviously we'll be keeping our purchase quiet, and as long as you can sell us *more* items than them, it shouldn't be a problem."

"I see. But we don't know how many items they will be demanding."

"At this point, no one knows how much . . . glassware you can produce," Seraphina explained. "If you can limit expectations, then we'll do our best to reduce their demands."

Suliel nodded. The guns were a new weapon, untested in a real combat. A few words from trusted courtiers could greatly reduce the interest shown by the crown. She would have to remember to seem more upset or his Majesty might suspect her of having another buyer.

She felt another pang of self-doubt and reached for Kelsey again.

<If you were truly evil, I wouldn't have been able to deal with you,> Suliel sent.

<Oh, you'd be surprised how reasonable evil can be. If I can get what I want by allying with you, why wouldn't I negotiate?>

<Like I am now? Am I evil?>

<You're asking me? Anton doesn't think you're evil.>

Suliel felt warmth flow through her. She didn't know if Kelsey was telling the truth, if she'd even asked Anton. But hearing the words, she knew it was what Anton would say.

"Two hundred . . . glass lanterns in two weeks," she said. "Five gold each, to be picked up from Kirido."

That was a ridiculous price for lanterns, but Suliel felt she had to keep the pretense going. The number of guns to make available was something that she and Kelsey had worked out beforehand.

"I'll try and limit . . . your competitor to fifty," she continued. "If I *can't,* then we can revisit that number."

Seraphina nodded slowly. "That seems acceptable," she said. "How soon can you have another shipment ready?"

"Another two weeks, assuming nothing has gone wrong with my—my husband's—investiture," Suliel said. "And we haven't discussed the . . . candles."

Seraphina frowned for a second before decoding her statement. "Ah. We had hoped to manufacture the candles ourselves."

"You might be able to," Suliel admitted. "I can't give you the recipe for the powder, but I'm told it doesn't involve any alchemy. The . . ." Suliel struggled to find the right word, before giving up.

"This," she said, taking out a round lead ball and handing it to the lady in front of her. "This might prove difficult for you to manufacture."

"It's so round," Seraphina said.

"The size needs to be exact too," Suliel said, parroting the words that Kelsey had told her. "Neither too big, nor too small."

"Hmm. It might be difficult. But I'm sure the blacksmiths have ways of making round things."

"I've been told that the easiest way is to build a tower and drip molten lead down a central shaft," Suliel said. "If the tower is high enough for the lead to solidify on the way down, you end up with lots of balls like this."

"The easiest?" Seraphina said, eyebrows raised. "It doesn't sound easy at all. And I don't recall a tall tower being reported as one of Kirido's new buildings."

Suliel shrugged, trying to cover her twitch at the news that Seraphina—that the Rose Circle—was getting reports about Kirido's construction efforts. "A long shaft works just as well," she said.

<They're going to want to make their own, just to make sure you don't have a hold over them,> Kelsey predicted. *<But they're not going to be able to beat our low, low prices!>*

"Our current price is one silver for one hundred . . . candles," Suliel said aloud. "If you prefer, we can sell the materials for a slight discount. It makes them easier to transport, but I suspect the costs of putting them together won't make it worth it for you."

<Can't beat the costs of a skeleton assembly line,> Kelsey gloated.

Seraphina nodded. "You may well be right, but we will see for ourselves," she said. "For now, shall we add . . . twenty thousand candles to the first order? And perhaps we can set up a weekly shipment without going through you each time."

"That should be possible," Suliel agreed. "I'll give you a letter of introduction to my people."

"Then we have a deal." Seraphina raised her cup as if she was giving a toast.

"Wait—" Suliel protested, "What can you tell me about the support I'll be getting?"

"Very little, I'm afraid. I can't give away who our members are."

"I suppose not," Suliel acknowledged. "But I can hardly supply your goods if I'm locked in a dungeon."

"That isn't going to happen," Seraphina assured her. "We can't show ourselves, but we can be very influential behind the scenes. You'll have your confirmation before the two weeks is up, I'm sure of it."

Suliel looked at her new partner doubtfully. "If you say so," she finally said. "Then, there's one thing I should mention, in light of our new relationship. Princess Elara invited herself to dinner with me tonight."

"Did she." Seraphina's face assumed a very complex expression that Suliel had trouble reading.

"Will that be troublesome?" Suliel asked. "It's not like I could have said no, but she didn't specify that it should be private. I could invite you if you wished."

"No . . ." Seraphina said slowly. "She no doubt *wants* a private meeting, so if you don't give her one, she'll just bully you for another dinner invite."

"Where does she stand on . . . this issue?"

"It's not really known," Seraphina said. "She *is* her father's daughter, but she was on quite close terms with her aunt before. Since her marriage, she's been . . . unpredictable."

"I see. So you don't know what she wants, then."

"I do not. Do let me know if you find out, won't you?"

Suliel laughed ruefully. That was the end of their negotiations for the day. There were a few small details to be ironed out, like where the coin was to be delivered, but that was all handled with a minimum of fuss. It wasn't long before Suliel was once again at the mercy of the gossiping ladies, but soon after *that*, she found herself in her carriage, headed home.

<Was that too easy?> she asked Kelsey. <Are we selling for too low a price?>

< There's the price it costs to make it and the price people are willing to pay for it,> Kelsey sent back. <We're way over the first, so it doesn't really matter if we're under the second.>

Suliel scowled. <We could have gotten more for it. That money goes towards hiring more men, and we need all the people we can get.>

The first sign that something was wrong was one of the horses screaming. Suliel had heard that sound once before and never wanted to hear it again. Almost in the moment she recognized the sound, there was a massive crash from outside of the carriage.

Then the crashing was coming from inside and all about, as one side of the carriage dropped to the ground, slewing to the side and throwing her. Suliel slammed into the seat opposite her and collapsed in a heap.

<What? What's going on? Suliel, are you there?>

Kelsey's voice was just a random noise in her head. Suliel didn't understand it, she didn't understand what was happening. She groaned.

<Suliel! Come on! Get it together! Look sharp, look around! What is happening?>

Suliel looked around, but nothing made sense. The cabin was all smashed up and lying on its side. From outside came a voice that she didn't recognize.

"Just go through the roof, then."

There was another crash, this time from the roof of the carriage. Suliel stared wide-eyed as an axe smashed a hole in what had been the roof. An unfamiliar face looked in.

"I *told* you she'd be fine," he said.

Suliel screamed, but it didn't drown out the voice in her head.

<Suliel! SULIEL! Stay strong for Anton!>
<Anton?> she thought back, her first coherent thought in a while.
<I can't believe that worked,> Kelsey said. *<Are you with me?>*

The man had pulled back from the hole, but only to make it bigger. The axe cut into the wood again, quickly enlarging the hole.

<Yes. I'm being . . . kidnapped? Attacked?>
<Something like that. Remember your gun?>

Suliel *did* remember. She reached into her sleeve and grasped the handle.

<Good. Remember that you've only got two shots, so make them count. Wait for one of them to get close. He's not going to be able to dodge if he's climbing through the hole, so get him then.>

Suliel wondered what happened to her guards. They were out there somewhere. Knocked out by the crash? Killed by whoever these men were?

The man returned. He didn't look like a rescuer or a guardsman. He looked like a thug. Suliel used *Nobility's Privilege.*

**Bram Bjornson, Level 16, Unmarried, Parents Dead, Three Brothers,
Loyal to: Aran Myaren, Human, Street Enforcer**

He looked back at Suliel and sneered. "Don't try anything now, little lady. One piece don't mean no damage."

He casually ripped off some more of the carriage roof and stepped carefully inside.

<Now,> Kelsey told her.

In one smooth motion, just as she had practiced, Suliel whipped out her pistol and shot the thug in the face.

CHAPTER TEN

Angel Flying Too Close to the Ground

SULIEL

G ah! My eyes!" The man fell back, yelling and cursing up a storm.

<He's not dead!> Suliel thought, panicked. <The gun didn't work!>

<Oh it worked,> Kelsey told her. <It's just a very small gun, and he must have a very hard head. Let's poke our head out and see what's going on.>

Cautiously, Suliel did so. The thug had fallen down on the cobblestones. Suliel's ears were still ringing from the sound of her shot, but she could hear him yelling without difficulty.

She saw one of her guards, fallen and unmoving as well. It looked as if he'd been thrown there when the carriage crashed. *Her other guard was . . . fighting,* she thought. She could hear steel clashing, but it was behind the carriage.

<Okay, this is good,> Kelsey said. <The Enforcer might not be dead, but he's out of the fight, and I don't like his chances long-term if he doesn't find a healer. Gunpowder burns are an underappreciated benefit of close-range fire.>

Suliel tried to let the words rush past her, but Kelsey wasn't done.

<Look sharp. That guy was talking to someone that you haven't seen yet. Look around until you find him.>

Suliel blinked. Someone else? She looked around wildly. She missed him the first time, but then she looked closer at some shadows. There was still light in the sky, but the high walls all around meant that there wasn't any direct sunlight anywhere near.

There was a man there, hiding. Not magically, just standing in the darkest spot.

Aran Myaren, Level ??, No Family,
       Loyal to: No One, Human, Cunning Ringleader

When he realized he'd been seen, he stepped forward. A wicked-looking curved blade appeared in his hand.

"That's a nice magical item you've got there," he said. As he stepped out of the darkness, his blade seemed to glimmer with reflected light. Suliel couldn't seem to look away from it. "I hate to do my own dirty work, but needs must as the gods decide."

<Hey! Snap out of it! Tell him to stay back!> Kelsey shouted in Suliel's mind.
<What?> Suliel asked. Her thoughts were scattered as if . . .

"Stay back!" she called out, pointing the gun in Aran's direction. He paused, his face twisting into a snarl.

"If we can't do this the easy way . . ." he called out. "Hurry up with that fool and get back here!"

<Looks like he's got some kind of mesmerizing trait.> Kelsey said. *<Tell him you're not afraid.>*

"I'm not afraid of you!" Suliel shouted. It wasn't the most confident of assertions, and the man didn't seem convinced.

"Oh you will be, once—" he broke off to look at his fallen minion. "Bram!" he barked. "Stop flailing around and get up!"

"I can't see, boss!" Bram said. He nevertheless started struggling to get to his feet.

"Do you stand on your eyes or your feet?" Aran asked acidly. "Get—"

"Boss! Trouble!" the shout came from the other side of the carriage.

"What *now*," the ringleader said. Before anyone could speak, the sound of an approaching carriage answered his question.

"Those fools were supposed to divert any—" He cut himself off as the new arrival came into view, veering around Suliel's wrecked carriage. It was already coming to a stop. It was well made, Suliel noted, but not especially decorated except for the small crest on the door.

"Move along!" Aran yelled at the carriage and gestured with his dagger. "There's nothing here that a pampered noble wants to get involved in."

Suliel frowned, trying to make out the design. It looked like—

Her view of it was cut off as the door opened and a young lady stepped outside. The first thing Suliel noticed was the lady's dress. Suliel could tell at a glance that it was at least the equal of the one that Suliel was wearing. The second thing she noticed was the rapier held in the lady's hand. Long and thin, it glittered even in the dim light.

"I don't believe I will, Mr. Myaren," the lady said. "It looks like something *very interesting* is going on."

Aran stared at the blade. "Anyn's teeth," he swore. "Two Tier Three items in the same holdup? It might be worth the risk . . ."

The lady raised an eyebrow, and two guards jumped down from the roof of her carriage.

"Ah, there you are," she said. "I was starting to think I might have to fight at something like even odds."

Aran cursed and spat on the ground. "We're running!" he called, immediately following his own advice.

"Not so fast," the lady said, dashing after him. Her guards winced but followed after.

"Boss?" the blind Bram called out, "I still can't see!" He'd gotten to his feet, but he was staggering from side to side. Aran left him behind without a word.

The lady lashed out at Bram with her sword as she passed him. Not a proper strike, just lashing out as if she was using a whip. Instead of crying out in pain, Bram just slumped.

"I'll just . . . lie . . . down . . ." he said. To Suliel's astonishment, he lay back down and seemed to go to sleep.

Suliel stared at him for a moment and then looked around. The street was empty. The fighting behind her had stopped as well.

"Eshara!" Suliel said suddenly, remembering her guard. Holstering her pistol, she ran over to her fallen guardswoman. She quickly determined that the woman was still breathing. The angle of her lower arm made it easy to tell that it was broken, but that was the limit of Suliel's medical knowledge.

Hearing footsteps approaching, Suliel looked up quickly, but it was just the lady and her guards.

"He got away," she called out as she approached. "Are your people all right?"

Suliel rose from where she had been examining Eshara and dipped into her deepest curtsy. This time, she had the presence of mind to use her trait and confirm what she already suspected.

**Elara Jiro, Level ??, Parents Alive in the City, One Brother,
Loyal to: Divided, Human, Dissident Noble**

"Your Highness," Suliel said. "You've arrived exceedingly early."

* * *

"I always like to arrive a few hours early to these things," Elara confessed. "It forces my host to greet me before they're ready."

It had been a few hectic hours since the holdup. Both of Suliel's guards had survived and been treated by a priest who had been fetched by one of Elara's guards. Suliel's carriage would never be *quite* the same but should be in working order in a few days. At least she hoped so. She had a lot of cash coming in, but those funds were earmarked for projects already.

"I had a prior engagement," Suliel complained. "What if it had gone on a little longer?"

"Oh, that would have been the *best*," Elara said smugly. "Your servants would have let me in, of course, and then I would have been here to greet you when you arrived."

Suliel smiled thinly. "I'm sure that would be very amusing for you,"

Inwardly, she flinched. That would have been a disaster. She had been looking forward to a few hours to decompress after her experience with Lady Seraphina and her coterie. The sudden terror of the attack hadn't been a *replacement* for an hour in a hot bath, but her interrogation by the gossip-hungry ladies now felt like an age ago.

"Perhaps, but there is a serious reason behind it," Elara said. "When I catch people off their guard, that's the only chance I get at seeing their true faces."

"You certainly caught me unprepared," Suliel acknowledged. "But does a princess have a reason to care about a backwater noble's true face?"

"I do," Elara said seriously. "You've seen my class."

"I did," Suliel said carefully. "I would have thought that class included measures to hide it."

"It does not," Elara said, "Or . . . if it does, I haven't been offered them. You see, Dissident Noble isn't a class like Scheming Chamberlain or Traitorous Courtier."

"It isn't?" Suliel asked, trying to hide her flinch at the mention of Lady Seraphina's class.

"No, it's right there in the name. I'm not scheming or traitorous. I *dissent*."

"I'm still not following," Suliel confessed.

"In order to dissent, I have to speak out. That makes hiding my class superfluous."

"Oh, I see. I can't imagine that makes your father very pleased," Suliel said.

"That would be a considerable understatement," Elara agreed. "But my . . . peculiar status protects me, as long as all I do is talk."

"I can't imagine it's a popular class, then," Suliel said.

"It isn't," Elara said. "There might be a few . . . backwater nobles who speak up from the safety of distance, but if you want to effect change, you need to be *here*, and very few can do that safely."

"I certainly couldn't," Suliel said. "Disagree with the King? Even if my life wasn't immediately forfeit, I need his approval for my marriage and inheritance."

"So few can," Elara mused. "Which is why I feel there is a need for me to speak up about injustices. As the only one who *can*, I feel a responsibility."

"I might feel more impressed with your nobility if your presence wasn't dragging me into the King's disfavor," Suliel said bitterly. "*I* can't afford to antagonize his Majesty."

"Is that a complaint?" Elara said. She spoke lightly and smiled, but the words sent a chill through Suliel's heart. She couldn't afford to antagonize *Elara*, either.

"Of course not," Suliel said with a false and brittle smile. "How could one such as I think to complain?"

Elara sighed. "I apologize. You need not fear my father's wrath. My antics are well known in the city, and everyone will know that you had no choice but to host me."

Suliel paused and the anger that was running through her stilled. The thought she was being *used* still burned, but Elara's regret seemed real. She remembered that her parents had told her that royalty never apologized. Elara had come right out and said it. Not "I owe," or "I should"—she had apologized.

"I accept your apology," Suliel said slowly, "in the spirit in which it is offered."

Elara sighed, this time in relief. "Thank you," she said. "I'm not as precious about it as my parents, but I don't apologize often."

"Noted," Suliel said. "But. It's not merely his anger I have to fear. I have a Sovereign class! When I go before him, I'm not only seeking acceptance. I need to beg forgiveness for trespass! Anything that gives him a negative view of me could mean my death!"

"I know," Elara said. "And I swear to you that my presence will help more than it hinders in that regard."

Suliel paused for thought again. Elara's words weren't necessarily untrue. Dissident or not, as long as the Princess wasn't *imprisoned*, she had influence in court. Her status as a *foreign* princess only increased her clout. The question was . . .

"Why would you spend your influence on me?" Suliel asked.

"Because I think that you can help me," Elara replied.

Suliel blinked. She could help a princess? "That's . . . going to require more of an explanation."

"Well, I'm not sure yet if you can," Elara temporized. "Before I go into that, might I learn more about you?"

Suliel knew she couldn't refuse. "Our evening meal is about to be served," she said. "I suppose personal history should make a fine dinner conversation topic."

Over food, which Elara praised effusively, even though she must be used to more refined fare, Suliel told the story of her father's death and her marriage. Which was one way to bookend the events that had occurred.

Elara let her talk without interruption, only speaking up when Suliel got to the end.

"I read the report of your mother's tale," she said. "There are surprisingly few contradictions between the two."

Suliel smiled ruefully. "It mainly hinges on our *interpretation* of the facts, I imagine," she said. "Though I doubt my mother mentioned that she was being influenced by Magister Tikin."

"She did not," Elara confirmed. "As you say, the difference lies in how you view the dungeon. She sees it as a purely malevolent force, while you see it as an entity that can be negotiated with."

"A person," Suliel said. "One that has been at war with the living, but is willing to accept a peace treaty."

"And you say *all* dungeons are similarly intelligent?"

"As I understand it, all dungeons have the potential to *develop* intelligence," Suliel said.

"Interesting. That's not generally known, though there have been rumors and speculation about it."

"The Adventurers Guild seems to know it for a fact, though Guild Master Nyer wouldn't confirm it until I had already met Kelsey. I don't know why they're keeping it a secret."

<Wizards,> Kelsey sent, speaking up for the first time.

"What?" Suliel said, startled.
"What?" Elara asked, confused.

<Wizards have got a vested interest in harvesting dungeon cores,> Kelsey said. <They must be the ones suppressing the information.>

Elara was watching Suliel closely. "Is something wrong? she asked.

CHAPTER ELEVEN

Modern Times Blues

N othing's wrong, your Highness," Suliel said. For a moment, she considered, and then discarded, the idea of keeping her link a secret. "One of my traits grants me a link to Kirido's dungeon, and it just . . . interjected."

<You can just call me Kelsey, you know.>
<I won't,> Suliel sent back. *<Not to the Princess, it sounds ridiculous. The Dungeon of the Endless Battle isn't much better.>*

"Interesting," Elara said. "A linking trait so early in Tier Two? An Epic class indeed."

"I'm sure it's nothing compared to some of yours," Suliel mumbled. The Princess might only have a Rare class, but she was twice Suliel's level.

"Perhaps," Elara agreed, swirling the remains of a fine vintage in her goblet. "What's it like, being linked to a dungeon?"

"It's a person," Suliel repeated. "A strange one to be sure, irreverent and lacking in respect for human life. It has a few people that it cares about and goals that it seeks."

"Such as?"

"Survival, for one," Suliel said carefully. She didn't even want to hint at what Kelsey's conversation with the god had implied. "Beyond simply managing to kill those who would come after her core, she sought to ally with Kirido for protection."

Elara raised her eyebrows. "And by implication, the wider Kingdom?"

Suliel bowed her head. "That would be for his Majesty to consider," she said.

"And what would the dungeon be bringing for his consideration?" Elara pressed.

Suliel raised an eyebrow of her own. "As I understand it, you count as a diplomatic representative," she said. "Is the Tiatian Empire deigning to open negotiations with Kirido?"

Elara froze and then chuckled ruefully. "Ah, that would be overstepping my role," she said. "Please, forget I asked."

"Of course," Suliel agreed. "Forgive me for asking, but what *is* your role, exactly? I have had only rumors to go on."

"I suppose I should explain a few things," Elara agreed. "Let me start by saying that, for the last decade or so, the Tiatian Empire has been toying with the idea of starting an expansionary phase."

Suliel swallowed. "I see. In *our* direction?"

"Westward, so yes, but not *specifically* at us," Elara explained.

Suliel let her grip on her goblet relax. She set it down and put her hands under the table.

"There are five sovereign nations between the Empire and Zamarra," Suliel mused. "I haven't heard anything about them being invaded, so what form, exactly, would this expansion take?"

"That is still being debated," Elara said. "Invasion is a possibility, but the generals have concerns."

"Concerns," Suliel repeated. "I was always told that the Tiatian Empire was vast and mighty, with more soldiers than their enemies could count."

"It's more complicated than that," Elara said. "It's not like they could send all of their forces, and by extending their supply lines so far, there is the possibility of disaster."

"When the military is stymied," Suliel said, repeating her old lessons, "that leaves—"

"Diplomacy," Elara agreed. "If one of the kingdoms were to join the Empire voluntarily, it would allow the Empire to use it as a base to expand further."

"You think the King will . . . will he?" Suliel asked aghast. A true king would never give up his sovereignty like that . . . would he?

Except he might be a False King. Who knows what such a person would do?

"He hasn't been asked," Elara said quickly. "Yet. If the Empire were to ask, and he were to say no . . . we'd be at war. So the Empire won't ask, not until either their forces are in position *or* they know beyond a doubt what the answer will be."

"We're not the only kingdom being courted, are we?" Suliel asked shrewdly.

"Of course not. And the first nation to get asked stands to get far greater rewards for signing up. The Empire only needs *one* friendly acquisition."

"Why only one?"

Elara frowned. "The reason that the Empire wants to expand is to provide new lands for freshly minted nobles. If the existing nobility get to remain, then there are no new lands to be had."

Suliel swallowed again. "That's why? So if every nation surrendered, the Empire would have to keep expanding?"

"Something like that," Elara said. "I doubt it would come to that, though. Not all the nations are on as good terms as we are. Dunust, for example, was mostly founded by refugees from the Unification Wars. They don't remember Tiatia fondly."

"So your former husband was here to . . . what?" Suliel said slowly. "Sound out the King? The court?"

"That was *part* of what Kaelan was here for," Elara corrected. "He was also engaged in normal diplomatic relations, but then he met me, and . . ."

"You're not the heir," Suliel said. "Marrying you wouldn't hand the Kingdom over—"

"But it would bring the nations closer together," Elara agreed. "It wasn't a political match, but his grandmother approved."

That would be the Empress, Suliel reminded herself.

"But then he was assassinated," Suliel said. "I'm sorry for your loss."

Elara inclined her head in acknowledgment. "He was indeed," she said heavily. "Which brings me to my main concern: finding those responsible."

"You don't believe the official story, then?"

Elara snorted in a most unladylike manner. "Dior was a fool, and smitten with me, but I doubt he knew *how* to contact the Shadowblades. Giving up a noble scion showed that my Father was serious about appeasing the Empire, and he did *confess*, but . . ."

"Confessions can be obtained," Suliel agreed. "Maybe not even with torture, but sufficient concessions to his family. . . . It's interesting that you mention the Shadowblades."

"Oh? I wouldn't have expected a country noble to know of them. You surprise me."

Suliel suppressed a grimace. "Country" noble was more polite than "backwater," but it still stung. "I happen to have one in a cell back home," she said smugly.

"You *what?*" Elara asked incredulously.

Suliel held up her hand placatingly. "He was badly injured in an attempt on the dungeon," she said. "I doubt I can hold him longer than he wants to be held."

"I suppose not," Elara said, sighing. "Still, if he's willing to talk . . . I would be in your debt."

"I can write a letter, but I can't guarantee that it would get there in time,"

Suliel said. "Nor can I ensure that he'll talk. He answered some of my questions, but I didn't know enough at the time to make good use of him."

"Still, I will be in your debt," Elara said.

"Could you not have found him in the city? He was a member of the Stormguard, and I heard that they were quite famous."

"Ah, Draven Blackthorn then? You're right, he is well known. He doesn't take contracts, but his class is available for anyone to see."

"Then why hasn't he been arrested?"

"He is protected—by a few things. For one, his deeds as a member of the Stormguard are well known and lauded. For another, his traits and his fellow team members make arresting him a fraught enterprise."

Suliel winced but didn't say anything. Someone else could publicize the news that the Stormguard were no more.

"And lastly," Elara continued, "he is still a member in good standing of the Shadowblades. So anyone who arrests him can expect a knife in their back at some point."

"That is quite comprehensive," Suliel stated. "I take it you considered going after him at some point in your investigations?"

"I was dissuaded, yes," Elara said sourly. "Father's men had long learned the futility of searching out those assassins."

"I see," Suliel said. "Then who do you think was responsible?"

Elara scowled. "Most of the noble families are somewhat supportive of the idea of Zamarra ceding to the Empire," she said. "They would keep their lands and titles. But the institutions that now serve the King would see some significant changes."

"You're talking about the Privy Council, the Merchants Guild . . ." Suliel said.

"And the Adventurers Guild," Elara said. "They have no equivalent in the Empire's administration. Even the city guard would have to be reorganized to fit in with a provincial government."

"So you think that one of those . . ."

"*Someone*, in one of those institutions, was corrupt enough to murder my husband to protect their current position. That's what I think."

"So what is it that you think I can do for you? Aside from writing that letter, of course."

"You're a noble from out of town," Elara said. "Young, without entanglements with the current order. I can *trust* you to not be already involved with the corrupt elements here."

I'm not entirely *free of entanglements*, Suliel thought guiltily, but she wasn't so foolish as to mention Elara's rebellious aunt to her.

"You've already shown your worth," Elara said excitedly. "No one from here would have *dared* to imprison Draven, even as politely as you have."

"I'm starting to wonder about that," Suliel said uneasily. "Am I going to be in danger from the Shadowblades?"

"I doubt it. They would have to become aware, and I doubt Draven would mention it."

"That's something. So you want me as a political ally, then? I'm afraid I won't be much use until I'm accepted by the court."

"That's true, but I don't see it being a problem," Elara assured her. "I'll speak to Father and get this all sorted out."

"Then I'd be happy to help in any way I can," Suliel said. She meant it, too. Rooting out corrupt officials sounded like the sort of thing Anton would approve of.

Not that I have any idea of how to go about doing that, but Elara seems to know what she's doing.

Elara smiled. "I knew I could count on you," she said. "Now, let's talk about that attempt on *your* life."

Suliel grimaced. "You don't think it was just a random robbery?"

"I do not. You didn't see, but they blocked off the street once you went through. They were after you, and were either hired or tipped off."

"Do you think that the fellow we captured will know anything?" Suliel asked.

"Perhaps, but that ringleader is probably the only one that knows who hired him." Elara grimaced. "We're probably better off working from the other end. Who would want to kill you?"

Suliel smiled wryly. "You wanted me for my lack of entanglements, but I seem to have a few. I don't think my mother would try to have me killed, though."

"You didn't think she'd lock you up, either," Elara said. "Filial piety only goes so far."

"I suppose," Suliel sighed. "I do feel, though, that Magister Tikin is more likely to seek my death. He didn't seem unwilling to stoop to underhanded methods."

"He's been keeping a low profile since returning to the capital," Elara said thoughtfully. "He was in my report, of course, but I haven't heard anything about him since then."

"Draven said that he was being backed by someone called Kalren Voss."

"I know him. He's Father's court mage," Elara said. "I'll point him out when you get introduced at court."

"Finally, I doubt that Captain Oldaw thinks fondly of me," Suliel said sadly. "I doubt that he hates me enough to kill me . . ."

"You never know," Elara said. "I should be able to have all of these watched. If they go near where that gang operates from, we'll know. All of them except your mother, that is. From what I've heard, she never leaves Lord Brankil's estate. If she's arranging something, she's using a go-between."

Suliel felt a small thrill at the mention of having people watched. Elara had an *organization*, capable of clandestine action.

I need one of those, she thought. First, though, she needed more people for her regular operations.

CHAPTER TWELVE

Bay City

They sent Zaphar in to infiltrate Verheti. The two street kids, Haris and Yaseen, whom they had picked up back in Denasti, went with him.

The pair had clambered around on the boat, both while it was being refurbished and during the quieter times at sea, to the point that Anton had some hope of them qualifying for the Sailor class. They probably already qualified for more than a few criminal classes. Right now, though, they were too young for a class, which was an advantage, according to Kelsey.

"No one's looking for them," she said when Aris objected to sending them into the city. "They've spent their lives living off the streets, looking for information and handouts. The difference now is that we're feeding them."

The boys certainly had no objection, far preferring a 'job' in the city to hanging around the fishing village with the girls. The rest of the team found a roadside inn a little way outside of the city and settled in to wait.

Anton, Aris, and especially Kelsey kept their faces hidden, but they didn't see any signs that the authorities were looking for them. After a full night and day at the inn without incident, Anton stopped worrying about being discovered and started worrying about other things.

"What do we do if they don't make it back?" he asked Kelsey.

"They'll make it back, don't worry," she assured him. "If they don't . . . I don't suppose you'll want to cut our losses at that point, will you?"

"I don't want to . . ." Anton said. "But if they capture Zaphar, won't they find out where we are?"

"He *would* crack like an eggshell," Kelsey acknowledged. "I suppose that means we won't be kept wondering long. They'll have a detachment of troops on our back before you can say Rumpelstiltskin."

"It's good to know that our capture and execution will be *quick*," Anton muttered sarcastically.

"Relax," Kelsey said easily. "First of all, nothing is going to go wrong. Second of all, if something does go wrong, we've got a pretty good view of the ground between the bridge and here, so we'll see a detachment of guardsmen riding hell for leather towards us long before they arrive. And thirdly . . ."

She trailed off.

"Thirdly?" Anton prompted.

"Thirdly . . . I think that's Zaphar coming now."

Anton twisted to look around.

"Is that . . . does he have a donkey now?" he asked.

They went out to meet him on the road. It was quicker, and there were less prying eyes. Also, Kelsey got to pet the donkey. She was completely unperturbed by the way it pulled away from her and bared its teeth.

"Could you . . . not . . . do whatever it is that you're trying to do?" Zaphar asked plaintively. He was using all his strength to hold the donkey back, and failing. Anton reached out and grabbed the leather strap. Suddenly unable to move back farther, the donkey brayed and tried to take a bite out of Kelsey.

"It's a loaner, so please don't kill it," Zaphar said quickly.

"I'm disappointed," Kelsey said, reluctantly leaving the donkey alone. "I thought you'd become a man of means, a merchant with his own donkey! And yet, it seems that you're merely living off the charity of others."

"Yes, yes, very funny," Zaphar said sourly. "Perhaps we could get to the inn, and I can tie this demon-beast up somewhere and have a proper conversation?"

"Too many ears," Kelsey said casually. "Fill us in out here."

"Fine, fine," Zaphar said. He made sure that Anton had a good grip on the strap, and then released his death grip. He moved carefully over to the donkey, trying to access its saddle bags without getting bitten. Fortunately, the beast still had its entire attention focused on Kelsey, so he was able to accomplish this easily. Smirking in triumph, he passed a bundle of papers over to Kelsey.

"I had a remarkably easy time of it, I did," Zaphar said. "Almost suspiciously so. At least some of the guards have an Inspection trait—they knew I was a merchant."

"They didn't ask for passes?" Kelsey said, flipping through the pages.

"They did, but I told them the story—that I had been robbed on the way and only had the sample bag I'd managed to run away with. Then it got weird."

"Oh?" Kelsey said. She passed the papers to Aris. Anton would have taken them, but he was busy with the donkey, which seemed to have decided that Anton was the only thing that could save it from the demonic Kelsey. It was hiding behind him while still trying to run away.

"One of the guards has an uncle who is an alchemist. The guard thought his uncle would be very interested in the glass jars you left me with, and suggested that I contact him."

Kelsey chuckled. "I keep forgetting how bad you guys are at glass making," she said. "So instead of disappearing into the slums . . ."

"It would have looked odd if I didn't follow the guard's advice," Zaphar said. "So I followed the directions and . . . he *was* interested. I have an order for five hundred more of the second type."

"The square ones?" Kelsey asked. "I *guess* I can fill that if we need to, but we aren't here for trade deals."

"He *was* useful," Zaphar said. "In between setting me up with a merchant's pass, which I didn't need, he put me up and told me about the city. I learned about the upcoming games from him. And he lent me this donkey and gave me two weeks' supplies for the trek back to my hometown that I was *supposed* to be eager to make."

Kelsey laughed. "Feels like your little green friend is looking out for you," she said. "Nothing like the luck of the fae."

"If that is so, it worked out better than last time," Zaphar said. "Last time, it was a nightmare."

"What are the games?" Anton said. "It sounded like they were important?"

"It's probably something to do with this," Aris said, holding up one of the sheets so he could see. Anton was getting better at Elitran script, but all he could make out of the writing was "Arena" and "Death." The eight pictures were more informative, or at least four of them were.

"That's Thalorin!" he said. "And Seraphin!"

"They're scheduled to fight to the death in a week," Kelsey told him casually. "Gonna be a big event."

"Oh," Anton said. "That's the trap."

"Exactly," Kelsey agreed. "Now all we have to do is spring it."

"That's not *all* of the trap," Aris said. She held up another picture. It wasn't as accurate as the ones of the captured townsfolk, but it was clearly supposed to be Kelsey. There were others for Anton and Aris.

"They're looking for us," Aris said. "I don't know why they didn't bother posting these outside the city, though."

"They don't want to warn us," Kelsey said. "If we'd just walked in, we would have been spotted before we even knew they had posters out of us. If we'd seen posters out here, it would be easier for us to get away."

"Speaking of getting away, where are the boys?" Aris asked. "You didn't lose them, did you?"

"No, no," Zaphar said. "They will be handling our entrance into the city."

Aris frowned. "Don't you have a pass now? Can't we all just walk in on that?"

"Yes . . . but also not at all." Zaphar said. "The pass belongs to a fake merchant who is expected back in the city in *four weeks*. If I return early, the guards will mention my arrival to the uncle and suspicions will start to rise."

"So what's the plan?" Kelsey asked.

Zaphar shrugged. "I bought a boat."

"This is a rowboat," Soraya said disdainfully. "And it leaks."

"All boats leak," Kelsey said.

"*Ours* doesn't. My father's didn't."

"When it comes to *my* boat, give it time," Kelsey said. "The sealant worked pretty well, but it won't hold forever. As for your father's *ships*, did you ever go down to the lowest deck? Where they kept the bad slaves?"

"My father's slaves were well treated," Soraya muttered. "But . . . no. I didn't."

"There you go, then," Kelsey said with amusement. "I know you don't like getting your feet wet, but suck it up, princess."

Soraya hesitated some more. "Maybe I could go back to the village with the other girls."

"No. A courl would stand out like a sore thumb," Kelsey said. "Anyone who passes through would have questions, and that might lead to attention."

Anton waited patiently on the middle seat for Kelsey to chivvy Soraya into the boat. He was new to rowing, but it wasn't particularly hard. This would be his second trip.

"Do you know where we're going?" he asked Tyla. She was behind him, at the front of the boat.

"I do; I saw where Zaphar led you," she said.

"Then we're off!" Kelsey said. "Soraya, try to keep the grumbling down to a minimum. If someone hears us when we get near the city, they might think we're up to no good!"

Soraya made a disgruntled snort but managed to keep quiet as she climbed in.

It should be fine, Anton thought. Zaphar's real purchase hadn't been the boat. Kelsey could have pulled out her Zodiac inflatable if need be, and Anton was pretty sure that it could be rowed just as quietly as this boat. What Zaphar had secured was a *dock*, out of the way, but still within city limits. Knowing now what Kelsey had taught Anton about criminal enterprises, Anton was sure that it had been used for smuggling many times before.

The boat cut through the dark water, Anton steering according to the occasional murmured directions from Tyla. It wasn't long before she whispered for him to slow down. Looking over his shoulder, he could see the dock looming out of the darkness, with Zaphar standing there waiting for him.

"This way," Zaphar said softly, once they had all disembarked. He led them down some narrow alleyways to a nondescript door. He knocked three times, and Aris opened the door to let them in.

"How much money did I give you?" Kelsey asked, looking about the place. They seemed to be in a comfortably furnished house. Four doors led off to other rooms, and this room had enough backless couches to seat them all.

"Ah . . . there was a downpayment for the bottles," Zaphar said.

"Nice," Kelsey said, testing the cushions. "I assume there aren't any servants we need to worry about?"

"It is all ours for three weeks," Zaphar said.

"Then let's get to planning," Kelsey said. "Zaphar, what do we know about the arena and the games?"

"The event will last a full day," Zaphar said, "with the death matches being the final event."

Anton swallowed. "They have to fight until one of them dies?" he asked.

"Yes. It is very unusual, I think. Rused has no arena, but from what I hear, one can normally surrender even if death is expected. But for these matches, no, which has increased the excitement."

"I guess if you own a person, you don't want them to die on you," Kelsey commented.

"That's . . . not inaccurate," Soraya mumbled.

"So is al-Kadir in the lineup?"

"He's not on the program, but it's said that he will be attending. They say that he will challenge the winner of the mainline tournament and also that he has offered to buy the freedom of any slave who lasts five minutes against him in a duel."

"That's a long time," Anton said.

Soraya shook her head. "It could be a minute and it would be too long," she said. "He'll make it interesting by drawing it out. Shallow cuts, letting them run, that sort of thing."

She shuddered. "He's a monster who loves pain and the roar of the crowd."

"Noted," Kelsey said. "Do we know the layout of the arena?"

"Not yet," Zaphar said. "But there are lesser events most days. I can get in and surveil."

"That's a start," Kelsey said. "But we're going to need more than the public areas. She beckoned for the two kids to come closer. They had kept quiet since rowing the boat out to meet them.

"I've got a special job for you two," Kelsey told them.

CHAPTER THIRTEEN

Karma Chameleon

SULIEL

At breakfast the next day, Suliel looked thoughtfully at Delir Nyer. He wasn't *her* Guild Master; he managed the Adventurers Guild in Kirido. He answered to the head of the guild here in Bures, and to the King, before he answered to her. But he had lived in her town for so long—all her life—that Suliel had trouble separating him from the other townsfolk. Her people.

She suspected he had the same difficulty. Certainly, he addressed her with the same respect that everyone else in town did. And he'd come here at her request, to help her with matters that had very little to do with Kirido's guild hall.

"How is the recruitment coming along?" she asked him.

He nodded in acknowledgment but waited to finish his mouthful of bacon before he replied.

"Well, my lady. We should have the first cartload ready by tomorrow."

Suliel nodded, pleased. Under normal circumstances, there was an ebb and flow to the population of the Kingdom. Part of that was the additional work required during harvest, but it was also a response to events—like the raid on Kirido.

Suliel had lost a good number of men on the walls, and these needed to be replaced. She could draw from the nearby villages, but that left those villages bereft of manpower. Eventually, word of work being available would draw in those looking for a job, or a home.

However, Suliel required many more workers than the natural flow could provide. She needed to expand her army, and Kelsey was promising her industries that no one had ever heard of. So she was tapping the much larger employment pool in the capital. Some of these people would find their way to Kirido eventually, but she needed them now.

Paying to transport immigrants was an expense, but it was one that Suliel was willing to pay. At the same time, she didn't want to burden her fiefdom with those unwilling or unable to work—Anton was sending her enough of those—so she needed an administrator with discernment. And discretion.

"Good. I'm sure I can rely on you," Suliel said. "There is another matter that's been troubling me, though. What can you tell me about Riadi?"

Suliel felt Kelsey's interest sharpen, but the dungeon didn't say anything.

"The Goddess of Reincarnation, my lady?" Delir asked.

The image of the blue-skinned and definitely *male* god flashed into Suliel's head.

"Yes. I can't say I've heard of . . . that goddess. What do you know of her?"

Delir looked thoughtful. "In my job, you collect bits of all sorts of lore. I'd heard the name before Kelsey looked it up and asked me about her. Since then, I've looked up what I could, which isn't much."

"What can you tell me?"

"No known priesthood in Zamarra or the neighboring kingdoms. No temples. Although . . ." he trailed off, thinking. "If what Kelsey surmised was correct and she has taken over the dungeon portfolio, every dungeon might serve as a temple."

"Do temples serve a special purpose for gods?" Suliel asked. It was surprising to her how little she knew about religion. The priests of Tiait handled most ceremonies for her demesne, and Suliel's education hadn't covered much on them beyond learning the proper way to pay respect.

"It's not really known," Delir said. "They may be no more than status symbols. On the other hand, most stories about gods manifesting have them do it inside a temple, so that may be a requirement."

<I reckon that was a manifestation we saw,> Kelsey sent. <There was a presence that humans could see.>

<Noted,> Suliel sent, but she kept on listening to Delir.

"Reincarnation is an odd portfolio," Delir said. "No one ever remembers doing it, and the only reason it exists as a concept is that several gods have mentioned that it happens."

"If it happens to everyone, but no one remembers it . . ." Suliel said, trailing off into confusion. "Does that make her a powerful goddess or not?"

"Indeed," Delir said. "Perhaps the most useful comparison is Enbanser, Goddess of Birth. But she is much more well-known and revered than Riadi."

"Everyone prays for a safe birth," Suliel said. "And her priesthood goes out into the countryside helping expectant mothers."

"Yes," Delir agreed. "But no one prays for a safe rebirth. How would you even know it occurred?"

"You wouldn't. So she must be a weak goddess, then."

"Perhaps. Though if she has picked up the dungeon portfolio, perhaps she has others that bring her more worship."

"Wouldn't we know her as the goddess of something other than reincarnation, then?"

Delir smiled gently. "She may operate those portfolios under a different name. Or in faraway countries."

Suliel sighed. "We don't know much, do we? Do we even know she's female?"

"Gods don't have physical bodies, so they are genderless in a literal sense," Delir said. "Most of them prefer to present a constant form, which includes a gender."

"Mel doesn't have a physical body, but she's definitely female," Suliel said.

"Who?" Delir asked.

<Mel's form may well be shaped by my expectations,> Kelsey sent.

"Mel is Kelsey's dungeon fairy," Suliel explained. She added on what Kelsey had told her.

"I see," Delir said. "That may be true for gods as well—they are influenced by their worshippers' beliefs. But gods are a completely different order of beings from fairies. I'd expect them to have more control over their form."

"If she hasn't manifested, though, then how do we know she's female?"

"I'm not sure," Delir admitted. "The book I read simply gave her gender as female without any explanation. Perhaps one of the gods mentioned it to their followers in passing."

"There are more books of lore in the capital, correct?"

"Indeed, my lady. The Adventurer's Guild here has an extensive collection."

"Then can I ask you to go through those books and let me know anything you find about Riadi?"

"Of course, my lady. Should this take priority over the recruiting?"

"No . . ." Suliel said, consideringly. "But you can't be spending all your time recruiting, can you? If we're keeping our efforts quiet."

"Indeed not, my lady. But going through old books—while an enjoyable pastime—takes a great deal of time."

"Focus on recruitment. But do as much searching as you can. Oh, and can you also check for any gods that have blue skin?"

Delir dropped his fork. It clattered on the metal plate.

"Did you say blue skin, my lady?"

"I did. What of it?" Suliel asked.

"Gods can take any form, my lady, but blue skin . . . it's a sign of demons."

"What?" Suliel asked.

<What?> Kelsey sent.

Delir begged leave to finish his breakfast and organize his thoughts before saying more. Suliel agreed, if only to avoid their food growing cold. She had to force herself to eat, though. The only thing that got her through was the training her parents had put her through about maintaining a pleasant composure during unpleasant events.

After the plates had been cleaned and they'd moved to the sitting room, Delir sat opposite Suliel, his face a picture of furious thought.

Finally, he took a deep breath.

"As I said, my lady, the administrator of the Adventurers Guild needs to know all sorts of odd things. Most people will never encounter a demon, but the odds are much higher for an adventurer."

Suliel nodded. That made sense. Adventurers encountered all sorts of strange things.

"Demons are creatures from outside of this world," Delir said. "That makes them part of the class of beings known as Outsiders—beings from outside of this world. Outsiders are generally considered to be of two types—demons, who are entirely inimical to mortals, and fae, who are more neutral."

"Is there not a class of Outsiders that are considered good?" Suliel asked.

"There is not," Delir said. "But I have only speculation of why that is. The most likely reason is the mistrust that the gods have for any being from the outside. They are unwilling to countenance the idea that an Outsider can be good, and assume that any actions that appear beneficial are either a product of capriciousness or deceit."

<It's racial profiling, that's what it is,> Kelsey sent. Suliel ignored the nonsense.

"So there might be good Outsiders, we just don't hear of them?" she asked.

"Perhaps. Another school of thought states that Outsiders come in *many* types. Demons and fae are just the most common, and they are the way they are because of their shared heritage and culture."

<I think that one's more likely,> Kelsey said.

"Well, she would," Delir said when Suliel reported her words. "Since she is, by her account, an Outsider who is neither a demon nor fae."

<I've met two fae now, and I'm definitely not the same as them,> Kelsey sent.

<Have we really eliminated the possibility of you being a demon?> Suliel sent back.

Kelsey replied with a very odd sensation. It took Suliel a moment to process it, but it was the sensation of her tongue sticking out.

Delir continued with his lecture. "Part of the reason we think this is that demons and fae refer to themselves as such, while some other Outsiders do not. Though some have, once the distinction was explained to them."

"Some do, some don't . . . this is getting complicated," Suliel complained.

"I'm afraid so, my lady. We have never received a comprehensive explanation of Outsiders. What I'm telling you is based on the recorded interactions with Outsiders, spread over hundreds of years.

"Over the centuries, demons have consistently displayed some characteristics. The most salient one is that they have a physical body. They are skilled with both illusions and shapeshifting, so that body might not look like their true form. But in every case that a true form has been revealed, it has had blue skin."

"In every case?" Suliel asked. "Wait, who does this revealing?"

"Whenever a demon shows up, a hero isn't too far behind," Delir said. "These heroes are often guild members, so we do get reports."

"Do heroes show up for fae as well?"

"Fae are best left alone," Delir said. "That's the advice we get. Be polite, don't ask for things, and they'll go away when they get bored. They rarely cause harm like a demon does."

"How do the heroes know to show up?" Suliel asked.

"Sometimes it is as simple as a request going out to a nearby guild. Other times . . . divine providence is assumed."

"What does that mean?"

Delir looked a little embarrassed. "Sometimes, a series of unlikely events occurs that leads to a hero being in the right place at the right time. When that happens, we assume that a god was responsible for arranging it."

<They do arrange things like that, long in advance,> Kelsey said.
<Do I want to know how you know that?> Suliel replied.
<Probably not.>

"So when it comes down to it, what does a god with blue skin actually *mean*?" Suliel asked.

"Hard to say," Delir said. "They could take on that form if they want to make a point. Or it could be a demon pretending to be a god."

"We need more information," Suliel decided. "Delir, is there anyone at the guild you can trust to search the records while keeping quiet about it?"

"Who are we keeping it a secret from?" Delir asked.

"Everyone," Suliel said sourly. "From the gods themselves if we can manage it."

<Pretty sure that ship sailed when you spoke all this aloud,> Kelsey sent. *<Our thoughts are private, but not much else.>*

Suliel grimaced. "I just want to know what we're dealing with before anyone else knows that we're dealing with it. I'll make some funds available, Delir. Try and find me some information I can use."

Delir bowed his head. "I will do what I can, my lady."

CHAPTER FOURTEEN

Follow the Leader

I don't like this," Zaphar whispered urgently. "I hate it. You're going to get me killed."

"Don't be ridiculous, no one ever got killed in a coffee shop," Kelsey said.

"It's a coffee*house*, and—and people get killed all the time in *all sorts* of places when they're wanted felons!"

Anton thought he had a point. The hooded robes they were wearing didn't look out of place and did a good job of hiding Kelsey's and his faces, but they barely counted as a disguise. As an additional concession to their criminal status, Kelsey had secured a table at the edge of the room. It overlooked the main area, which made Anton's job a lot easier. He got to work cataloging classes, while Kelsey convinced Zaphar to go downstairs and *mingle*.

"Look, you're dressed like they are," Kelsey said softly. "Your class matches. No one will suspect a thing, and the best part is you don't *want* anything from them. You just need to blend in."

"I'm not cut out for this," Zaphar muttered. "And that's only part of it. You *know* that every time I try this, something *weird* happens."

"That's fine," Kelsey said. "Trust your patron, you know? It will all work out, and you'll get some experience."

"The least you could do would be to stay close to get me out of trouble," Zaphar whined.

"Are you crazy?" Kelsey said with a grin. "We're wanted felons; we need to get off the streets as soon as possible."

"Do you really think he'll be all right?" Anton asked as they slipped into an alleyway that took them away from the bustling street.

"He'll be fine," Kelsey said. "Ultimately, he doesn't have anyone looking for him, so even if he gets into some kind of trouble, he'll be able to worm out of it."

"And how was your day, dears?" Kelsey asked as Soraya, Aris, and Tyla staggered into the safehouse. Soraya glared at Kelsey before she replied.

"Exhausting," she said bitterly. "Why do we have to trek down *every* single alleyway in this two-bit town?"

"You need to know the ground," Kelsey said placidly. "We'll make maps and plans, but it won't do us any good unless you can follow the route without stopping."

Aris stepped over to Anton and hugged him, recharging by resting her head on his chest. Then she moved over to the table and started adding to the map of the city streets, adding some alleyways and correcting mistakes that had been made. Tyla joined her, adding her own contributions in a hushed voice that didn't interrupt Soraya's complaints.

"What route? We've been going every which way!"

"We need to get the whole picture before we can plan the route," Kelsey said.

Soraya's eyes narrowed. "And why force me to do it?" she asked. "Aris is much better at it, and she has Tyla to help her. My presence is unnecessary."

"You are pretty useless," Kelsey agreed, grinning at Soraya's reaction. "But you need to know the area more than anyone else."

"Why?" Soraya asked suspiciously.

"Because that's where you'll be fighting," Kelsey said smugly. "Or . . . something like that."

"Fight? I can't fight!" Soraya exclaimed.

"You're part of the team now, remember?" Kelsey said. "Don't worry, it's all part of my master plan."

"A plan that you still haven't explained," Soraya complained.

"I'm still working out the fine details," Kelsey said confidently. "You'll understand soon enough."

"Does this mean I get a gun, at least?"

"Mnm . . . maybe? Are you sure you want one? You'll be washing the gun smoke out of your fur for weeks after you fire one."

Soraya wrinkled her nose in distaste. "Well, I want *something*. If you're going to throw me to the wolves, I need some kind of weapon."

"I'll consider it," Kelsey said. "I'll let you know when it's time."

"We found it, we found it!" Yaseen yelled.

"*I* found it," Haris said scornfully. "You were in the wrong tunnel."

"We split up to cover more ground! So we both found it!" Yaseen declared.

"Boys, boys," Kelsey said. "What did I say about coming *here* after visiting the sewers?"

"That you'd have the spiders eat us," Yaseen said fearfully. "But! But! They wouldn't let us in the public bath anymore, *even though* we had money!"

"Well, at least you tried," Kelsey said. Then her voice turned cold. "But close only counts in horseshoes and hand grenades, so it's spider time!"

"Kelsey," Anton said firmly. He didn't think Kelsey would *kill* the boys over a stink, but she was quite capable of scaring them with a "little nibble." The boys didn't scream and run, so they must have doubted her murderous statement as well.

"Fine!" Kelsey said, with what Anton hoped was fake disgruntlement. "Clothes in the basket, get in the tub!"

As she spoke, she made the mentioned items appear, throwing soap in after them when they complied.

"Now scrub!" she said. "Spiders can't smell you, but I can."

"Even the hair?" Yassen complained.

"Especially the hair," Kelsey commanded. She made a bucket of water appear and poured it over their heads. "Scrub!"

Kelsey only started asking them questions once they were clean, dry, and dressed in fresh clothes.

"So what did you find?"

"We found the gladiator cells!" Yaseen said.

"*I* did," Haris objected.

"How do you know?" Kelsey asked.

"To start with, it was around about the right place," Haris said. "And we spoke to 'em!"

"Spoke to them how? Did you get into the prison?"

"Nah, nah," Haris said. "The cells are underground, see? So they're real close to the sewers. Reckon they're built right on top! Gladiators are slaves, so they don't rate a toilet. They just have a grate right on top of the sewer. Probably smells pretty bad, but slaves don't get to complain."

"They could hear us when we shouted!" Yaseen said proudly. "They didn't speak good, but we got their names."

"Great work, kids," Kelsey said. "I'm taking you to the brothel tonight."

"Kelsey," Anton cautioned.

"What? No brothel?" Kelsey asked incredulously. Anton just gave her a firm look, not bothering to respond to her nonsense. "Wine with dinner? No? Extra dessert?"

"Extra dessert is fine," Anton said over the boys' disappointed noises.

"You're weird," Kelsey declared. "This is much riskier than infiltrating a coffee-house, but you don't mind it at all."

Zaphar glared at her. "Can you keep it down?" he asked quietly. "I don't normally meet clients in the middle of a job, but if I did, I'd wager they wouldn't give me away by talking."

"I am being quiet," Kelsey grumbled, but at a much lower volume, Anton noted. "Have you got the goods?"

Zaphar nodded and held out the medallion. "He should be asleep for the rest of the night."

"Won't take me that long," Kelsey boasted. She made the medallion disappear.

"I thought using the . . . machine shop took longer," Anton said quietly.

"It does, but I already knew what I was making, at least the rough outline," Kelsey said. "So I have everything prepped. However . . ."

She frowned. "Looks like I'm going to have to make a mold, and that takes time. Let's just spend the mana."

She held out her hands, and a medallion appeared in each of them. They looked identical, right down to the ribbon that they dangled from.

"Whadda ya think?" she asked Anton. He used *Delver's Discernment.*

Lala Rank Medallion, Item, Great Quality, Tier 1
Lala Rank Medallion Duplicate, Item, Great Quality, Tier 1

"That one's the fake," he said, pointing. Kelsey grimaced.

"How can you tell?" she asked.

"The name is different," Anton said, shrugging. "Says it's a duplicate."

Kelsey growled under her breath. "Stupid magic system," she muttered. She made the fake disappear while staring intently at the real one. Then she relaxed, and a new medallion appeared in her hand.

"How's that?" she asked.

Anton blinked, but used his trait again.

Lala Rank Medallion, Item, Great Quality, Tier 1

"It's got the right name now," he reported.

"We need you to kill a wizard," Kelsey said.

Tyla looked up from her meditation. It still gave her a small amount of experience, so it was worth doing when she was out of mana for spells.

"Will wizards give me more experience than other foes?" she asked.

"Maybe," Kelsey said. "But Mel tells me that wizards power up their cores by absorbing other dead cores."

Tyla considered the notion. "Don't you find that disturbing?" she asked. "Robbing the corpses of your fellow numina?"

"I am a necromancer, after all," Kelsey said.

Tyla shrugged. "I don't think it's necessary right now," she said. "I don't have the traits to make full use of the power of this stone as it is. Adding a few extra *types* of mana would be nice, but I think my priority should be to work on my level."

"Killing a wizard does that, too," Kelsey pointed out.

"I suppose. I shall keep an eye out then," Tyla said. She hesitated for a moment before speaking again.

"Do you suppose . . . that this stone has already absorbed other cores?"

"Maybe," Kelsey said. "Tikin might have known its history, but he's not exactly available for questioning right now."

"Maybe I am just imagining things," Tyla admitted. "But when I think about how it feels when communing with the core . . . there might be three entities in there."

"Interesting," Kelsey said. "But I still want you to kill a wizard."

"The time has come," Kelsey intoned. "Zaphar, go and stand in front of the door."

"On this side, yes?" Zaphar asked, his eyes narrowing with suspicion.

"Yeah, yeah, unless you have an allergy to knowing plans," Kelsey said. "This isn't your plan, though—it's hers." She pointed at Soraya.

"Are you finally going to tell us what we've been mapping the ghetto for?" Soraya asked.

"Yep!" Kelsey said brightly. "What we've been doing, Soraya, is mapping your escape route."

"Escape from what?" Soraya asked. The answer came to her as soon as she asked. "Oh no. There is no way . . ."

"Part of the team, Soraya, remember?" Kelsey said with a grin. "Al-Kadir is our biggest problem. He's going to be waiting for Anton and me right near the cells, ready to pounce the moment we try something."

"Can't you just kill him?" Soraya asked weakly. "You'd be doing the world a favor."

"I gave it a red hot go, back at the docks," Kelsey said regretfully. "Maybe if we'd had the deck sweeper set up, we could have done more, but as it is, I don't think we can be sure of killing him. What we can do is make sure he stays out of our way."

Soraya looked at the exit, but Zaphar was, as instructed, standing in front of it, looking confused. He probably wouldn't try and *stop* her, but by the time she got past him, Kelsey would have grabbed her.

Her shoulders slumped. "If I don't agree, you'll just trade me for concessions, won't you?"

"Honestly, I doubt they'd go for it," Kelsey said. "Al-Kadir may be their big bad menace, but I don't think he's got enough pull to get our prisoners free in return for you."

"Some small mercy then," Soraya said softly. "But I *can't* get captured by him, Kelsey."

"You're not going to," Kelsey assured the despondent courl. "He's going to chase you around for a bit, and then you're going to get away."

Soraya laughed nervously. "Are you joking, or just insane? If he chases me, if he *sees* me, it will be all over."

"Have a little faith in yourself, why don'tcha? You won't be doing this alone, anyway. You'll have support from Tyla and Aris."

Tyla stood up. "I'll do whatever I can to help, Numen." Aris just stayed where she was, raising her eyebrows.

"Ooh," Kelsey joked. "She doesn't look happy about saving you. Maybe you shouldn't have eaten all that human meat in front of her."

"That's not fair—" Soraya started at the same time as Aris blurted, "I wouldn't—"

They both stopped and looked at each other. Kelsey just grinned. "Don't worry!" she said. "I've got a plan. We'll do a run-through and some setup tomorrow, and then al-Kadir will learn for himself why you shouldn't bite down on every tasty bit of bait that's dangled in front of you."

CHAPTER FIFTEEN

Gonna Make You Sweat

They walked in the front gate. Out in the open, as if they didn't have a price on their heads. Anton and Kelsey just walked in with the rest of the crowd. They did cover their faces, but Kelsey's considered opinion was that they didn't *need* to. It did threaten to be more trouble than it was worth, though, so she wore the hood.

Everyone else was already in the arena. Anton and Kelsey were last, to give them a chance to get into position before the trouble started. They came out of the entrance tunnel and paused on the main concourse to get their bearings.

"There," Kelsey said, nodding in the direction she meant. "The nobles' section, where all the guards are. That's where he'll be."

Anton was looking for Aris. Soraya and Tyla were too notable to have their heads uncovered, but she was just another dark-skinned girl. Third pylon, go back . . . and there she was. She'd been keeping watch on the entrance and their eyes met. She smiled, and Anton couldn't stop himself from smiling back.

"I found Aris," he reported. "She's—"

"I see her," Kelsey said shortly. "You ready?"

"Yeah," Anton said.

It was a long walk to the nobles' section. While you could get there from the main entrance, the rich had their own entrance, far away from the one the rabble used. The fights weren't due to start for another hour, but the stands were already crowded. Anton and Kelsey forced their way through, until they came to an obstacle that wouldn't be moved. Guards, blocking the way forward.

"Al-Kadir," Kelsey said. "We're here to see him."

She threw back her hood, and Anton could see the moment when half the guards recognized who she was. The other half must have been asleep at the briefing or something; they just gaped at her unusual skin coloring.

"Don't start no trouble, there won't be none," Kelsey said in response to the tightened grip on spears and the cautious half-steps backward. "He wants to see us, we're here."

She waited patiently for the courl in charge to figure out what to do. After a brief pause, he stepped forward.

"Hand over your—"

"No," Kelsey said firmly.

The courl looked uncomfortable. Anton looked him over.

Hazan Khetar, Level 23, Courl, Steadfast Sentinel, Warrior/Trustworthy Guard/Steadfast Sentinel, S: 31, T: 29, A: 23, D: 23, P: 24, W: 22, C: 5

That was a little bit higher than most of the other guards. Anton was pretty sure all the guards were Tier Three, but not too many levels higher than him.

Kelsey wasn't carrying any visible weapons, but Anton had his sword, and his hand was on the hilt. He could take one or two, but Kelsey's guns would be the wildcard in that fight.

From the look on Hazan's face, he had been warned about the guns.

"Farl, go warn the Captain. The rest of you, contain them. *Carefully.*"

He paused a moment to make sure his instructions were obeyed. Then he addressed Kelsey again.

"Follow me," he said abruptly. Turning on his heel, he walked slowly forward, leaving the guards to shuffle sideways or backward as they maintained a ring around Anton and Kelsey.

Kelsey matched Hazan's pace and Anton followed her lead, moving deeper into the nobles' section. Richly dressed courls and humans looked down at them as they walked slowly towards their destination, a walled-off section of the stands.

Just before they reached the wall, Hazan spun to face them again.

"Halt!" he barked.

"Let them through," a deep, silky, familiar voice called out. Hazan winced.

"Sir, they have not been checked for weapons," he protested.

"As if that would have any meaning," the voice said. Anton could tell that the speaker had stepped forward and would soon be coming into view.

"The girl has her own dimensional storage," al-Kadir said as he stepped around the corner. "So your search would do no good."

He looked scornfully at Anton. "And while the boy is armed, his blade will not serve him against mine."

He held out his hand and a sword appeared in it. It was long and thin and flickered with a green iridescence. Anton couldn't help identifying it.

Viper's Edge, Enchanted Weapon, Excellent Quality, Tier 3

"Very nice," Kelsey said. "I'd say we look forward to taking it off you, but I'm not sure poison would fit with the theme Anton has got going on."

Al-Kadir's face curled up in disgust. "What *are* you, puppet? Where is your master?"

"Still haven't figured it out yet, huh?" Kelsey smirked. "But that's not the question you really want to ask, is it?"

"The reason I haven't killed you already," al-Kadir agreed. "I will have an answer. Necromancy is a rare evil, but not an unknown one. Priests with power over the undead have been found and stand ready to bind you. The answers I seek will be torn out of your flesh!"

Al-Kadir controlled his anger with some obvious effort. "I only hope that there is a mind in that shell to feel the pain it causes. Now. Where. Is. My. Bride?"

"She's right over there," Kelsey said, pointing across the arena.

Anton looked where she pointed. He knew where to look, and what he was looking for. It was a long way away, though. He could barely make out Soraya, hood off, standing upright, looking right at them.

Al-Kadir had a much higher Perception than Anton did. The Tier Four Champion growled deep in his throat as Soraya jumped down off her seat and started to run.

"Capture them alive," was all al-Kadir said before blinking away. His teleport didn't take him far, only to the edge of the stands. Anton had one last glimpse of him jumping down into the main arena before he had to focus on the guards.

"Here! Catch!" Kelsey said, tossing a metal cylinder at Hazan. He didn't catch it, of course. His spear was in his hands and he used it to bat the item away. That didn't help, as the item was already spewing a cloud of white, toxic smoke.

Anton was already donning the mask that Kelsey had provided at the same time. Kelsey was doing the same. She didn't have to breathe, but if she didn't, she couldn't *talk*, which was an unacceptable condition.

At first, the guards were put off by the cloud of smoke, but as Kelsey dropped more cylinders, they realized that their chance of capturing the pair was going to be lost. Shouting in defiance, they charged in.

That proved to be a mistake. The smoke wasn't *just* smoke. It wasn't alchemical, according to Kelsey, but it burned the mouth and lungs if you breathed it in, and it burned the eyes if you held your breath. The yells turned to choked cries and hacking coughs and the guards started falling to their knees. Anton had to use *Uncanny Evasion*, but only once.

"I've got this!" came a cry from behind. A wind sprang out of nowhere, blowing the smoke away. Unfortunately, it had already done its work. The guards were no doubt grateful that it had stopped, but they were still incapacitated, at least for the moment.

Anton used *Quick Attack* to send the tip of his sword through the throat of his closest opponent and looked back to see where the voice had come from. He saw a small crowd, four or five people in robes rushing forward. The one in the lead was clutching a glowing round object hanging around his neck.

"Oh, a wizard, is it?" Kelsey said, speaking loudly to be heard through her mask. Screams from the crowd all around distracted her. The smoke that had been pushed away from her was now dispersed into the crowd. Even dispersed, it was still a burning, choking smog, and the crowd didn't like it. At all.

Anton could see that the guards rushing towards them were slowed, but the real victims were the rich spectators in the nearby sections. Unlike the guards, they weren't motivated or trained to push through the pain.

"Bit of an own goal there, hey?" Kelsey said to the wizard. Anton wasn't sure if he could hear her. The other robed figures next to him had started holding their hands out towards Kelsey and were chanting something. One of them spoke a little more clearly.

"*Bind Undead,*" he chanted.

Kelsey cocked her head to the side and waited a beat, but nothing happened. The robed figures started to look a little uncertain.

"Yeah, I'm not undead, sorry, guys," Kelsey said. Then her guns swept up and started firing.

Anton went back to executing guards as they started recovering. He slashed at Hazan, but the courl used a trait to block. He was stronger than Anton, but he was still coughing and weeping from the gas. Anton pulled back, putting the courl off balance and used *Uncanny Evasion* to slip past the courl's wild counterstrike. It put him too close to use his sword, but a shove and a leg sweep put the guardsman on the ground, his spear clattering away.

Another *Quick Attack* took the courl's life and a decent amount of experience.

More guards were running up to replace them, though.

"Kelsey!" Anton called out. Kelsey had broken away from him and was bent over the body of the mage.

"Sorry!" she called back. "Couldn't miss this!"

She held up the courl's mage core before sending it away to storage. Another metal cylinder replaced it.

"Let's get this party started again!" she said, throwing it at Anton's feet. Smoke billowed around him as both Kelsey and a fresh set of guards approached.

Once she reached him, she handed him another cylinder.

"You can throw farther," she said. "Let's spread the love, right?"

They had a few moments. The fresh guards were holding back, wary of entering the cloud. Anton took the smoke bomb and pulled the release as he'd been shown. Then he threw it, as far forward into the stands as he could.

Another canister, another throw. This one went in the opposite direction. People started to scream. People started to move. People started to panic.

"Let's make for the nobles' entrance," Kelsey said. "If we block it off with smoke, they'll have to flee through the commoner sections."

Anton felt it when it happened. Well, he didn't just *feel* it.

You have reached Level 5.
Please allocate free Ability points.

"He did it," Anton told Kelsey. He'd been worried it wouldn't count for him since he wasn't the one who'd freed the prisoners. But he'd been a part of the plan, and it couldn't have happened without the distraction he'd provided. That was, apparently, enough to count. Added to all the deaths he'd caused, it was enough to put him up to the next level.

Strength and Toughness, he thought, playing to his strengths.

Applying Benefits for Level 5
Strength + 2
Toughness + 2
Agility + 1
Dexterity + 1
Perception + 1
Willpower + 1
Charisma + 1

"Let's get out of here," Kelsey said. They had reached the exit by then, keeping it clear by dint of a constant supply of choking smoke. Several attempts had been made to charge them, but no one had found an answer yet. Even a Tier Four had been forced to retreat when a simple cloth mask had proved ineffective.

Anton knew they were running out of time, though. Kelsey had warned him that the masks could only be used for a brief time before the filters wore out. Changing masks was possible, but it would mean exposing his nose and eyes to the gas.

So they left. No one was willing to stay near the gas, so they didn't have to worry about a perimeter. Anton was a little surprised there were *no* guards, but after they travelled a little farther, they got a view of the *other* entrance.

"Yeah, let's steer clear of *that* carnage," Kelsey said.

Anton nodded. He handed his mask to Kelsey and they headed for the rendezvous point. The kids had found the spot where the sewers entered the river.

"I don't see the girls," Anton said nervously.

"Don't worry, they'll make it," Kelsey assured him.

There was a sudden sharp boom from nearby. Anton jumped in surprise, but he knew what the sound had to be. The sewers were kept locked off by a thick iron grate, with bars as thick as his arm. They were no match for Kelsey's demolitions, though.

Anton looked over the wall that separated the sewer from the slightly less smelly docklands. It wasn't long before he saw Zaphar, accompanied by the two kids and a host of other figures, stumble through the stream of waste towards daylight.

Kelsey threw a rope ladder over the wall. You could get out through the river, but you'd have to swim. Zaphar was the first one up. He was already complaining.

"Why do I always—always—get the worst jobs?"

Free Fallin'

TYLA

Tyla knew what she had to do. They all did. It had been explained; they had gone over every step. For most of the steps, they had practiced exactly what they had to do.

It was hard, though, to remember anything when al-Kadir started heading their way. He was too far away for his aura to work, but when his eyes had swept over them, Tyla had felt the fear that a small animal feels when a hunter has marked them as their prey.

It was worse for Soraya, of course. Aris and Tyla had been noted, but the hunter's attention had merely brushed over them. They had been dismissed. Soraya was this courl's prey.

She froze, but Tyla was expecting that. Kelsey had predicted it.

"She's not a fighter," Kelsey had said. "When the fight starts, she's going to freeze up, try to work out what's going on before she makes a move. Aris might, too; she's used to combat happening at a distance."

Tyla knew that combat didn't happen at a distance. If you didn't move, the raiders took you. If you didn't fight, they held you down and . . .

Tyla moved. She grabbed Soraya and pulled her down from where she'd been standing. She'd been making herself visible, but now they had been seen, and they needed to move.

Aris was moving on her own, which was good. Soraya made some noises, some protest, but she quickly realized what was happening. They ran. Not for the exit. They ran *up*.

The walls of the arena rose two man-heights over the highest level of the stands. Then a roof rose *farther*, angling inward to provide some shade. Exiting the stadium over the roof was not *impossible*. Anton or Zaphar could do it, clinging to the wall like a spider and climbing out.

Or Tyla could cast a spell.

True flight was beyond her, much to her dissatisfaction. She could slow someone's fall, or cause them to rise gently into the air. She cast the spell on Aris first. She was a higher level than Soraya, better suited for catching the roof and climbing over. She didn't wait for Aris to start rising, but immediately cast the spell on Soraya.

Al-Kadir was running across the arena sands. He was coming.

Even as Soraya rose into the air, Tyla cast the spell on herself and jumped. They didn't have much time. Even as they clambered up and over, Tyla was acutely aware that this obstacle wouldn't slow al-Kadir at all. They weren't sure how his blink step worked, exactly. It might be that he would have to blink up to the roof and follow them. Or he might be able to blink straight through the wall. A fall of fifty feet or so would not bother him.

It would bother them, though, so Tyla couldn't simply cancel her spell. Instead, she cancelled it for *her* and grabbed on to the other two. Her weight dragged them down and prevented them from drifting off, while their lift kept her from falling. They drifted down, far slower than Tyla would have liked, but when the ground came up to meet them, Tyla realized it was faster than was safe.

She knew how to roll with a fall. She cancelled the spells on the others just before she let go. Soraya had the breath knocked out of her, but Aris was there, helping Tyla get Soraya moving again. They didn't have much time. They needed to get to the alleyway before al-Kadir made it out of the arena.

Get to the alleyway, but don't get in it.

"Al-Kadir is a gladiator," Kelsey had said. "He doesn't have tracking traits; he's never had to hunt someone down across anything other than ten yards of sand. If you get out of sight, he's screwed."

She'd made a face at that. "If he loses you too soon, he'll come back to get answers out of me, and he might be able to fight through the gas. So you need to keep him on the hook."

They reached the alleyway, and Tyla held back. She held Soraya back, too. Soraya made a soft complaining sound, much like a cat would. She didn't want to wait, but she didn't struggle. She knew they had to stay in sight.

Al-Kadir might not remember Tyla, but he would recognize Soraya. They didn't have to wait long. Al-Kadir appeared on the roof of the arena.

So he can't teleport through walls, Tyla thought. *That is important information.*

It didn't take long for him to notice them. As soon as he started moving, Tyla released Soraya and they ran.

The chase was on. They rounded the first corner, and Tyla cast her next spell.

Alleyways have trash. This hadn't had enough for Kelsey's purposes—they'd had to bring some in, stacking it in precariously piled heaps. Now, as they ran, Tyla tugged at the piles as she passed, bringing them down in a crashing, clattering tumble.

Ostensibly, this was to delay pursuit. Anyone else would be slowed by having to pick their way over and through the scattered garbage. Not al-Kadir, though. He was too fast and too strong to be meaningfully impeded. The real reason Tyla was scattering trash behind her was to leave a trail. They had other ways to slow al-Kadir down.

A crash of metal into stone and an angry snarl was the sound of al-Kadir running into her earlier spell.

It was strange, but the kind of mana that Tyla knew as Water was used for many other things than just that. It covered most liquids. Not *all* liquids, Kelsey had pointed out with irritation. Blood was covered by Human or Animal mana despite, as Kelsey put it, being practically the same thing. Molten earth and metal were still covered by Earth. But Tyla was able to create wine, water, and vinegar with a spell. And oil. It didn't last for very long, disappearing into thin air when the mana was used up. But it lasted for long enough to make the flagstones treacherously slippery on the first turn.

"Faster!" she called out to Soraya ahead of her. The courl was already running out of breath. Tyla was not. She couldn't run as fast as al-Kadir, but she could keep this pace up for an hour at least. She needed to.

Ahead, Aris took a right. *They* needed to turn left, and Soraya did it as they'd practiced. Splitting up was one way to evade pursuit, but they were pretty sure that al-Kadir was only interested in Soraya. That gave Aris an opportunity.

After the left, a right, and then they were out of sight. Tyla pulled down another pile of garbage to let him know where they'd gone. She didn't bother oiling the corner—he wouldn't be fooled a second time that way.

A loud crack from behind them told Tyla that al-Kadir had rounded the corner and Aris had taken her shot. Tyla didn't stop running, but she listened. There hadn't been any further shots by the time they reached what Kelsey chose to call the danger house.

The number of shots was a signal. They had thought that Aris would only have time to get one shot off before al-Kadir was out of sight. It would have been more if she was firing pistols, but putting distance between them was important. If al-Kadir had turned on Aris, she would have fired as many times as she could get off. If she fired a *second* shot, it was a signal that al-Kadir had dodged the first.

"I don't think he's got a danger sense," Kelsey had said. "In all his fights, he's been facing the other guy, and he's known his opponent is trying to kill him. I'm not sure there's anything that danger sense would have done for him that basic situational awareness wouldn't do."

There was little hope that Aris would be able to kill him, even with a rifle shot to the back. Kelsey had described how her shots were *deflected*, just slightly, turning a lethal wound into a flesh one.

If he'd had a danger sense, he would have dodged, and Aris would have fired a second shot to let them know that. That meant the danger house was going to work. Probably.

They hadn't been able to put any traps in the alleyways. Kelsey had *wanted* to but had been convinced that regular townsfolk setting off the traps would have been detrimental to their chances. Even if it would have been funny.

So they had rented a house. Not a *nice* house. It was large, with ten rooms and two stories, but it had fallen into disrepair. The walls were still strong, but all the furnishings, doors, and windows were rotting. The floor of the upper story was ready to give way at any moment. The merchant who'd rented it to them had barely been able to conceal his glee at getting some money for the barely habitable building. Tyla wondered if he would still be so pleased once the week was up.

Kelsey had drilled them, again and again, about lifting their feet as they went over the threshold. She'd made them do it blindfolded. Soraya had been the most vocal complainer at the time, but it was all worth it now, as she stumbled up to the building. Exhausted, she still managed not to trigger the bomb.

Tyla was right behind her. She didn't dare look back to see how close al-Kadir was behind *her*. There were no lights in the building, and all the other doors and windows had been boarded up. Tyla could see perfectly well in the dim light, though, and both of them had been drilled on the path they had to take through the maze of debris-ridden rooms.

They were halfway to their destination when the bomb went off. Kelsey had suspected that he would be on the lookout for the large boxes of explosives that she'd used before. This bomb was much smaller. Kelsey had promised that it would turn any normal person into "stew." Against the supernaturally tough gladiator, she was less certain.

From the howl of pain and rage that resulted, Tyla gathered that some damage had been done, but al-Kadir was very far from finished. Tyla could hear crashing sounds from the front that suggested their hunter was still active. But they were here.

Soraya stumbled forward, towards the pit. She knew where she was going, but she was tired enough to make mistakes. Tyla caught her before she could fall, and directed her to the ladder. Under almost any other circumstance, the young courl would have balked at climbing down in the darkness, but she moved without protest.

Al-Kadir was still stumbling around in the outer parts of the building. Tyla got on the ladder and grabbed at the rope for the trapdoor. Kelsey's skeletons, disturbing as they were, did good work. They had drilled and dug through to the sewer network, installed this ladder and the concealed trapdoor that Tyla now pulled over herself. Debris had been stuck to the other side, to make it look like it was just part of the ruined floor. It wouldn't fool determined scrutiny, but in the dark of the interior it would last long enough.

At the bottom of the ladder, Soraya pulled out a light-stone. Relief and disgust warred for supremacy on her face.

"We're not safe yet," Tyla said. "This way."

They didn't have to wade through human refuse; there was a walkway. The smell was bad enough as it was, but they didn't have much choice. After a minute's brisk walk, they came to the plunger. Kelsey had just left it sitting on the floor, the wires fixed to the wall and ceiling, leading back the way they had come.

"You do it," Soraya said. "I'm too tired."

Tyla nodded. It took some strength to push the plunger down. You had to do it quickly or it wouldn't work. She put her full weight behind it.

The explosion was separated from them by both a layer of earth and an entire floor of the condemned building. Putting the explosives on the second floor meant that al-Kadir would never get a chance to see them before they went off. So all they heard was a muffled, but still loud, boom. Closer to them, there was the clatter of some rocks falling down the shaft they had come in from.

Tyla got some experience, but not nearly enough.

"We stopped him," she said. "But I don't think we killed him."

Soraya nodded glumly, and they headed off to the rendevous point.

CHAPTER SEVENTEEN

Express Yourself

Aris leaned against Anton's arm as the wagon carried them slowly back to the village where their boat was moored. Kelsey had arranged for the covered wagon ahead of time, of course. They'd waited until nightfall and then slipped across the river under the cover of darkness. Patrols had been light and easily evaded by people with Darkvision.

The three separate explosions that Aris had heard from different parts of the city might have had something to do with *why* the patrols were so light. Aris hoped that, since the explosions were purely a distraction, collateral damage had been kept to a minimum, but Kelsey's impish grin when they'd gone off made that hope slim.

She didn't ask. Asking questions like that was how she'd learned the term *collateral damage.*

The wagon was slow but unobtrusive. They'd escaped the security cordon before getting to it, and now they could rest while the oxen pulled them the rest of the way. Kelsey was making some noises about replacing them with untiring undead, but that would be more than a little obtrusive.

It was a little cramped, and a little hot. Kelsey had assumed that they'd pick up a few extra gladiators, but Zaphar had exceeded her expectations. It was going to be crowded on the boat back as well. At least Kelsey kept them well supplied with ice-cold water. And Aris didn't mind an excuse to sit close to Anton.

On her other side, Soraya was trying to keep as much distance as possible between herself and Aris. She was exceedingly uncomfortable being put into close quarters with "sweaty humans," which was Kelsey's current source of amusement.

"So are you going to pick one, or what?" Kelsey asked Soraya.

"One what?" Soraya said warily.

"A class." Looking at the others, Kelsey explained, "She's topped out Tier One, but she's still a Merchant Apprentice."

"Congratulations," Aris said, trying to inject some real warmth into the word. Soraya was part of the team now, but she was still part of the family that had enslaved Cheia. And she ate human meat as if that was perfectly normal. "If you wanted advice, Anton has studied up on different classes."

Anton stirred when she mentioned his name but didn't say anything. Soraya bristled, which on a courl meant that some of her fur did stand up.

"I don't need advice on *classes*. It's perfectly clear what they entail from the names. I'm just uncertain of what my future holds, so I'm finding it difficult to determine what class I should get."

"Talk to us, sweetie," Kelsey said with a grin. "I'm curious about what you qualify for."

Soraya glared at her but sighed. "I suppose it will pass the time," she said. "And the shame is greatly reduced in *this* company."

"Very classy," Kelsey laughed. "Is that a fancy way of saying that we already know all the terrible things you did that got you better classes?"

Soraya stared at Kelsey evenly for a long moment. "Yes," she said shortly.

She sighed again and closed her eyes briefly. "Obviously, having completed Merchant Apprentice, I qualify for Merchant. That's a Fine class, and what I always thought I would be. However, I'm no longer sure that I will be able to practice that trade in the near future."

"So what else have you got?" Kelsey asked eagerly.

Soraya frowned. "I did qualify for Thieving Merchant and Penniless Merchant as well. Those are both Fine as well, if decidedly inferior."

"Don't be so snobbish," Kelsey said. "I'll bet Thieving Merchant would be a lot more useful to you right now, and I imagine *other* merchants who have lost everything would find Penniless Merchant to have useful traits. I think *you* can skip that one, though. I can bankroll you like I did for Zaphar's momentary career as a bottle seller."

"If you should have a *need* for a merchant, which seems unlikely," Soraya muttered under her breath. "My other options are more . . . disturbing. To start with, there is Charming Grifter. I don't know why a criminal class like that is *Rare*, but it is."

"Charming Grifter requires that one of your marks is in love with you," Anton said, his deep voice rumbling through Aris.

Soraya leaned forward to look around Aris. "*What?*" she asked intensely.

"One of the people that you've . . . conned," Anton said. He seemed taken aback. "I suppose it could mean your father? He was the one you tricked out of the ransom, after all."

"I suppose," Soraya said. She released Anton from her glare and faced forward again. "I'm not sure that makes me feel any better, though. The other Class of note is Deadly Poisoner. Another Rare."

"Oooh, take that one!" Kelsey said immediately. "I will give you a shiny thing if you do! Or . . ." She thought for a second. "Here! A tasty sweet if you pick Deadly Poisoner."

"Don't be ridiculous," Soraya snapped. "I'm not going to make a decision that determines my *life*, for a sweet."

"Two sweets!" Kelsey said. "Three! But that's my final offer."

Soraya turned her nose up in response. "I don't even know why I qualify for that," she said.

"You poisoned those guards, remember?" Anton said. "And they died."

"Not from the poison!" Soraya exclaimed. "Tyla stabbed them!"

"But they would have been able to resist if they weren't poisoned," Anton said. "So you helped, at least."

"I don't believe I ever thanked you for your help in that matter," Tyla said flatly. She was farther down the line, but everyone in the wagon was aware of the current conversation. "So, thank you."

Soraya's ears went back, flat to her skull. She struggled to control herself. "I didn't—they weren't supposed to—"

She cut herself off and took a deep breath.

"I bet Deadly Poisoner qualifies you for some Alchemist traits," Kelsey said enticingly. "I can provide reagents and a lab . . ."

"Don't you have enough poisons?" Anton asked.

"Bite your tongue, there's no such thing," Kelsey said, pouting.

"I'm *not* taking Poisoner," Soraya stated firmly.

"Boo!" Kelsey said. "Charming Grifter would be useful—would have *been* useful—but as you know, we've already got a con artist."

"It's bad enough that I've engaged in such acts," Soraya said snippishly. "I don't particularly care to advertise the fact."

Kelsey shrugged. "Grifter will probably have something to disguise your class, same as Zaphar's Fae-Touched Rogue."

"It seems wasteful to spend a trait just to conceal your class," Soraya said. "And I won't get any trait until my second level. I'd have to . . . *grift* without that advantage."

"True, true," Kelsey said. "But we wouldn't be having this discussion if you were just going to take Merchant and be done."

"Well . . . it is a Rare class," Soraya said wistfully. "You don't just set that aside."

Aris nodded. She remembered how excited she was to get her Unique class and how much Suliel was willing to risk for her Epic class. Higher rarities meant higher abilities, and rarity almost never went down when you made it to the next tier.

"Suliel says . . . that there is a need for merchants in Kirido, but she doesn't know how well a courl merchant would do, trading in Zamarra," Kelsey said thoughtfully. "Maybe trading in a hostile environment would be worth a better class?"

"There *is* such a class," Soraya said glumly. "Determined Merchant. It's well known and revered, but it's hard—the conditions have to be very hostile and you have to do *very* well. Aiming for it deliberately is considered foolish."

"There's Adventurous Trader," Anton put in. "It's a Rare Tier Two class, meant for delvers who want to trade with what they take in the dungeon. The easy way to get it is to have had both the Adventurer and Trader Classes, but I think just Trader will do if you've delved a dungeon."

Soraya shuddered. "No thanks. I have no wish to see what Kelsey is truly like."

Kelsey grinned. "Aw, these days I'm a soft little pushover, letting anyone just walk all over and in me."

"I don't believe that for a second," Soraya muttered.

"You can always go back to Merchant when you get a chance to become one," Aris suggested. "You should probably consider which class will get the most experience from what comes next."

"And what will that be?" Soraya asked bitterly. "We're not expecting any trouble on the way back, are we? And once we are in Kirido, I'm not sure what use I'll be."

"Well . . ." Kelsey said temptingly. "If you were a Poisoner, I could set you up with a lab and you could make all sorts of pretty poisons. And everyone you kill with them will be a nice chunk of experience."

"I don't *want* to kill people!" Soraya protested. "I just want to make a lot of money and live a life of ease!"

"Whoa, that's crazy talk!" Kelsey said. "*Not* killing people?"

"You might want to just take Merchant, then," Aris said gently, ignoring Kelsey's performance. "I'm sure Suliel will be able to find some role for you."

"Would that be . . . allowed?" Soraya asked softly, looking at Kelsey.

"Hmm? Oh, you think I'll *make* you choose Poisoner? Honestly, do you think I'd be offering you my valuable sweets if I was going to do that?"

"I wasn't sure," Soraya said stiffly, "if that was all an elaborate joke at my expense."

"I would never!" Kelsey protested. Aris was fairly sure that meant it *was*. "I'm not clear on the etiquette on these things, but Suliel got *all kinds* of upset when her mother tried to force her away from her class. I kinda figured it wasn't the *done thing*."

Soraya stared at Kelsey for a second, as if waiting for her to change her mind. "Then I will take Merchant, unless someone has more advice."

"Penniless Merchant might be the way to go, I think," Anton said thoughtfully.

Soraya looked at him. "Why?" she asked.

"Variant classes like that may have equivalent abilities, but they generally offer better traits. At the very least, traits more appropriate to the situation the class refers to, and . . . you don't have any money."

"How much better?" Soraya asked.

"I don't know. Merchants, more than anybody, keep their traits secret," Anton said, scowling as if they were keeping secrets from him, specifically.

"Then . . ." Soraya said, sighing. "I suppose that's what I'll do."

You didn't get traits on your first level, so there were no immediate revelations about Soraya's choice. The rest of the journey was uneventful.

Uneventful, that is, until they reached the village where they had left the boat.

"What happened here?" Soraya asked.

The village looked wrecked, reminding Aris uncomfortably of her hometown when the raiders had come. Fires had damaged about half of the buildings. Smoke and bodies were everywhere. Most of them wore Elitran uniforms, but not all of them.

The remaining villagers were gathering bodies and cleaning up desultorily. Several of them looked at the wagon as they approached, but no one hailed them or came near.

"Cheia," Aris whispered. "We should have brought her."

"At least the boat is still there," Kelsey said, pointing beyond the village. The *Whiskerwind* was floating out in the bay. They had *left* it tied to the small jetty that was all that the fishing village boasted, but it was still here.

"Cheia!" Aris shouted, jumping out of the wagon and running into the village. She headed for the jetty, but she kept an eye out for anyone she knew. She recognized some of the villagers, but they shied away from her, ducking around corners or into ruined buildings.

Something about the damage to the buildings impinged on Aris's mind. There was more general fire damage, that was true. But a lot of the buildings had holes in them that didn't look like sword or axe or spear damage. The bodies she passed had familiar-looking gunshot wounds.

By the time she got to the pier, the *Whiskerwind* had started moving. Aris could hear the throb of its engine as it clumsily turned towards the jetty.

As it got closer, Aris could see that it was packed with her fellow townsfolk.

"Cheia!" she yelled, and a small figure came forward, waving. Aris sobbed with relief.

By the time the ship reached the dock, the others had caught up. Cheia was the first to get off the ship, and Aris grabbed her before the younger girl got both feet on dry land.

"Cheia! I was so worried!" Aris sobbed.

"It's fine, sis, everyone is fine," Cheia said. She managed to pry herself free and looked nervously at the group.

"I can explain," she said.

CHAPTER EIGHTEEN

I Beg Your Pardon

SULIEL

Suliel rode in the carriage to what, she explicitly reminded herself, was *not* her doom. She was wearing a dress more expensive than any she had ever owned. It was not to her taste, nor had the dressmaker been pleased by her requirements.

Fashion in the capital ran to elaborately billowed dresses in rich reds, blues, and greens. Suliel knew her slight frame would be lost in one of those, so she'd asked for a gown with a thinner, more elegant silhouette. That had been bad enough, but the dressmaker had despaired when Suliel had asked for it in black, with silver highlights.

"Oh no, no, no," the dressmaker had said. "You don't want that! Your skin will be lost against it, and besides—"

The woman cut herself off, not wishing to point out that Suilel's skin was just a shade too light for *proper* nobility. It was dark enough to not be scandalous, but it was noticeably lighter than both her parents. Something that implied interesting things about her ancestry, but Kirido *was* a dungeon town, after all. Adventurers came from all over.

Suliel had insisted, though. People talking about her skin tone was not even the least of her concerns. If they were talking about *that*, then they wouldn't be talking about any of the things she *was* worried about. Skin tone wasn't going to get her executed.

Glinting over the dark fabric were some of her mother's jewels, left behind when she'd fled. Suliel had needed advice from both Seraphina and Princess Elara—solicited separately, of course—on what portion of her mother's collection to wear. No noble wore *all* of their jewelry, naturally. That would be gauche. Suliel needed to wear as much as she could, without appearing to be the young, inexperienced, nouveau riche baroness that she was.

It would have been easier to wear *less*, to call on a simple elegance that went with the gown, but Suliel needed to wear *more*.

She was a sovereign, after all. Ignoring or trying to hide that fact would not go down well with the King.

The carriage pulled up in the courtyard, and Suliel took a deep breath. This was where it started. The important people were inside, but there were watchers in the courtyard who would take what they saw here and report it to those waiting, and to those courtiers who were absent from court today.

The door opened, the steps went down, and Suliel stepped out into view, accepting the steadying hand of the royal footman who was there for that purpose. His eyes widened in surprise when he saw her, but he didn't let anything show on his face as he bowed with consummate professionalism.

Then the skeletons stepped out behind her, and he drew back in fear.

The skeletons had been outfitted in Anat livery. Just tabards—they hadn't managed to find a way to attach pants. Scabbards had been a challenge as well, but they had hung them from a strap going across the body, over the opposite shoulder. They still carried their original shields, but they had been painted with Anat heraldry.

Suliel wondered if her mother would die of shame when word reached her of what she had done to the family colors.

Nodding to the footman, Suliel strode forward, her skeletons falling in behind her. As a baroness, she *was* entitled to two guards while at court. Few made use of the privilege. For one, it was discouraged, and for another, it served little purpose. The King's guard outnumbered them all, and disagreements between nobles were not settled with violence in the King's house.

Suliel wasn't expecting the skeletons to protect her. For all Kelsey's promises of their exceeding skill, the Lazybones were only Tier Two trash monsters. The guards and many of the nobles had nothing to fear from them. Their grinning faces did make a statement, though.

Suliel stopped at the top of the entryway stairs. She was supposed to be escorted in, but there was no one to greet her. She looked around. The guards were looking at her with concern but not making a move.

"Sir!" Suliel called out. "Do you intend to leave me waiting at the gate?"

There was a pause. Then the royal page slunk out from behind the guards, staring at her sullenly. Suliel just looked back with her best impression of an imperious stare. If the stakes weren't so high, she would have laughed. The page was barely older than she was, and he'd clearly been spooked by the skeletons. Suliel quickly looked him over.

**Tainan Dorel, Level 4, Father, Mother and Two Sisters All in Bures,
Loyal to the Lord Chamberlain, Human, Page**

"Well?" she asked.

He bowed shakily. "Please follow me, my lady," he said reluctantly. He flinched as the skeletons clattered into motion behind her.

Tainan led her through the palace, but he kept edging away from her, clearly unwilling to be near her guards. It would have been amusing, but Suliel had to concentrate on maintaining her dignified pose and bearing. It had gotten easier since her Agility had improved, but she still couldn't move quickly.

"Tainan!" she barked. He yelped and stood at attention, giving her a chance to close the distance.

"Do I have to have my guards hold you in place, or are you going to escort me *properly*?" Suliel enquired. She tried to keep her tone gentle, but more than a little irritation seeped in. She had better things to worry about than this!

<I am genuinely turned on by how much you're intimidating this poor kid,> Kelsey sent. *<Can you make him piss his pants?>*

Suliel ignored her vulgar partner.

"I—I'll escort you properly, my lady," Tianan stammered.

"Good," Suliel said, allowing the boy to resume his duties.

"Baroness Suliel Nos!" the herald proclaimed loudly. He hesitated for a moment before continuing. "Sovereign of the Crypts!"

Suliel stepped forward into the sudden silence. It wasn't *usual* to have the herald call out your class as a special title. It would get a little boring with all the "Nobles" and "Ladies" that would be called. But when your class was as unusual as Suliel's, the rules changed.

Suliel had two options. It might have been wiser for her to not draw attention to her class. To pretend it did not exist, to meekly bow and scrape to the King, and hope that he did not take offense by her mere existence.

That did not seem like the right course to Suliel. The King *knew* about her class. Half of this room had *Nobility's Privilege* and was a higher level than her. *They* would know, by the simple expedient of looking at her. There was no hiding her class, even as a pretense.

Instead, with Kelsey's enthusiastic support, Suliel had decided to *own* her class. She glided forward. Every eye was on her while every part of *her* attention focused on walking with effortless poise while her eyes roved widely, looking for familiar faces.

She saw Seraphina, casually speaking with another noble lady, carefully *not* looking at Suliel as she passed. It was best that they weren't seen as being close.

She saw her mother, standing next to her liege lord, Count Brankil. They watched her go by, their faces expressionless. Lord Brankil had refused to meet with her until she had been accepted into court, which was unsurprising. Should she live past today, she would have to call on him.

She didn't see Princess Elara until she drew near the King. She was seated on the dais behind him, along with the rest of the family and a few court officials. She gave Suliel an encouraging smile.

They were nearing the end of the carpet, so with a mental nudge from her, the Lazybones stopped and knelt. She carried on another ten feet to the pre-scribed distance and looked up at her King.

Ranon Kalond IV, Level ??, Wife, Son, and Daughter All in Bures, Sovereign, Human, Wise King

She knelt without hesitation. That had been the plan, but even if it hadn't been, she would have. Even if her inspection had shown her that he was a False King, she would have. King Kalond's presence was too majestic to do otherwise.

That's the power of a double Charisma progression, Suliel thought with awe. *A counterpoint wormed its way into her mind. One day, I'll have that much Charisma.*

It was said that the rulers of both empires had Charisma scores so high that they could not be looked upon by lesser folk. They were cordoned off, served by high-level officials with strong Willpower and slaves whose minds had been lost to adoration. The King's Charisma was not that high, but Suliel started to believe that such a thing was possible.

"Suliel Nos," the King said. "You got married."

"I did, your Majesty," Suliel said. If that was where the King wanted to start, then that was fine.

"And yet, he is not here," the King said. "He is the Baron, now, is he not? Why is he not here for my blessing?"

Suliel was pretty sure the King knew the answer to this question. Assuming he listened to the reports of his judge, anyway. But court was more performance than anything else, so she answered the question without hesitation.

"He is a hero, your Majesty. He sailed south, having sworn to rescue as many of his fellow townsfolk from the raiders as he could."

"A hero, you say? Our last report has him as a mere adventurer."

"He has reached his third tier," Suliel said proudly. There was a murmur of response from the listening nobles.

"And how does he fare on this mission of his?" the King asked.

"The last report I have states that he has rescued the last group of captives and is heading home."

Another murmur from the nobles. The King's face was impassive.

"And what is the source of your reports?"

"A trait from my class," Suliel stated. That should be the end of it. It was rude in the extreme to inquire about a person's class. To do so in front of all the gathered nobles . . . it *was* within the King's privilege, but Suliel doubted he would press her.

"A potent trait for a Tier Two class," the King mused. "Epic classes really are a different beast. My own class is only Rare; I can't help but feel jealous."

He hadn't asked a question, so Suliel stayed silent.

"A potent class indeed," the King continued. "One wonders if we should cut off this growing bud before it flowers into a threat."

Suliel swallowed nervously. "There is no need, your Majesty," she said. "As a loyal subject of yours, any growth on my part serves the Kingdom."

"Does it?" the King asked. "Can you say with honesty that all your actions have been in accordance with my will?"

"I—" Suliel started, but he was still speaking.

"You imprisoned and exiled your mother. You imprisoned my captain for a crime he did not commit. And there is, of course, your class."

"I released Captain Oldaw as soon as there was evidence clearing him," Suliel said hastily. "Given the nature of the crime, I'm sure you agree I had to act swiftly according to the knowledge I had at the time."

"Now would be a good time to replace that sword you took," the King said mildly. Suliel winced.

"That sword has been reforged," she admitted. "And . . . lost, on my husband's adventures. It is no longer available."

<If he's going to be a baby about it, I can make another one,> Kelsey sent.

Suliel didn't respond. The Glimmering Sword was more a historical artifact than a useful weapon. The King could afford to commission his own Tier Two weapons. Tier Three would be a different matter, but she knew that Kelsey couldn't make those. Yet.

The King stayed silent, so Suliel continued with her defense. "My mother's actions were equally egregious, and my response to them was within my prerogative as Baroness."

She didn't elaborate on what her mother had done. The King knew already.

"Finally," she said, "you have set no law on what classes may be taken. I recognize that the name might seem to be . . . competition, but there is no such clash."

She pointed behind her, and the Lazybones stood up and saluted.

"My class may have the word 'Sovereign' in it, but *that* is my domain," she said. "It is a domain that lies outside of yours and one that you have no wish to lay claim to. I am neither a usurper nor a secessionist, but a loyal subject of your Majesty."

The King was silent for a moment. The moment lasted for about a thousand years as far as Suliel could tell.

"A loyal subject?" he asked wryly. "There is a first time for everything, I suppose."

The court tittered at the King's joke.

"I will withhold judgment on your actions, Baroness," the King said, "until I can get a better grasp on your character. For now, be welcome in this court."

Suliel felt a surge of relief. Relief and . . . something else.

You have reached Level 5.
Please allocate 2 free Ability points.

Agility. Agility, Suliel thought immediately. After being clumsy for so long, she was addicted to the improvement in grace that went with an Agility increase.

Applying Benefits for Level 5
Strength + 1
Toughness + 1
Perception + 1
Willpower + 1
Charisma + 2

"Growing quickly indeed," the King said, his face unreadable. "We will call upon you again, Baroness, for a more private discussion. Until then, you are dismissed."

CHAPTER NINETEEN

Having an Average Weekend

I can explain," Cheia said nervously.

Kelsey grinned and looked around at the devastation like a proud parent. "No need," she said. "One look at you tells me all I need to know."

Cheia laughed nervously and glanced at Aris. Aris narrowed her eyes.

"Anton," she said calmly. "What does her status say?"

"Her status?" Anton asked. Then he looked.

Cheia Lucina, Level 10, Human, Original Gunner's Apprentice, Doxy/ Original Gunner's Apprentice, S: 11 T: 4 A: 15 D: 16 P: 15 W: 15 C: 14

"Oh," he said. "Level ten already?"

"It's not my fault!" Cheia protested. "We were attacked!"

"Oh, Cheia, no," Aris said. "*You* did all this?"

"Not all of it," Cheia said, looking around. Anton noticed that the sullen glares from the villagers had increased. Most of them were directed at Cheia.

"Oh, Cheia," Aris remonstrated. "I didn't want you getting into . . . all this." She gestured at the village.

"I was just doing what you would, sis!" Cheia insisted. "When those troops came, I had to protect everyone!"

"I really want to hear all about it," Kelsey said. "But maybe not on the dock? Should we move to the ship, or do we still have a place here?"

"The hut is still there," Cheia said. "They haven't tried to kick us out. No one wants us here anymore, but they're too scared to say anything."

"Perfectly handled," Kelsey said with a grin. "No notes."

"Kelsey!" Aris scolded. "That's not the sort of impression we want to give!"

"Nah, it's fine," Kelsey said unrepentantly. "Fear will keep them in line, fear of this battle station!"

"Is that another word for boat?" Anton asked. Kelsey stuck her tongue out at him.

"We thought it would be best to move back onto the boat," Cheia said. "Aside from the villagers not liking us anymore, we weren't sure if any of the soldiers got away."

"So you're all ready to leave?" Kelsey asked. "That's fortunate. We should get the guys on board and head out then. There's nothing left here for us."

"I'm not sure we're going to have enough beds on board," Cheia said, looking at the ex-gladiators getting off the cart. "Oh! Hi, Thalorin!"

"People can share bunks," Kelsey said dismissively.

"Kelsey!" Aris exclaimed. "It's too soon—they shouldn't have to—"

"Plus the beds are too small to be comfortable doing that," Cheia said matter-of-factly.

Kelsey looked at them both. "What I *meant* was, you can sleep in shifts, and each bed can be used by up to three people. I don't know *where* you're getting your ideas from."

"Oh, right," Aris said. "That makes sense."

It took a while to get underway. Kelsey insisted on going over the engine before they left.

"Let me tell you," she said to no one in particular. "It's a real pain to fix one of these when you're drifting with the current into some rocks."

"Is that an experience you've had?" Anton asked. "I thought this was your first sea voyage."

"It's a general admonition," Kelsey said, waving vaguely. "Applies to a lot of things."

With all the arrangements to be made, it wasn't until the evening meal, supplied by Kelsey and eaten on the deck, that Cheia got around to explaining.

"Everything was fine until the soldiers showed up," she said. "I don't know if they were looking for us, but they were looking for *something*. We kept to huts, hoping to stay out of sight until they were gone, but they saw the ship and insisted on searching it, and the village."

She stared into the middle distance, remembering. "The villagers argued with them, but the soldiers just did what they wanted. They split up into small groups and went around all the huts. When they found us, they tried to drag us out of there."

"Did they recognize you?" Kelsey asked.

"I'm not sure. I don't speak the language that well," Cheia said. "They were mostly excited to have found 'women.' There's a couple of reasons they could be happy about that. They didn't get much time to express what they were here for."

"What happened?" Anton asked.

"Well, we were armed," Cheia said. "They weren't expecting that, didn't *recognize* that. So when they started dragging us out, they were surprised by what happened."

"I'll bet," Kelsey said. "I'm going to need to combine an ammo check and a level check, see who got the most experience for the least number of shots."

Cheia nodded absently. "That was just a small group, though. There were other groups all over the village, and one group that was headed for the boat. They'd all heard the shots, even if they didn't know what they were. We thought the best plan was to make for the boat."

"Always secure your escape route," Kelsey said.

"It was pretty scary," Cheia said. "Moving while trying to avoid the soldiers, headed right for a bunch of them. And we only had so many shots. Fortunately, they didn't know that. We . . . killed . . . the group that was between us and the boat, and kept the ones closing in on us back. They'd figured out that we were carrying weapons by then, so they ducked back whenever we waved a gun at them."

"So that left you trapped on the boat," Anton said.

"I'm not sure if 'trapped' is the right word when you could just leave on the boat," Kelsey said. "But you didn't."

"We thought about it," Cheia admitted. "But aside from leaving Aris and the others behind, we knew that the boat only had a day's worth of fuel. And we didn't have a map."

"You could go a long way in a day," Kelsey stated. "But I guess without a map, you wouldn't know where to go."

"Exactly," Cheia agreed. "So we pulled off but stayed in the bay. And then we had another problem."

"Which was?" Anton asked.

"We realized that we couldn't let any of the soldiers escape," Cheia muttered, looking down with shame.

"What? No! Why?" Aris pleaded.

"If we let them go, they would have passed word that we were here," Cheia explained. "Their superiors would have sent boats, or mages, or siege weapons or . . . something that could capture us."

"Very well reasoned," Kelsey purred. "So what did you do?"

"They were yelling at us from the pier," Cheia said, remembering. "Not a hundred yards away. They didn't have any bows, and none of us were good enough shots at that range. Not with the small guns."

"Go on," Kelsey said, her eyes wide.

"They didn't realize what we were doing," Cheia said. "Not until it was too late. They never got a good look at our guns, and the deck sweeper doesn't look like them. Not really. So they just stood there while I set it up like you showed me, and then . . ."

She swallowed.

"I mowed them down. Not all of them. Once they realized what was going on, they jumped in the water, which made it difficult. Some of them managed to swim back to shore."

"Cheia . . ." Aris interjected, but the younger girl pressed on.

"I got a trait," she said. "All of the ones available had strange names, but I took the one that said Targeting because that was what I was having trouble with right then. It made it so I could see a . . . light, wherever the gun was pointing."

"Targeting Reticule, maybe?" Kelsey asked. Cheia paused.

"That word, yes, that's what it said. So I could aim over longer distances, and we *still* needed to make sure that the soldiers didn't report back. So I kept shooting."

"But not at the villagers, surely?" Aris asked. "They were trying to protect you!"

"At longer ranges," Cheia said, "the deck sweeper doesn't hit exactly where it's pointed at. And the soldiers started hiding."

"So, an important distinction that hasn't been needed up to now," Kelsey said, "is the one between *hard* cover and *soft* cover. Hard cover will stop a bullet, while soft cover will only block the shooter from *seeing* you. It won't save you if they shoot right through."

Cheia nodded. "The village was all soft cover," she said. "It didn't save them. But there was . . . unexpected damage."

Kelsey nodded. "It's not that unusual for machine guns to start fires," she said. "Bullets are surprisingly hot. And there's all sorts of potential for broken oil lamps or debris from a cooking fire that gets hit."

"I tried not to hit the villagers," Cheia said miserably. "And I think I got all of the soldiers. But once the fires started, it got really confusing."

"It sounds like you stepped up, Cheia, and did what was needed," Kelsey said. "I'm proud of you."

"She shouldn't have needed to!" Aris said. "You said they'd be safe here."

"I'm pretty sure I put a 'probably' in there," Kelsey said. "Nowhere in this world is totally safe. And hey! Nobody died!"

"That was pure luck!" Aris said.

"It was pretty miraculous that none of us died," Cheia agreed.

"Who's the god of surviving rapidly escalating firefights?" Kelsey asked.

Anton thought for a bit. "Butin?" he suggested. "He's the God of War, at least for Zamarra."

"Huh," Kelsey said. "We did just try to curry favor from his church back in Bures. I wonder if he did intervene?"

"Do you think he did?" Anton asked.

"I hope not!" Kelsey said. "Aside from the fact that it would mean that Cheia needed help, we were counting on getting that help in Bures."

"I didn't see anything that looked like divine intervention," Cheia put in. "Nothing that I couldn't explain."

"Well, maybe we've got that favor still on the books then," Kelsey said.

She looked over at the crowd of ex-slaves still eating. It wasn't everybody. Tyla was steering the boat on the heading that Kelsey had provided, and the sleeping in shifts had started already. Despite the celebratory mood, everyone was keeping their voices down in consideration of the sleeping passengers. It was difficult enough to sleep with the throb of the engines a constant presence.

Kelsey ignored those considerations, of course.

"You did good, girls!" she shouted. "They came to take you away again, and you showed them their graves! I can see that some of you got levels from it as well. Nice!"

The response she got was positive, if a little muted. Except from Aris.

"Kelsey!" she half-whispered urgently. "People are sleeping!"

Kelsey waved her off. "This is important," she insisted. "We're starting something here, and everyone's a part of it. Even the ones that are sleeping."

She looked out over the group again.

"Most of you are from Kirido," she said. "Some of you are from elsewhere on the north coast, captured in a different raid. Some of you were born in the Empire and decided to take your chances as free men. All of you have good reason to hate the Empire."

Anton's gaze searched out Zaphar, who was quietly sitting in a corner, eating his food. Of all the people here, Anton thought, Zaphar should hate the Empire the least. He was just a criminal, and Anton doubted that he felt singled out for punishment like the others. Although there was Soraya.

She was looking distinctly unhappy as Kelsey started outlining the crimes of the Empire that she'd once called home. Most of the crimes were slavery-related, after all, and Soraya still felt part of her family.

"Whether you stay in Kirido is up to you," Kelsey continued. "Some of you have got families to get back to, some of you want to seek your fortune elsewhere. But Kirido needs you."

She paused to look them over again.

"Kirido needs you to fight. To fight against the ones who enslaved you." She looked at Soraya. "To fight against the ones who *want* to enslave you."

She grabbed Anton's arm and held it up. "This one wants to fight for you!" she shouted. "To fight for freedom! Freedom for everyone!"

It wasn't a roar. More of a buzz. A susurration of excitement as people responded but were too polite to forget about their sleeping comrades.

Kelsey dragged Anton to his feet. "Okay, big man," she said. "Time to make your pitch, Baron Nos."

Anton looked at her in surprise. They hadn't discussed this. He looked over the small crowd of expectant faces. He took a deep breath and started to speak.

CHAPTER TWENTY

Limelight

SULIEL

Like a fish that was too small to eat, Suliel had been released back into a pond full of predators. The King's words hadn't been reassuring, but they had been within Suliel's expectations. Her fate would be decided by the *private* meetings the King would hold with her. Most likely, she would live or die based on her ability to meet the King's demands for the new type of weapon.

That was fine; she was prepared for that. Now that she had been recognized, she was permitted to attend court, and it was no longer a minor scandal for a lady or a courtier to speak with her. Given the gossip swirling about her, Suliel might have expected to be swamped by fops and favor-seekers at this point.

She wasn't, thanks to the two skeletons standing behind her. They rose when she did and maintained a respectful distance of two paces behind her. Suliel doubted they would intimidate any serious noble, but the court was full of frivolous timewasters.

It was a shame that she wouldn't be able to bring them on future visits. *Once* made a point. Bringing them again would make her seem standoffish, and the one thing Suliel couldn't afford was to be isolated. She would have to enjoy the use of them while she could.

Looking around, she could see a few people she'd like to talk to, like Princess Elara. The fact that she'd slipped away from her chair behind the King and was mingling was a clear invitation to approach. There were a few people that she had to talk to, like Lord Brankil. Suliel also noted a few of the ladies from her party with Lady Seraphina. She should probably pay her respects to them.

As she moved away from the center of the room, Suliel's eye was drawn to a powerful-looking figure who was standing, straight as a spear, at the edge of the room.

That has to be . . . she used Nobility's Privilege to be sure.

Idran Sehhur, Level ??, Wife and Three Children in Bures, Loyal to King Kalond IV, Human, Paramount Strategist

Suliel shivered. She didn't need Anton's Inspection trait to tell her she was looking at a dangerous man. General Sehhur, the Sword and Shield of Zamarra, was no longer as young as he once had been. But he still stood tall and strong. It looked like he was wearing armor, light plate under loose robes trimmed with gold. That would have told Suliel his rank even if she hadn't known his name.

He was looking not at Suliel, but at her guards. She hoped he wasn't going to ask for a spar. The Lazybones might be skilled, but they couldn't hope to stand against a Tier Four.

Deciding that rank held the privilege of going first, Suliel made her way to Princess Elara. Not directly, of course; that would have been gauche. Ideally, Suliel would have stopped to greet or introduce herself to the other nobles, skipping from group to group like a honeybee visiting flowers. Moving randomly, but always with an eye towards her goal. When she finally intercepted her target, both of them would express surprise at running into each other.

That was the theory, at least, as Suliel's mother had explained it to her once. Suliel had never had the opportunity to try it for herself, and she suspected her attempts at misdirection would be easily seen through. She was finding herself with another problem, however. No one wanted to talk to her.

It was a subtle thing. Ladies neglected to meet her eyes as she approached; lords simply turned their backs. Some of the younger nobles shied away as she merely turned in their direction. It seemed that she'd overdone the intimidation.

None of this would stop her from talking to anyone she needed to, of course. If a noble turned his back, she could simply tap him on his shoulder.

Well. She could tap him on his elbow, that was much the same thing. Why did the elite defenders and rulers of Zamarra have to be so *tall*?

Suliel wasn't worried about Princess Elara refusing to talk with her. The problem was it wouldn't look *natural*. If Suliel just walked towards the Princess, with every other noble scrambling out of her way, it would be a statement as strong as the one she was *trying* to make. People would think she was challenging the Princess to a duel.

She couldn't just stand on her own and wait for the Princess to show up, either. That would make her look weak and isolated. There were a few people that she could expect to talk to, but moving directly to them would single them out, and snub the Princess besides. That just left . . .

Suliel suppressed a sigh. *I really hope it doesn't come to a duel,* she thought.

"General," Suliel said, dipping her head and dropping into a curtsy. "It seemed to me that you had some questions about my escorts."

General Sehhur looked down at her, dark eyes glittering, missing nothing.

"A few," he said, his low voice rumbling. "Why are they not armed with the new weapons I've been hearing so much about?"

Suliel quailed under the weight of his regard. He didn't have a noble's Charisma, but he was close.

"I brought—" Suliel started, and then forced herself to start again. *Without squeaking.* "I brought them here to make a point, not because I thought I needed protection."

"You don't think your life is in danger?" Sehhur asked mildly.

Suliel swallowed nervously. "I'm only on my second tier, General," she said. "There's nothing I can do to directly confront the forces against me. All I can do is throw myself on the mercy of his Majesty."

"A bold strategy," the general said. "Perhaps your best option, given the circumstances."

"High praise from the most renowned strategist in the nation," Suliel murmured. "If you had some advice . . ."

"Ha! Bold suits you, my lady," Sehhur laughed. "But my wisdom is in service to another. However, I would hear your account of the weapons you're bringing."

Suliel wondered if the general knew the truth about the King.

Is that the right way to phrase it? she wondered. If the King is true, then there is nothing to wonder about. Unless he has been fooled by the Rose Circle and believes the King false. If the King is false, then I wonder if he knows the truth.

The more Suliel thought about it, the less likely it seemed that she would ever figure out the truth.

<You're tying yourself in knots,> Kelsey sent. **<Just focus on the sales pitch.>**

"The guns fire a small piece of metal, very fast. Too fast for me to see," she explained, miffed that she'd needed the nudge. "It hits hard enough to be fatal up to at least Tier Three, depending on where it hits."

"Fascinating," Sehhur said. "So it is a threat across tiers, is it?"

"Yes? Is that so unusual? A Tier Two sword can kill a Tier Three warrior, can it not?"

"True," the general rumbled. "But a Tier One warrior cannot hope to hit a Tier Three opponent without very special circumstances. That doesn't seem to be the case for these weapons."

"I'm sure that the other classes will find themselves with traits that counter guns eventually," Suliel said.

"Perhaps," the general allowed. "In any case, I look forward to seeing them in action when—"

"General!" another voice interjected. "Have you been bullying the latest entrant to our father's court?"

Suliel turned to see Princess Elara inserting herself into their conversation.

Oh good, that worked, Suliel thought. Staying in one place let the Princess come to her. A side effect of her rescue, though, was that the Princess's Charisma was absolutely *dazzling.*

She must have been holding it back the other night, Suliel thought. *She's—*

<**Stay strong, kid,**> Kelsey interjected.

General Sehhur was still talking.

"I am not, your Highness," he said. "I was simply—"

"I won't hear of it! She's far too young to be subjected to your harassment."

"She is in her second tier," the general said mildly. "And I was not—"

"I won't put up with a moment more of this," Princess Elara stated. "I'm rescuing her."

She started dragging Suliel away. Suliel resisted for a moment until her mind caught up with what was happening.

"Can you really talk to the Sword and Shield of Zamarra that way?" she asked, scandalized.

"Oh, Sebbey's practically an uncle," Princess Elara said with a giggle. "He knows I wasn't serious."

She glanced behind them. "Your skeletons are quite good at this," she said. "I thought we'd leave them behind."

It was fortunate that her guards were under Suliel's control and not under orders, as they might have reacted badly to the Princess grabbing Suliel. That was also the reason they'd dashed after the pair, managing to maintain distance without losing too much of their dignity. There was a limit to how fast the Princess could drag Suliel without tripping her.

"If you wanted to leave them behind," Suliel said dryly, "you just had to ask. I didn't know anywhere to leave them safely, though."

"Good point," the Princess agreed. "You may as well keep them around. I'll just introduce you to the less cowardly nobles."

What followed was a whirlwind introduction to the Zamarran royal court. Suliel quickly gave up on remembering names; they would be available with a glance when she met them again. She focused on trying to gauge reactions.

On the whole, it didn't *hurt* that she was being introduced by a princess. It partly made up for the deliberately intimidating look she'd been attempting. Memories of previous trips to the capital were starting to come back to Suliel.

She was remembering more names and faces. Old playmates, friends of the family, and other nobles that had been mentioned but never met. Suliel was putting faces and voices to names.

Kelsey assured her that she was keeping track of everyone that Suliel saw. Dungeons had a perfect memory, apparently.

"It must be exciting, making so many new friends!" Elara enthused.

"Overwhelming," Suliel replied. "Do *you* ever get introduced to thirty people at once?"

"Occasionally," Elara said with a wink. "Duties of a princess and all. My wedding was quite crowded with new faces, as I recall."

"Of course," Suliel said, her face growing hot. "I should have realized."

"It's nothing," Elara assured her. "And now, there's just one more person that you need to be introduced to." She indicated with a slight shift of her head whom she was talking about.

"I already know Lord Brankil," Suliel said, her mood dropping a bit. "I don't need to be introduced."

"Perhaps not," Elara admitted. "But a little support goes a long way. I know you haven't been looking forward to speaking with him."

"I do have to, though," Suliel said. "I don't suppose that your father would accept my vassalage to him directly, would he?"

"A promotion to Earl? Or Countess, I suppose in your case. You'd have to sell him the guns *very* cheaply."

<*Sell the guns for cheap, and jack up the price on the ammo,*> Kelsey sent. <*That's the holy scripture of capitalism.*>

Suliel shook her head. "It was just an idle thought," she said.

It was a short walk to their destination.

"Count Kinkin Brankil, I present to you Baroness Suliel Nos," Princess Elara said.

Suliel bowed her head and curtsied.

"My liege," she said.

Lord Kinkin Brankil was tall and slender. He had sharp features and neatly groomed black hair with just a few streaks of silver. He looked down at Suliel as if deciding what to do with her.

"My dear," he said, "I was so sorry to hear about your father."

"It was a great loss to us all," Suliel said, sending a special emphasis Kelsey's way.

<*Feels like I'm being called out,*> Kelsey sent back with a wry emotional tone. <*He did have it coming.*>

Suliel didn't feel up to rehashing that old argument again.

"A tragedy," Princess Elara agreed. "But not one that should be compounded with another, should it?"

"Another tragedy, your Highness?" Count Brankil asked.

"The estrangement of a daughter from her mother," the Princess replied. "Surely, as her liege and her relation, you have a duty to reconcile the two."

The Count looked from Princess Elara to Suliel's shocked face. "Were that possible, we would all rejoice," he said smoothly. He gestured to someone behind him.

One of his entourage stepped forward, dressed in a new gown that she had not left the castle with.

"Hello, Mother," Suliel said.

CHAPTER TWENTY-ONE

Can You Feel It

TYLA

Let me start by saying, I don't really know how this works," Kelsey confessed.

She and Tyla were belowdecks, facing each other, sitting crosslegged in the very front of the boat. It was cramped and a little uncomfortable. Anton had reduced the engines to the minimum, and they'd all gotten used to the *thrum thrum* of them enough to think it was quiet. The only other people down here were the ones sleeping.

It was as close to a private meeting as possible, under the circumstances.

"I've never seen it happen," Kelsey continued. "Mel *has*, but she never stuck around to see the results. Not that some dungeon raider was going to stick around and detail them for her to hear."

Tyla nodded. It seemed appropriate, even if she had no idea what the numen was talking about. Kelsey hadn't yet seen fit to mention what "this" was, but Tyla paid rapt attention nonetheless.

Kelsey gave her an unimpressed look. "That was a warning," she said, "A warning that I don't know what I'm doing, but you're just going to follow my advice willy-nilly, aren't you?"

"I'm not sure," Tyla said carefully, "what wisdom or knowledge you think I have that you do not, numen, but I shall carefully consider all my options before I follow your advice."

Kelsey snorted. "That was awfully close to humor, Tyla, are you sure you're all right?"

She continued without waiting for a reply.

"What we *do* know, from what we've heard, is that a wizard can absorb other dungeon cores into his own, to grow stronger."

She pulled out another dungeon core. Tyla stared.

"I picked this up while you were leading al-Kadir around by the nose," Kelsey said. "There was a wizard, but none of his spells included protection from lead."

She held out the core to Tyla. At Kelsey's encouraging nod, Tyla reached out to take it.

Then she stopped.

"What's wrong?" Kelsey asked.

"It feels . . . like I am not supposed to have this," Tyla said. "It feels wrong to touch it."

"It's rejecting you?" Kelsey asked, leaning forward.

"More like . . . I'm rejecting it? This feeling comes from within me," Tyla said. "Or maybe . . . it comes from my core?"

With all the meditation she had done, and her constant contact with her core, Tyla often felt as if the core and herself were more than just connected. Sometimes, she felt as if the core was part of her.

"Interesting," Kelsey said. "Mel says that the wizards never touched the core directly, they touched it with their own core."

"You didn't mention that before," Tyla said reproachfully.

"I didn't know it was important," Kelsey said. "We don't have a lot of data points here, Tyla, and you might be the only wizard I see for a while. I want to get as much information about the process as possible."

"Does that mean," Tyla said slowly, "that you want me to touch it?"

Kelsey paused to consider. "Do you *want* to touch it?" she asked.

"No." Tyla shook her head. "But . . . I will if you ask it of me, numen."

Kelsey blew air through her teeth. "That attitude is going to get us in trouble someday. Let's stick with your instincts. They're a much better guide than whatever theories I'm working with."

"As you wish," Tyla said, bowing her head. "Then . . . I should touch it with my stone?"

"Yeah," Kelsey said after another pause. "Feel free to stop if it feels wrong or anything."

"I will," Tyla said. She fished her core out from under her robe. It was still tied to the chain around her neck, so Kelsey held the core close enough for Tyla to touch it.

This time, Tyla felt no unease. Her hand practically moved forward on its own, gently touching her stone to the one Kelsey held out.

Both stones started glowing brightly, too brightly to look at. Tyla closed her eyes, but she didn't pull away. She didn't feel that she should.

She felt a pulling sensation as if she was being drawn into the stone. Or . . . no. The stone was being drawn toward *her.*

There was a final flash of light, bright enough to shine through her eyelids. Then darkness. Tyla opened her eyes.

The other stone was gone, without even dust remaining. Kelsey was looking at her expectantly. And Tyla was . . . full.

"I—I need to meditate," Tyla said. She held the stone on her lap and tried to focus. She tried to ignore the protests of the wakened crew members, of the other crew coming down to see what had happened. Kelsey was shooing them away. Tyla didn't need to worry about them.

She needed to understand what was in her.

The warm presences that she felt had been joined by another. That only made sense. The magic that swirled around them and seeped into Tyla was stronger. Too strong for the controls she had placed on it to hold. She needed to reestablish her command of it.

The first step was establishing what had changed. While everything was roiled up, only some of the kinds of magic had actually increased in strength. She needed to—

Tyla paused. There was a new kind of magic within her. It slipped out from under her grasp like quicksilver. For a moment it appeared to be Earth, then it slid away like Water, before fading away into Air. It was—

Illusion, Tyla realized. *Always seeming to be what it wasn't.*

With a rush, the knowledge of how to use it came to her. There wasn't very much of it, but when she got stronger, she could use it to become invisible, to change her appearance, to shift her apparent location.

You have completed Level 5. Please select a new Class.

Tyla hadn't even noticed the experience coming in. She perused the list of classes, but there was only one that she wanted. The one on her path.

Dungeon Witch (Rare, Tier 2)

Select Dungeon Witch, she thought.

Applying Benefits for Level 1
Strength + 1
Dexterity + 1
Perception + 1
Willpower + 1
Charisma + 1

Assign free point:

Tyla brought up her status to see where she should spend the free point.

Tyla Greenwalker of the Padascar Tribe, Dungeon Witch (Level 1)
Overall Level: 13
Paths: Padascar Hunter (Broken)/ Doxy (Broken)/Apprentice Dungeon
 Witch/Dungeon Witch
Strength: 12
Toughness: 8
Agility: 10
Dexterity: 18
Perception: 20
Will: 15
Charisma: 10
Traits:
Persistent Tracker
Silent Shot
Danger Sense
Sense Magic
Cast Lesser Charm

Kelsey had told her that Willpower was the most important ability for wizards. But what she had right now had served her well. She still wanted to fight with a bow or the guns that Kelsey supplied, so more Dexterity would be useful. On the other hand, her Agility was being left behind.

Agility, she thought.

Agility + 1

"How'd it go?" Kelsey asked as she returned and saw that Tyla's eyes were opened.

"It went well," Tyla answered. Knowing that Kelsey would want specifics, she added, "I gained strength in Destruction, Control, and Perception magic, as well as Animal. And I gained Illusion magic."

"Nice," Kelsey said. "Still no Creation magic?"

Tyla shook her head.

"It's a gap," Kelsey admitted. "But we'll get over it. And I can see you got a new class, so there's no need to be modest about it. Welcome to full adulthood!"

Tyla grimaced. "I feel like I reached that milestone some time ago, and it wasn't pleasant," she said.

Kelsey was entirely unabashed. "That doesn't count," she said. "You think events are what make you an adult? Hardly. It's arbitrary counts on a mystical system that make you a man. Or a woman. Now get upstairs so everyone can congratulate you on making it to Tier Two."

Tyla bowed her head. "Yes, numen," she said.

It wasn't a *party*. Kelsey had very specific notions about what constituted one, and this did not qualify, as she loudly declaimed to anyone who would listen.

Kelsey's notions didn't exactly match up with Tyla's idea of a celebration, but she had to admit that this didn't qualify for *that*, either. There was no bonfire, no feast of roasted meat. There *were* drinks, Kelsey saw to that, but Anton had insisted that the mead and wine be rationed. He didn't want widespread drunkenness on board.

That much matched with Tyla's memories. She was old enough that she hadn't been *forbidden* alcohol, but the tribe mothers had looked askance at her if she asked for more than one cup.

Kelsey had protested, once again mentioning the lack of conformance with her party standards, but even she had eventually agreed that the loss of coordination and emotional control were not welcome aboard a small ship at night. It would be all too easy for someone not in control of themselves to fall overboard, perhaps without anyone even noticing.

Because people were slipping off into the darkness, trying to find a private place on the all-too-small boat. Everyone had started on the main deck when the *gathering*—Kelsey insisted on calling it that—had started. There had been congratulations on reaching her second tier that Tyla could have done without. Too many people, in too close quarters.

Although it had sent a thrill through her when Baron Anton shook her hand and thanked her for all that she'd done for them. As if *he* hadn't saved *her*. The man had a presence to him, and he seemed to be getting just a bit bigger and more muscular at every level.

Tyla had made her exit once everyone had finished congratulating her. The words and the feeling weren't fake, but there were only so many times she could be thanked and greeted without it getting repetitive. Tyla didn't want to distance herself. The girls that she had gone through slavery with were more important to her now than her friends back in the tribe had been. But there was only so much she could take.

Her climbing skills and her Darkvision allowed her to claim the crow's nest. On a bigger ship, it would have been a platform, perhaps including some shelter. On this boat, it was a handhold, conveniently nailed so that she could hold it and sit on the mast's crossbar.

Even so, she felt comfortable here. It was the closest she could come to being perched on a tree branch. There weren't any other ships to be wary of, no rocks or shores in sight, so there was little need for her to be alert. She could relax and watch over everyone below.

The boat wasn't big enough for privacy, but people were trying. For most, the darkness made it feel as if you were alone with the person you were softly talking to. It was pretty amusing to see one couple, looking for a spot, stumble into one pair after another.

People were pairing up. No one was having *sex*, no one was *that* comfortable with the very limited privacy that the darkness provided. And Tyla thought that many, if not all, of the girls weren't ready to be reminded of their previous class.

With Baron Anton taken, and jealously guarded by Baroness Aris, Zaphar had, without even trying, attracted the attention of most of the rescued ladies. He had been a part of their rescue, and he got more dashing with every level. He hadn't *done* anything with that attention, mostly because he was more skittish than a scared cat. Now that the boys had joined them, though, he was no longer the only game in town.

Some of the girls had been reunited with sweethearts, and some of the girls were looking for someone to protect them. Zaphar had watched his bevy of beauties start to slip through his fingers. He'd been forced to *act*, to decide which of them he wanted to spend time with.

Tyla could see him now, talking intensely with Lyra in a quiet corner. That was probably as far as it would go tonight, with both of them lubricated by only a single cup of wine. It was a scene duplicated many times around the boat. A lot of quiet talking, a little bit of kissing. The occasional embrace.

Right now, both sides wanted to share their story with someone. Tyla didn't imagine that the boys' experience had been much better than theirs. The rest would come in due time. Tyla knew that her fellow rescuees were strong. They would recover.

And if any of the boys wanted to try something before her sisters were ready, Tyla still had her knife.

CHAPTER TWENTY-TWO

Don't Dream It's Over

SULIEL

Just so we're clear,> Kelsey sent. *<If you want to pop a cap in her . . . face, I will support your decision one hundred percent.>*

Thanks to the nature of mental communication, Suliel understood what the phrase meant. Even though the words made no sense and she had never heard them before. She also understood that the last-minute change that Kelsey had made was not the normal formulation, which rather buried the point of making the substitution in the first place.

What was even the point of bringing scatology into it? For the briefest of moments, Suliel imagined a world where murder by guns was so common that people needed to add depravity to their gun-related threats.

It was a distracting thought and helped Suliel keep her anger at bay when she looked at her mother again.

<No thanks,> she sent back. *<I intend to get through today without killing even one person.>*

<That kind of repression isn't healthy,> Kelsey sent right back. *<You need to let loose more.>*

Suliel checked that her smile was still in place. She had frozen, slightly, while her mother returned her greeting. Distracted by Kelsey, she'd paused for a bit too long, and everyone was now waiting for her to say something. Not ideal, but not out of line with the icy persona that she was projecting.

"Obviously, I'd welcome rapprochement with my mother," she said. "But I'm not sure the issues that need reconciling should be aired in front of the entire court."

"There are private chambers for just such an occasion," Lord Brankil assured her. "Shall we?"

Suliel nodded assent, and the entire group started moving. Murder *was* still an option, Suliel thought to herself. She was still carrying her derringer, and while the Princess must have speculations, she didn't know what Suliel could do. No one else had the faintest clue.

Of course, by suggesting murder at the first opportunity, Kelsey had made it far harder for Suliel to give in to the urge. Suliel had primed herself to regard any suggestion that Kelsey made with suspicion.

It was possible that was why she had suggested it. For a remorseless killing machine, Kelsey could be quite subtle at times.

A feeling of amusement from Kelsey was a sign that Suliel's thoughts were leaking. She tamped down on them.

The private chamber was as richly appointed as the rest of the palace. The main furniture consisted of two couches, wide enough to seat three, facing each other across a low table. Narrow tables and a few chairs were set around the walls.

Lord Brankil and Suliel's mother took one of the couches, while Suliel and the Princess took the other. As a friendly gesture, Suliel directed the Lazybones to stand by the door, instead of directly behind her.

The rest of Lord Brankil's entourage took seats around the edge of the room, as far away from the skeletons as possible.

<*Should I be worried about listeners in the walls?*> Suliel asked Kelsey. She got laughter in return.

<*I mean, sure, but you've got servants right in front of you that are probably reporting to someone.*>

Suliel blinked and focused on the two maids who had been in the room when they arrived. Suliel had *noticed* them, but they were just a part of the room. Suliel was used to allowing servants to overhear her, but they were *her* servants. She trusted them.

"Do you think we could do without refreshment for the length of this discussion?" Suliel asked. "I don't fancy the servants overhearing this discussion."

She was amazed by the looks of surprise she got. Her mother looked at her as if she had not even considered the possibility that a servant could be a spy. A similar look from the Princess made Suliel feel dismay.

Shouldn't she know about this already? Suliel thought.

Lord Brankil did not show any surprise. Instead, he looked at Suliel speculatively.

"That would be wise," he said. "Wait outside," he told the servants.

<*Now we know who attended Intrigue 101,*> Kelsey sent. <*I guess he didn't say anything before because none of his secrets were on the line.*>

Since Lord Brankil was looking at her, Suliel cast a glance over at his entourage and raised her eyebrow.

"I suppose I could," he allowed. "Will you be sending your attendants out as well?"

"If you wish," Suliel replied. "They still follow orders once out of my sight—"

<*So jelly,*> Kelsey sent.

"—but I cannot predict the reactions of those that see them unattended."

"A fair point," Lord Brankil conceded. "I suppose they aren't likely to go tattling to the gossip mongers."

He inclined his head towards the door. His followers took the hint and filed out.

<*He's got them well trained,*> Kelsey noted.

"Now that we're *in private*," Lord Brankil said, "I should start by expressing my displeasure that Baron Nos has sent his *wife* in his stead."

"My lord has—" Suliel started, but Lord Brankil waved her to silence.

"I'm aware of the reasons," he stated. "I just want to make sure that he *intends* to show up at some point to make an account of himself."

"He does," Suliel promised. "As soon as he returns from his mission."

"Very well," he said. "Now, where should we start with . . . this."

"Perhaps with an apology," Suliel said icily. Her mother bristled.

"I will not apologize for trying to protect my daughter from her own foolishness!" she insisted.

"Now now," the Princess said, laying a hand on Suliel's shoulder to restrain her hot response. "No one could deny a mother's desire to protect her child, Lady Anat, but there are limits are there not? My understanding is that you locked her in her room *after* she attained her new class."

"She only did that to defy me! To break off the marriage arrangements that I was finding for her!"

"Still," the Princess said. This time there was a touch of steel in her voice. "It *was* a Tier Two class, was it not?"

"It was—" Suliel's mother broke off under the Princess's firm gaze. "It was," she admitted.

"A class that she earned by her own efforts, with no fell magics granting it unduly?"

<Can magic do that?> Kelsey asked.

<There are stories of demons doing it,> Suliel sent back. <I've never heard of a historic case.>

"There was! Just look at it!" Lady Anat pointed at the animated skeletons. "The foulest of magics, that has festered under our town since time immemorial!"

<I want to say flattery won't get you anywhere . . . but it's working,> Kelsey sent.

"Dungeons aren't—they aren't Outsider evil," Princess Elara said patiently. "They are sent by the gods to test us, and provide us the resources we need."

"It's been killing my family since the beginning," Suliel's mother said bitterly.

"But they don't cheat the system," the Princess said. "Suliel earned those levels, earned that class. When she confronted you, she *was* an adult, and the inheritor of the estate."

"Now, now, it's not so clear cut as that," Lord Brankil interjected. "Lady Suliel's status as an adult was established, yes, but she was about to marry the lad that was there. He should be considered the presumptive Baron."

"He may have *presumed*, but I was *never* going to marry him," Suliel spat.

"Had it been a few days earlier, you would not have had a choice," he said flatly.

"But it *was* a few days later," the Princess put in. "She was an adult and considered capable of making her decisions."

"But one cannot *blame* a distraught mother for ignoring something that just happened, and was the result of a choice she rejected."

"One can forgive a mistake, but first it needs to be acknowledged that a mistake has been made."

The two nobles stared calmly at each other. The Count was the one to back down.

"A mistake was made," he admitted.

"What? No!" Suliel's mother protested.

"Clena, face facts," the Count said. "You meant well, but you were in the wrong. If we want to maintain a relationship with our dear cousin, we will have to admit to wrongdoing."

"But I—"

"And we *very much do* want close ties with our family, do we not?" he said firmly.

Lady Anat didn't say anything further, just stared at her lord. He stared back, implacable and calm. Finally, she slumped.

"I was wrong to lock you in your room, my daughter," she conceded.

"And you were wrong to capture the castle," Suliel said coldly.

"Yes, that was a mistake. I'm sorry," Lady Anat admitted.

"And you were wrong to try and kill Anton," Suliel said.

"That was an honorable duel . . ." Lady Anat said, looking at Lord Brankil for support.

He shook his head.

"Yes, wrong," Lady Anat said. "I'm sorry for that."

Suliel felt a strong wave of emotion flow through her.

"I think we can agree," Lord Brankil said, "that the acts that *Lady Suliel* committed against her mother, while regrettable, were the acts of a wronged noble seeking to regain her inheritance. No permanent damage was done to those represented here. The Mage Guild and Captain Oldaw might disagree, but they are outside of this discussion."

"I think we can agree to that," Princess Elara said.

"Wonderful," Lord Brankil said. "Then, Baroness, I think it is your turn."

"I—" Suliel started, before choking up. The words wouldn't come. There was so much anger, she couldn't let go of it.

<I'm not saying you should do it,> Kelsey sent. **<Branky-boy has clearly got some ulterior motives. But you will feel better if you accept the apology.>**

<What ulterior motives?> Suliel sent back. Speaking this way didn't require her to breathe.

<Dunno. Maybe he wants the guns as well? I wouldn't worry too much about it. We can always murder them later.>

Kelsey's answer to everything. Suliel felt a spike of amusement shoot through her. She didn't laugh aloud, but it skewered the knot tying up her throat.

She took a deep breath.

"I accept your apology, Mother. I forgive you."

It did feel better.

"Excellent," Lord Brankil said. "I hope we can—"

He was interrupted by Clena lunging across the table to embrace her daughter.

"I'm sorry! I'm sorry!" she sobbed. "I didn't know what to do!"

Suliel hugged her mother back. "It's done with now, it's all right," she said. She felt tears forming in her eyes.

It felt a bit anticlimactic to continue with the meeting after that, but there were still a few things to discuss. For one, her mother would come back to Kirido with Suliel, but she would continue staying with Lord Brankil for now.

Suliel promised to stay in the city until Anton could get there and meet his new lord, but she insisted that she could take care of any baronial business that the Count had for her. Some of the notes in her father's study had concerned the tax arrangements for the barony.

She was able to get assurances that the previous arrangements would continue, once she established that she knew the details of them. Lord Brankil looked a little disappointed but did not complain. Suliel expected that he'd have even less to complain about once the tax revenues started being collected. She expected the new industries would more than make up for the losses from the raid.

She didn't mention this yet, of course. There was no point in promising revenue that might not materialize. The Count didn't press her, admitting he expected a revenue hit.

He didn't mention the guns.

By the time the meeting was over, the dry and tedious discussion had wiped away the emotional moment that it had started with. Suliel felt nothing but tired when she was done.

"Thank you for your help," she said to Princess Elara as they were leaving.

"It was my pleasure," she replied. Then she made a face. "Well, the first bit, anyway. The second half was enough to make me glad that I don't have any land-holding responsibilities."

"Just your presence was a help," Suliel murmured. "I don't know if Lord Brankil would have been as accommodating if you hadn't been there."

"Perhaps," Elara allowed. "We should go out on the town to celebrate. I can—" she cut herself off as a servant dressed in a higher quality of livery approached.

"Lady Nos," the man said, bowing. "You are summoned to meet with the King."

CHAPTER TWENTY-THREE

Fade To Black

SULIEL

If you would follow me, the King will see you now," the servant said. Despite his livery, he was dark-skinned enough to pass as a noble, and the arrogant sneer on his face made Suliel think that he just might be from a noble family. Royal servants were apparently a cut above the rest.

Suliel inclined her head. She wasn't going to show too much deference to a servant, even if he did serve the King. She activated *Nobility's Privilege*.

Selvin Marak, Level ??, ??,
Loyal to: Ranon Kalond IV, Human, Loyal Servant

Suliel blinked at the blank family section, but she only read him to get the man's name. Marak led her through a bewildering maze of antechambers before stopping at the door to another one.

"If you'd leave your . . . attendants in here, my lady. They will not be permitted to attend a private audience." He raised a supercilious eyebrow. "I take it that they can be ordered to stay in place and not take action?"

"Of course," Suliel said. She entered the room and looked around for the best place to leave the Lazybones. The room was furnished as richly as any of the other rooms she'd passed through. This one featured an embroidered divan, faced by two stuffed armchairs.

"I take it that they will remain undisturbed for the duration of our meeting?" she shot back. The room was currently empty, so it should be simply a matter of locking the door.

"Of course, my lady," Marak said.

Suliel gestured for the skeletons to stand at attention against the wall, next to an ornate side table. Then she turned to Marak. "If you would direct me."

"Just one more thing," Marak said. "Sleep."

Suliel frowned. Was that a directive? She felt . . .

Everything went black.

<blibawarble garble songanaoh I think you're coming back. Can you hear me?>
<I hear you!> Suliel sent frantically. *<What's going on?>*
<Try opening your eyes and have a look.>

Embarrassed, Suliel took the suggestion. It took a moment to focus on the fabric surface an inch from her face, but she quickly realized that she was sprawled on the divan in the same room that she'd blacked out in.

Twisting around to survey the rest of the room, Suliel saw that she was indeed still in the same room. The only notable change was the dead stranger lying on the floor.

Suliel let out a strangled "Eeep!" and pulled her legs up on the couch.

<Well, this is interesting> Kelsey sent. *<You know this guy?>*
<You've been looking through my eyes since I arrived here. How would I know him if you don't?> Suliel sent back.
<Well, I don't know, but I thought I'd ask just in case,> Kelsey said. *<Looks like he was stabbed through the heart, from behind, by a large-bladed weapon.>*
<Like the . . .> Suliel twisted around to look for the Lazybones. They stood in place, grinning at her.
<Good call. I'd tell you to check their swords, but whoever it was cleaned off the murder weapon on the guy's robes.>

Suliel looked back. It was difficult to tell. The stranger's robes, made of fine linen, were a very dark blue. But there was a clear stain on the lower part.

<Fortunately, the Lazybones are the fastidious type,> Kelsey sent. *<Cleaning off the weapon is something they would do.>*
<What's the other type?> Suliel asked. Even as she did, she knew it was a bad idea.
<The meat-envy type,> Kelsey replied. *<The fastidious types don't want anything to sully their pure bones, but the other kind just loves to drape themselves with flesh or drench themselves in blood.>*
<I've heard of that,> Suliel sent. *<The stories describe it as a kind of taunt they do sometimes.>*

<No, they don't require an audience. They just . . . do it. Not that they often get a chance. I clean that stuff up as soon as the delvers leave.>

Suliel put the gross, disgusting thought aside. *<What do I do?>* she asked.

<Good question. First, can you find out if the Lazybones killed the guy?>

Suliel made a face. "Did you kill this man?" she asked aloud, pointing at the corpse. For complex commands or questions, it sometimes helped to say them out loud.

The impression she got back was nonverbal.

<I think so?> she sent back to Kelsey. *<There's a sense of satisfaction from following orders, but I never ordered them to kill.>*

<You were asleep,> Kelsey replied. *<They have orders to protect you when you sleep.>*

<That . . . makes sense, but what happened to Marak? And why was this guy attacking me?>

<I'm guessing they're one and the same.>

<How?> Suliel asked. *<They don't look anything alike.>* The stranger even had paler skin than Marak.

<Last I saw, Marak seemed to be casting a spell on you. If we assume he was a wizard, then he could have had an illusion making him look like a servant. When he died, the illusion ended, same as your sleep spell.>

<So he's . . . a wizard?> Suliel asked.

<Let's find out, shall we? Turn him over.>

Suliel looked doubtfully at the corpse. There wasn't much blood, but there was a stain on the man's back and a small pool underneath him. Already thinking past the moment, Suliel knew that she couldn't afford to get any of his blood on her.

She gestured the Lazybones forward.

"Make sure you don't get any blood on you," she said aloud.

The skeletons approached cautiously. One of them grabbed the man's feet, the other his shoulders. Holding him by the blood-free ends, they rolled him over.

Suliel's eyes focused on the telltale bulge on the man's upper body.

<Oh ho ho!> Kelsey sent. *<Me wanty!>*

"Can you get the core without getting blood on yourselves?" Suliel asked.

The skeletons peered at the corpse from several angles. Then one of them reached out with both hands for the light chain that went around the man's neck. A sharp tug broke the chain and the skeleton drew the mystic bauble out from under the corpse's robes. Unfortunately, while the upper half of the chain was blood-free, the core was soaked in it.

Sensing Suliel's disapproval, the first skeleton carefully lowered the core into a fold of cloth—the lower part of the corpse's robe—held by the other Lazybone. They wiped it off as best they could. The chain, with too many nooks and crannies to be easily cleaned, was simply removed and dropped back on top of the corpse.

The bauble that was presented to her was mostly clean. Suliel took hold of it carefully.

<You qualify for a Wizard class now,> Kelsey sent. <Dread Witch Queen may well be in your future.>

<That's thinking a little too far ahead,> Suliel sent. <What do I do now?>

<Hmm. I presume we want to avoid being connected to the death? Or do you want to claim it in self-defense?>

Suliel stopped in the middle of her answer. She had been going to say that she didn't want to be connected, but was that the best plan? Whatever was going on, casting spells on nobles was not something that a wizard could do legitimately. Assuming the King hadn't secretly ordered it, Suliel had been well within her rights to kill the wizard.

<Let's save a claim of self-defense for if we get caught,> she decided. <It's easier if no one knows what happened.>

<Good call. Then put the shiny away and get out of her. Don't forget to check if anyone's on the other side of the door.>

Suliel nodded and carefully wrapped the core in her handkerchief. Slipping it into a side pocket, she carefully checked that she didn't have any blood on her. Then she checked the skeletons. With everything clear, she had everyone carefully back away from the body and then follow her out the door.

The first room she checked was empty, so Suliel entered it calmly. The next room . . . which room had she come through?

<Left,> Kelsey told her.

<Are you sure?>

<I am a maze,> Kelsey replied, sending her amusement along with the words. <I'd be in a fine mess if I couldn't remember six different rooms.>

Suliel shrugged and accepted the guidance. Also at Kelsey's direction, she squared her shoulders and strode forward as if she knew where she was going.

No one stopped her, but it was still a relief to make it back into the main audience chamber.

<Do you think the Princess is still around? We should take her up on that offer she tried to make.>

<I just want to get back home,> Suliel replied. She was intensely aware of the weight of the core in her pocket. Mages could sense magic, couldn't they? Would they be able to tell she'd robbed one of their colleagues? **<But you're right.>**

<I'm always right,> Kelsey sent smugly.

Suliel ignored her. She drew her *Aura of Nobility* around her at full pitch and attempted to wander in a purposeful manner as she looked for the Princess. Her heart was starting to hammer with nervousness by the time she finally found Elara.

She angled her approach so that the Princess would see her as she drew near. It wouldn't do to interrupt an important conversation. To Suliel's relief, the Princess gestured for her to approach as soon as she came into view.

"Lady Suliel," Elara said. "Has my father finished with you already?"

Suliel curtsied. "It was a quick conversation, your Highness."

The Princess's eyes glittered as she studied Suliel.

"If you'll excuse me, Lord Angout," she said to the older man. "I promised the Baroness a dinner date in the city, and we will be late if I delay any further."

Recognizing the name, Suliel realized that she was interrupting the Lord Chancellor, and curtsied again.

"Think nothing of it, your Highness," the Lord Chancellor said, bowing. "I wouldn't dream of interfering with a young lady's introduction to the delights of the capital."

Suliel stared at him, wondering if he was insinuating something. But he simply bowed again and took his leave. Elara took Suliel by the arm and started leading her towards the exit.

"Was Father rough with you?" she asked. "You seem distraught."

"I didn't meet with your father," Suliel said softly. As softly as she could while expecting the Princess to hear her.

The Princess frowned, but she didn't say anything more until they left the palace.

They travelled together, in the Princess's carriage, while Suliel's empty carriage followed. The Lazybones rode on top of their carriage, which amused the Princess no end. Once they were underway, she let her jollity fade.

"This is as private as we can reasonably expect," Elara said. "Why didn't you see my father?"

"I don't believe I was summoned by him," Suliel answered. "The servant proved to be in disguise."

"That's not possible," Elara dismissed. "I recognized him; he was one of Father's messengers."

"He *looked* like him," Suliel told her. "But he was actually a mage."

She pulled out the core. "And I killed him."

Elara stared at the core. "How?" she asked. "And . . . why?"

"Luck," Suliel admitted. "He thought that my guards would stay put if I didn't direct them. He didn't realize that they had standing orders to protect me when I'm sleeping. So when he spelled me to sleep . . ."

"They killed him," Elara finished. "I had no idea they were so deadly. My advisors tell me that they are only level five."

"They are more *skilled* than the average skeleton," Suliel explained. "That doesn't always make a difference, but it can."

"So you're telling me that there's a dead wizard in a random waiting room in the palace," Elara said. "That should cause no end of trouble once it's discovered. Do you know who the mage is?"

"It wasn't your court mage," Suliel said. "He was wearing very dark blue robes, while I saw Master Voss was wearing crimson today."

"Most days, he does like the color," Elara agreed. "Dark blue is what the Mages Guild tends to wear, so I suppose we can assume it was they who wanted to capture you."

"I don't know why," Suliel said, "Unless Master Tikin is influencing them."

Elara frowned. "I would have thought that Tikin wants you dead, not captured," she said. "Well, whatever their ploy, you seem to have foiled it. You can relax for the rest of the evening."

"Yes, your Highness," Suliel lied. She didn't think she'd be able to relax ever again.

CHAPTER TWENTY-FOUR

Welcome to the Jungle

SULIEL

Nothing happened in the time it took for Suliel to return to the town-house. No announcements were made, there was no sudden flood of troops sealing the city, and no one searched her or the Princess out. The absence of any reaction hung over Suliel for the rest of her evening meal and followed her back to her temporary residence.

<It makes sense,> *Kelsey told her.* <If they were going to lock something down, it would be the palace, and you wouldn't see any signs of that here. As for searching you out, they don't have police here, do they?>

Suliel frowned at the image that came with the unfamiliar word. <The City Guard do something like that,> she sent back. <But they certainly wouldn't do that in the palace.>

<So who's going to be doing the investigation?>

Suliel thought about it. <The King will appoint someone,> she decided. <A trusted noble or one of the judges, perhaps.>

<Amateur hour, then,> Kelsey sent, along with a smug feeling. <Although those judges can be pretty pesky with their Truth-Telling trait. Are there any other classes we need to worry about?>

<Not that I'm aware of,> Suliel sent. <We use trackers, but there won't be any tracks indoors.>

<Yeah, nice work staying out of the blood, you and the Lazybones both,> Kelsey sent. <Then the only thing that ties you to the crime is that core.>

<Yes, which I should store somewhere. I can't keep it on me.>

Suliel rang for her butler.

"Yes, my lady?"

"Arelon . . ." Suliel said, pausing as she said it. She didn't know the man that well, and it felt overly familiar to refer to the dignified man by his first name. "Did my father entrust you with the keys to the safe in his study?"

"He did, my lady. His custom was to empty it before leaving for home and leave me with the keys in case of need."

It was cautious of him to not leave any documents behind, Suliel noted. Wise, for someone engaged in treason.

"Excellent," she said aloud. "I'll need the keys, then. I have something that needs keeping."

"As you wish, my lady," Arelon said.

When he brought the keys to her in Father's—her—study, Suliel looked at them suspiciously.

"Are these the only keys to the safe?" she asked.

"Your father had another copy that he kept with him," Arelon said. "You would know its location better than I do."

Suliel thought about it. There had been some keys in Father's study back home. They had been labeled, though, and she didn't remember seeing one marked "townhouse safe."

Perhaps Mother . . .

"Arelon," she said. "I have had something of a rapprochement with my mother. She may come to visit. If she does, she is not to have access to this room, understand?"

"I do, my lady. That is good news about Lady Anat. It is always troubling when families are split asunder."

"I suppose so," Suliel agreed. She sent him out of the room before she pulled out the core. She trusted her butler, but he didn't need to know about this.

<Will it be all right, in here?> she asked Kelsey nervously.

<It won't turn into a dungeon, if that's what you mean,> Kelsey said. <I'm not aware of any special storage requirements.>

Suliel used the cloth she'd used for a wrapping to make a padded base for the core to rest on. She didn't want the thing to get scratched by the metal.

She had barely closed the safe when there came a knock on the door to the study.

"My lady, a message has arrived."

"So late in the evening?" Suliel wondered aloud. "Come in, then."

Arelon entered, cradling the folded and sealed note carefully, with both hands. "My lady," he said reverently.

Suliel's lips quirked at her servant's sudden formality, but she understood when she saw the royal seal.

She reached out and relieved Arelon of his burden. Breaking the seal, she read what was inside.

"My lady? Are there any instructions?" Arelon asked.

Suliel sighed. "Make sure I'm ready to leave for court in the morning," she said. "I've been summoned to speak with the King. Privately."

"I'm glad to see that you left your guard dogs behind, Lady Suliel."

Suliel bowed her head in acknowledgment. "Bringing them yesterday made a point, my liege. Bringing them today might imply I felt unsafe in your company."

As part of that same message, her dress today was much less severe, a closer match to the colors in fashion at the moment. It didn't fit in completely, however. It was a little too plain to be considered in tune with the mood of the court ladies.

If the Princess had worn a dress like this, it might have started a new trend, but on Suliel it should simply mark her as someone who was trying, but not quite able to match up with the whims of the court. It was only to be expected of a mere country baroness, after all.

The King chuckled. "Do you feel safe, then?" he asked. "Here, at the palace?"

"Are we all not kept safe under your protection, your Majesty?" Suliel answered automatically. The King's question would have been odd, under normal circumstances. Coming after the discovery of a murder on the palace grounds, it was . . . less odd.

It wasn't quite the question that Suliel would expect to be leveled at the murderer, so she chose to relax. And, too, the murder had not been announced, so it would be best to proceed as if she had no idea what the King was talking about.

"Ah, but what will my protection be worth, once these guns of yours become commonplace?" the King said. "From the demonstration provided to Captain Oldaw, a fellow could pull one out during an audience and kill me from across the room."

Suliel swallowed. Talking about killing the King was *pretty much* a death sentence, but she supposed it was all right if the King did it. She resolved to be very careful about what *she* said.

"With respect, your Majesty, while the rifles are certainly dangerous, I don't believe the threat is that grave. Even if guns should become commonplace, your Majesty should have no problems banning guns from your immediate presence, much as you already do for other arms."

Suliel carefully kept her thoughts away from the small pistol strapped to her forearm. For the moment, they were only selling rifles. Pistols were next, but the clumsy, bulky examples that Kelsey had shown her were a far cry from the revolver that Aris carried or the two-shot that Kelsey had given Suliel.

"Furthermore, I believe that your Majesty would survive a shot from a rifle unless it were well-aimed or very lucky. You might be severely wounded, but Your Majesty does not stand alone. Even if an assassin got close enough to shoot you, you would have others to pull you back to safety, to go after the assassin, and to heal your wounds."

"You think so? I suppose it will be a while before we find out," the King conceded. "But it puts more power in the hands of the powerless, does it not?"

"It allows people to fight up a tier," Suliel agreed. "Maybe even two. Much as a magic weapon does."

"These weapons will be much more common, though," the King pointed out.

"My notions of how common magic weapons are may be a little skewed from growing up in a dungeon town," Suliel admitted. "It seems that every adventurer carries at least a Tier Two sword."

The King chuckled again. "I suppose so," he said indulgently. "Now, let us determine just how common these weapons will be."

A lady did not stagger. A lady did not *crawl*. So despite how Suliel felt, she kept her back straight and her head up as she made her way back into the main court area. She could feel the eyes on her, and she wouldn't give them the satisfaction of seeing her fall.

"My dear, how nice to see you back in court so soon!"

The voice was familiar. Suliel turned to see Lady Seraphina with a concerned look on her face.

"You look like you need to get off your feet," the older lady said, moving closer to wrap her arm around Suliel's. "Before you trip over them. What have you been up to, dear?"

"I'm fine," Suliel said. It wasn't a lie. Physically, she was fine. Mentally was another matter. "I've just come from a meeting with the King."

Suliel could now confirm that, False King or True, King Kalond had traits that were worthy of a King. He had at least one that let him *command*.

"Ah, he can be a trial, can he not?" Seraphina murmured. "This way."

She led Suliel to an antechamber that held four comfortable divans with screens around them for more privacy. Suliel was guided to sit on one of them.

"Feel free to lie back if you need to," Seraphina said.

"I really am fine," Suliel assured the courtier. "The King was just very . . . forceful."

She hadn't planned on denying whatever demands the King had for the new weapons. She hadn't realized that resistance wouldn't be an option. All she could do—and even that was with Kelsey's prompting—was point out when he was asking for the impossible. And *ask* that her barony get repaid for its contributions to the defense of the country.

It helped that *Kelsey* controlled the supply of the guns, not Suliel. If Kelsey insisted there was a limit on production, what was Suliel to do? If Kelsey demanded compensation, Suliel had no choice but to pass that along.

Even that had strained her mind to the breaking point. She'd felt an urge to confess everything to the King. Her father's treachery, the overtures from the Rose Circle, everything. Only Kelsey's reminder that confessing would get her—and Anton—killed kept her from blurting out the truth.

"The King chose to limit himself to one hundred units," Suliel said softly.

Seraphina's brow twitched in what was almost a frown. "More than we'd hoped," she said. "You can provide us with more, though, can't you?"

Suliel looked at the older, more experienced woman. The King's trait was still running through her, she realized. She wanted to say no, to denounce this traitor.

"It's hard, isn't it?" Seraphina said. "So hard, he doesn't think anyone can stand against it. Let me distract you with a little story."

The words were still stuck in Suliel's throat as she fought with herself over what to say. Lady Seraphina gently stroked the hair on the side of Suliel's head.

"The strangest rumor has been flying about since this morning," Seraphina said. "A mage was found dead in one of the rooms of the palace."

The words Suliel were going to say were gone, washed away by a cool blue panic.

"Can you imagine?" Seraphina said. "A mage, stabbed in the back in a room that was not supposed to be open. A single strike to the heart, the clear work of a master swordsman."

<Breathe, Suliel,> Kelsey said.

Suliel started, as she realized she'd forgotten to. She took a breath and swallowed. She could speak again, but she wasn't sure what to say.

"Do they know who he was?" she tried.

"They do," Seraphina said. "He was a member of the Mages Guild. Which member, I haven't been able to find out. Yet. But the bigger question is what he was doing here."

"Do the mages not visit the court?" Suliel asked.

"They do, but aside from our dear Court Wizard, they do so only by invitation. Our dead friend was not invited on this day. It is no surprise that he made it into the building—mages have their ways, of course. But what he was doing is still a mystery."

Suliel swallowed again. "You're right, my lady, that was a most interesting diversion. If you learn any more about the matter, I would be glad to hear it."

"Would you? I worry that my little tales would only bore you."

"You could not possibly bore me, my lady. To answer your earlier question, we can have two hundred ready, at the price discussed, before the King gets his shipment."

"That's excellent news, my dear. I'll set the wheels in motion."

CHAPTER TWENTY-FIVE

You Gots To Chill

Anton's fingers tightened on the wheel.

"So the Rose Circle is *blackmailing* her now?" he asked.

"No, not exactly . . . but kinda," Kelsey said. "It's a gray area."

"How is it gray? Either they are or they aren't."

"They *aren't*, because Suliel was already going to trade them the guns. They *are*, because letting slip that they know about the murder, and that Suliel is connected to it, suggests that they know she did it. So it's both."

"Did they do that? You said they just told her that they know about the murder."

Kelsey sighed. "Suliel just *got* this instantly, you know. Seraphina *implied* that Suliel was connected to the murder by mentioning it to her."

"Did she?" Anton asked, confused. "I don't see how one follows from the other."

"It's how nobles work," Kelsey explained. "You've got to listen to what they *aren't* saying."

"They aren't saying a lot of things," Anton grumbled. "They aren't saying they were behind it all, or that it was all the plan of their rabbit overlords. So why aren't they saying that particular thing?"

Kelsey sighed. "Possibly, you had to be there," she said. "Non-verbal cues, Suliel's emotional state at the time, the timing of the revelation . . . it all adds up. If you were there, you might have picked it up. Might."

"Okay, but if they don't need to blackmail her, then why did they?" Anton asked.

"They might be worried she was getting cold feet, planning on reporting them to the King," Kelsey said. "To be honest, if he'd *asked* her if she'd contacted the Rose Circle, she probably would have told him."

"Why didn't he, then?"

"He doesn't want word of the Rose Circle getting out. If Suliel hadn't known about the Circle, he would have told her by asking the question."

"Politics is complicated," Anton complained.

"You'll get used to it, *Baron*," Kelsey said archly. "Fortunately, Suliel seems to know what she's doing. To get back to the blackmail, since they aren't making demands, it also comes across as an offer to *help*."

"Help . . . us?" Anton asked, completely lost now.

"They know about the incident, possibly more than we do," Kelsey explained. "They probably have some sort of in with whoever is doing the investigation. They can help us find out why the Mages Guild is after Suliel."

Anton frowned. The wooden steering wheel creaked alarmingly in his grip. "We need to get there faster," he growled.

"Sure, but you need to be informed before we get there," Kelsey said. "If you don't have all the information, you won't be pointing your sword in the right direction."

"What *else* do I need to know, then?"

"You should probably decide if you're supporting the Rose Circle or the King," Kelsey replied.

"But . . . I don't know if the King is false or not," Anton protested. "Is that—will my loyalty be a problem?"

"What do you mean?"

"Well, I'm supposed to meet the King, aren't I?" Anton said. "And he's got *Nobility's Privilege*, so he'll see the same thing that Suliel did, won't he? That my loyalty is to Kelsey?"

"I'm not sure it will, now," Kelsey said. "Back then, you were going along with whatever I said, but I think we've grown past that. I'm more like an advisor, don't you think?"

"Maybe," Anton said. "I thought it was the geas that made it say that, though. The geas is still there."

"No, the geas doesn't make you do what I say," Kelsey said. "Back then, you were lost and looking for purpose. You were chained to me, so it only made sense that you'd look to me for direction. Now . . . you've grown. Freeing the slaves was your idea—you dragged me along for it."

Anton looked at her suspiciously. "Wasn't this all part of your master plan?"

Kelsey laughed. "My plan is mostly blank spots," she said. "I need you to grow, which won't happen if I control every little thing. I have to let you do what you want, and then try and keep you alive through the consequences."

"So what will my loyalty read as?"

Kelsey paused. "Suliel says that heroes often read as 'Independent.' That sounds like it suits you right now."

"Won't that be a problem for a baron?" Anton asked.

"You're still a hero," Kelsey pointed out. "Suliel says it's not great, but it's not disqualifying."

"Unless the King decides it is," Anton mused. "It really would be helpful to know if he was false or not. If he was a true king, I think I could be loyal to him."

"Yeah, well, we all have wishes," Kelsey said. "I'd like to know how to make a really great battery. Lithium polymer, sure, but which polymer? Do you know how many of them there are?"

Anton was spared from responding to Kelsey's nonsense by a call from the crow's nest.

"Ship ahead!" Tyla called down. When they looked up, she pointed in a direction that was almost directly in front of them.

"Take the wheel," Anton told Kelsey and made his way to the mast where Tyla was climbing down.

"I do not think it is an Elitran ship," Tyla told him, handing him the binoculars.

They only had one set. Kelsey had complained long and hard about how hard it was to grind the lenses. Anton took the device and clambered up the mast, his trait making easy work of the climb.

Once up, he peered through the binoculars, looking for the ship. It didn't take him long to find it. Even through the binoculars, he couldn't make out much detail yet, but it was close enough for *Delver's Discernment* to work.

Imbube's Pride, Tiatian Windreaver, Excellent Quality, Tier 3, Windcatcher Enchantment

That was all. He couldn't get a bead on any of the crew. He did make out what looked like huge crossbows attached to the deck.

"It's a Tiatian warship," he told Kelsey when he got back to the wheel. "Do you think we can avoid it?"

"We can . . . probably. The problem is that it's between us and Kirido, so any evasion we do will mean it takes longer to get home."

Anton frowned. Some of the others were starting to gather near. Soraya and Aris joined him on the raised platform.

"What's a Tiatian warship doing out here, anyway?"

The question was for Kelsey, but from her silence, it wasn't something that Suliel knew much about. Soraya was the one to answer.

"Tiatia thinks they own the entire sea," she said scornfully. "Now that we are out of Elitran waters, it makes sense that we should see a patrol."

"Do they . . . attack other ships?" Anton asked.

"Not peaceful trading ships, Suliel says," Kelsey said thoughtfully. "But if they think you're a warship . . ."

Everyone except her glanced involuntarily towards the front of the ship.

"So they'd leave us alone?" Anton asked hopefully. Even if they were worried about the deck sweeper being recognized as a weapon, they could store it away.

"In our case, they might have a few questions about how we're not using sails or oars," Kelsey said wryly.

Everyone looked at the sails, which were still tied up tightly to the masts. No one had touched them since the trip had begun. Anton had considered trying to use them for more speed, but Kelsey had convinced him that without the knowledge of how to use them, they could well slow the ship down.

"That's the sort of technology . . . er, *magic*, that the military might want to get its hands on," Kelsey went on.

"So what do we do?"

Soraya pointed forward. "That weapon made short work of the pride of the Elitran navy. I'm sure that they could do similar to the ships of that barbaric Empire."

"I don't know . . . that ship was Tier Three," Anton said, prompting a stifled gasp from Soraya. "I didn't check, but is that normal for Eltiran ships?"

"Mostly Tier Two," Kelsey told him. "I'd still put my money on the machine gun."

"And they had what looked like big crossbows on the deck," Anton said.

Kelsey drew in a breath consideringly. "Ballistae," she said. "Primitive, but effective. With our new gunner, we should outrange them, but we don't want to get hit by them."

"Won't attacking a Tiatian ship have some sort of consequences?" Aris asked.

"If we can sink it without a trace, then hopefully not," Kelsey said. "No witnesses means they don't know who to blame."

She winced, reacting to something they couldn't hear. "But, I *suppose*, if a new powerful ship shows up, they *might* suspect it was responsible for the earlier, mysterious loss of one of their ships."

"So we don't want to fight, we don't want to run, and we don't want to approach them," Anton said. "Does that about cover it?"

"We're going to have to do *something* we don't like," Kelsey agreed. "What's your decision, Captain?"

Anton grunted with annoyance. Partly at the decision that needed to be made and partly because he was being forced to make it.

"Letting them approach is the only option that doesn't inevitably lead to something bad," he said.

"Hey, c'mon! Sinking the ship only might lead to something bad!" Kelsey protested.

"Sinking a Tiatian ship *is* bad. I want to avoid it if we can," Anton said. "Not just because of the stuff Suliel said. They're not like the Elitrans, they don't raid us."

Soraya sniffed. "As if they could be compared to our glorious Empire."

Kelsey gave Soraya a wry look. "Brownnosing them when they're *not here* isn't going to get you back any sooner."

Soraya's ears went back and she dropped her head. "Sorry," she said. "But while they may not have raided your coast, they have sunk many Elitran ships."

"Aw, now you've got me all turned around. Maybe we *shouldn't* sink them."

Kelsey returned Soraya's glare with an innocent grin.

"I'd rather not sink *any* ships if we don't have to," Anton said. "Tyla, is there anything you can do to help?"

"Magic, you mean?" Tyla said. She thought for a moment. "I could shroud the ship in mist. If we don't move too fast."

"How fast?" Anton asked.

"I'm not sure. We'd have to experiment," Tyla confessed.

"Um," Aris put in. "Wouldn't a fog bank kind of stand out right now?"

They all looked out over the water. It was getting late in the afternoon, but the sun was still out, and the weather was fine. There was nothing but clear blue water all around, with not a fog in sight.

"Perhaps," Tyla admitted. "I could . . . hide the deck sweeper. If it doesn't move."

"With Illusion magic, right?" Aris asked. "Could you make it look like we have sails?"

Tyla looked up at the masts. "I could, but . . . I can't make them move. They would look strange, even at a distance."

"That wouldn't fool them," Kelsey said. "They've got to have someone with an Identify trait that works on ships. We'll show up as special."

Anton blinked and turned his trait on the deck beneath him.

Whiskerwind, Kiridan Steelcutter, Good Quality, Tier 3, Fireheart

"Tier Three as well," he noted. "But 'steelcutter'? It's made of wood."

"I didn't pick the name," Kelsey said. "The engine's steel, though. Cutter is a fast boat, or maybe it's referencing breaking chains. I dunno."

"Fireheart refers to the engine, I guess," Anton mused.

"Pretty poetic for a humble four-stroke," Kelsey said. "But it isn't inaccurate."

"Do it anyway," he told Tyla. "Hide the gun and make fake sails. It will keep them guessing."

"Couldn't we just use the real ones?" Aris asked.

"We don't know how to put them down," Anton said, waving vaguely. He was aware there was a special word for it, he just didn't remember what it was. Furl? Spoke?

"And once they're down, we don't know how to get them up," he added.

"Reduce our speed a bit," Kelsey suggested. "It will make us a less attractive target and surprise them if we have to run away."

Anton nodded. They already had a top speed in reserve, but it wouldn't hurt to have more. Though it hurt to slow down. He bore with it, telling himself that slowing down was better than turning back.

Tyla did her magic before returning to the crow's nest. It wasn't long before she had an update.

"They've adjusted course. I think they mean to intercept!"

"Well, this is another step," Kelsey said. "Your first parley as a ship's captain."

She stopped suddenly, struck by a thought. "You need a hat!" she exclaimed.

"I have a hat," Anton said. Just about everyone was wearing straw hats, provided by Kelsey, to keep the sun off them. The only exception was Soraya, who said they pinched her ears.

"A *fancy* hat!" Kelsey corrected him. "I've been working on this for a while, but I didn't think we'd get a chance to use it."

She produced a hat, made of . . . Anton didn't know what it was made of. He tried using *Discernment*.

Tricorne Hat, Clothing, Good Quality, Tier 2

"Is this really necessary?" he asked, eyeing the skull and crossed bones insignia that Kelsey had affixed somehow. It was probably too late to go back on it, seeing as he'd allowed the flag to carry it.

"Absolutely," Kelsey assured him. "Can't be taken seriously as a captain if you don't have a fancy hat."

Anton sighed and put it on. "How do I look?" he asked.

"Arrr!" Kelsey said. "Splice the mainbrace and shiver me timbers!"

CHAPTER TWENTY-SIX

Fool's Gold

SULIEL

Anton is coming home.

The thought stayed with Suliel as she worked diligently for the betterment of her barony. *His* barony, now. She was working on behalf of her husband. That thought sent a thrill through her that she wouldn't have understood a year ago. Back then she'd been fuming at the knowledge that she was to be married off to some noble who would inherit her father's lands. That her duties would be reduced to managing her household and serving her husband in the bedroom.

That all changed when it was *Anton*. The boy that she'd dreamed about was now the man that was her lord. Even more wonderfully, he trusted her with Kirido. To rule it in his absence. Not in the paternalistic way that her father had let her play at command, being watched over and evaluated. Anton admitted that she was more suited for the role and supported all her decisions.

The link that they shared via Kelsey wasn't the most reliable of communication channels, but Suliel knew that, had he wanted to, Anton could have had her pass all the decisions to him. Instead, he'd let her make the calls and only asked Kelsey for the details after the fact.

It filled Suliel with a fierce sense of pride as well as a burning desire to make sure that his trust was not misplaced. Now that her introductions had been completed, Suliel could make most of the arrangements needed by correspondence. She spent much of the morning writing letters. Lunch and dinner were for making connections with her fellow nobles.

Invitations were flowing in now that she'd been accepted by the King. Most of them were meaningless, just distant cousins looking to capitalize on a connection, or fellow vassals of Lord Brankil looking to sound her out on the minor factional disputes within the county. For the most part, Suliel could just attend, smile, and nod.

Her retainers would prefer that she did not attend at all, on account of some trifling kidnapping attempt.

"Honestly, my Lady, do you really have to go?" Syon said despairingly. "You're trying to project an aloof persona, it wouldn't hurt to skip a few parties."

"I need to be *seen* to *be* aloof," Suliel replied. "If I don't go, I merely seem unsociable."

Syon's face twitched as the desire to scold her warred with his sense of propriety. As her father's chamberlain, he had often been the one to catch and discipline Suliel when she got into childish mischief. Now *he* served *her*. He never forgot himself, but sometimes he looked like he wanted to.

"Bah! Can you talk some sense into her?" Syon asked his companion.

"I fear not." Guild Master Delir Nyer bowed to her. He was not one of her retainers, but he'd been acting as one. "Though I would add my cautions to those of my colleague. Someone is clearly trying to capture you, my lady. You should not make it easier for them."

"I'm confident in the protections you have in place," Suliel said airily. Delir sighed.

"Then at least accept this," he said, holding out a bracelet. It was a simple thing: a large stone, or more likely cut glass, dangling from a silver chain.

Suliel raised her eyebrows in surprise. "You have a lot to learn about giving ladies jewelry, Guild Master," she said.

Delir gave her a sour look but kept his feelings to himself. "It's a security precaution, my lady. The stone glows in the presence of magic."

Suliel looked at him doubtfully but reached out to take the bracelet. As she did so, the stone started to glow. Faintly at first, then growing stronger as she grasped it.

<*Is it reacting to our bond?*> Kelsey sent, and had her answer immediately as the crystal glowed more strongly.

"An obvious magical effect might explain why I'm wearing something so obviously out of fashion," Suliel allowed. "But I'm not sure of what use it will be if it always glows."

"It's additive," Delir explained. "It will glow more strongly if it detects additional magic."

"Oh, I see," Suliel said. She reached out to the Lazybones. They weren't in the room with her, but she could still give them orders. The stone brightened as the link grew stronger. "But . . . I'm making it glow with a trait, not magic. Does that mean my traits *are* magic?"

"Most traits hold a little bit of magic," Delir told her. "Some are more magical than others, and yours are . . . very magical. A wizard's magic is even stronger."

"I doubt they'll send another wizard after me," Suliel said. "Not after what happened to the first one."

"Perhaps," Delir admitted. "If it's the Wizards Guild after you, though, they might have wizards to spare, and not much else in the way of options. As it happens, I have some news on that front."

"Oh?"

"Since that first attack on the carriage, I've been asking around about any contracts that might be out on you."

Suliel frowned. "I thought you were looking for information on blue gods."

"You can't just talk about one thing if you want to be subtle," Delir said, winking. "People will think you're after something."

"I suppose that's true," Suliel admitted.

"As you might suspect, the guild doesn't accept jobs involving kidnapping or murder."

"Of course not," Suliel agreed. Bounties and town defense were one thing, but if adventurers became nothing more than murderers for hire, there was no point in licensing them.

"However, some adventurers *do* take such jobs, and they talk about them. Not in the guild hall as a rule, but in taverns where other adventurers can hear them. *Those* adventurers will sometimes report on what they've heard."

"And what have you heard?" Suliel asked warily.

"That there is, indeed, a contract for your capture. One hundred gold. Alive."

Suliel thought about it. That wasn't a *princely* sum. Many nobles could afford to pay more to have their enemies disposed of in that way. Few did; the risks of failure or discovery were high unless you contracted with . . .

"Are the Shadowblades going to get involved?" she asked. That would change things.

"It's unlikely," Delir assured her. "The Shadowblades only deal in murder, and this party wants you alive."

"Why?"

"I can only speculate, but aside from concerns about their image, the Shadowblades are probably worried about crimes that involve surviving witnesses."

"No, I mean, why do they want me alive?"

Delir shrugged. "Again, I have only speculation. A week ago, I would have assumed it meant your mother was behind this, but you have come to an accord, have you not?"

"To an extent," Suliel said thoughtfully. It could be her mother. She would want Suliel alive. But when the King had accepted Suliel's class, he had destroyed most of her mother's position. The marriage was done, now, and her mother seemed to be trying to come to terms with that.

Who else? It could be the King, suspecting her of treachery but not wanting to make an overt declaration. He could seek to imprison and question her secretly.

Would the King operate through street-level thugs, though? Suliel didn't think so. He had access to far more dependable resources. The wizard seemed more like the sort of person the King would hire. Could there be two groups after her?

Suliel shook her head. This speculation was getting her nowhere. "Can we get any information out of the Wizards Guild?" she asked.

"No," Delir said flatly. "Not if they're behind this, and even if they're not . . . they don't allow outsiders to pry into their business."

"I suppose we'll have to rely on the Rose Circle for information then," Suliel said. She didn't like that idea, but perhaps she should think of it as a chance for the secret society to prove themselves trustworthy.

"Then, will you wear it, my lady?" Delir asked, looking pointedly at the bracelet.

"I suppose so," Suliel said. "It has to be a bracelet, though?"

"You won't be able to see it on a necklace," Delir pointed out. "A ring would work, but—"

"No," Suliel said. "It's gaudy enough as it is. If it was a broach, I could pin it to my sleeve . . . no, a bracelet will do."

"Thank you, my lady. Just remember to keep it in sight."

Suliel slipped the bracelet on, looking at it disdainfully. "Since you mentioned your efforts at the guild, have they borne any fruit?"

"I'm afraid not, my lady," Delir said. "While I haven't exhausted every avenue yet, thus far I haven't found anything to contradict what I told you the first time. Demons are blue-skinned, gods are not."

<Interesting,> Kelsey sent. **<I wonder if it's just my local god that's being impersonated by a demon or if they all are?>**

Suliel felt her stomach churn at the thought.

"My lady?" Delir asked in alarm.

"It's nothing," Suliel told him. "Just something Kelsey said. Is it possible that all the gods are nothing more than demons?"

"Surely not," Delir said. His face showed his doubt, but his words were clear. "The enmity of the gods and demons is long established, as is the benevolence of the gods versus the malevolence of the demons. It's possible that they might have a . . . common origin, but the differences between them are as night and day."

<Does he reckon that a demon can impersonate a god, then?>

"Perhaps to humans," Delir said when the question was relayed. "Or to an isolated dungeon. Not to the gods, though . . . surely."

"What about the fairies?" Suliel asked. "Mel seemed . . . worshipful of Riadi in that scene you showed me."

<Good question,> Kelsey sent. *<Mel doesn't see things the way we do. Descriptive elements like blue skin . . . she wouldn't notice if that changed. If a demon took over the role of a god, I don't think she'd notice.>*

"That's a terrifying thought," Suliel said. She spoke aloud so Syon and Delir could hear her. "Maybe we should take this to one of the churches."

<Whoa, are you crazy?> Kelsey asked. *<We don't know that the other gods aren't up to their blue-skinned elbows in this!>*

"I know, but if they are, we don't lose anything, do we?" Suliel asked. "They already know that we're on to Riadi. And if they aren't, we can get help."

"I think we should get help regardless," Delir said. "The problem is, if they are secretly demons, that help will be primed to sabotage us somehow."

<And that help would only be indirect anyway, wouldn't it?> Kelsey asked. *<They don't do anything directly.>*

"That might change with a demon impersonating them. It might be operating on the same . . . plane of their existence." Delir said thoughtfully. "A demon impersonating a god. There are stories, legends that I can look up."

"That tell of how to deal with a demon?" Suliel asked hopefully.

"There are such stories," Delir said. "They are always couched in vague terms. Myths, rather than instructions."

<We'll take what we can get,> Kelsey said. Suliel relayed her words.

Delir nodded. "I'll see if I can get you a text on the subject, but in simple terms . . ." He paused for thought. "To start with, you need a hero."

<We've got one of those. Or will soon.>

"The hero has to draw the demon out," Delir continued. "How he does that varies in the stories. When the demon comes forth, the hero confronts the demon. They may fight, but the conflict is never decisive. The demon always retreats, but somehow the hero gets a trail to follow."

"Somehow?" Suliel asked.

"It varies. Sometimes the demon leaves a trail of blood, sometimes it taunts the hero with clues to follow. Or the hero might glean some clue from the demon's appearance. However he does it, he follows the clues to the place."

<*The place?*> Kelsey said. Suliel could feel that Kelsey was suddenly very interested.

"Again, it varies, and is almost always vaguely described," Delir said. "It's a place from which the demon can't run."

<*Does the hero go alone?*> Kelsey, or rather Suliel, asked.

"Oh no, he almost always gathers a questing party to follow him," Delir said. "Depending on the legend, there's specific symbology for each of the hero's followers."

"And then?" Suliel asked.

"They fight the demon and win," Delir said. "I don't think the win is automatic, though. They just don't write legends about unsuccessful heroes."

CHAPTER TWENTY-SEVEN

US Forces

H o! The ship!"

Anton didn't think the cry made much sense, but he took the meaning. "Ho! Yourself!" he called back. He'd already reduced his speed to a crawl, allowing Imbube's Pride to draw near.

Up close, he could appreciate just how much skill went into piloting a sailing ship. The other ship's captain, Anwar Kaelan according to *Delver's Discernment*, was trying to have his ship come alongside the Whiskerwind. Unlike Anton, he couldn't control his speed by pulling a lever. He was at the mercy of the wind, and so he had sailors opening or closing sails to get the speed he wanted.

It was a complicated and tricky process, and not at all like the illusory sails hanging from the Whiskerwind's masts. They just hung there and did nothing. Anton could feel the disbelief radiating from the sailors on the other ship whenever they got a second to stare at the fake sails.

Part of Anton thought that they should have left the masts bare, but he reminded himself that they were always going to attract attention. The sails were to divert it, not hide from it.

With the ships close enough, and their velocities nearly matched, the other ship started throwing ropes over to them to bind the ships together. Since this was a peaceful boarding, the crew of Anton's ship caught the flung ropes and . . . stood there, not knowing what to do with them.

"Oi, quit standin' there like a fish outta water! Run that line through the fairlead, then belay it proper on the cleat!"

Thalorin, the former gladiator slave, stared blankly at the sailor who was yelling at him. He pointed at the rope questioningly.

With a curse, the sailor untied a rope on his ship that was attached to the end of one of the . . . branchy out thingies on their main mast. He stepped back and took a running jump, swinging on the rope across the gap between the ships. Anton stared in amazement.

Tariq Amane, Level 18, Human, Master Sailor, Deckhand/Sailor/Master Sailor, S: 28 T: 28 A: 17 D: 15 P: 15 W: 1 C: 3

Tariq grabbed the rope off of Thalorin and started to tie it to part of their ship, berating the man all the while.

"You need a good double half-hitch 'round the bollard or we'll be driftin' apart like the girl you left back home. And mind yer slack! We don't need any more drag than we've got already."

He was speaking the same Tiatian Trade that they spoke back in Zamarra, but no one understood a word. A few started copying his actions, though. Only one managed to satisfy the sailor with his results. The other gladiator got shoved out of the way as Tariq redid it.

"Listen here, mate, a ship's only as strong as the hands that haul her lines. You slack on those ropes, and she'll buck you like a wild beast in a storm. Keep 'em tight, steady, and never let a knot slip. A loose line's the fastest way to lose a mast—or worse, your life. So haul hard, keep your eyes sharp, and remember— every pull could be the one that keeps ya afloat."

Deep booming laughter came from the bridge of the other ship. Anton looked up—the Pride's deck was ten feet higher than Whiskerwind's—to see the captain, Anwar Kaelan. He was a large and muscular man with short, stubbly grey hair. Like the rest of the crew, his skin was a rich chocolate brown.

"Your crew are no sailors, that is for sure," he called down. "But I think that you do not need them to be, hey?"

Anton shrugged. "We've managed fine so far," he said.

"So it seems! Will you join me on board, or shall I come down to you?" At the captain's words, a simple rope ladder was tossed over the side of the Pride.

Anton didn't look at the front of his boat, where the deck sweeper was covered in an illusion of tied-down barrels and crates. Some crewmembers were strategically placed to ensure that any of the Pride's crew that came aboard stayed away from the area.

As far as Anton was concerned, the fewer of the Pride's crew that came aboard, the better.

"I'll join you," he said. Eschewing the ladder, he climbed directly up the side of the Pride. Kelsey headed up as well. She took the ladder.

Anwar stepped back to give Anton room as he clambered on board.

"Well met, Captain," he boomed. "I am Anwar Kaelan, as I think you might know, captain of this ship. This is my first mate, Suri Ralan."

Anton nodded at the tall, lean woman with tightly braided hair and deep, piercing eyes. Her skin was darker than the others, almost obsidian.

"My first mate has keen eyes, you know, keener than most," Anwar said.

Anton nodded. He'd been expecting this. Kelsey had expected that *someone* on a military ship would have an identification skill.

"What do your eyes tell you about her?" he asked, pointing at Kelsey, who was coming up to join them by a less direct route. The sailors in her way were standing aside, looking at her suspiciously.

"Nothing," Suri said, after a pause. Her voice wavered, and she looked at the captain. "Nothing, Captain."

Kelsey smiled as she joined them. "No trait is perfect," she said. "Just because it always worked doesn't mean it always will."

The Captain snorted. "My own eye is for boats, but I would be greatly taken aback if I saw something on the water that I didn't recognize," he said.

"This is Kelsey," Anton said. "She's . . . my comrade."

"So pale," Anwar said, looking at her. "Is she a ghost? Is that why Suri's eye doesn't work?"

"A ghost wouldn't have to climb that ladder," Kelsey pointed out. "I'm pale because I'm from the Frozen Coast."

"If you say so," Anwar said doubtfully. "We have sailed that far north, but I've never seen your like."

He shook his head, breaking off his gaze. "But strangeness is to be expected when dealing with heroes," he said, looking back at Anton.

Anton shrugged. "There's been a bit of strangeness," he admitted.

"A bit!" Anwar exclaimed, throwing up his hands. "We see an Elitran trader, but what has happened to it? Steelcutter? Fireheart? Those are not Elitran names. We get closer and we see it is full, not of Elitrans but of . . . Zamarrans? Is that where you hail from?"

Anton nodded. "And where we're headed for," he said. "Most of these people have escaped from the Empire. We're heading home."

The captain's eyes narrowed, but it was Suri who spoke. "Some of your crew still hold Slave classes."

"Some of them don't want to do Tier One again," Kelsey explained. "They'll finish the class and take a Tier Two that they qualify for."

"Finish the class?" the captain said doubtfully. "Will they be practicing their current profession in Zamarra?"

"They don't have to," Kelsey said. "Slaves can get levels from killing monsters, same as anyone."

"And where will you find these monsters?"

"There's a dungeon near Kirido," Kelsey said. "Maybe you've heard of it?"

"I have not," Anwar stated. Kelsey frowned. "I have better things to pay heed to than the geography of foreign nations."

"It's on the coast," Kelsey said, her voice rising slightly. "Isn't it your business to know what's there?"

"Kelsey," Anton said warningly. She looked at him, her eyes flashing. "It's not important," he told her. She stared at him for a long moment, and then she sighed.

"I suppose not," she said.

Anwar looked at her for a moment and then turned to Anton. "Now, this boat," he said. "Where did it come from?"

"We bought it," Anton said. "And then we made some improvements."

"We?" Kelsey said.

"We have a mage travelling with us," Anton spoke over her.

Anwar raised his eyebrows and looked at Suri. She shook her head.

"We did not see this mage of yours on board," Anwar said.

"She hid herself," Anton answered. "We needed to keep some of our cards hidden."

"And yet you tell me of her?" Anwar asked. "I'm not sure you have thought this strategy through."

"We're not keeping her existence a secret," Anton said. "We're keeping her location a secret. In case things take a turn for the worse."

The captain looked at Anton levelly. In truth, Anton wasn't too worried about things going badly. Between the deck sweeper and the personal firearms that Kelsey had distributed, Anton liked his side's chances of winning any fight that broke out.

Winning that way, though, would be almost as bad as losing. Suliel had told him, in no uncertain terms, what would happen if his first report as a freshly minted Baron was to tell the King he'd started a war with the Tiatian Empire. Not to mention that casualties would be all but certain. Guns could erase the gap between the first and second tiers of his crew versus the second and third tiers of the Pride's crew, but they couldn't protect people. Anton didn't want to be bringing corpses back home.

It was the captain who looked away first. "Perhaps that is fair," he said. He looked at Kelsey, perhaps wondering if she was the mage.

Kelsey just grinned, as if daring him to ask.

Anwar shook his head again. "Ships and wizards don't mix," he said dourly. "You need your boat to be reliable on the water, not subject to the whims of some fellow with a robe."

"I couldn't agree more," Kelsey said. "But I notice you have an enchantment on your ship?"

"Not the same," Anwar claimed. "That is the work of the navy's Legendary Shipwright. Craft, not magic. Reliable."

He cast his eyes up at the Whiskerwind's false sails and snorted. "Unreliable," he said. "How is it that you are sailing on the right heading?"

Anton shrugged. "We have a map and a compass. Kelsey knows how to use them."

Anwar looked at Kelsey with new respect. "How does a ghost know these things, when she is not a sailor?"

Kelsey just smiled. "I used them in a previous life," she said.

"And where did a group of escaped slaves get such a thing? Or a boat, for that matter?"

"I had funds for a boat," Kelsey said. "The map and the compass . . . let's just say the people that tried to stop us leaving don't have any use for them anymore."

Anwar narrowed his eyes. "Fierce, aren't you? That's no small amount of funds, though. Have the northern kingdoms decided to intervene in the slave trade?"

"*I* have," Kelsey said. "I don't represent any kingdoms, though. I'm just a humble merchant."

The captain laughed. "Aye! A humble merchant taking on an Empire! Though . . ." He looked over at Anton. "Such a merchant would do well to fall in with a Heroic Liberator. I've not heard of the class before, but the name paints a picture."

"I can't claim any great victories against the Empire," Anton said. "I just wanted to bring back my people. We got a few more than that, but it's just a drop in the ocean."

"You're young yet," the captain said. "I'll wager your victories are still ahead of you."

"Speaking of which, Captain," Kelsey said. "Were you planning on stopping us?"

The captain laughed. "Just itching for a fight, aren't you? No, the Tiatian Empire has no quarrel with ex-slaves wanting to return home. We stopped you because you were a strange Elitran ship, but we aren't blockading Zamarra."

"Then, if you'll excuse me, Captain, I'm in a rush to get back to my wife," Anton said. He gave a quick bow.

"Ha! Another sign you're not a sailor. Go on then, be off with you. Mayhap we'll meet on the seas again someday."

He shouted over the side. "Get those lines untied, Tariq, and stop fraternizing!"

Anton and Kelsey couldn't get off the Pride fast enough to suit them.

"I can't believe that worked!" Anton said as they watched the warship sail off.

"Meh, I'm a little disappointed," Kelsey said.

"Why?"

"He didn't say anything about your hat!"

CHAPTER TWENTY-EIGHT

I Still Haven't Found What I'm Looking For

Land ahoy!" Tyla shouted from the top of the mast.

Anton checked in the direction she was pointing and adjusted their course slightly.

"What does 'ahoy' mean?" he asked no one in particular. Soraya was on the bridge and assumed he was talking to her.

"She's using it wrong," Soraya said with a sniff. "It's 'ship ahoy' and 'land ho.' You can't mix them up like that."

"But what does it mean?" Anton asked. "For that matter, what does 'ho' mean?"

Soraya pressed her mouth closed, and her tail lashed with frustration. She didn't want to admit that she didn't know the answer.

"Sailors are drunk most of the time," Kelsey said, coming up to join them. "Most sailor lingo can be explained by someone getting blitzed and forgetting the names of things."

She thought for a moment. "And when I say someone, I mean *the entire crew.*"

Anton looked at her doubtfully. "I don't think that's the reason," he said. "And if it was, I don't think you'd know."

"Trust me, I'm always right," Kelsey said, smiling easily. "Did I hear that we'd be making land soon?"

"It's been sighted," Anton said. "She didn't call out that she'd seen Kirido, though."

"We've got a compass, not GPS," Kelsey said. "On dead reckoning, we might have hit Zamarra, but getting our heading close enough to land on Kirido first try is asking a bit much."

"What do we do, then?" Anton asked. "I don't think any of us have travelled far outside of town."

"It's not complicated," Kelsey assured him. "We look for a town, and if we don't see one, we pick a random direction and sail until we find a town. They should be able to tell us which way to go after that."

"Oh, that is pretty simple," Anton agreed. He supposed it might be a little annoying to go one way and then be told that they needed to sail back the way they came, but that's all it would be. Kelsey was providing them with fuel, and they had enough food.

Despite Kelsey's warning, Anton felt a surge of excitement when he saw the dark green line rise about the horizon. He inched the engine into the danger zone before thinking better of it and nudging it back. They waited patiently for the land to resolve itself . . .

It didn't look at all familiar. Not that it was *strange*—it had the usual rocks and trees and grass—but Anton didn't recognize where it was in relation to home. Nor did any of the crew from farther afield. And there wasn't a village in sight.

"Pick a direction, Captain," Kelsey said.

Anton picked west. Some of the girls were from farther west; if they'd did happen to be west of Kirido, he might be able to drop them home. When they got to the next coastal village, it turned out that they were east of Kirido.

Anton kept the boat headed west. Home was getting closer.

"Check that out," Kelsey said as they passed the mouth of a river.

"Check out what?" Anton asked. The only unusual thing about the river was that it didn't have a settlement at the mouth. The river had cut through a ridge to get to the sea, making the ground nearby unsuitable for building. Looking upriver, though, Anton could see some boats headed in their direction.

"We'll be taking that river up to the capital after we drop off everyone," Kelsey said.

"We aren't taking the roads? I thought that was the fastest way."

"It's more direct, and going upriver is slower than going down," Kelsey allowed. "But that only applies to boats without a fireheart."

"Sounds good," Anton agreed. "I didn't really want to walk all that way."

The Whiskerwind cut through the waves, and it wasn't long before Kirido came into view. Well, *something* came into view, at least.

"Is *that* Kirido?" Anton asked.

"It looks a little different, huh?" Kelsey said.

It did. The most obvious difference from the seaside was the tower that guarded the sea approaches. Anton could count himself a world traveller now; he'd seen higher and larger fortifications. When he saw it looming over his hometown, though, it looked bigger.

From here, Anton couldn't see much of the town wall, but he'd already known that it was going up, wider and higher than before, helped by Kelsey's construction techniques.

The jetty had changed as well. Now a stone—or concrete, Anton supposed—pier jutted out into the sea, with smaller wooden jetties branching out for ships to tie on to. Suliel had doubled the number of boats that could use the harbor, Anton judged. Given that one of the ships moored was bigger than any he'd ever seen at Kirido, he guessed that it could take larger ships than before as well.

"It's looking good," Kelsey said, looking around with satisfaction. "I haven't been able to monitor things recently with Suliel being in the capital, but everything seems to be progressing nicely."

They had been noticed, of course. The tower would have sighted them early enough to have word sent down to the docks, and Anton could see a party waiting for them. He could see that it included guards, which was new. Old Kirido hadn't bothered to inspect ships when they arrived.

Since they hadn't recognized the ship, and since they couldn't have had any idea of what to make of Kelsey's flag, there was a certain tension in the group as the Whiskerwind approached. Then one of them pointed, and they started talking excitedly.

"I wonder which of us they recognized?" Kelsey wondered. The group on the docks sent someone running back into town while the rest of them waited. They were still tense, but it was a different kind of tension.

Anton slipped the Whiskerwind into what looked to be a convenient berth, easily ignoring all of the issues that would have plagued a regular ship. Anton just lined up with the dock and steadily reduced speed as he approached. At the last moment, he briefly threw the engine into reverse, leaving them motionless.

The welcoming party watched in amazement, and one of them gave a small cheer. Anton's crew threw ropes to the shore, and they were hastily tied to the jetty posts.

The guards saluted him as he stepped ashore. Anton hadn't intended to be the first to step off the boat. It had meant an awkward pause as he made his way along a deck crowded with his fellow townsfolk eager to get home. They all insisted, though, gesturing for him to come forward and refusing to step on the gangplank until he did.

"Welcome home, Lord Nos!" the senior guard said. Anton didn't need to use *Discernment*; he'd known Ramal Drakos since he was a kid. This might be the first time the man had addressed him as Lord Nos, though.

"As you were, Ramal," Anton said, repressing the urge to berate the man. Drakos—Sergeant Drakos, if Anton was reading the new insignia right—was ten years his senior. Hearing the older man call him Lord felt like a joke.

He knew it wasn't, though.

"It's good to be back," he said instead.

"In case you weren't aware, my lord," Ramal said, "Lady Nos has left for the capital. We've sent word ahead to the castle for them to prepare your welcome, sir."

"That's good, but I think we're going to need a bigger welcome," Anton said. He glanced up at the ship, his gaze catching on Aris and Cheia standing together near the prow. "There's a whole crowd here that needs to be reunited with their families and some strangers that need a home. Spread the word that there will be a feast at the castle to go along with some announcements. For now, though . . ."

He motioned for the welcoming crowd to clear the way.

"Everyone who knows where they're going, head out!" he called. "Those that don't, stay here with me."

There wasn't a rush. Everyone had learned to step carefully aboard a ship. But they surged forward as fast as they felt they could. When they stepped on solid land, some of them bowed, and some of them shook his hand. Some of them just nodded with tears in their eyes as they rushed past him.

Aris and Cheia were two of the last to leave. Aris embraced him. "We did it," she said.

"Go on, go find your parents," Anton said. "I'll take care of things here."

They raced off to be replaced by Kelsey. Anton had hardly noticed the pang of fear when she'd been out of his sight, but he noticed when it eased.

"Got everything in hand?" she asked. Anton nodded. He'd hashed a plan out with Suliel through Kelsey's link. It was enough to seem like he knew what he was doing.

"All right, everyone that's left, follow me to the castle. We'll see about getting you a bed, a bath, some food, and fresh clothes!"

That got a cheer from the remnants of his crew. With his new citizens at his back, Anton led the way up to the castle.

"So soon?" Belan Lucina asked plaintively.

"First thing in the morning," Anton said. "Kelsey tells me that the tide doesn't matter, so we'll head out as soon as it's light."

"We," Cheia said firmly, looking sternly at her father.

"You don't have to go," Belan said. "You only just got back!"

Anton took a moment to wonder when he'd started thinking of Aris's father as Belan instead of Master Lucina. He had a moment; this discussion wasn't one he wanted to be a part of.

"I'm a gunner now," Cheia said proudly. "I'm part of the crew, so I'm going with Anton!"

"Lord Nos," Etase, Cheia's mother, corrected her.

"Anton is fine," Anton reminded them. "You're family, remember?"

"It's hard to," Belan said. "I can't believe that you're the same boy that Aris would steal muffins for."

"They weren't *stolen*," Aris protested. She'd been leaning her head on Anton's shoulder, half asleep from wine and talking. "They belonged to the Lucina family, and I was giving them to him!"

"You're changing the subject," Etase said. "Which is supposed to be about Cheia staying here!"

"That's not happening, Mom!" Cheia said. "I'm an adult now, and I can make my own decisions."

Anton tried to keep the wince off his face. Becoming an adult from killing so many people . . . Thus far, they'd managed to keep the story from her parents.

"I don't care if you're Tier Two, you're still my little girl!" Etase exclaimed. "Aris went to get you back, but you want to leave as soon as you get here!"

"We won't be long," Anton tried to assure her. "Just up to the capital, pay honor to the King, and be back again. There shouldn't be any danger."

"Then why do you need a gunner?" Belan asked.

Cheia rolled her eyes. "Someone has to keep the gun maintained, Dad. It's not magic; it will rust if we just leave it under the tarpaulin."

This wasn't . . . strictly true, but Anton held his tongue. Kelsey *could* disappear the gun and have her skeletons service it.

The argument continued, but Anton managed to stay out of it. To his surprise, Aris didn't join in either. She and Cheia had argued about it on the trip almost nonstop. Her silence must mean that she'd become convinced, or at least resigned to Cheia coming with them.

Anton let them argue and looked around the courtyard. This feast was a little different from the one held before they'd left. That one had been paid for by Kelsey, hosted at the largest inn in town, and featured wine more than food. This one had involved Anton breaking open the barony's store of provisions. Meat and vegetables, bread and cheese. Basic food, served on trestle tables in the courtyard. Anton had wanted to get everyone together, celebrating and eating, sharing each other's joy of reunion.

He nudged Aris fully awake. "We'd better get to bed," he said. "We've got a long day's sailing ahead of us tomorrow."

CHAPTER TWENTY-NINE

Left to My Own Devices

SULIEL

It started with the rain.

Suliel didn't think anything of it. Rain was not an unusual occurrence in Bures, or anywhere in Zamarra for that matter. It wasn't a storm; there was no lightning or dangerous winds to go with it. Just heavy rain that weighed down on everything.

Suliel had known that Seraphina's garden party would be cancelled long before she received word. Much of the business and politics of the city continued, of course, but no one wanted to go outside any more than they had to. Meetings went on, sheltered from the rain, but many smaller matters could be delayed and were.

That left Suliel with some correspondence to respond to, but otherwise, she had the day to herself. Normally, her mood would have been brought down by the oppressive weather, but today, she was brimming with barely repressed excitement. She joked with Syon and Delir over breakfast that she had changed her mind three times when the maids were dressing her.

Anton would be arriving soon. Perhaps today, but most likely tomorrow. Kelsey had not been able to provide a more precise estimate. She had bemoaned the lack of good information on currents, channel depths, or even the actual length of the river. As she had explained to Suliel at great length, all she had was a line on a map. It was unlikely that the river ran such a straight course, so the distance they had yet to travel would be unknown until they arrived.

Suliel wasn't able to help with her own resources. Trade and trips to the capital had always been over land for her family. She had offered to see if better maps were available in the city, only for Kelsey to offer some biting comments about the cartography skills of "this backward kingdom of pig farmers."

Suliel let the secondhand insults go. Despite her rough and ready ways, Kelsey was a perfectionist, and she was never more annoyed than when she had to *guess* at something she felt she should *know.*

Suliel didn't mind. What did it matter if Anton arrived today or tomorrow? The important part was that he was coming. Kelsey had kept her promise and kept him safe. The fact that he'd succeeded in his quest was good, too. It would cement the affection that the townsfolk had for him and be an impressive achievement to present to the King.

Suliel had already written to the Court about her husband's imminent arrival. He wouldn't have to wait as long as her to see the King.

The day passed uneventfully, the gloomy weather doing its best to wear Suliel down and failing. Kelsey relived the boredom with the occasional acerbic comment about the many failings in Zamarra's understanding of what constituted a "navigable" river.

As night approached, Kelsey decided to accept that they weren't going to make the trip in one day.

<Sorry, Suliel, it will have to be tomorrow,> she sent. *<This glorified stream is too crowded with useless wastes of wood.>*

<The rain can't be helping either,> Suliel sent back.

<Rain? No, it's clear where we are.> Kelsey paused, probably talking with the others. *<There's a town up ahead; we'll dock and get to you tomorrow.>*

<All right. I'll see you soon.>

Filled with a sense of anticipation, with just the tiniest twinge of disappointment, Suliel went and had dinner. She read until it was time for bed.

She woke in the middle of the night. It was dark; the curtains were drawn. She could hear *something* . . . struggling? She reached for the light-stone beside the bed and uncovered it.

The first thing she saw was one of the Lazybones. Its sword was drawn, but its other hand was covering its mouth with a single finger . . . the gesture for silence? It wasn't looking at Suliel—the command for silence must have been meant for the other one.

Suliel looked over and saw the other Lazybones struggling with a man dressed in black leather with a mask covering his face. Struggling might be the wrong word. The Lazybones' sword had been pushed through the man's torso, and while he was still moving, Suliel doubted he was long for this world. The animated skeleton seemed to be holding the dying man up, preventing him from falling.

Suliel screamed. That was the job of the lady of the house when faced with intruders. She had to be the focus of the defense, so her first duty was to let her defenders know where she was and that she was in distress.

There was a sudden crash from outside the window. The unencumbered Lazybones quickly went to investigate, poking its head through the gap in the curtains.

<Oh, okay, that doesn't sound like it will be solved with a glass of water. What's going on?> Kelsey's thoughts came quickly, with no sense that she had been sleeping. She never slept. Suliel opened the connection wider, giving Kelsey access to her sight.

<Who's that guy?> Kelsey asked.

Suliel didn't have time to answer. An arrow screamed out of the window, punching through the heavy curtains and embedding itself in the wall behind her. When she turned to look, she saw that it had impaled a scapula bone and pinned it to the wall.

She heard a loud shout from somewhere in the house.

<Okay, I'm going to take this as "we're under attack,"> *Kelsey sent calmly.* **<Dunno if we'll get there in time, but we're on our way.>**

Suliel tried to calm down enough to send a coherent response, but events were still moving around her. The injured Lazybones stumbled out from behind the curtain, its glowing eye sockets fixed on its missing bone. The other skeleton approached the window, holding the dying man up in front of it. When it pushed the man past the curtain, there was a muffled impact of another arrow strike. The man screamed in pain, but he was quiet when the next two hit.

There was a scraping sound, followed by a muffled thud from outside. When the skeleton emerged from the curtain, he wasn't carrying a body anymore.

<Tch. Wasting a perfectly good human shield like that,> *Kelsey complained.*

The uninjured Lazybones went over to the injured one, who was ineffectually tugging at the arrow with one arm. Between them, they managed to pry it free and release the scapula. Suliel watched as they reattached it.

<Okay, you want to try and secure that window,> Kelsey sent. **<Then either fort up here or go looking for the others.>**

Suliel looked at the skeletons and thought about what they needed. The skeletons looked at each other and then returned to the window. This time, they approached from the sides, sliding under the curtains. A few moments later, Suliel heard the shutters *clack* shut.

"Do they still lock?" Suliel asked aloud. That wasn't the sort of detail she could get through feedback, so she pushed the curtains aside to look. The locking mechanism was still attached, and the Lazybones had just latched it in place.

Suliel looked at it doubtfully. The shutters had been in place when she went to sleep, so she was unsure of how long they'd stop those outside.

"Let's go," she said to her skeletons.

She let the skeletons lead. They didn't need the light from the stone she was carrying, and she trusted them to follow her desire and not attack any of the house staff. Their first encounter was not an unfortunate servant coming upstairs to see what was going on, but something altogether more sinister.

As Suliel rounded the corner, a step or two behind her skeletal guards, the light from her stone did more than relieve the darkness. For an instant, a knot of shadows seemed to resist the light, gathering darkness into itself. Then it burst, and a man appeared out of nowhere.

He snarled a curse and started to run, but the Lazybones overcame their surprise at his appearance and were quickly on to him. Suliel made haste to use *Nobility's Privilege* while he was still a valid target.

Kiran Falke, Level 18, Unmarried, No Family,
Loyal to: The Grey Oaths, Human, Wayward Scout

Suliel looked away as her skeletons dealt with the intruder. She stared at where he'd appeared from. It was close to the door to Syon's room. Holding her light high, she opened it.

To her relief, the room wasn't awash with blood. The windows were open, the curtains moving gently in the wind, and a figure was lying on the bed, struggling to get up.

There were still shouts coming from somewhere else on this floor. By a process of elimination, she assumed they were coming from Delir's room. But she still needed to check what had happened here. Checking to make sure the Lazybones had finished, she directed them to enter the room.

One of them closed the shutters, taking care to avoid being shot, while the other guarded Suliel as she approached the bed. It was Syon. He'd been tied and gagged.

The skeleton grinned as he made short work of the binding. Syon gasped for air when the gag was removed.

"I'm sorry, my lady, I couldn't fight him!"

"You're my chamberlain, not a soldier," Suliel said. "Did he say anything?"

"He put a knife to my throat and threatened to kill me if I made a sound," Syon said, shuddering at the memory. "I'm sure he was after you, my lady, but he said nothing of his plans."

"All right. Gather yourself as soon as you can and join us. No, wait."

Suliel paused for a moment, as a thought struck her. "Stay on this level, and uncover all the light-stones. Leave the doors to the rooms open so we can see if any have gone dark."

"I—I can do that, my lady. Just give me a moment to compose myself."

"That's fine," Suliel said. "Scream and run if you see anyone that isn't staff."

She turned and moved towards Delir's room. The sounds of a struggle were still going on, so she let the Lazybones go first. They rushed in, swords raised and . . . paused.

Their grins never wavered, but they managed to look uncertain as they stood there. Suliel entered the room and took a look for herself.

Delir was wrestling with another intruder. They were rolling around on the floor exchanging blows. The intruder seemed to be trying to disengage and reach the dagger that had been flung into a corner, while Delir seemed to be mostly concerned with keeping his opponent on the ground while landing as many punches as possible.

"Think you can . . . write me off . . . cause I've got one leg? I'll show you, you punk!"

"Take him alive, please," Suliel said. She checked *Nobility's Privilege.*

Corvin Thale, Level 14, Unmarried, One Sister,
Loyal to: The Grey Oaths, Human, Rootop Infiltrator

Both of the combatants froze at her voice, but Delir recovered more quickly. He snuck a furious punch past Corvin's guard into his stomach.

"Take that, you stray mongrel! You weren't good enough to sign up for the guild, don't go thinking you can beat an ex-adventurer!"

The Lazybones put their swords away and just grabbed Corvin's arms, pulling him up as he tried to retch. Delir lay on the floor and took deep breaths.

"Delir," Suliel said. She stepped over to the small table beside the bed.

"My lady," Delir said. "I'm sorry, you've caught me at an inopportune moment."

"That's quite all right," Suliel said. She grabbed the Guild Master's leg and handed it to him. "Get that on. We need to see to the rest of the house."

"As you say, my lady." He started strapping the artificial leg onto his stump. "What do you want done with that?" he asked, nodding at the captured infiltrator.

"Can you tie him up? If he didn't bring ropes with him, there are some in Syon's room." Suliel looked consideringly at the Lazybones. "I don't think knots are one of their skills."

"Certainly, my lady," Delir said, hauling himself to his feet. "May I ask what the situation is?"

"Three men came in through the locked windows," Suliel said. "There are archers covering at least this side of the house. And I haven't seen any sign of the two guards that were supposed to be on duty tonight."

"Ah," Delir said, his face falling. "They were good lads. I'll be mighty sad if they haven't made it."

He braced himself and sent another blow into the stomach of the defenseless Corvin.

"Not as sorry as this scurvy piece of scum is going to be, though," he said. "You can let him drop now, boys," he said. "Let Uncle Delir show you how to hogtie a sow for the slaughter."

CHAPTER THIRTY

To Live Is to Die

SULIEL

Where are my guards? Suliel thought. To herself—Kelsey wasn't going to know where her men were.

Most of them should be asleep in the carriage house. They only had two guards on watch at night. That struck Suliel as foolish *now*, but Bures was supposed to be kept safe under the King's watchful eye. Massed assaults from mercenary soldiers were *supposed* to be unheard of.

The two guards on duty should either be on patrol around the house and grounds, or keeping watch from the rooftop parapet. The second possibility was easier to check.

"Delir, go downstairs and let everyone know what's going on. We need to get someone to the carriage house, but it might not be safe to go outside. I'm going to finish checking up here."

Delir looked as though he wanted to protest, but he looked at Suliel's skeleton guards and just nodded while he finished tying up the intruder.

"Aye, my lady. Shall we send someone across anyway?"

Suliel swallowed. Tonight was the first time she'd lost one of her people. She'd seen death and its aftermath during the raid, but this was the first time she was *responsible*.

"Wait for me," she said. "I'll send the skeletons down. They're less . . . vulnerable to arrows."

<*I can't believe you'd spend the Lazybones' lives so easily,*> Kelsey sent as Suliel headed upstairs. <*They have kids, you know?*>

<What?> Suliel sent back, distracted.

The stairs that led to the parapet were a part of the guards' patrol route. So they were kept lit at night. The golden light that filled the space was reassuring, but all it meant was Suliel wasn't going to get ambushed by another shadowy stalker.

Kelsey started sending images to Suliel. Not of scenes she was seeing, but *mental* images. Pictures of what were probably meant to be the Lazybones, with other skeletons. Two of the other skeletons wore dresses, and there were four more . . . little skeletons?

<Little Riblet and Bonita will be devastated if you get their dad killed,> Kelsey sent.

Suliel paused at the top landing, her mind spinning. *<That's not—>* she started, before reconsidering. *<I want to say that's not possible, but if I do, you'll find a way to make it happen, won't you?>*

<That does sound like something I'd do,> Kelsey admitted. *<Don't go through that door; send the bones in for a look.>*

"Oh, *now* they're expendable?" Suliel said aloud. It was good advice, though. She thought she'd be safe if she stayed low to the ground, but there was no need for her to risk herself.

She ordered the skeletons to check, including a directive to keep down. They obeyed, scuttling out into the open air. They didn't take long to find what they were looking for.

Suliel heard two arrows hitting the roof, and then the skeletons were back. One of them was holding a bloody arrow. The other was carrying two rifles.

"They're not . . ." Suliel wasn't sure how she was going to finish that sentence, but the skeleton seemed to know what she meant. It shook its head and used its arrow to point at first its neck, and then the chest of its companion. It shook its head again, its ever-present grin adding a macabre sort of consolation.

"Right, I should . . ." Suliel trailed off. She winced as she realized that she didn't know *which* of her guards had been on duty that night. Two of her men had died and she didn't know which ones.

"I need to see them," she said softly. The skeletons shook their heads again. It wasn't that they could stop her, but it was good advice.

"Bring them in, then," she said. The Lazybones nodded and dropped their current burdens on the ground. Suliel picked up and examined one of the rifles while they were gone.

It was loaded and charged, ready to fire. Or would have been, if the powder hadn't gotten wet. They had been struck down before they realized they had an enemy.

The Lazybones dragged the two corpses laboriously over the threshold. Suliel sometimes forgot that, for all their skill, the Lazybones' strength wasn't all that high. They'd managed to complete the task she'd given them, though. Suliel looked down at the fallen.

Jarek was a veteran who had served with her father. Talin was from one of the branch families, a distant cousin of Suliel's, who had been brought in as part of the expansion of her forces.

"I don't . . ." Suliel said. "I won't . . . I won't let your deaths be in vain."

She looked at them for a moment more and then took a deep breath. She handed the rifle to the nearest skeleton.

"Get those weapons dried and reloaded, soldier," she said firmly. "We're going to need them."

They were all waiting for her in the great hall downstairs. Arelon Marr, the maids, the cook, and Darik the groundskeeper. Syon was there too, the upper floors were all blazing with light now.

"Sorry to wake you all," Suliel said wryly. "I take it that everyone is up to date with the situation?"

They all nodded nervously. Valia, one of the maids, raised her hand.

"Is Talin all right?" she asked.

Suliel shook her head. "I'm afraid not," she said. "He was one of our first casualties. Has anyone heard anything from the carriage house?"

"Nothing," Syon said. "It's screened off from the main house by the gardens, so they may not have seen or heard anything amiss yet."

"Would that our enemies were so uninformed," Suliel muttered. "We needed to light up the house, but now they must have realized that their first assault failed. What's their next move?"

Everyone looked at one another, but one by one they all settled for looking at Delir. The Guild Master grimaced but gave the matter some thought.

"It depends on what they're after, and what their resources are."

"I've *heard* of the Grey Oaths," Suliel said. "Enough to know that they have more men than we've seen."

"Your *Nobility's Privilege* gave you that, did it?" Delir asked. "Aye, well, they're a mercenary company. They run from somewhere between fifty and two hundred warm bodies depending on the season."

He scowled. "They haven't got the best reputation, but I hadn't heard anything that said they'd go against the King's peace like this."

"What do you think they'll do?" Suliel asked.

"They've got the men for a direct assault, if they're desperate," Delir mused. He looked soberly around at the whole group. "If they try that, then they'll need to make sure there's no witnesses."

Suliel smiled thinly. "My husband already knows what I do. It's scant comfort, but if the worst does happen, he'll be able to point the King's men at the perpetrators."

<Yep. Although, side note, I don't know if he'll be that interested in bringing the King in. If something happens to you, he's going to take that personally.>

Suliel blushed at the concern that Anton showed and Kelsey passed on. Did he really think so highly of her? She almost missed Delir's response.

"It's always good when your enemy makes a mistake, my Lady. But if we're to repel an assault, we'll need to make preparations."

Suliel nodded. "Barricade the doors and windows?"

"Aye, but we need those guards. Two skeletons and myself aren't enough to cover one side of this place."

"How?" Suliel asked. "We know their archers have the front side covered."

Darik put his hand up. "Out the front is the quickest way, my lady, but if we go out of the kitchen entrance and come around the side, we should be covered most of the way."

Suliel tried to visualize it, but she didn't know the grounds well enough. That there were a lot of trees and bushes on that side of the grounds was as far as she could get.

"All right," she said, "We'll send . . ." She trailed off, looking at the Lazybones.

"All due respect, my lady, you're talking about stealth," Delir said. "Ain't what those fellas are good at. There's not much light out there, but those two practically glow."

"The archers must have night vision to have been so effective," Suliel allowed. "But if not them, then who?"

"I can do it, my lady," Darik spoke up. "I know the way better than anyone."

"You're not one of my men, Darik," Suliel said. "You were hired to be a gardener, nothing more."

"I doubt that will matter to these fellows," Darik said bitterly. "I'm your man now, my lady, and one way or another I'll be fighting for your life and mine."

Suliel hesitated. She looked at Delir. In times past, he would have been more than suitable for the role, but with his leg . . .

"Very well," she decided. "I'll put my faith in you. The rest of us will get working on those barricades. We'll leave the kitchen door open for you to all get back."

"Yes, my lady, I won't let you down." Darik saluted her before heading for the kitchens.

The rest of them got to work putting furniture in front of the first-floor windows. The rest of the *humans*, that is. The skeletal warriors proved strangely inept at moving furniture. They were a little bit stronger than the maids but didn't seem to be able to grasp Suliel's orders. They kept trying to destroy the furniture, or they would slam whatever they were carrying into the door or window in question.

After a few mishaps, Suliel took them upstairs to watch over the front gardens. Standing well back from the second-story windows, the Lazybones had a good view of the grounds without exposing themselves to archers.

< It's actually crazy how many things they do have routines for,> Kelsey sent, *<But they don't have routines for everything.>*

<You mean everything they've done tonight was rote behavior?> Suliel asked. *<It seemed so natural!>*

<Yeah, they seem alive until you run into one of the missing spots,> Kelsey sent. <I guess whoever was responsible didn't think they'd be moving furniture.>

<But dragging bodies is . . . oh, I guess I can see the need for that,> Suliel admitted.

<I gave up trying to follow the logic of it a long time ago,> Kelsey said. <You can work around it with detailed and complex orders, but it's a pain.>

A shout came from the kitchens before Suliel could answer. Valia had been sent to watch the door once she'd been overcome with exhaustion from the unaccustomed physical labor.

"Miss! Miss!" she called. "Darik's back! And he's brought the guards!"

A surge of relief went through Suliel. With her soldiers here, they might have a chance.

"Sergeant Mirok," she said to the first of them to stumble through the kitchen and come into the main hall. "You're out of uniform," she said with a wry smile.

Sergeant Eshara Mirok dropped what seemed like her own body weight of gear and saluted.

"Apologies, my lady! It seemed like speed was of the essence, so we didn't wait to dress!" She was a lithe, agile woman with dark brown skin. Suliel was used to seeing her hair braided with silver charms in it, but she must have let it out when she slept. "We brought everything over instead!"

"Good. I think I'll defer to you on the placement of everybody. We're expecting an attack from the front, but we'll need to have at least some coverage on the back and sides."

"Yes, my lady. Do we have any information about the opposing forces?"

"The Grey Oaths mercenary company, numbers unknown," Suliel said. "We just need to hold out for a little while before the Baron gets here."

<I wish I could give you an ETA, but this pissant kingdom has neglected to

put signposts on the waterways,> Kelsey said. **<We haven't reached the city yet
is all I can tell you.>**

"Yes, my lady. Those archers are going to be a problem. I'd like to get up on
the roof and see if I can take them out."

"They have Darkvision, too—"

Suliel stopped as a shot rang out from upstairs. She and the sergeant
exchanged glances.

"It's starting," Suliel said.

CHAPTER THIRTY-ONE

If A Tree Falls

SULIEL

Is that one of *my* trees?" Suliel asked, outraged. After everything that had happened, this felt like a final, personal insult.

"Probably, my lady," Sergeant Mirok said glumly. "It's traditional to make siege equipment with whatever you have on hand."

Suliel stared out at what had been, until tonight, her ornamental garden, screened for privacy by a thick copse of trees. Now, it was the staging ground for an invasion force.

It was hard to make out in the darkness. The mercenaries had brought lights, but they must have realized that light would make them targets for arrows. Their lanterns were stuck on poles, widely spread, and the dim light they provided barely made it through the rain. Nevertheless, the long shape they were clustering around could only be a ram.

"Why did you ask for the Lazybones to stop shooting?" Suliel asked.

"The . . . skeletons fired when the mercenaries came out of cover," the sergeant explained. "They dropped two of the soldiers carrying the ram and caused it to be dropped. At first, I didn't want to waste ammunition until I knew what was happening. Now . . . this is what we want."

"We *want* mercenaries in my garden?" Suliel asked, raising her eyebrows.

"Not as such, my lady, but we want them milling around, not doing anything. This battle is about delay, is it not?"

"Is it?" Suliel would rather the battle be about wiping the stain of this insult off her lands.

"They outnumber us, my lady, by a considerable amount. And your husband is coming to reinforce us. Right now, they're doing nothing, and it isn't costing us anything."

"I see. You don't think we can defeat them on our own? Are the rifles not enough?"

"They are powerful, my lady, but this is the first time they've been used against opposing troops. With your life at stake, we need to be cautious."

"All right," Suliel said. "So what's our next move?"

"That depends on what they do," Sergeant Mirok told her. "We're using the time gained to set up positions covering all the approaches. It looks like they'll eventually try a charge from the front, but they seem spooked by those shots."

She looked quizzically at Suliel. "Something about those shots has got me puzzled as well."

"What's that?"

The sergeant pointed at the dropped ram. "You can see, they had screens up?"

"Those big wooden shields?"

"Aye. They're a bit light for shields, but they protect against arrows well enough. The rifles went right through, as I'd expect, but how did the skeletons hit the target?"

<Skellies can sense life,> Kelsey explained. <A thick enough barrier will block it, I guess those screens weren't thick enough.>

"Ah," Sergeant Mirok said, once Suliel passed the explanation on. "That might prove useful later on."

They settled in to wait. The arrangement they ended up with seemed strange to Suliel, but Sergeant Mirok assured her that it was suited to the nature of this assault. The top two floors were empty but blazed with light to deter any further assassins. The rooms below were dark, to preserve the soldiers' night vision and to help keep them hidden from the watching archers.

The ground floor, meanwhile, had been fortified with makeshift piles of furniture, sourced from every floor of the mansion. The ordinary staff were gathered here. They had been armed from the house's inventory, not so much as a final line of defense as a way of slowing any invaders that made it in long enough for the soldiers to come down.

Suliel stood on the second-floor landing. Centrally positioned, she could hear any shouted warning from this floor or the one below. Suliel felt that the limited utility of this command position was only highlighted when her sergeant left it to take up a position at the front of the house.

The wait dragged on, with the sound of falling rain the only thing Suliel could hear. The orders had been given, the positions had been taken. Even the mercenaries outside were quiet, no doubt trying to avoid attention from any passersby.

Finally, the call came from the front of the house. "They're moving!"

"Steady!" Sergeant Mirok ordered. "Flanks and rear, keep an eye out in case this is a distraction!"

Suliel found she couldn't hang back and wait. She rushed to the front rooms.

"Stay back, my lady!" Sergeant Mirok managed to keep to the proper forms of address, but her tone betrayed her irritation.

"I am standing back!" Suliel shot back. And she was. She didn't enter the room; she hung back at the door, close enough to get a view of outside. "What's happening?"

Yesterday, this had been a sitting room with pleasant views of the front garden. The wide windows had no glass, but they had shutters, now flung wide open. Most of the furniture had been dragged downstairs, but a couch with a high back remained, positioned so that two soldiers could hide behind it and rest their guns on the back.

The other room held two more soldiers, and both rooms had their own skeleton. The Lazybones ignored the more comfortable firing positions. They stood there with their guns raised, untiring.

"The main force is coming in ahead of the ram," Sergeant Mirok said shortly. "Must be hoping to keep us busy while—"

She broke off, intent on the scene below. "Cover your ears, my lady. Ready volley! *Volley Fire!*"

Four rifles fired as one, the sound ringing out like thunder. Suliel had just managed to protect her ears, but the sound still rang through her. Two more shots came slightly after, like an echo. The skeletons didn't have the soldiers' trait that let them fire as one.

"Reload!" Sergeant Mirok yelled.

Smoke filled the room. Despite Kelsey's claims, the rifles weren't exactly *smokeless.*

<It's smokeless, not smokenone,> Kelsey said, catching the stray thought. <Believe me, it's less.>

Suliel crept forward to get a better view. A dozen . . . no, *two* dozen men were lying on the ground, just behind the fountain. The ram had been readied, just in the cover of the trees, but it wasn't being brought forward.

How did we get so many? Suliel wondered. Then she saw that they were moving.

"Hold fire!" Sergeant Mirok commanded. "Let's not teach them how fast we can reload."

They watched as the invaders scuttled back, shields held high. Three of them were left on the field. Sergeant Mirok made a disappointed sound.

"We hit more than that on the volley," she said. "I guess some of them can still move."

"Why were they all on the ground?" Suliel asked.

"They were counting on shields and a *Parry* trait to save them," Sergeant Mirok explained. "Bullets go too fast for that, though. When the volley hit and men started going down, they all panicked, diving for cover like they were gonna be the next ones shot at."

The sergeant grinned. "Likely they don't know how many guns we've got," she said. "Anyway, once they dropped, they lost momentum for the charge. They must have figured it was better to fall back and try again."

"And you held back the second round to delay them further," Suliel said. Sergeant Mirok nodded.

"Aye, every time they get a shock, they run around in circles for a bit," she said. "Right now they think we can't do a second shot in the time we have, so I'm thinking they'll try and push through the gauntlet. When the second volley hits, they'll freak out all over again. Hopefully."

"Hopefully," Suliel agreed. "There are so *many* of them, though."

Sergeant Mirok shrugged. "That's why it's a delaying game," she said.

"So now . . ." Suliel trailed off. She already knew the answer.

"We wait," Sergeant Mirok confirmed.

Suliel sat down. With the only chair in the room occupied, she had to sink down to the floor, leaning against the doorjamb. For the first time, she registered that she wasn't properly dressed. She'd grabbed a robe to cover her nightdress back when she was in her room, but that was hardly a substitute for proper clothes. At some point she'd accepted a short sword in its scabbard and belted it around her waist, making for a somewhat incongruous ensemble.

I should get dressed, she thought. *I don't want to go to my death—or kidnapping— dressed improperly.*

She smiled wryly to herself as the opposite impulse hit her. Why bother? It's not like there's a proper gown to be kidnapped in.

"Get back, my lady," Sergeant Mirok warned. "They're making another try."

With reluctance, Suliel allowed herself to be shooed away. The sheer unpleasantness of being in the room when they were firing was a major factor in her decision.

"Ready volley . . . *Volley Fire*! Reload!"

The noise was much less deafening from here. Suliel waited tensely for some indication of how the volley had gone.

"Ready volley . . . *Volley Fire*! Reload! They're breaking again!" The sergeant's voice was filled with triumph. "Fire at will, squad! See how many we can get on their way back."

This time, a ragged fusillade sounded out, as soldiers fired as soon as they were ready instead of waiting for the slowest. *Volley Fire*, Suliel had been told, had a greater impact on enemy morale, but some of the soldiers had traits that allowed them to fire faster, or more accurately, if they weren't using *Volley Fire*.

It would be a little while before the next charge, Suliel thought. She headed downstairs to find her maids. They were on the ground floor with the rest of the servants, clutching their smallswords nervously. Suliel tried to project an aura of calm.

"I think the menfolk can spare you for a bit," she said. "Come upstairs with me."

"Yes, miss," Shana Veris, the older of the two, said. "Should we . . ." She awkwardly held up the sword in its scabbard.

Suliel's smile almost slipped. "Bring the weapons," she said. They shouldn't need them, but *shouldn't* wasn't *wouldn't*.

Suliel led them up to her rooms on the third floor. Everything up here was well lit, and she had a feeling that if the enemy had more infiltrators, they would have used them by now.

They got to her room. The maids had followed her here without a word of explanation, but Suliel could feel their questioning glances.

"Since we have a moment between attacks," she explained, "I thought I should get dressed properly."

Both maids stared at her. Suliel gave them a questioning look of her own.

"What? You think I should welcome my husband's arrival in a nightgown?"

"Ah, no, miss. What would you like to wear?"

"Something practical, I think . . ."

After some discussion, they settled on a dress intended for hunts. It was one that Suliel had brought with her and not up to the dictates of court fashion, but she didn't think that Anton would mind. Helping her into it seemed to calm the girls' nerves, and Suliel had to admit that the familiar activity soothed her own anxiety.

They were almost done, when the first *crack* of a volley sounded. They all froze.

"Come on, let's get this finished," Suliel said. The girls nodded and busied themselves. Then the second *crack* sounded.

The final piece, her sword belt, fit much more easily over the sturdy linen than it had over her nightgown. Suliel paused as the third *crack* sounded.

There wouldn't be a fourth. Sergeant Mirok had explained that they would only have time for three volleys before the enemy came too close to the house. Firing at them then would require going up to the windows, which would expose them to the archers. Instead, the plan was to go down and man the barricades, fighting in close hand-to-hand. A single pair would remain upstairs, to hold off the ram.

Suliel swallowed. "Let's go down. And . . . make sure you bring your swords. We might need them."

"Yes, miss," the maids said. Their voices trembled as they cast anxious glances at the sounds coming from downstairs.

<I've got some news for you,> Kelsey cut in, her mental voice terse.

Suliel sent a feeling of receptivity as she headed down the stairs.

<We've reached the rainstorm,> *Kelsey sent.* **<And it's not natural.>**
<What do you mean?>
<I mean someone used magic to put it in place. A wizard. One more powerful than Tikin.>
<Why would a wizard make it rain on me?> Suliel asked incredulously.
<To cover their tracks,> Kelsey replied. **<Discourage witnesses. I don't know why, but it seems like a good portion of the Wizards Guild is after you.>**

CHAPTER THIRTY-TWO

It Won't Take Long

Yeah, it's magic," Kelsey said, staring at the sky.

"Why?" Anton asked. "Why just make it rain?"

They were in sight of the city walls now. The rain had started abruptly as they approached the city as if they had passed through a curtain. Anton could see a faint glimmer of magic in the clouds, but it was Kelsey who knew what they were looking at.

"I guess . . . they don't want the spell to be noticed? If a sudden storm sprang up, people might wonder. But rain . . . who cares about a little rain?"

"Why do it at all, then?"

"To hide?" Kelsey speculated. "It reduces visibility, people don't want to go out. . . . It won't keep them from being found out, but it should give them more time before the alarm is raised."

Anton didn't have time to respond, as Zaphar called out *another* submerged hazard from the front of the boat. Anton grunted with frustration as he veered the boat out of its way.

"The main thing is, this tells us who we're dealing with," Kelsey said thoughtfully. "They might have a wizard with them that we need to look out for."

Anton grunted again, his eyes peering through the darkness. Finally, he saw it. Dark shapes of ships loomed ahead of him. They had reached the docks.

"Take the wheel," he told Kelsey. "Tie her up . . . there." He pointed to where a small hut stood on the jetty.

"That's gotta be where the harbormaster is?" Kelsey said questioningly. "Do we have time to go through customs and all that?"

"No," Anton said. He slowed the engine to something more reasonable and let her take the wheel.

They were passing ships now. Darkened hulks were flaring up with light as the night watchmen realized that something was bearing down on them. Curses started flowing as people saw them barreling past at unsafe speeds.

It helped. Kelsey, Anton and Zaphar all had night vision, but the farther away a ship could be seen, the more easily it was avoided.

Anton joined Zaphar at the prow of the ship. He drew his sword.

"Hey, hey," Zaphar stammered. "I did good, right? We didn't hit anything on the way here."

"It's not for you," Anton chuckled. "Help Kelsey tie up once we've stopped."

A lantern had been lit in the hut that Kelsey was aiming for, as someone came out to see what all the noise was about. Anton didn't think it was the harbormaster. Someone with such a significant title wasn't going to be stuck on a jetty at night in the rain. The man emerging to peer about in the darkness was probably just a guard.

Regardless, he was probably the one in charge here. Anton had to time it just right. He could leave it to later, but he didn't want to wait for Kelsey to carefully nudge the *Whiskerwind* up to the dock. Not that she was being particularly careful. The dock was coming up quite fast.

"Slow down, you maniac!" Zaphar called back to the helm. Anton ignored him. It was time.

Leaping Attack.

The hapless guard screamed and dropped to the ground. He needn't have bothered. *Leaping Attack* required an *attack*, but it didn't have to be on anything living.

Anton's sword chopped deeply into the doorframe, some little distance above where the guard's head had been. Anton landed on the wall of the hut, which shook with the impact but didn't collapse. Anton was grateful for that. It would have been embarrassing to have the whole structure collapse around him.

The guard squealed so loudly that he might have been stabbed instead of frightened. Anton looked down at him and leapt down off the wall. He picked the man up by his collar and drew him to his feet.

"I am Baron Nos of Kirido," Anton said.

"Mercy, my lord!" the man cried.

Anton shook him. "Are you paying attention?" he asked.

The man nodded fearfully.

Anton growled under his breath. He didn't have time for this.

"I am here at the orders of the King," he said, which was technically true. "*Right now*, I am on my way to rescue my wife from *criminals* who are assaulting my mansion."

Something of the man's regular routine seemed to assert itself. "But—but, you can't tie up at night, my lord. There are fees and customs—"

Anton shook him again. "We'll take care of that later. *Right now*, I'm going to find my wife and *you* are going to fetch the guard."

"The guard, y—yes, my lord."

"Bring as many as you can find, understand?" Anton demanded. "Take this as high as you possibly can. Either because you believe me when I say that there is a mercenary company assaulting my mansion, or because I need to answer for the damage and the injuries that I've done here."

"In—injuries, my lord?" the man asked, trying to sound ingratiating. "You haven't done any injuries here."

"I believe that's my cue!" Kelsey said, jumping from the now tied-up Whiskerwind to the dock. "You want his legs broken, or just his arms?"

"Mercy, my Lord!" the man cried, attempting to flinch away from Kelsey.

"That was a joke," Anton said, glaring at Kelsey. "No one is going to hurt you. Do you understand what to do?"

"Y—yes, my lord."

"Take this as high as you can," Anton warned him. "It might be expecting too much to have the King wakened tonight, but I want him to be aware. This is his peace that these mercenaries are breaking, and I want them to answer for it. I'm going to be at the townhouse that used to belong to Baron Anat. Bring them there."

"Yes, my Lord. I'll—I'll try."

Anton let go of the man. He stumbled, almost falling, and then bowed hastily.

"Well? What are you waiting for? Get moving!"

"Y—yes, my lord!" the man said, and dashed off.

"Kelsey, Aris, you're with me," Anton said. "Zaphar and Soraya, you need to stay on the boat. Let's not have foreigners running around tonight."

"Aye aye, sir!" Zaphar said quickly. He gave Anton something that might be a salute.

"I'm not a foreigner!" Cheia said brightly. "I can come!"

"You're the ship's gunner," Anton replied. "You need to stay with the ship."

"What!" Cheia gasped. "You're using my job to keep me out of danger? That's not fair!"

"Fair or not, get used to taking orders," Anton said. He looked at Aris, who gave him a grateful smile. "Let's go, everyone. Kelsey, which way do we go?"

Kelsey looked at him quizzically. "Why are you asking me?"

It turned out that Kelsey didn't know the streets, because *Suliel* didn't know the streets.

"She takes a carriage everywhere!" Kelsey said. "Sometimes she looks outside, but it's a very disjointed experience of the outside, let me tell you!"

That didn't exactly matter, because they knew that the townhouse was in the Noble's Quarter, which was in the upper half of the city. All they had to do was head uphill.

"We should find ourselves a carriage, though," Kelsey said. "Not only will it be faster, but it's their job to know where everything is and the fastest way to get there."

Anton agreed, if only because it would mean getting out of the rain. He didn't know how he was supposed to tell a carriage for hire from one owned by a rich family, but the point was moot. There weren't any carriages about.

They'd moved well out of the dockyards before Anton saw a carriage. It wasn't just one, there were four of them parked outside of what looked like a pub. He quickly headed for the entrance.

There was a boy outside, sitting under an overhang, just barely out of the rain.

"Are those carriages for hire?" Anton asked. The boy looked at him and blinked slowly.

"Normally, yeah," he said. "But no one wants to drive in this weather. The drivers are all inside; they paid me to watch the horses."

For the briefest of moments, Anton wondered if it was okay to leave the horses out in the rain while the drivers stayed inside to get dry and drunk. Then he remembered that he had more important things on his mind. He pushed his way inside the building.

It was warm and dry inside, a sharp contrast to the cold and damp he'd come in from. Anton pushed farther in, allowing the girls room enough to share the warmth. The smell was less welcome, though it wasn't all that unpleasant. Anton knew the smell of stale beer from the pub back home.

There was a small stir when he entered. People looked his way and then turned back to their conversation and drinks. Anton thought there might have been more of an effect if he hadn't been blocking their view of Kelsey and Aris.

"Is anyone here a carriage driver? We need to get to the Noble's Quarter!" he called out. That got attention, but not much of it seemed positive. Some people turned to see what would happen next, but none of the drivers that Anton knew must be here chose to speak up.

"Ain't no one wants to drive in this weather, boy," someone called out, "They'd rather—"

"We'll pay one gold for the trip," Kelsey announced. She stepped around Anton and held up a single coin.

Anton wasn't sure that the men in here could tell it was really gold. In the dim light of the lanterns, even a silver piece would glint yellow. But the *promise* of it motivated an immediate response.

"That's a lot of money to be flashing around, girl," a seedy-looking man said, jumping out of his chair and approaching. His eyes fixed on the coin, he didn't seem to notice Anton until Anton stepped in front of him. He tried to push Anton out of the way and seemed surprised when Anton didn't move.

"What of it?" Anton asked. He gently grabbed the man's wrist and removed the man's hand from his shoulder. He moved it slowly, giving the man every chance to resist, but Anton's Strength was much greater. The man stumbled back, the naked greed in his eyes replaced by fear.

"Ah, nothing, nothing. Must be nice being rich and all," the man spluttered, backing away.

Four men, at three different tables, stood up. Two of them were at the same table, and it was the closest of the three. They made it a race to get in front of Anton, while the other two cursed and gave up.

"I need to get to Baron Anat's townhouse," Anton said.

"Aye, I know where it is," one of them said, just ahead of the other. Anton looked at Kelsey.

"He seems a little less drunk than the other one," she said.

"Good enough. Let's go."

Things went much faster by carriage. Even the gates of the inner city are swung open wide for a fast-moving vehicle. Anton had told the man to hurry, and if the rattling and swaying as they went around corners was any indication, he had obeyed.

Then the carriage shuddered to a halt, the driver pulling back on the horses and leaning on the brake. They stopped so suddenly that Anton had to catch Aris to stop her from being flung forward.

"Are we there?" Anton asked, poking his head out the window.

"Nope," Kelsey answered.

"Reckon this is as far as we go," the driver said, pointing ahead. Two hundred yards down the street, four soldiers with pikes were standing in front of a gate.

"That's the gate to the Baron's estate," the driver said. "But that ain't any noble's livery that they're wearing."

Anton looked up. The sky was still covered and dark, and the man had spotted the mercenaries from this distance.

"Good eyes," he commented.

"Wouldn't be driving at night if I didn't have a trait for it," the man said.

"Fair enough. We'll get out here."

Stepping out of the carriage, Anton felt the rain start to drench him again, negating the efforts of the warmed towels that Kelsey had provided in the carriage. He ignored it, focusing his attention on the soldiers.

"Pay him," he said to Kelsey, leaving one scrap of awareness for the man who had got him here.

"Should I shoot them from range?" Aris asked.

"No," Anton replied. "Let's see how close we can get before they raise the alarm."

CHAPTER THIRTY-THREE

Potholes in My Lawn

Charging spearmen was normally a terrible idea. Anton ran forward anyway, leaving his companions behind. Kelsey could probably keep up with him, Aris could not. Both of them preferred to fight at a distance anyway, and Kelsey preferred to let him do the fighting, only stepping in when she needed to.

Sometimes, that annoyed Anton. Her excuse that he needed the experience wasn't wrong, but it still irked him to do all the work while she sat back, perfectly capable of ending a fight with a well-placed gunshot. Not this time.

Anton had never been in the city before. He'd never seen the mansion that he had been told he owned. He had a hard time seeing the mercenaries as invaders of his *home*.

But they were threatening Suliel. His family. *That* he could get angry about.

He quickly used *Discernment* against the four mercenaries guarding the gate as he got up to top speed.

Balin Torrek, Level 18, Human, Veteran Spearman, Warrior/Soldier/
Veteran Spearman, S: 25 T: 24 A: 22 D: 21 P: 5 W: 5 C: 6
Erwyn Karse, Level 17, Human, Veteran Spearman, Warrior/Soldier/
Veteran Spearman, S: 23 T: 24 A: 22 D: 19 P: 6 W: 6 C: 4
Rheda Lyns, Level 17, Human, Veteran Spearman, Warrior/Soldier/
Veteran Spearman, S: 22 T: 23 A: 21 D: 21 P: 7 W: 6 C: 4
Marvok Drent, Level 14, Human, Soldier, Warrior/Soldier,
S: 21 T: 18 A: 17 D: 18 P: 4 W: 4 C: 6

Not too bad. All of them were under his level. They did have classes that were optimized for combat, and they would have traits that helped them in exactly this situation, but Anton wasn't too worried.

The mercenaries had mismatched armor, but they all wore the same grey tabard. It had a marking on it, but Anton couldn't make it out. One of them had a long-sleeved mail shirt; the others had bits of plate strapped onto a leather jerkin. Loose plate, it was sometimes called. One of the soldiers must have had a trait that sensed for danger, because they were taking him seriously. Even though he was just one man, they leveled their spears at him, the shafts moving in eerie unison.

That was probably a formation trait at play. Not uncommon for soldiers; they had probably been grouped up because they all had the same one. Anton kept running. It must have looked suicidal—he hadn't bothered drawing his sword yet.

"Halt!" Balin called out. "This area is off-limits! You—"

That was as far as he got before Anton struck. At the last second, when he was close enough to see the edges of the spears pointed at him, Anton kicked his feet forward, letting them fly out from under him.

He'd expected to roll, but he hadn't reckoned with the slippery cobblestones. *Spider Climb* worked on any hard surface, vertical or horizontal, so he hadn't noticed how slick the road was. Instead of tumbling, he slid, dodging under the spears. They dipped down to catch him, but they were far too slow.

Anton crashed into the legs of the middle of the formation, sending Erwyn and Balin tumbling to the ground. He was moving so fast that he ended up behind them as they fell. He even had some momentum left.

Planting one foot on the ground, Anton used *Spider Climb* again, affixing the foot to the stone surface. His forward motion halted, and Anton felt himself shoved to his feet as his momentum was converted into upward movement.

It was looking a lot less like suicide now. Two of the mercenaries were on the ground, having let go of their spears. The other two were slowly turning, still not sure what had happened.

Quick Attack. Quick Attack.

Anton's sword lashed out twice, scoring hits both times. One was slightly off; it skittered off Rheda's spaulder before cutting deeply into Rheda's collarbone. The other sliced into the side of the neck of the lowest leveled soldier, Marvok. Both of them fell away, blood spurting from their wounds.

They were all down now, but two of them were getting up. Anton prepared for another strike.

"Mercy, lord! We surrender!" Balin said weakly. He held his hands up placatingly.

Anton paused. The two uninjured ones still had short swords at their belts, but they didn't seem inclined to reach for them.

"How many of you are there?" he snapped, his sword still raised.

"There was a full half company when we started—fifty men," Balin said quickly. "I don't know what our losses have been, but they weren't light."

"Where is the wizard?"

The man stared fearfully at Anton. "How do you know—with the commander. In the forest."

He pointed vaguely at the grounds. Where he was pointing wasn't in line with the gate, so it didn't mean much to Anton.

"Where are the *archers*?" Kelsey said as she caught up. Aris was only a few steps behind. Balin stared at them both, but answered the question.

"I—I don't know, exactly, he said. "There are three groups, two in the corners at the front, one on the rear side. They'll be in the trees."

"Can you take this squad prisoner?" Anton asked. He didn't want to delay any longer than he had to.

"Sure," Aris replied, pulling out her pistol. Balin looked at it warily.

"Is that . . . one of the guns we've been hearing?" he asked.

"Something like that," Aris said. "Please don't make me use it. Anton wants us to stay quiet."

"Shall we treat their wounds as well?" Kelsey asked idly.

Anton looked at the two injured. The woman he'd struck in the shoulder didn't seem too badly off, but the young soldier, Marvok, was clutching at his neck frantically. From the blood leaking through his fingers, he might not last long.

"Sure," Anton said, turning to leave.

"One sexy skeleton nurse, coming up!" Kelsey chortled. Then her voice turned serious. "Watch out for those archers. They're focused on the house, but they could easily turn around on you."

Anton nodded and entered the grounds. Of *his* house, strange as that thought was. Once he was past the gate, there wasn't much of a mystery about where he had to go. Fifty men had trampled quite a beaten path into the forest that shielded the corners and edges of the estate.

Anton had worried that the noise of his earlier attack would alert the rest of the forces, but as he crept along the trail of the invaders, he learned that there was never any danger of that. The command post of the mercenaries were not keeping their voices down.

"—need support, dammit!"

"Fifty men, and yet you can't capture one back-country noble girl?" The cold and arrogant voice that spoke was dripping with scorn.

"*And* her guards. The forces here are *nothing* like we were told to expect!" This voice sounded more natural to Anton's ears.

"Are they not? Ten human guards. Two skeleton warriors, a well-known and *weak* type of undead. How *exactly* did they pose a problem for your company?"

"*Something* took out our infiltrators," the frustrated voice replied. "And those new weapons are deadly! They can't be blocked or parried!"

"No one has knowledge of the new weapons yet," the arrogant voice said. "You should be grateful for the chance to see them in action before anyone else."

"Yeah," the frustrated voice said sarcastically. "It's been an *educational* experience for all our casualties."

"The possibilities of *losses* were accounted for in our contract."

Anton was close enough now to peer through the undergrowth and see who was talking. The arrogant voice belonged to a man in robes. Anton didn't need to guess that he was a wizard. He could see a halo of magic surrounding the man as well as a glimmer of magic from the core hanging beneath his robes.

The other man was wearing heavy chain. He must be the company commander. He had the lighter skin of a half-breed like Anton, and he looked as frustrated as he sounded.

"Yeah, yeah," he said. "This isn't *about* the contract. If this goes on, we might not be in a position to pull out all our bodies."

The other occupants of the clearing weren't taking part in the conversation. They were wounded. A dozen men nursed shattered limbs or bleeding torso wounds while a single woman moved among them, doing her best to staunch the bleeding.

The wizard rounded on the commander. "You *have* to," he insisted. "If any of your fallen are identified, then—"

"It'll come back to the Grey Oaths. If there's enough evidence for the King to send his investigators in, we're not gonna stand up to *that*. Your involvement will come out."

"Unacceptable," the wizard hissed. Then he stiffened. "However, it may be too late. He turned to look directly at Anton, hidden in the bushes.

Anton cursed to himself. He quickly used *Delver's Discernment* to see what he was dealing with.

Veylan Corbraith, Level 19, Human, Magister, Apprentice Mage/Mage/ Magister, S: 3 T: 5 A: 4 D: 25 P: 41 W: 30 C: 6

Okay, what? Anton thought. Did all wizards have such a high Perception? No wonder he'd been spotted.

He stepped out of the undergrowth and started walking calmly towards them.

"It is too late," he agreed. "The King has been informed, and it's only a matter of time before you're all hung as bandits."

He spared a quick glance around the clearing. None of the wounded looked as if they were going to interfere, and from the way the medic was furiously concentrating on her tasks, she wasn't going to take action either. That left the commander.

**Rhenar Vhorrin, Level 27, Human, Commander, Warrior/Soldier/
(Broken) Sergeant/Commander, S: 25 T: 24 A: 22 D: 21 P: 5 W: 5 C: 6**

Anton swallowed silently. This one wouldn't be so easy. The wizard had a clear weakness when it came to combat, but Rhenar almost matched Anton in combat stats. He had more levels than Anton, as well. He'd taken the long way around to get to Tier Three, following a path of Common and Fine classes. It was, strictly, an inferior method, but it had gotten him to the same place that Anton was now.

Anton kept walking forward. Magic was always best at a distance, so he wanted to close the range. The wizard wasn't a fool, though.

"That's close enough!" he snarled, pointing a finger at Anton. "Any closer, and I'll smite you!"

Anton took that step. "I can make it go easier for you," he said. "If you surrender and inform the King of just who is after my wife, I can call for clemency."

"Your wife?" Rhenar blurted out.

"I'm Baron Nos," Anton said. He tried to make the words sound natural. "This is my estate that you're trespassing on."

He took another step.

"You're—you're not supposed to be here," Rhenar said. "You're supposed to be out of the country!"

"I just got back," Anton said. "Why so surprised? Isn't the hero always supposed to show up at the moment of greatest need?"

He took another step.

"It doesn't matter," the wizard sneered. "You're just another witness we need to eliminate!" Anton could see the magic flare up around the wizard. That had to mean he was casting a spell.

Uncanny Evasion.

Anton triggered the dodge at the same moment the spell was released, which was fortunate as the lightning bolt flashed through the space he had been faster than he could have possibly reacted. The wizard screeched in rage. The commander drew his sword.

It didn't matter. Wizards knew to start casting before the swordsman got in range, but Anton's range was a lot longer than Veylan Corbraith thought it was.

Leaping Attack.

For once, Anton used the trait without trickery. This was *Leaping Attack* as it was meant to be used. A flat, fast trajectory, directly at his target. As his sword swung in, he felt some kind of protective spell. The air itself tried to push him back.

It wasn't enough to stop him. Anton's blade cut through the wizard's arm, raised up to ward him off, and cut deep into the man's torso. The wizard fell to the earth with a cry of pain.

Anton landed, sure-footed, but he had to quickly twist to parry the attack that came from his left side. Anton had the higher Strength, but the commander had a trait that strengthened the attack. Without a trait to counter it, Anton had to give ground, stumbling to the side.

"Nothing personal," the commander said, following up his attack with strong blows from a variety of directions. "I just can't allow my men to be executed."

The rain had stopped, Anton noticed. He gripped his blade more firmly and readied himself to receive the commander's attacks.

CHAPTER THIRTY-FOUR

Critical Beatdown

Just call off the attack and run," Anton said. He pointed at the fallen wizard. "I have what I need."

Rhenar grimaced, but gripped his sword more tightly. "The Grey Oaths don't abandon our clients," he said. "We always see things through to the end."

"Is that normal for mercenaries?" Anton asked, his eyes narrowing.

"Not at all," Rhenar admitted. "It's our selling point. It's why we're called the Grey *Oaths*."

"I didn't think that meant anything," Anton confessed. "I took you for common bandits."

"Have a care, *Baron*," Rhenar snapped back. "Our contract called for your wife to be taken alive, but there are many things that can happen to a person before they die. It's our honor that protects her."

Anton felt the anger flow through him. Oh yes. He was angry enough to do this now.

"Talk about honor when you're not thieving on my lands," he said. Then he jumped.

It wasn't *Leaping Attack*. Rhenar had seen him use that; he was almost certainly ready for it. As experienced as he looked, he was probably ready for this fakeout as well.

Anton's strength let him leap farther than one would expect, even without using his trait, but he made sure to fall well short of the commander. He dived to the ground and rolled under the man's guard. Not a trait, just long practice under the eyes of his parents.

The commander was a veteran of many battles, but adventurers fought differently. He seemed to sense the move coming, but he couldn't get his sword down in time.

Normally, Anton would be in no kind of position to attack. His sword, while still in his hand, was out of line, and Rhenar was now too close for the long blade to be used effectively. None of that mattered, though. Anton just needed to have his feet under him. It was just a matter of finding the right timing as he tumbled . . .

Leaping Attack.

Too close for the sword, Anton used his hand, launching himself up and planting a fist deep in Rhenar's stomach. The chain mail protecting the mercenary yielded to the blow. The metal links dug in at him, but Anton had *Stone Skin* and thirty Toughness. His hand was stronger than mere steel.

Sadly, Rhenar was nearly as tough. The hit knocked the wind out of him, driving him back with a *whoof.* But when Anton tried to follow up with his sword, it was blocked by a parry that had all the hallmarks of a trait.

Undeterred, Anton launched *Quick Attack* after *Quick Attack*, hammering the mercenary's defense. But he held firm, and a shimmering field sprung up around him, reducing the force of Anton's blows.

"Low blow, Baron," he gasped as his breath came back. "But I started on the lines. You don't come out of that without a defense. I think you'll—"

Whatever he was about to say was lost, as a sharp, searing pain exploded across Anton's back, causing all his muscles to spasm violently. Crackling energy surged through him, leaving his nerves screaming in agony and his vision swimming with bursts of light. His legs buckled under the shock, and he collapsed forward, his breath catching in his throat as the acrid smell of burnt fabric and flesh filled the air.

Rhenar stared at him for a moment before catching up to what was going on. "Or," he said, "my wizard client could finally pull himself together enough to cast a spell."

He looked behind Anton.

"You doing all right there?" he called out to the wizard. Anton could hear weak cursing coming from behind him. "Yeah, you'll be fine. Liria, can you see to our client? Can't have him dying."

Anton rolled over onto his back. Under the circumstances, he considered it a triumph. His muscles were still trembling from the spell.

Rhenar looked back at him. "Shame," he said. "That lightning would have killed most people. Guess you're too tough to let that happen."

Anton didn't bother replying. He needed to focus on getting up.

Rhenar sighed. "I really don't want to have killing a noble on my record," he said. "But you are another witness. Tough or not, a sword through the throat will kill you."

Anton thought that might *not* be true. With an ordinary Tier One sword, it would take significant strength to push it through the skin of his throat. Rhenar had the strength to do it, though. Easily.

Rhenar raised his sword. Not overhead, ready to slash down, but held up to his chest, the point facing down. He was going to thrust it right through Anton.

"Sorry to have to do this, but I took an oath."

He drove the blade down. Anton dodged.

He shouldn't have been able to. His body was still a twitching mess. But *Uncanny Dodge* didn't care about that. It moved his body the way it *needed* to, not how he wanted to.

Anton convulsed. It felt as if every part of him had moved randomly. Some of them in ways they weren't meant to. The result of all that randomness, though, was that his throat moved just enough to the side for Rhenar's strike to go wide. The blade plunged deep into the earth. Rhenar hadn't been holding back.

"What the?" Rhenar said. His eyes were wide with surprise. "How?"

He tugged on his blade, trying to retrieve it. For a single second, the earth held onto it. In the second second, Anton was.

"Hey! Let go!" Rhenar objected. In the heat of the moment, there was no time to point out how silly a command that was, and Anton's voice wasn't up to the task anyway. Instead, he just glared at his would-be killer and focused on his *other* hand.

To his surprise, Anton was still holding his sword. He'd been *drilled* to do that, to always hold onto his sword, no matter what. Now, he had it clenched in a death grip. He wasn't sure he *could* let go of it at this point.

Anton swung his sword. It was possibly the *worst* swing he'd ever made, surpassing the pathetic efforts of his childhood. But it *was* a swing, made with some portion of his strength, and the blade *was* sharp. Rhenar had no choice but to let go of his sword if he wanted to avoid injury.

Anton tried to chuckle. It came out as a crackling rasp. But now *he* had both swords. He grabbed the hilt of Rhenar's and tried to use it as leverage to get up.

Rhenar backed away. "Liria. Get me a spear."

"But sir!" a voice that must have been Liria's protested. "I need to—"

"That's an order, soldier!" Rhenar barked.

Anton ignored the byplay. He was trying to stand up, and that took everything he had. He climbed laboriously to his feet and looked around. Not much had changed. The wizard was still on the ground. Liria had left her bandaging job unfinished and was rummaging around in a pile of supplies.

Rhenar was trying to stand between Anton and his two allies, but the angles were too disparate. He couldn't cover both of them.

"Holding a spear makes you a combatant," Anton rasped. Everything felt better, now that he was up. His legs seemed to be remembering what to do. His arms were still weak, but he was getting there. With a wrench, he pulled Rhenar's sword out of the ground and held it pointing backward, resting on his shoulder. From there, he could easily throw it.

Liria froze.

"Demon's tears, girl, this isn't the time!" Rhenar shouted. He moved to stand in front of her. Anton looked at the wizard, and Rhenar cursed and moved back.

"I'm just a medic!" Liria cried. Anton wasn't sure if she meant that she shouldn't be attacked or if she meant that she shouldn't have to fetch equipment. Not that it mattered. As long as she wasn't moving, Rhenar didn't have a weapon, and Anton had more time to recover.

"Just run," Anton suggested. "I don't have time to hunt you all down."

"Grey. Oaths. Don't. Run." Rhenar snarled.

"I bet you do, when the time is right," Anton said carefully. Just as carefully, he took a step forward. Just to see if he could. The results seemed promising, so he took another step.

"If you run now, you *might* get away," Anton said. His voice was almost normal now. "I already sent for the King, so you're going to be hunted. It's not a matter of witnesses any more. They *know*."

"Might be better to—" the man muttered before breaking off. "Liria!" he shouted.

The girl yelped and then dashed into the pile of supplies. Anton threw a sword at her, but he didn't bother trying to aim. He needed to finish the commander.

Leaping Attack.

Predictable or not, it was all he had at this point. He needed a trait to move his body; he didn't trust it on its own. Rhenar must have seen it coming; he was cursing furiously as he raised his arm to block.

Blocking a trait-powered blow with your forearm, even if it is wrapped in chainmail, is not a wise move. Rhenar did his best. The shimmering barrier sprang up again, reducing the damage. And his natural toughness helped.

It wasn't enough. Anton's sword sliced through the mail and into the man's bones. He didn't sever the arm, but he came close. Rhenar screamed in pain, which panicked Liria. She popped out of the pile clutching a spear, but after one frightened look at Anton, she screamed and took off running.

Still clutching the spear, though. Good discipline, Anton noted. Then, the arrow struck him in the shoulder.

Now it was Anton's turn to scream. The arrow didn't punch through; it lodged in the muscle of his shoulder. It felt like liquid fire every time he moved the arm, but he had to. The archers were assigned in pairs.

Uncanny Dodge.

Anton twisted out of the way of the second arrow, screaming with the pain of moving. More would be coming, Anton knew. He needed cover, and the best bit of it was standing right there, clutching his almost severed forearm.

Rhenar didn't react when Anton grabbed him and held him in the direction that the arrows had come from. Not in time, at least.

"Where'd that come from?" he asked groggily, looking at the arrow in Anton's shoulder. "Is that one of ours? Couldn't you have made it a bit earlier?"

He called that last out into the darkness. Not waiting for an answer, he dropped to the ground, or tried to. Anton held him up.

"Call for them to surrender!" Anton told him. Rhenar ignored him in favor of clutching at his wound and trying to stem the bleeding with his good hand.

"Come out without your weapons, or he'll bleed to death!" Anton called out.

"Grey Oaths . . . don't surrender," Rhenar mumbled.

"He doesn't have much time!" Anton shouted. He glanced around at the other possible combatants. Liria had stopped running and was hiding in what she thought was darkness. The wizard was still on the ground. Casting that spell had taken everything out of him, it seemed. Anton kept an eye on him, looking out for a surge of magic.

There was a tense pause. Then Liria screamed.

"What's the matter, haven't you ever seen a skeleton before?" a familiar voice called out. Liria backed away from it, back into the clearing.

Four skeletons walked out of the forest, grinning.

"Careful," Anton called out. "There are archers in the trees."

"Wasn't it *me* who warned you about *them*?" Kelsey asked. "Don't worry, I got it."

She stepped out of the forest, holding a contraption. It took Anton a moment to realize that it was a bigger version of her *torch*. The only reason he made the connection was that it immediately lit up with a dazzling light. A bright beam shot across the clearing and illuminated the trees.

"You see them now, right?" she asked.

"Yes. Yes, I do," Aris said. She stepped forward and raised her rifle to her shoulder.

CHAPTER THIRTY-FIVE

Bring Your Fine Self Home

Anton winced as the bony fingers probed into his wound. "We don't have time for this."

"Anton, you're *injured*," Aris scolded. "Are you going to run into another fight with an arrow sticking out of your shoulder?"

"At least he didn't try pulling it out," Kelsey said. She had placed herself strategically so that she could keep an eye on both the "sexy nurse skeleton" and the four skeletons guarding the prisoners. "Barbed heads are barbaric. Well, *arrows* are barbaric. Stick-powered weaponry!"

"The house is being attacked *right now*," Anton protested. "We can't stop just because I need a bandage!"

"Bandage, he says." Kelsey rolled her eyes as the skeleton nurse pulled the arrow out with a wet *schlick*. "Suliel is . . . fine, for now. This commander guy must have been giving his men a buff because they backed off the moment he fell. They must have felt it."

"So they've stopped?"

"Eh, pulled back to re-evaluate," Kelsey said. "They're in the building. Suliel's people have fallen back to the second floor. Sergent Mirok thinks they're going to bring in the archers to sweep the second-floor landing. They might send someone back to see what's happened to their commander."

"So there are more forces incoming?" Anton asked. He struggled to get up, but the nurse was still bandaging him. When he tried to get free, she jammed her finger bones directly into his wound, causing him to cry out in pain.

"Don't worry; her fingers are quite sterile. We boiled them just before she came over," Kelsey said.

"I don't know what that means," Anton said. He took deep breaths to work through the pain. "Are you *sure* you're keeping their murderous nature suppressed?"

"Mostly. Don't struggle so much; it makes their job harder. Anyway, if they send someone, Aris can take care of them. We don't have to wait much longer, anyway."

"Why not?"

In the distance, trumpets sounded.

"That's why not," Kelsey said smugly. "At least . . . I *think* so? I can't imagine who else would be playing trumpets. Hang on."

Anton looked at the prisoners. The ones who were still conscious had started to look distinctly worried. *More* worried, that is. Most of them were injured and in considerable pain.

"Okay, Suliel's confirmed it," Kelsey said. "The King's forces *do* announce their arrival with trumpets. Sometimes."

"Why?" Anton asked.

Kelsey shrugged. "I guess sometimes it helps if the people you're coming after know who's after them."

"We announce our approach because we have nothing to fear from any force residing in this Kingdom," a new voice said.

A tall, imposing figure walked out of the darkness. Anton gulped.

Idran Sehhur, Level 38, Human, Paramount Strategist, Scion/Reckless Knight/Gallant Captain/Paramount Strategist, S: 36 T: 37 A: 35 D: 38 P: 50 W: 44 C: 50

"And sometimes you use them to make it sound like you're far away when you're really pretty close!" Kelsey said brightly. "How sneaky!"

General Sehhur, famously known as the Sword and Shield of Zamarra, looked at Kelsey for a long time. Then he turned to Anton.

"Baron Nos," he said.

"General Sehhur," Anton said. His voice faltered, and he scrambled to his feet in order to bow. "I, uh, I suppose that my message managed to reach a high rank after all."

"Indeed," the man said. He looked as though he'd dressed in haste. He was wearing a polished breastplate that had been strapped over a simple arming doublet and leggings, and he wasn't wearing a helmet. "An invasion of the capital from one of the King's vassals does raise the alarm."

"It was—is, still—an emergency, General. I need to—" Anton stopped as the general held his hand up.

"Haste leads to mistakes, young Baron. I heard your—" The general broke off and gave Kelsey another long look. "—*companion* say that the danger is not immediate."

"I feel so *seen*," Kelsey said with amusement.

The general gestured, and a squad of five men came out of the forest.

"Take charge of these," the general ordered, gesturing at the prisoners. "While the Baron briefs me on what has happened here."

"I suppose we don't need my skellies anymore?" Kelsey inquired. She gave . . . Anton supposed it was a salute. Just one that he'd never seen in Zamarra or the Elitran Empire. "Permission to withdraw them from the field, sah!"

The general gave her a third long and unamused look. "Granted," he grated.

The four skeletons formed up in a line and marched towards Kelsey. As they reached her, she touched them and sent them back.

"Do you want to keep the medic?" she asked. "There's one among the prisoners, but . . ." She dropped her voice in a fake whisper. "I don't know if she can be *trusted*."

"*That*," the general said, looking with distaste at the skeleton nurse, "is a *medic*?"

Anton was largely inured to Kelsey's antics by now. He was even reasonably sure that this particular affront could not be laid at her door. The costumes the skeletons wore were part of their *race*. The nature of monsters was determined by the gods. Kelsey had complained about their shortcomings enough for Anton to know that if she influenced that, it was only in minor ways.

That said, Anton was *also* reasonably sure that whatever Kelsey *could* have possibly done to make this affront worse, she had.

The stiff, *pink* fabric of the skeleton's short—*scandalously* short—dress did a good job of concealing the fact that there was no flesh underneath it. Not a perfect job; it hung strangely and didn't always move when the nurse did. The bodice, while plump, held nothing but air, and the short, flared skirt revealed nothing but bone. It didn't hide the truth so much as parade a lie proudly.

"A *sexy* skeleton nurse!" Kelsey said. She dropped her voice again. "If you want to spend some special time with Trixie, General, I'd normally charge, but nothing's too good for you! Just say the word and—"

"Get rid of it," the general growled, his composure breaking for the first time.

He didn't wait to see if she complied. Turning to Anton, he glared at him.

"Baron Nos, *report*."

"Kelsey has a link with Suliel, sir, so we knew when the attack began. We were just a little way out, so we left immediately. The attackers were a mercenary company known as the Grey Oaths. They were hired by a wizard."

Anton pointed the man out.

"I took his dangly bit away, and I'm keeping it safe!" Kelsey announced.

"We, uh, confiscated his core," Anton translated. "We took out the guards at the gate and captured this command post. We were about to move on the main force—"

"And they're running!" Kelsey announced. "They tried to hide it, but it was only going to be so long before Suliel noticed. They're booking it!"

Anton looked at the general, who was glaring at Kelsey again. He didn't seem upset by the news, only by her continued existence. Anton took that to mean that he had secured all the approaches before blowing the trumpets.

Muttering something under his breath, the general turned back to Anton.

"You must be eager to check on your wife," he said. "Let's go."

"Right!" He started heading toward the house. Aris and Kelsey fell in with him, as did the general. Anton wracked his memory for what Suliel had told him about etiquette.

"Uh, welcome to the Nos estate," he tried. "My apologies for the state that it's in."

The general snorted. "Torn-up gardens can be forgiven," he said. "Your actions are another matter. We have *standards* for our nobility, Baron Nos. Rules of propriety, precedence, and procedure. Your wife can fill you in."

"She's been trying," Anton confessed. "There hasn't been much time for talking."

"*Make* time," the general commanded. "I heard of your quest to bring back those captured in the raid. Was it successful?"

"A few died before we could reach them," Anton admitted, feeling a pang of guilt. Failing to bring every person back, as he'd promised, still stung. "But we brought back every person that was still alive."

"Not a bad result," the general said. "No operation goes perfectly, even one of mine."

"That's not what the stories say, General," Anton replied.

"Ha! You'll see for yourself, soon, just how little stories can be trusted," the general laughed. "Was your wife caught up with the murder in the palace?" he asked suddenly.

"What?" Anton asked, caught off guard.

"The wizard that was murdered in the palace," the general said, looking at Anton closely. "Probably some kind of connection there with the wizards that attacked your wife."

"I heard rumors about a murder in the palace," Anton said carefully. "They were passed on through Kelsey."

The general grunted. "Fair enough," he said. "I wouldn't want to commit anything based on what *that* told you."

"Rude!" Kelsey objected. "See if I give *you* any more free passes to the skeleton bordello!"

Anton was spared from further comment by his first sight of his townhouse.

In some ways, it was more impressive than the castle, which also belonged to him. It didn't have the castle's high wall or impressive defensive position. It was less fortified overall, a fact which the attackers had made full use of. But it was just as large as the castle, with wider doors and windows that were currently blazing with light, illuminating the battered and wrecked lawn and garden outside.

A hacked-up tree, used for a ram, had been abandoned on the front steps. The doors had been caved in, and broken furniture had been scattered all over the steps and lawn. Fortified shutters on the lower floor had been pulled off; protective bars had been pried away.

"Not too badly damaged," the general said.

There were no bodies left outside. The mercenaries had dragged off their casualties, and whatever casualties Anton's people had suffered were suffering inside. Anton stepped forward into the light, then hesitated. He didn't want to get shot by a surprised defender.

"Go on," Kelsey said. "They're expecting you."

He nodded his thanks and started moving more quickly. He couldn't *run*; he had to pick his way through the debris of the failed siege. He made his way up the steps, Kelsey and Aris right behind him.

Suliel was waiting inside. She was standing on the second-floor landing, behind an improvised barricade and a small knot of Kirido soldiers. She was trying to see past them, and they were trying to stand between her and any potential threat that came through those doors.

"Anton!" she cried.

"Suliel!" he shouted back. He rushed forward. The stairs were slippery with blood and . . . oil? He didn't stop to wonder why, he just triggered his *Spider Climb* to climb the stairs sure-footed.

He jumped right over the barricade. Not with a *Leaping Attack*, just a normal jump powered by his not-so-normal strength. Then he had reached Suliel, and she was throwing herself into his arms.

"You're here," she mumbled into his chest. "I was so frightened."

Anton held her as tightly as he dared. She felt warm and vital in his arms, but also terribly fragile. "You're too brave to be frightened," he murmured into her ear. One of his hands stroked her long hair. "You drove off an entire mercenary company."

"That was our people," Suliel said, "and Kelsey's skeletons. I didn't do anything."

"I don't believe that for a second," Anton said. "I'll have more to say about it once I've heard all the reports. Look forward to being scolded for putting your life in danger."

"Yes . . . my lord," Suliel said. It was hard to tell with her face buried in his chest, but Anton thought she *was* looking forward to it. When she started speaking formally in private, she was in a particular mood.

"I'm glad to see that you're all right, Lady Nos," General Sehhur called out from the floor below. Suliel stiffened in Anton's grip.

"Put me down!" she whispered urgently. Reluctantly, he did so.

Once on the ground, Suliel curtsied in the general's direction. The soldiers blocking the view had all disappeared. Some of the barricade had already been removed.

"Thank you for your timely aid, Lord General," Suliel said. "I apologize for the circumstances we find ourselves in, but our gratitude for your rescue knows no bounds. Please permit us to offer you our hospitality at a later date, when it is not so constrained."

The general bowed. "No thanks are necessary when I'm conducting the King's business," he said. "To dispose of ruffians threatening the peace of this city is nothing less than my duty."

Suliel looked as if she was going to reply, but the general held up his hand. "I will leave your household to clean, take stock, and repair," he said. "I have but one duty remaining to me."

He pointed at Anton.

"Baron Nos, you are charged with appearing before the King tomorrow. To answer for your actions this night, to be assessed of your fitness for the title you hold, and to answer any questions the King might ask about certain events that have troubled him. Ninth bell. Do not be late."

CHAPTER THIRTY-SIX

My Love Is Alive

SULIEL

Anton was home. Not *home*; that would have to wait until they returned to Kirido. But he was here. With her. Suliel stood up straight, poised and unmoving until General Sehhur made his exit. The excitement running through her made her feel as if she was vibrating, but she ruthlessly suppressed any outward sign.

Until he was gone and Suliel let herself relax. She gave a small sigh. Anton took a step towards her and took hold of her again.

He always knew what she needed. She leaned into his comforting warmth.

"It's over," Anton announced to the gathered household. "The King's forces are gathering up what remains of the mercenaries. You all fought well, and you won."

A ragged cheer went up from all of those who had fought for her.

"Cleanup comes next," Anton said, and the cheers turned into exaggerated groans. Anton laughed.

"That can wait until tomorrow," he assured them. "For now, let's take care of the wounded and get everyone a bed. Somehow. I saw most of my furniture was on the front lawn."

The remark caused about half the room to chuckle ruefully.

"Sir," Sergeant Mirok said. "The carriage house was untouched, I think. We should be able to find beds for just about everybody there."

"Good thinking, Sergeant. Let's get everyone that we can over there. The rest of us will find something in here. That includes me."

Anton gave a fake chuckle. "I can hardly let a few mercenaries kick me out of my own home, can I?"

"No sir," the sergeant agreed. She saluted him with a faint smile.

"Oh, one more thing," Anton added. "We need to send a runner down to the docks, let Cheia know that everything is resolved. She'll probably cause an incident if we let her stew all night."

Suliel stopped paying attention at that point. Aris came up the stairs and peeled Suliel away from Anton and into a hug of her own. Suliel didn't mind too much. Aris was taller than her, and Aris's hug meant that Suliel's head was resting against Aris's very ample bosom. She smelled of gun smoke and leather.

Suliel relaxed into her soft pillow and let Anton take over. His deep voice washed over her as he gave more orders. She only snapped out of it when Kelsey spoke up, the sound of her real voice startling Suliel into paying attention.

"I can take care of keeping watch," Kelsey said. "The cleanup as well. I'll get it all done while you get some sleep."

She winked. "Or, you know, *sleep*. If you know what I mean."

Suliel felt her face grow warm. She was certainly too keyed up to fall asleep right away.

Suliel's bed—the bed in the master bedroom of this mansion, which she had always thought of as her parents' bed—had been commissioned by her grandfather. Suliel knew this because his name, and her grandmother's, had been carved into the headboard. Suliel had consigned it to the barricades without any hesitation. The heavy, carved wood had been perfect for holding the doors in place. The straw mattress had done an excellent job of shielding them from arrows until it had been dragged out through the windows.

Suliel regretted it now, and not just because she needed somewhere to . . . sleep. There was history in that bed, her family's history, and she had let it be shattered and scattered across her lawn. She resolved to ask Kelsey if something could be done to repair what Suliel had sacrificed.

Not right now, though. Right now, Kelsey was making them a *new* bed. *Delivering* one, rather, from one of her rooms in the "hospitality section."

"Feast your eyes, and your asses, on this!" Kelsey crowed. She had made an entire metal-framed bed, complete with mattress and bedding.

Anton frowned in confusion. "I thought there was a limit to the size of things you could do that with?" he asked.

"Upgrades!" Kelsey said. "I got spatial manipulation, which—among other things—lets me increase the size of my storage space. I was waiting for an appropriate time to show it off, but I suppose I should have known I'd first use it for something bed-related."

"Isn't it the same as the one we used before?" Aris asked.

"You were distracted then," Kelsey said loftily. "So I'm not offended that you didn't notice then how amazing it was."

"It's soft . . ." Suliel said, pushing on the mattress. "Not like straw, but . . ." her face got hot again. The thing it most reminded her of was Aris's breasts.

"Yes . . ." Kelsey said, drawing out the word salaciously and giving Suliel such a knowing look that Suliel had to check that her mind link was locked down. "Feel the decadent luxury of a society that your primitive minds cannot even conceive of! Rubber latex!"

"It's just a bed," Anton said, sitting down on it. "A really *comfortable* bed," he admitted.

Kelsey cackled in triumph. "I'll leave you kids to enjoy it," she said.

Aris looked at Kelsey in surprise. "You're not staying?" she asked.

"Too much to do," Kelsey replied.

<Do leave that channel open, though,> she sent to Suliel. **<I promise not to giggle at the embarrassing bits.>**

Then the door shut behind her, and they were alone. There was a *thunk* as Aris released her gunbelt and let it drop to the floor. Then a similar noise as she threw her heavy coat off.

"Were you up when the attack started?" Aris asked. "Everyone was dressed in armor thrown on over night robes, but you were fully dressed." She started undoing the fastenings on her shirt.

"There . . . wasn't much for me to do before the fight started," Suliel said. She couldn't take her eyes off Anton, who was removing his leather armor. "I thought if I was going to meet my fate, I'd do it properly dressed."

"It met you instead," Anton said, smiling. His chest was bare now, the warm brown skin calling to Suliel. His pants were still on, which was a mistake that had to be corrected . . .

"Do you need help with that?" Anton asked, pointing at her dress.

Suliel tried to say yes, but her mouth had stopped working. She felt a soft warmth from behind as Aris embraced her.

"I'll be your maid tonight, shall I?" she murmured softly in Suliel's ear. The warmth pulled away, and then Aris started unlacing Suliel's dress.

"What? But . . . you're . . ." was all that Suliel managed to say.

"Kelsey's been teaching me things," Aris purred. "About . . . what *I* can appreciate, and about what *Anton* appreciates."

Then Anton was standing right in front of her, his chest within . . . licking distance.

"Maybe you can help me out with my clothes, as well," he rumbled.

"Y—yes, my lord," Suliel stuttered. Aris's warm hands slid down Suliel's sides, taking her dress with her. Suliel could feel Aris's breasts again, soft and warm with a hard, hot nub, rubbing against her shoulder blades.

Suliel pulled at the lacings of Anton's leggings, then at the pants themselves. His member, already hard, swung free.

"My lord?" Anton asked. "I thought we were closer than that. Is that really what you want to call me?"

"Husband . . ." Suliel breathed. "*Anton.*"

Then Aris pushed Suliel gently down her knees in front of her husband. His staff was right in her face, smelling of sweat and arousal.

Aris squeezed Suliel's small, dark breasts. Suliel gasped and swallowed her husband's heat. Her mind went blank. She could hear Aris talking to her as the girl's hands caressed Suliel's body, but she couldn't tell what the words were. The only things that mattered were her husband's groans of pleasure and the slickness and warmth of him as she took him in as deep as she could.

She only came back to herself when Aris pulled her away.

"Wait! I want—" She struggled weakly, but Aris was stronger.

"You're supposed to be getting him ready, not finishing him off," she chided Suliel. She drew the smaller girl up on the bed, pushing Suliel onto her back.

"I'll give you a taste later," Anton chuckled, "But there's a husbandly duty that I've put off for too long."

"You're ready, too," Aris said. Her hand snaked down between Suliel's legs, and Suliel felt the slick wetness there. She hadn't even noticed what Aris was doing.

Now she looked up at Anton, her legs spreading of her own accord.

"Y—yes," she managed to say. "I wa—"

Then he plunged down into her, and Suliel had no more words. She felt his heat spreading her apart, splitting her open, and drowning her in ecstasy.

She gasped and moaned, and then he let his weight fall on her, and it was all she could do not to scream. His hot flesh rubbed against her ebony skin. Her face was buried in his chest; she tried to pull him even closer.

"She wants it harder," someone said. Suliel was grateful to whoever it was. She did want it harder. She wanted to be pounded into complete submission by her husband.

Someone was screaming, but she didn't have time to work out who. Tension was building up inside her. The white heat between her legs was spreading out to encompass all of her. Everything was going . . .

She convulsed with the power of her orgasm. Whole-body spasms shook her body, sending white-hot fire through her brain. She lost herself again.

When she came back to herself, she could feel his still-warm seed inside her. Anton had rolled himself off of her but taken her with him, cradled in his arms. Now, she was resting on top of him.

She had to let him go out of her to slide up his body to kiss him. His arms pulled her closer into the kiss, teasing her with his strength.

Not just *his* arms. "Back with us?" Aris said. Her hands teased Suliel as well, running down Suliel's back and sides, caressing her buttocks. "You must have really needed that."

Suliel broke off from the kiss, but she hadn't entirely regained her speech. "Nghl," was all she could manage.

"Did they teach you that in elocution class?" Aris teased. "You know, Anton promised you a taste, but I think I'll get one before you."

"Wha? Nooo . . . I wan . . ." Suliel tried, but she wasn't quite capable of speech yet.

Aris giggled. "Do you? I'm afraid you can't have this. It's all mine." She rolled Suliel over on her back again, away from the blessed warmth of her husband. Suliel couldn't resist, her body was limp and spent. All she could do was moan in disappointment.

Anton obligingly leaned over and kissed her. His hand found her breast and squeezed it gently. Suliel's moans became something other than disappointment, but Aris wasn't done.

"If I want a taste of my husband's seed, all I have to do is go where he left it," she said smugly. Suliel didn't understand what Aris meant until she felt a warm tongue slip between her legs.

Suliel's back arched as the hot liquid sensation engulfed her.

"Wait!" she gasped. "That's . . . Kelsey . . . does . . . ahhh!"

Aris pulled her face away. "Mhmn, delicious. I told you, didn't I, that I'd been learning from Kelsey? I learned how good this feels . . . and I learned how much it excites Anton, to see the woman he loves lose control."

"Wait, I—hhnnng!"

Aris had started again, licking and teasing. Suliel couldn't resist; couldn't stop her legs from opening and welcoming Aris in. Anton leaned over and kissed her again.

"You're so beautiful, Suliel," Anton said. Suliel could only pant in response. She'd lost all composure, all control. Anton's hand caressed her face as he stared into her eyes.

"I want you to come for me, Suliel," Anton said. He guided her hand down to him, stiff and ready. "I want to make up for lost time and make you come until you can't anymore."

Suliel could feel it building again. It wasn't the same; it wasn't the mind-destroying pounding that she'd welcomed before, but it promised to be just as good. It flowed through her, filling her to the brim, getting her ready to burst. It would just take a touch . . .

Anton kissed her, and she exploded.

CHAPTER THIRTY-SEVEN

King of Rock

Everything looked better in the morning. Much, much better.

"Did you work all night?" Suliel asked Kelsey incredulously.

"If by work you mean walking around touching things, then yes," Kelsey said loftily. "I didn't even have to bend over."

"But there's . . ." Suliel looked around. "The windows are fixed!"

"Most of them," Kelsey acknowledged. "I have people for that."

"Skeletons, you mean," Anton put in. "Which you've explicitly told me *aren't* people," he said before she could retort.

"You're stepping on my bit," Kelsey complained. "After everything I've done for you?"

"Yeah," Anton said, unabashed. "But this place . . . my home . . . you really cleaned it up. Thank you."

"You're welcome, I guess," Kelsey said awkwardly. "I've got . . . crews working on the furniture, seeing what can be repaired. It will be a few days before that is sorted out."

"That is only to be expected," Suliel said. "Thank you for your efforts, Kelsey."

Kelsey didn't blush, but she looked as though she wanted to. She glanced around for a new topic of conversation and lit upon Anton.

"You're looking fine this morning," she said. "Did you get *any* sleep?"

"Some," Anton said. Now it was his turn to look away awkwardly. "You could have . . . I mean, we—"

"Forget about it," Kelsey said, waving him away. "Is the wound all right?"

"It's fine," Anton said, looking down at his bandage. This was the first time he'd been able to appreciate his super-human constitution. He didn't regenerate like al-Kadir, but just a few hours of sleep had greatly reduced the severity of the arrow wound.

"Good, because it would be a shame if you bled all over the fine clothes that Suliel bought you," Kelsey said with a grin.

"Oh, you found those?" Suliel asked. "We had to use the wardrobes for—"

"Found them, spruced them up, and have them ready to try out," Kelsey said. "I know you want to look your best for your audience."

"I don't know . . ." Anton said, edging away. "I'm more comfortable in my usual clothes, and we don't want to keep him waiting . . ."

He took another step towards the front door.

"Hold it," Aris said, grabbing ahold of his arm. He would have pulled away, but he'd never managed to break free when Aris held her body against him. Her soft warmth was irresistible. "Did Kelsey say something about dressing you in fancy clothes?"

All in all, there were worse things in this world than being fawned over by three beautiful women. While Kelsey's contribution was mostly confined to smirks, leers, and the production of new outfits, his two wives were very interested in dressing him in new clothes, and then undressing him. Anton put up a token resistance, but he didn't mind the attention.

They would have gone for much longer if they hadn't had a hard deadline to meet with the King. Since they did, Anton soon found himself riding in a carriage for the first time, wearing stiff and uncomfortable clothes. Some kind of sweet-smelling oil had been applied to his hair, and a mysterious lotion had been applied to his skin.

It wasn't magical, so Anton wasn't sure what the point of it was, but the girls had been in favor of it.

Anton had never been to see the King before, so he didn't realize how quickly he was passed through all the normal checks and procedures that separated his Majesty from his subjects. At least, not until Suliel spoke up.

"This is ridiculous," she said. "At this rate, we might see him before the tenth bell."

"The appointment was for the ninth bell," Anton reminded her. They had shown up earlier than that, of course, but the hour had been rung while they were going through protocol.

"Normally that would mean late afternoon," Suliel told him. "This is—"

She stopped as the chamberlain approached. Having him handle the appointment personally was apparently a big deal.

"I'm afraid your companion will *not* be granted entry, Lord Nos," the man said without preamble. "She is, in a word, too dangerous."

"Fine by me!" Kelsey declared. "Just put me in a room with some snacks and I'll be good."

Anton frowned. This wouldn't be a problem, not since he'd gotten *Unwavering*, anyway. He should be fine as long as she wasn't too far away, but he'd miss her . . . wisdom wasn't the right word. Her unique perspective on things.

I'm already talking like a courtier, Anton thought.

This was the King, though, so a frown was all that Anton could do. He didn't protest as Kelsey was led away. He could still contact her through Suliel.

The chamberlain returned and bowed to them.

"This way, my lord."

Anton and Suliel followed the man deeper into the palace. Suliel had guessed that this was going to be a private audience, but precedent had been departed from so violently she couldn't be sure.

It turned out to be a semi-private meeting. A high table, with the King and five other people sitting on it, overlooked two smaller tables, set at an angle to each other.

"Don't use *Discernment* here," Suliel whispered, looking around the room.

Anton nodded. He hadn't been planning to. He had gotten better at using it to identify enemies, but it still felt rude to him. He looked around for himself. The main light source of the room was the pair of light-stones in the center, leaving the walls deliberately unlit. Anton's eyes could pierce the darkness, though, and he noted that the walls were lined with alcoves, some of which were covered by curtains, while others held darkly dressed figures.

Some of them were clearly guards, while others were harder to identify. They could be servants, wizards, or even assassins. All Anton could tell was that they didn't carry obvious weapons.

They were led to seats at one of the smaller tables. They sat, and Suliel pulled Anton down to whisper in his ear.

"You know the general, of course." Anton didn't *know* Idran Sehhur, but he remembered the tall warrior with deep black skin from their brief interaction last night. Even if he hadn't, the shining breastplate and gold-trimmed robes would have made his identity clear.

"I don't know the woman next to him, but sitting next to her is Prince Driecht."

The woman in question was older, with tightly braided hair. Prince Driecht was a tall, lean man with obsidian skin and glittering eyes. Suliel skipped over the King as he didn't need an introduction.

"Next to the King is Lord Chancellor Whiden."

Anton wasn't sure of the difference between a chamberlain and a chancellor but resolved to try and remember which older gentleman was which. Suliel didn't know the final person at the table, but they could both tell from his deep midnight blue robes that he was a priest of Tiait. The heavy gold medallion around his neck told them he was a high-ranking one.

They all sat in silence for a few moments. None of the high-ranking nobles wished to speak, while Suliel and Anton didn't dare. About a minute later, three more men were shown into the chamber. They wore robes and—Anton quickly used *Sense Magic*—they had dungeon cores around their necks. To Anton's magic sense, the cores glowed brightly enough to be seen through the robes. Wizards, then.

"This hearing will now come to order," Lord Whiden drawled. "At issue is the charter of the Grey Oaths mercenary company, who broke the King's peace with an attack on the mansion belonging to Baron Nos. The charter of the Wizards Guild, who are said to have ordered this attack. And the title of Baron Nos, yet to be confirmed by the King, over the events of his accession and the events of last night."

Anton gulped. He didn't think he'd done anything wrong, but it sure sounded as if he was being thrown in with these other criminals. The chancellor looked around as if waiting for someone to speak up. The middle wizard looked as though he wanted to. He was red in the face and he was holding his mouth firmly shut, but he was glaring at the chancellor.

"We'll start with you, General," the chancellor said.

General Sehhur shrugged. "It seems pretty clear cut," he said. "We caught them in the act, casualties and the remains of siege weapons strewn all over Baron Nos's lawn. We captured their commander, Rhenar Vhorrin, and most of the survivors. Some of them slipped our net. Vhorrin has requested that his men be spared in return for his testimony against his employer."

The general turned and gave the wizards a predatory look. "But we captured his employer as well, so any testimony he gives is of dubious value. An . . . informal conversation established that he doesn't have any surprises for us."

"And this was the Grey Oaths?" the King inquired.

"Except for the wizard, every one of the attackers was registered as Grey Oaths," General Sehhur confirmed. "From what we can gather, the force was about a third of the Grey Oath's nominal capacity and half of what they are supposed to have active in the city. Vhorrin tried to claim that the contract was for his squadron alone, and the rest of the company were unaware."

"Yeah, that's nonsense. The captain is either in collusion or incompetent, leave it to the courts to find out which. Revoke the charter and charge the ones we have in custody. The others will have to take their chances."

That was bad news for the rest of the Grey Oaths, Anton knew. Without a charter, mercenaries were little more than bandits and were often treated as such. Some of them might join another company or individual mercenaries could beg leave from a lord to stay in their demesne. Some of the delvers in Kirido had been of that persuasion, but they'd mostly been pressed into military service before the raid.

"Moving on," the chancellor said. "We have the matter of the Wizards Guild charter." He looked expectantly at the wizards, who glowered.

"I beg leave to speak on this matter, my lords," the middle wizard said, looking as if he was choking.

"Proceed," the chancellor replied.

"My order is shocked by the actions of the traitor, Corbraith. We disavow all knowledge of his actions and request the return of the item he stole from us."

"And what item might that be?" the chancellor asked.

"His—the core that was in his possession," the wizard said. "His . . . *use* of it was contingent on his membership, and so, once we became aware of his treachery, he was no longer permitted to carry it. He stole it, and we would like it returned."

"Hmmm." The chancellor turned to General Sehhur. "No mention of a core was made in your report, General."

"That is correct," Sehhur said easily. "No core was found on the scene."

"But that's—" The wizard stopped with a sudden realization. He turned slowly to Anton. "You have it," he said coldly.

Anton looked at the angry wizard, and then at the nobles sitting in judgment, trying to work out where he stood. There seemed no point in denying it, Kelsey had already mentioned it to the General.

"Kelsey has it," he admitted.

A small muscle started throbbing on the side of the wizard's head. "A . . . that *dungeon* has another one of *our* cores?"

Anton thought about what he knew of the laws regarding wizards. Laws were not his strong point, to put it mildly. But he did have an interest in the laws as they pertained to adventurers, and wizards—some of them—were adventurers.

"Only the one," he said. "She awarded the other to a mage in my employ."

"She—" The mage turned stiffly towards the main table. "Your majesty, I must insist that this unknown mage be inducted into the guild!"

The King blinked slowly. "Nobles have the prerogative of hiring a court mage who is not in the guild," he said. "You know this."

"But—but—she *stole* the core!"

"Ah," the King said. "A worrying accusation indeed. The events of that day have yet to be fully accounted for. However, they took place on the lands claimed by Baron Nos."

The wizard just looked puzzled. Anton did too, but that was because he was wondering who Baron Nos was, and why he was claiming Anton's barony.

"Should Baron Nos be confirmed," the King explained, "he will have the right to judge the righteousness of the events that took place on his lands."

"But that's—he can hardly be considered an impartial—"

"To question my noble's judgment is to question *my* judgment," the King cut in firmly. "Is that what you wish to do?"

"No, your Majesty."

"Of course, that just goes to show *why* we must consider such questions carefully. I believe the matter of Baron Nos is next on the agenda, Lord Whiden?"

"It is, your Majesty."

"Excellent. You can go," he told the wizards.

"What? I mean, I'm sorry?"

"You can go," the King repeated. "The Wizards Guild has no interest in the lands of a minor noble, so you may leave. Seek out Baron Nos once his fate has been decided."

The wizard's face worked furiously as he held back whatever he wanted to say. Eventually, he just bowed his head. "As you say, your Majesty. By your leave."

They all left.

"Now," the King said. "Let us discuss the matter of *you*."

CHAPTER THIRTY-EIGHT

Political

What just happened?" Anton asked.

King Ranon Kalond of Zamarra, fourth of his name, looked at Anton with a raised eyebrow. Suliel, sitting next to him, poked her husband in the side.

"Uh, Sire?" Anton added hastily. "Was that a trial?"

"Not at all," the King told him. "Trials will be held for the Grey Oaths, and there will be further negotiations with the Wizards Guild, but this hearing is to establish the facts."

"Isn't that . . . what a trial is for? . . . Sire?" Anton asked, adding the last at another prompt from Suliel.

"Yes . . . but a trial is public. It behooves me to know the facts *before* they become widely known."

"I see. Sire." Anton was at a loss for what to say next. Fortunately, the King took charge of the conversation.

"So! Who do I see before me? I'd call you a promising young lad, were it not that you are already married and in your third tier."

"It's been an eventful year, sire," Anton said helplessly.

"You're no doubt hoping it will slow down soon," the King said. "The truth is, you can't afford to rest."

"I can't?" Anton exclaimed in dismay. "Sire?"

The King chuckled indulgently. "You know that each level comes harder, but you don't *feel* it yet. No matter what you do, your pace will slow. But if you don't do *enough*, it will come to a halt. Where do you plan to go from here?"

"Go? I—" Anton thought about it. "I don't know. I rushed back because Suliel was in danger, and every part of my life has been like that since the raid. I have a barony that I grew up in, but I've barely seen it since I took charge. It needs . . . so much, but I don't even know what. I . . . I . . ."

"Enough," the King said. "I'm not averse to you returning to Kirido, though I doubt you'll stay there for long. Events have a way of reaching people with destinies."

"Thanks—I mean, thank you, your Majesty," Anton said. "Does that mean my title is confirmed?"

"Not quite yet," the King said. His demeanor changed. In an instant, the warmth flowed out of him. He still smiled, but it was colder and more cruel. "There are a few details to be sorted out."

Then it was back to warmth. Anton would have thought he was imagining the changes, but Suliel clutched at his arm. It would have been painful if he'd been someone else. He looked down to see her lips were pressed together with anxiety.

"The first matter is a minor one," the King said. "Your wife made certain representations about providing some of the new weapons to our forces."

"I—" Anton started. He paused because Suliel was still holding on to him. He reached across with his other arm and laid his hand on hers reassuringly. "I'm sure that whatever Suliel told you is correct," he said.

"So quickly? You're not even going to ask what they were?" the King asked.

Anton took a deep breath and made sure to speak carefully. "I'm sure that your Majesty isn't going to lie about what she said, and that is the only concern I could possibly have."

The King didn't respond, so Anton went on to clarify. "She has far greater knowledge than I of both the politics involved and the process of making the guns. I'd be a fool to contradict her."

Was that what Suliel had been worried about? She was still holding on to him, but her grip had relaxed slightly. He quickly looked down at her. Her lips were still pressed tight, but he thought he detected a smile. It was hard to tell against her sandalwood skin, but he thought she was blushing.

"I see," the King said. "Then let us move on to your dispute with the Wizards Guild."

"I'm not sure, sire, what issue they have with me," Anton said. "Magister Tikin fought against us during the . . . events. He was exiled, and I understand if he holds a grudge against us. Is that enough for the guild to act as it has?"

"Perhaps. Perhaps it has to do with the questions your wife has been asking, or tasking others to ask."

Anton looked at Suliel. "Is it wrong to ask questions? Sire?"

"That does depend on the question. The Wizards Guild have many secrets they'd like kept quiet."

"Secrets about dungeons?" Anton asked, belatedly adding, "Sire."

"Of course. Dungeons are the source of their power, after all. I understand you know many things about dungeons that wizards would prefer you didn't."

"Is that . . . something you want me to tell you about, Your Majesty?" Anton asked.

"Now, that would anger the guild." The King spoke the words approvingly, but he shook his head as he did so. "I said this audience wasn't public, but it's not exactly private, is it?"

He gestured at the shadowed alcoves and at the men sitting at the table with him.

"The people here can serve as witnesses for those topics that need to be proclaimed while keeping silent on matters best kept quiet. They serve my purposes, not the guild's. The wizards would be quite upset if my servants knew what you know."

"I'm confused. Sire. I don't know what you want me to say."

"Just answer the questions. Such as: Is there a connection between the guild's recent antics and the murder in my palace?"

"Murder, sire?" Anton asked.

"Your wife must have filled you in. A wizard was stabbed in my very palace. A very severe breach of my peace—in my very home."

An intensity had built up around the King. The warm and friendly uncle had vanished again, and the cold seemed to flow from the King and surround Anton in ice.

"I did hear a report about it," Anton admitted. He looked down at Suliel. She seemed . . . angry, now. She was hiding it, but he could see it in her eyes.

"Then tell me," the King said, his voice like stone. Anton could feel the pressure building, forcing him to answer. "Did your wife have anything to do with it?"

This is the King's Charisma, Anton finally realized. He'd never had it used against him before. Suliel had mentioned the pressure, but she had said that the King had held back the full effect. He had gone easier on her because it would cause trouble with the other nobles if the King was in the habit of bullying them.

He wasn't going easy on Anton.

But Anton was *Unwavering*.

"No, Your Majesty," he said calmly. "I don't believe that she did."

And just like that, the pressure was gone. Anton took a deep breath. He saw that the Prince was frowning, but the others at the table had schooled their expressions before he could look.

"Very well," the King said. "Let us move on to the attack on your property. What compensation do you seek from . . . the guild, should it prove responsible?"

"Should it . . . Your Majesty, didn't you just say that they were the ones attacking me?"

The King waved his hand dismissively. "As you heard before, they intend to scapegoat this Corbraith fellow. It remains to be seen if we shall accept that."

"You don't . . . already know?" Anton asked.

"Ah, it is a complex matter, ruling a kingdom," the King sighed. "This is not the only point of contention between ourselves and the guild. As negotiations proceed, I may seek concessions from them in other areas in return for accepting their story about a traitor. You see?"

"I . . . think so," Anton said doubtfully.

"You will learn. The balancing of necessity with justice is easier for a baron, but the same kinds of decisions have to be made. Now, reparations."

"You're talking about payment in coin, is that right, sire?" Anton asked. When the King nodded, he shrugged. "I'm not familiar with the politics of the matter, or what would be an appropriate amount. I'd rather accept whatever your Majesty thinks is fair."

"That certainly leaves me with negotiating room," the King said approvingly. "But it might well leave you feeling shortchanged."

"Perhaps when I've been living in a castle for a year, it will seem that way," Anton said. "But right now, it feels like I've been handed more wealth than I know what to do with. What I really want from them . . . is for the attacks to stop. Can you negotiate for that?"

"I can't," the King admitted. "Oh, I could get them to promise it, but the attacks are already outside of the law. If their oaths to the Kingdom didn't stop them before, new oaths won't help."

"Forgive me, your Majesty, but why do you tolerate such disrespect?" Anton asked.

"Wizards are needed," the King said. "It's not that they possess a power greater than their tier, but they have so many ways they can use it. Scrying classes are rare. Weather control is rare. Wards for privacy and protection can only be done by mages . . . there are so many things they are needed for, that some accommodations must be made."

But you're the King, is what Anton wanted to say. Some part of him wanted to insist on the simple truth that the King was in charge and everyone had to do what he said. However, Anton knew that wasn't true. He'd lied to the King only a little while ago!

That's because he could be a false King, was the simple rejoinder. But again, the adult part of Anton knew that even a true King could give orders that Anton would not follow. There had to be a check against his power, or he would rule as a tyrant.

"Now, let us talk about that boat of yours," the King said. "I've heard very interesting things about it."

"I think I should start by saying the boat requires a special fuel that can only be made in the dungeon," Anton said quickly.

"What is this fuel, and in what quantity can Kirido supply it?"

Anton looked at Suliel, who had kept quiet through all this. Anton wasn't sure *why*; it was either because she was playing the role of the dutiful wife, or because of some formal etiquette requirement.

At his urging, she spoke up. "The dungeon says that it is a special type of oil that is thinner than water and burns twice as hot as lamp oil. She has no plans to increase production and says that widespread use would risk . . ." She frowned. "The destruction of human society through temperature increases?"

"I . . . don't know what to say to that," the King said.

"She says . . . that it was a temporary solution to an emergency situation. Better solutions exist and are under development."

"Perhaps we should revisit this discussion then. I gather we can look forward to many developments with Kirido and its dungeon."

Suliel bowed her head. "If the gods allow."

The King paused for a moment, and then shook his head slightly. "Well, Lord Nos, it seems that my questions have been answered. I am hardly in a position to claim that someone with a Heroic class is unfit to rule, so my final question is simply this. Will you serve under me?"

"I don't—" Anton stopped, unable to articulate what he was trying to say. "I don't know, your Majesty. What does *Nobility's Privilege* say of me?"

"That you are independent. Not all that rare, in the wider scheme of things, but vanishingly so when it comes to my nobles and the court. More common among heroes, of course."

"I suppose it would be," Anton agreed. "I'm sure it has changed a few times over this year. Not because I've been fickle, but because I've learned so much about the world and my place in it. I don't think I can go against my own heart when it sets a course."

Suliel poked him, but Anton had to continue.

"With that said, I don't think you are the type to give me orders I can't follow. So I will serve as your baron, if you'll allow it."

"You will uphold my laws, fight in this nation's defense?"

"I will," Anton said firmly. This, at least, he had no problems with.

"Then go forth a baron of this land, Lord Anton Nos. Manage your demesne wisely and well in my name."

CHAPTER THIRTY-NINE

Talkin' Bout a Revolution

I thought that went well," Anton said when they were in the carriage on the way back.

"Yes," Suliel said shortly.

"But . . . you seem upset about something," Anton pointed out. He put his arm around her and pulled her closer.

Suliel sighed. "It's just . . . you remember I said that the King couldn't use his traits to bully nobles, because they would revolt."

"Yeah, his Charisma did feel a little intense."

"Is that all?" Suliel chuckled ruefully. "I'm sure that was King's Command, or some facsimile thereof. That you could just brush it off, well . . . I suppose he should have known better than to use it on a hero."

"So you're mad that he used it on me?"

Suliel frowned. "*Technically*, you weren't a noble at the time."

"I wasn't? But wasn't the only reason I could marry both of you was because I *was* a noble?"

Suliel waved her hand dismissively. "Grey areas like that are adjudicated by the nobles, typically the nobles involved. The King could have stepped in, declared your candidacy invalid and your marriages false."

"He could?" Anton asked in alarm. He hadn't realized his marriages were on the line. "But . . . since he didn't, I am a noble, and it's all right because I *say* it's all right?"

"Exactly," Suliel said with satisfaction. "The House of Nos is established now, as noble as any other."

"Woot!" Kelsey said from the seat opposite. She was lying on her back, but there wasn't room for her to stretch out. Instead, her legs were resting on the carriage wall, in a position that *had* to be uncomfortable. "Does this mean you get to paint a shield with something?"

"If you're talking about a coat of arms, in cases like this, it's common to simply adopt the female insignia," Suliel said. "Or if you like, we could get a consultation from the heraldic college while we're in the city."

"That's the last thing on my mind right now," Anton said. Truthfully, he had no idea what they were talking about. He would have asked, but it didn't sound important, and he did have a lot of things at the forefront of his mind.

"Can you tell me now why I wasn't supposed to use *Delver's Discernment*?" he asked.

"Sorry, it was a last-minute thought, and I panicked," Suliel apologized. "It was just . . . you know the Rose Circle told us that the King was a False King."

"Because his older sister is secretly still alive and took the class first," Anton confirmed.

"Yes. A False King must have a trait that conceals his class from identification traits," Suliel said. "But . . . even if it's the first trait you get, you need two levels before you get it."

Anton didn't know much about concealment traits. They were mentioned in the books he'd read, but they were traits for criminal and deceptive classes. The owners of such classes were notorious for not divulging the nature of the traits, and so the authors of those books had to rely on secondhand accounts and speculation.

"Not only that," he said slowly, "but they can often be seen through if the investigator has a higher level. That varies with the rarity of the trait, but still."

"Do you know the tier of False King?" Suliel asked.

"No," Anton admitted. "King is Tier Three, so wouldn't it be the same as that?"

"Maybe," Suliel said doubtfully. "If so, he would have been at least level fifteen before he took it. But there would still be many people in the capital with higher levels."

"So what?" Kelsey put in. "He got away with it, we don't need to know how."

"We do need to know," Suliel insisted. "Because I think it means that in the early years, he was *protected*."

"Who can protect a King?" Anton asked. "I mean guards, obviously, but they can't stop an inspection. Not if the King shows himself."

"I can think of two possibilities," Suliel said. "One is a conspiracy of high-level nobles that kept him isolated from anyone that could expose him. The other is that a wizard cast a spell."

"Wizards *are* always casting spells," Kelsey commented. "That's the simplest explanation."

"But the King is at odds with the Wizards Guild!" Anton protested.

"And yet . . . he does not act against them," Suliel pointed out.

"He explained that . . ." Anton said, trailing off uncertainly.

"He provided *an* explanation, not necessarily the correct one," Suliel said. "And it need not be the entire guild, just a single wizard."

"Although," Kelsey drawled, "if *I* were a wizard responsible for the King being in the position he was, *I'd* want to be made head of the Wizards Guild."

"Anyway," Suliel said. "I didn't want you to use *Discernment* because either the King or his wizard might have been able to tell you were using it, and *that* would have tipped them off to the idea that we are suspicious of them."

"Might have been worth it, if it worked," Kelsey said.

"They would have thrown us in a cell," Suliel said sourly.

"Then Aris and I would have come to your rescue at the head of an army of undead, wielding rolling thunder," Kelsey declared. "The castle wouldn't have stood a chance."

"Don't even joke about such things," Suliel ordered.

"I'm not joking," Kelsey said seriously. "You've never had the chance to see Aris in action. Anyone standing between her and her man will fall like so much wheat in the harvest season. And her little sister has a mean streak a mile wide."

"What about General Sehhur?" Suliel asked.

"Well . . . he might be a problem," Kelsey admitted. "But I—"

"You're right, Suliel," Anton cut in before the conversation could get more treasonous. "Better to avoid that sort of situation."

Suliel huffed in frustration. "All of that, though, was predicated on the King being an usurper."

"We really need to figure out if he is not," Anton agreed. "We can't keep sitting on the fence."

"Do we need to?" Kelsey asked. "Just pick a side and go with it. In the end, it's the winner who decides who's right."

A sharp rejection rose in Anton's throat, but Suliel spoke up before he could find the words.

"That was what my father would have done—did, in fact. I doubt he knew the truth before he joined the Rose Circle."

"Your father's decision isn't good enough for you?" the woman who had killed Suliel's father asked. No, Anton reminded himself. The woman-like creature.

"It might be," Suliel admitted. "But I know it isn't good enough for Anton." She looked up at him. "I know he wants to make sure he's on the *right* side and make sure the *right* side wins."

"Well, sure," Kelsey griped. "He always wants to do things the hard way."

"Yes," Anton said. "So how do we find out?"

Kelsey blew air through her lips rudely. "Hell if I know. Kidnap the King and get him inside me? I'd be able to tell pretty quickly."

Suliel choked back laughter. "*That* will never happen," she said. "Not without a war."

"Hey, we're brainstorming!" Kelsey protested. "There are no bad ideas at this stage."

"If you say so," Suliel said with an almost expressionless face. Then she dismissed her amusement and started thinking about the problem. "There are people in the city who *know* the truth, but we don't know who they are or if any of them can be trusted."

"We know some of them," Kelsey pointed out. "The King and whoever the Rose Circle has set up to be Queen. They have to know, one way or the other."

"Unless they themselves are being manipulated," Suliel mused. "Which isn't out of the question if a wizard with mind magic is involved."

Kelsey shuddered. "Let's not go down that rabbit hole," she said. "Especially since we can't trust either of them."

"The King is obviously out of the question, and they won't risk us meeting Syrelle—or Queen Syrelle—until we've committed to their faction," Suliel agreed. "There are others . . . people in the palace, at least someone in the Rose Circle, at least one wizard . . ."

"Truth potions are illegal, right? Or wait, you said that judges can tell when people are lying!" Kelsey drummed her feet against the side of the carriage.

"They can, but they all swear loyalty to the King," Suliel replied. "As for the potions . . . it's tricky for nobles, but for what you're thinking, we'd have to kidnap someone to administer it. *That's* illegal."

"Hmm," Kelsey hummed. "Truth spells are a little too powerful for Tyla right now, but when she gets a few levels . . ."

"What about the palace staff?" Anton suggested. "Someone might have seen something, or someone might have an identification trait that the King didn't know about."

"If there's a commoner that knows something, he's been keeping very quiet for a long time," Kelsey said. "Or he didn't, and now he's been permanently silenced."

"I wonder if necromancy could solve our problem," Suliel said.

Kelsey laughed. "I'm not a real necromancer, remember?" she said. "You're already closer to being one than I am. No, I—"

She paused. Suliel started to speak, but Kelsey held up her hand.

"Wait," she said. "Witnesses. Someone who saw something. Suliel, did the King ever delve?"

"Of course," Suliel said. "It's a common way for nobility to gain levels, especially if they're going into a knightly order. There's a dungeon near the city, so almost certainly."

"Did he delve . . . *after* he became King?" Kelsey asked with urgency.

"I don't know," Suliel said. "I mean, he was seen—still is seen—as a warrior king, so I suppose he might have."

"There will be records, right? At the guild, those guys keep records of everything."

"Maybe not *every* delve," Anton said, "But any nobility or royalty would be recorded, yes."

"So we can find out," Kelsey said. "And you're a noble; you can get a slot delving the local dungeon, right?"

Anton looked at Suliel, who nodded.

"I suppose," he said. "Why is that important?"

Kelsey levered herself upright on the carriage seat and cackled. "If you don't see it yet, there's no way that *they* will. We'll ask the dungeon!"

"What?" Suliel asked.

"He wouldn't have been trying to hide from the dungeon, and even if he did, I'll bet that it would have been able to see through it!"

"But dungeons can't talk," Suliel said. "You're the only one who—"

"The fairy!" Anton blurted. Kelsey pointed at him with one finger and tapped her nose with the other hand.

"Ding ding ding!" she shouted.

"Kelsey could talk to the dungeon fairy of a dungeon we visited," Anton explained.

"I can see Kelsey's fairy. She didn't seem very talkative," Suliel said wryly.

"She's just shy," Kelsey said with a grin. "Next time, try letting her sniff your fingers."

"That's cats," Suliel replied. Kelsey only shrugged.

"Anyway, it's perfect," she said. "Our adversaries won't find anything suspicious in Anton visiting a dungeon. It's what heroes do, after all. They'll never suspect he's going to interview a witness."

"I wouldn't count on that," Anton said. "They know I talk to you, after all."

"Pish and tosh," Kelsey said dismissively. "I'm a known exception."

"To sense and good taste, perhaps," Suliel said. "But even if they do realize, they won't be able to do anything about it."

"Maybe," Kelsey said. "I'd say not to lower our guard, but we'll be in a dungeon."

"Guards should be fully up," Anton agreed. "I guess I should be the one to put the request in. We should have our team settled first, though."

"Oooh, we're putting together a delving party!" Kelsey said enthusiastically. "Let's see, we've got the fighter." She pointed at Anton. "Aris can pass for an archer; we've got a wizard and a thief."

She looked at Suliel speculatively.

"Count me out," Suliel said hastily. "I'd just be a hindrance, and I have more than enough business to handle up here."

"Aww, come on, Suliel!" Kelsey pouted. "The family that slays together, stays together! Or something. You can be the healer."

"I appreciate the noncombat role, but I can't heal people either."

"You can carry the healing potions!"

"No."

"What's your role going to be?" Anton asked, trying to change the subject.

"Me? Isn't it obvious?" Kelsey struck a stylish pose. "I'll be the bard, of course!"

Anton and Suliel both stared at Kelsey, but it was Anton who spoke first.

"Why would we take a bard into a dungeon?"

CHAPTER FORTY

Money for Nothing

Kelsey threw down the heavy ledger in disgust. "This is ridiculous!" she exclaimed.

Anton looked up from his own book and made placating gestures at the archivists, who were sending disapproving glares their way. None of them dared to approach Kelsey, but they made their displeasure known.

"The Archive Vault is supposed to be a *quiet* place, Kelsey," he said in a low tone.

"I can be as quiet as you like, but it won't make this garbage make any sense," Kelsey muttered. Her angry glare didn't go away, but she grumbled more quietly, which was enough to placate the guardians. Anton relaxed a bit more.

The next available opening for a delve in The Hungry Depths was in three days. Suliel had taken it upon herself to outfit the other party members, so Anton was researching the dungeon and its history. Kelsey had also expressed an interest.

Anton was glad his old Guild Master had come to Bures to help Suliel. His rank opened many doors in the Bures guild, and Anton was not sure he'd have found the Archive Vault on his own. In addition, it had taken all of Delir's diplomacy and Anton's noble rank to convince the Archivists that Kelsey should be allowed to browse the records.

Access was not normally restricted, but a number of the caretakers had felt that an exception should be made for dungeons. Kelsey's attitude hadn't helped, as she ranged from pointlessly combative to muttering cryptic statements like, "Ain't no rule that says a dungeon *can't* play basketball."

They got there in the end, though. Confirming the King had delved *The*

Hungry Depths after his coronation had been easy enough. Now, Anton was researching the types of monsters reported, while Kelsey was researching . . . something else.

"What is it?" Anton asked in a low voice.

"These numbers!" she whispered insistently, tapping at the page.

Anton looked at the record. "Of monsters fought?"

"No, of treasure earned!" Kelsey exclaimed, still keeping her voice low. "Silver for the first floor! That's crazy!"

"Uh, well, Kelsey," Anton said evasively. He could sense that they were approaching a dangerous conversational zone. "You said yourself that every dungeon determines its own rewards according to how much it wants to encourage visitors."

"Well, yeah, but this is off the charts," Kelsey insisted.

"What is?" Delir said, approaching close enough that he could join in the quiet conversation.

"I've been collating the amount of treasure awarded over different expeditions," Kelsey explained. She pulled a sheet of paper out of nowhere and handed it to Anton. It had . . . a lot of numbers on it, written in a neat, spidery hand that Anton did not associate with Kelsey at all.

"How is this . . . there's just one number for each floor?" Anton asked. He passed the sheet over to Delir to see if the Guild Master could make more sense of it.

"These are the mana costs," Kelsey said. "I can get away with manufacturing a good amount of my rewards, but most dungeons have to magic them up. Here—" She handed Anton some more sheets of numbers. "These are the costs involved in respawning each floor, based on the numbers and tiers of the monsters reported. And the maintenance costs are *here*."

Anton looked at the charts, his head swimming. "Um . . ." he started to say.

Delir was studying his paper with intense interest, but his expression held more than a little confusion. "This is fascinating, Kelsey. We've never had a chance to see this side of the equation. How confident are you that these numbers are accurate?"

"They can't be accurate, that's the thing," Kelsey growled. "Hang on."

After a short pause, she produced another sheet.

"This is the calculated mana expenditure for each of the expeditions I studied, next to the amount of mana I'd expect a dungeon to generate each day. You have daily expeditions going in, which makes things easier to calculate."

This sheet of paper was a little simpler. There were only three columns, one labeled "Generation," one labeled "Costs," and one labeled "Reserves." The Reserves column started with a number that was quite high, but it dwindled quickly and soon ended up negative.

"I see," Delir said once he'd studied the paper. "So, where do you think the inaccuracy lies?"

"How good are your numbers?" Kelsey asked, tapping the ledgers.

"Quite good," Delir answered. "Our officials pride themselves in their accuracy, and the records are used for tax purposes, so there is considerable incentive to get them correct. If adventurers are managing to fudge the numbers, I'd expect the inaccuracies to go the other way."

"That makes sense," Kelsey agreed. "There are some traits that you can take that make spending mana more efficient. Cheaper summons, extra treasure, and so on."

She paused with a doubtful look on her face. "I've never taken them because they're not great. Like, five percent bonuses . . . they do add up, though. I've got Charley running the numbers."

"Charley?" Anton asked.

"All my accounting skeletons are called Charley," Kelsey said matter-of-factly.

Delir raised an eyebrow. "You have accounting skeletons?"

"Oh, I've got all sorts," Kelsey assured him. "Mostly, I use them for engineering calculations, but sometimes mana costs need to be calculated."

"I see," Delir said. He held up the sheaf of papers that Kelsey had generated. "Can I—can *we* keep this information?"

Kelsey narrowed her eyes. "Those numbers would be pretty valuable to you, wouldn't they?"

"Of course," Delir agreed. "They're everything I could have hoped for, back when you first decided to open communications with us. It might well win over the disbelievers in the guild."

"Disbelievers?" Kelsey asked.

"There are some who say that you're not what you say you are and others who don't believe in your good intentions," Delir said. "Fools, of course, but they do have influence."

"Hmph," Kelsey snorted. "I guess I don't mind. They're not *my* secrets."

"Very generous of you, my lady," Delir said, gathering up the rest of the papers. Kelsey frowned.

"You don't like the term?" Delir asked hastily. "It was meant as a sign of respect, I assure you."

"No, that's not it," Kelsey said. "Just Kelsey is fine. What's not fine is this."

She pulled a final sheet of paper out of the air.

"This is the first scenario we tried that made the numbers work," she said grimly. She put the paper down on the table and tapped it.

"They need to have taken *Generous Rewards* at least *ten times* for these numbers to work," she said. "That's over half their traits spent on giving more treasure to invaders!"

"Well . . . at least it's *possible* that they might have done that?" Delir said, looking at the sheet. "Could they have managed it with the cheaper monsters trait?"

"Look at how much they're spending." Kelsey went back to the earlier pages. "So much more on treasure. They'd need to pick up two *Bountiful Spawn*s for each *Rewards* they lost. So even if they spent *all their traits* on it, they'd still need two *Generous Rewards*."

"The first scenario is more likely," Delir admitted.

Kelsey stared at him suspiciously. "You said you established communications with this dungeon," she said. "Has it said anything about this?"

"We've only managed the most basic of interactions," Delir said. "We try to establish our good will, convince the dungeon to lower the danger. We *theorized* that dungeons might have traits, but we've never known what they could do or what traits this dungeon might have."

"Well, someone does." Kelsey stared at the ledger. "And I know *someone* who knows secrets about dungeons and doesn't want others to know them. A whole group of someones. These accounts don't mention any Wizards Guild delvers, why is that?"

"The Wizards Guild doesn't delve, though they sometimes send a member down with a group," Delir said. "But they do regular inspections. Those aren't for experience, so they follow a capable group down and let them kill the monsters and take the treasure."

"They never did that with *me*."

"You have a reputation," Delir said carefully. "Among other habits of yours, you routinely respawn monsters on a floor the delvers have already cleared."

"That's just good sense," Kelsey said with a smug grin. "Get them when they're at their weakest."

Delir coughed. "We try to discourage that in dungeons that we've established a rapport with. The point is, it wouldn't be safe for a wizard team to follow behind a party delving you."

"I should think not," Kelsey agreed. "The last thing I want is for a wizard to feel safe."

"Or anyone," Anton pointed out.

"True," Kelsey admitted. "I am an equal opportunity death factory. So why do they do these delves if not for experience or treasure?"

"They may get some," Delir allowed. "While they choose strong parties, not everyone makes a full clear. The wizards are supposed to make it to the very bottom to do their inspection."

"And just what are they inspecting?" Kelsey asked.

"They are supposed to be checking for the conditions that lead to a dungeon break," Delir explained.

"That's . . . probably not true," Kelsey said thoughtfully. "The only condition that *requires* it is when you get too much mana."

"What other circumstances can lead to a break?" Delir asked.

"Oh, we can do it whenever we like," Kelsey said. "And the mana thing . . . there are ways to manage that. Even if you're not getting delved, you can spend the mana on other things, you know?"

"I don't, but I can imagine," Delir said eagerly. "So how does a dungeon get too much mana?"

"Not being delved will do it if you're dumb. But if that's happening, you just need to check how many monsters are dropping cores."

"I thought cores generated randomly?"

"They do, but they're how monsters absorb extra mana. If you've got too much surplus, more monsters grow cores."

"We do keep track of how many cores are found," Delir said. "It can be inaccurate as many parties don't search properly. *The Hungry Depths* isn't known for dropping many cores."

"I'd be surprised if it was, with the amount of mana it's spending on treasure," Kelsey muttered. "Anyway, say your monsters are full, and you're up against the floor cap, *and* you don't want to make adjustments, *and* you don't want to generate more treasure. If all of those are true, it can be easier just to let the monsters out. Another way—"

"Getting back on topic, if the wizards *aren't* checking for signs, what are they doing?" Anton said. Delir gave him a hurt look.

"Dunno. That's one more thing to ask about. How often do they do this?"

"About once a month, depending on if they can find a decent team to follow," Delir said. "There should be a note in the entries . . . there."

"Inspection team followed," Kelsey read. "It doesn't look like there's anything different about the delve itself . . . or the one after."

She started flipping through the book, running her finger along the entries fairly quickly.

"Are you reading that fast?" Anton asked.

"Sorta," Kelsey said. "I've got Charley copying the relevant details as I go along. I can do some statistics on the numbers once I've gathered them all. If we go back far enough, I could work out when this all started."

She paused and looked speculatively at the book she had open. Then, she looked at the other ledgers.

"This would go faster if I could have my skellies each take a book and start copying," she said.

"Ah! Well . . . the books are supposed to remain here at all times," Delir said hastily. "And there are archivists watching, you know. They would have objections if any books were to vanish."

Kelsey scowled. "What if I brought a bunch of Charleys here?" she asked.

"That also would not be seen in a positive light," Delir said, his voice pitched a little higher.

"Ah, well, it's not like we aren't stuck waiting for a few days," Kelsey said philosophically. "I just wish I'd invented data-entry skeletons already."

CHAPTER FORTY-ONE

Back in Black

TYLA

Tyla adjusted the fit of her new armor once more. The newly purchased leathers had been chosen to be as close as possible to her tribe's customary outfit. It wasn't a copy by any means, but it had been made for someone with the same needs as her tribe.

Those needs were to provide as much protection while restricting the movements of the wearer. The basic design was the same. A vest with flared shoulder guards, a stiff kilt to cover the upper legs, and tightly fitted bracers, vambraces, and greaves to protect the limbs.

There were differences. Her old armor had been made from deerskin, edged with the fur of smaller creatures for both comfort and silence. Her new outfit was made from something called a marluk, a terrifying creature found in the dungeon they were about to enter. The monster's skin was both stronger and lighter than simple deerskin. It boasted large natural scales that had been softened by boiling and shaped into the stiffer parts like her greaves.

And it was enchanted. Only the smallest of magics, but it was a revelation to her that the city could provide such things when a client requested it. Tyla had opted for a silencing enchantment. It didn't make *her* silent, just the armor. There were other options, like self-cleaning or additional protection, but Tyla was bombarded with enough extraneous noise. She didn't need it from her own equipment.

Zaphar had opted for the self-cleaning enchantment, but his armor was all soft, flexible leather from something called a vinelurker. It left him vulnerable, but he said he was more alert when he was nervous. It was still a step up from the loose robes he'd been wearing when he wasn't in disguise.

He was much more enamored of his new dagger. Larger and more vicious-looking than his previous knives, it was Tier Two and enchanted to boot. *Invisibility* was a choice that Tyla would not have made, but he seemed pleased with it. He'd already spent a few idle moments making the dagger and its scabbard fade from view.

It wouldn't be of much use against the animals in the dungeon—at least, not more than a dagger normally would be. Zaphar was excited about it because it would enable him to carry a weapon in places where that would not normally be acceptable.

Tyla much preferred the sensible nature of the enchantment on her own weapon. Protection against damp, cold, and heat seemed liked a small thing—if you had never had to care for a bow. Kelsey had been scathing of Tyla's choice, but she hadn't forbidden it. Tyla knew that she was always going to be more comfortable with a bow than with the deadly, loud new weapon.

Aris's gear was mostly unchanged. It had already been of high quality, and Kelsey insisted that it was important for maintaining Aris's "idiom."

That left Anton—*Lord Nos*, as Tyla resolved to think of him, even if he preferred to be addressed without a title. A great deal of his time over the last three days had been spent attending social functions with his wife. Despite that, he had managed to find time to outfit himself in a manner more suitable for his station.

For most of the time she had known him, Lord Nos had dressed like an Elitran mercenary. Mismatched, dusty armor, with the gaps covered over by coarsely woven robes. His new gear was finely crafted chain mail, worn over an embroidered gambeson. His arms were covered by the same marluk scales that she wore, but backed with leather to provide more protection at the cost of added weight. They were also decorated with finely crafted inlays.

His gear was still only Tier Two, but Tyla had heard that he was getting a Tier Three suit of armor commissioned. Armor of that quality had to be custom fit, and that took time. He could have replaced his sword with one of higher tier, but his current sword seemed to have sentimental value. Kelsey had stated that a new sword would come along when it was "thematically appropriate."

Tyla wasn't sure what the words meant, but she was pretty sure that Kelsey expected Lord Nos to pick up something suitable in the upcoming dungeon. That was what dungeons were *for*, after all—to reward the worthy. The only doubt in Tyla's mind was that delving deep enough for a Tier Three weapon would be . . . difficult. Not for Lord Nos, of course. And it was difficult imagining a monster that Lady Aris's firepower couldn't overcome. It was Tyla and Zaphar that she was worried about. They were only Tier Two.

Tyla took another look at her status.

Tyla Greenwalker of the Padascar Tribe, Dungeon Witch (Level 1)
Overall Level: 13
Paths: Padascar Hunter (Broken)/Doxy (Broken)/Apprentice Dungeon
    Witch/Dungeon Witch
Strength: 12
Toughness: 8
Agility: 11
Dex: 18
Perception: 20
Will: 15
Charisma: 10
Traits:
Persistent Tracker
Silent Shot
Danger Sense
Sense Magic
Cast Lesser Charm (10)

She had been practicing magic diligently since gaining her second tier, but she was still on the first level of Dungeon Witch. Each spell she cast gave her a small amount of experience, but second-tier levels were much harder to achieve. She'd hoped for a new trait before they delved, but it was not to be.

Even without that trait, Tyla believed that Lord Nos could protect them, and she had faith that Kelsey would not lead them into challenges that they could not overcome. Even when Kelsey was being . . . whimsical.

"Oh, this is just lovely. Nothing says 'Welcome, brave adventurers!' like a gaping, ominous hole in the ground. No ambience, not even a proper threshold enchantment. Just damp rock, bad lighting, and the distinct aroma of 'you're probably going to die.' Honestly, would it kill this place to invest in a foyer?"

Lord Nos stared incredulously at Kelsey as she stood frowning with her arms crossed. "Your first level stinks of actual decomposing flesh, and you want to talk about a foyer?"

"You're comparing durians and ginkgo fruit," Kelsey said smugly.

"I have no idea what either of those two are," Lord Nos countered. Kelsey waved him away.

"*I* make an effort to discourage visitors," she said smugly. "This one is supposed to be all lovey-dovey with wizards and adventurers and so on. It should be welcoming! Instead, it's just . . . meh."

Lord Nos sighed. "If we establish contact, then I guess you can exchange design tips all you like," he said. "Is everybody ready?"

They all indicated that they were. Lord Nos nodded.

"Very well then, you know the formation, let's go."

Tyla was first into the cavern. Both she and Zaphar were acting as scouts. Both of them could see in the dark, but she had the better perception. Not that the cavern was *completely* dark. The cavern walls were slick with moisture, which made an excellent growing environment for lichen and fungi. Some of the varied species scattered across the walls glowed just enough for her eyes to see.

Everyone in the party, except for Aris, could see quite well in the dark. There had been talk of getting potions for her and doing the delve entirely in darkness, but they already had light sources. Tyla and Zaphar could range far enough ahead to stay out of the area lit by the light-stone, and Kelsey promised to light up any targets for Aris with her torch. Blinding their enemies seemed like a better option than engaging them on equal terms.

It wasn't long before Tyla came across the first trap, a snare fashioned out of roots. Concealed as well as it was, Tyla would need to stay back and point it out to the others as they approached. Or she could trigger it safely and leave the way clear.

However, according to the briefing she'd received from Lord Nos, that would alert the sliggs and provoke an attack. It posed a tricky dilemma, or at least it would have if any of them had been in Tier One. As it was, she just had to signal to Zaphar, a few yards back, that the fight was starting. Notching an arrow to her bow accomplished this well enough.

He nodded and drew his dagger. This shouldn't take more than the two of them.

Tyla concentrated on the trap in front of her. Her mind gathered the energy from the core strapped to the small of her back. Mages customarily wore it around their necks, but that made Tyla look as if she had three breasts. Men stared enough.

Lord Nos had told her of fire spells he'd seen that unleashed a pillar of fire reaching as far as twenty yards away and two feet thick. Tyla couldn't manage that. Instead, a thin tendril of fire lashed out and laid waste to the triggering loop of the snare.

With a *thwipp-crack!*, the rest of the root trap disappeared into a crack in the walls. If Tyla had been standing in the loop, she would have been pinned, unable to respond.

She took a step back.

The sliggs boiled out of more cracks in the walls ahead of her. They were small, humanoid creatures between three and four feet high. Their dark grey skins blended in with the rock walls, even to the extent of dripping slickly with water. These ones were only armed with their claws, but that would change.

Tyla loosed an arrow and took a step back as she drew another one. The shaft sank directly into a charging sligg, sending it flying back and causing the others to chitter in fear or anger. Despite their loss, they kept coming, and Tyla kept firing.

She had downed two more before she drew level with Zaphar, who was ready to engage them in hand-to-hand combat. Their slick, leathery skins were tough but no match for his dagger. It was only a moment later before all seven of the creatures were dead.

"Easy," Zaphar said, taking deep, shuddering breaths. "That—that was easy."

A patch of bright light announced the main group's arrival.

"I should hope so; they were just level two," Kelsey said.

Zaphar glared disrespectfully at the numen. "I've never had to fight monsters that came down from the ceiling," he objected. "It's creepy."

Tyla wasn't sure that he'd ever fought any kind of monsters. In the forest, creatures attacked from the canopy all the time, so she hadn't been greatly perturbed by it.

"Are the corpses of any value?" she asked.

"People buy the skins and claws, but they're just Tier One," Lord Nos replied. "Even if we were here for that, it wouldn't be worth the time for us to collect them."

"I'll take 'em!" Kelsey declared. "Always got a use for fresh meat!"

"Um . . . should you?" Lord Nos asked. "Don't you prefer it when delvers leave the corpses?"

"It's not a big deal, but it does save on costs if I can recycle," Kelsey agreed. "Oh, wait, are you saying this is an etiquette thing? Like, dungeons shouldn't take other dungeons' stuff?"

"Should they?"

"I . . . dunno," Kelsey admitted. "Mel thinks . . . Mel won't say. She says that dungeons don't talk to one another because none of them ever took avatars, which I *know* isn't true. Oh, and now she's refusing to talk to me. Very mature."

Everyone stared at Kelsey, but no one said anything, allowing Kelsey to ramble on, apparently having a conversation with herself.

"Yes, I am telling everyone that. Yes, including Suliel. The next time she sees you, she's going to know what a brat you are!"

"Um, Kelsey? The etiquette?" Lord Nos asked.

"Oh." Kelsey made a face. "Tell you what, I'll take them, but I won't *process* them. That way, I can give them back if Deppy objects."

"Deppy?"

"That's another thing they can object to if they bother to make contact," Kelsey said. "Honestly, what's taking them so long?"

"I don't know," Lord Nos said. "We'll just have to go deeper."

CHAPTER FORTY-TWO

Way Down in the Hole

ARIS

The tunnels kept on going down. Aris didn't like it. The darkness and the twisting tunnels were not a good fit for her weapons. The intense noise they caused when she fired them was also a problem. The sharp retorts of her fire reflected off the closed-in walls and sounded many times louder than they should. Anton and herself had magical protection, and Kelsey sneered at the possibility of harm, but Zaphar and Tyra were vulnerable.

Both of them had better than normal hearing, and just one shot in these tunnels seemed to cause them physical pain. So, for the moment, Aris kept her pistols holstered and let the two scouts take care of the threats.

Not that sliggs were very threatening. They grew larger and sophisticated as the party descended, graduating to poison-tipped spears for their weapons. But they were still only first-tier creatures. Tyla and Zaphar dispatched them without difficulty.

"I feel useless," Aris confessed. As the only party member who needed a light-stone to see, she felt they were making concessions to accommodate her.

"Don't think like that," Anton told her. He held her arm to help her past a slippery and complicated slope. "It's standard practice to let the lowest-leveled member take on the early levels. They won't get much experience, but they'll get more than anyone else would." He kept holding her arm as they continued, which Aris rather liked.

"Zaphar is a higher level than I am," Aris pointed out. "I'm only thirteen, the same as Tyla."

"That's why he's backing her up," Anton said.

"Also, Zaphar needs more practice fighting," Kelsey said. "Most of his life has been spent running, not knifing. He's got the basics, but he needs more work."

"Most of *my* life has been spent baking," Aris said.

"Yeah, but you have a humdinger of a combat class," Kelsey said smugly.

"Humdinger?" Aris asked.

"You know, a doozy. A barnburner of a class. A ripsnorting sockdolager of a class."

Aris giggled. "You're just making words up now."

"I *wish* I was," Kelsey said. "Anyway, the point is that you'll get your chance once we get out of the kiddie pool."

Sounds of fighting came from ahead. Aris got her gun ready, but they didn't charge forward. They kept moving forward cautiously, as the plan called for.

Soon enough, they found the bodies. Most had an arrow sticking out of them. Kelsey removed the bodies and had her skeletons pull the arrows out. When Tyla ran short, Kelsey would be able to provide a fresh quiver.

"They're getting bigger," Aris commented as Kelsey made the corpses disappear. It was hard to tell with them curled up on the ground, but she thought that at least some of them were as big as a human.

"I thought they might be a tier upgrade, but they're still Tier One," Anton said. "They're Sligg Reavers."

"They've been the bosses for the last two floors, but they're every second monster on this one," Kelsey said. "Are we going to see a bigger one for the boss on this floor?"

A muffled roar sounded from ahead of them.

"Yeah," Anton said. "According to the accounts, it's called a Sligg Tyrant."

They rushed ahead, but they needn't have worried. Tyla had it under control.

They burst out into a large, irregularly shaped cavern. For the first time since they'd come down here, the illumination from Aris's light-stone didn't reach the walls or ceiling.

From what they could see, the floor was irregular as well, pockmarked with pools and puddles. A few sligg corpses were scattered about, most half in the water. The real action was outside of the lit area. Aris could see shadows moving, one much larger than all the others.

The roar came again, much louder, as they moved forward, carefully avoiding the rock pools. Kelsey's torch shone ahead of them, picking up a massive sligg, more than seven feet tall and with four arms. He howled ferociously and lashed his arms out at Tyla and Zaphar . . . but there was something wrong.

The two fighters were able to easily keep out of his reach as they finished off the smaller Sligg Reavers that surrounded him. As the party approached, Aris could see why.

The Sligg Tyrant had his feet frozen in the ground.

He must have been standing in a pool that had, for reasons that escaped Aris, frozen solid with his feet in it.

"Oh, Tyla's using her magic! Good girl!" Kelsey said.

Even as Kelsey spoke, Tyla finished her opponent and took a few steps back from the Tyrant. She had switched to melee for the fight, but now she sheathed her short sword and took a few deep breaths.

Aris looked back at the Tyrant. His roars now seemed pathetic instead of threatening. Under normal circumstances he would have seemed fearsome with his his height, his reach, the four arms. He had even picked up mismatched pieces of adventurer armor and weapons. He reminded Aris of the monstrous zombie, cobbled together from parts, that she had fought in her first delve.

Tyla took another breath and then shot it in the head. It toppled like a tree, crashing to the ground and cracking the ice below it with a *snap*. The Reaver that Zaphar was fighting howled in despair, giving him the opening he needed to finish it off.

"Still no level," Tyla said. "But I am getting close."

"It was only level eight," Anton told her. "We have a way to go before the gains kick in."

"Until then, we'll have to console ourselves with material gain," Kelsey said. "To the victor, the spoils!"

She walked up and disappeared the corpse of the Tyrant. Aris noticed that the ice had already melted.

"You're looking awfully pleased about getting some corpses and some trash equipment," Anton said.

"The armor looks trashy, but two of the pieces are Tier Two," Kelsey informed him. "Once I get them cleaned up, they'll be fine. But it's not about the *having*, it's about the *taking*."

"You enjoy stealing this dungeon's treasure?" Aris asked.

"Normally. I'm on the other side of this scenario," Kelsey told her. "Having adventurers come and take my stuff. It's nice to be on the other end of the transaction."

"I seem to recall you taking the things of *quite a few* adventurers, right down to their bodies," Anton said dryly. "You don't get to claim it was all one-sided."

"And I enjoyed myself when I got to do it then," Kelsey agreed. "Anyway, let's see what the floor reward is."

She strode over to the chest at the back of the cavern.

"Shouldn't Tyla or Zaphar open that?" Aris asked.

"There's no experience for opening a chest," Kelsey shot back. The chest and its lid were made of stone, which made it hard to open, but her strength was equal to the task. She flipped the lid open and looked inside.

"Huh," she said. "Two gold and fifty silver. At least it's not mad at us. This is just over the average take for this floor."

She flipped a coin to both Tyla and Zaphar that flew straight to them in a glittering arc.

"Here, a souvenir. Your first gold earned from a dungeon."

Tyla pocketed her reward without comment. Zaphar looked down at his.

"Technically, my first dungeon gold was when you paid me for our first job together," he said.

"That might be true, but no one likes a smart aleck, Zaph," Kelsey said. She pushed the chest out of the way. There was a small hole underneath with a lever. Pulling it opened a hidden door.

"This is the end of the sliggs, right?"

"Right," Anton confirmed. "The next floor is where the root jungle starts. We'll need to close up, keep everyone in sight of each other."

"No scouting?" Tyla asked.

"You'll see," Anton said. He led them through the passageway. There was another lever that closed the first door and opened another one.

"Ah, the old airlock gambit," Kelsey said. "But when you make it obvious like that, adventurers start to think there's some benefit in keeping both doors open."

"Is there?" Anton asked.

"Not really. It just prevents mana loss. So if you think pissing off the dungeon is a benefit . . ."

Anton looked at Kelsey for a long beat. Aris was sure he was waiting for Kelsey to say that they *should* piss off this dungeon to make the fairy appear. She didn't, though, and Anton moved on.

As they moved through the second door, the glow from Aris's light-stone showed a complicated tangle of roots and vines. There were pathways through it, but the roots were so densely packed that Aris couldn't tell if they were following natural passages through the rock or if the whole area was one massive cavern.

"Oh!" Tyla exclaimed. "This is more like the mazes we have at home! Except for the part where they are underground."

"Interesting," Anton said, carefully examining the plants in front of him. "Did your mazes also do *this*?"

He stabbed one of the vines with his sword and then leapt back. The vine he had stabbed twitched violently, coiling around itself to try and entangle whatever had stabbed it. A second later, it had coiled up so much that it had withdrawn from the edge of the light.

"Wait for it," Anton said.

With a *crack*, the vine whipped back to where it had been before. In the process, it set off several other vines that all did the same thing, except for one that released a puff of smoke or poison or something.

"Well, obviously, you don't step on the strangleweed," Tyla said. Four more *cracks* announced the return of the second wave of vines. These ones didn't set anything off, either through chance or because they were designed that way.

"That would not be wise," Anton agreed. "I think Kelsey and I are strong enough to not have to worry about getting dragged off, but the rest of you are vulnerable. And Zaphar . . ."

"I am not strong," the thief agreed. "Not strong at all. I would be wrapped up and delivered wherever it is they take me."

"What does the smoke do?"

"Different things," Tyla answered. Some types make you drunk, others burn the skin. The vines look different from what I am used to, so there may be other types."

"Just avoid the vines, and any smoke if possible," Anton told her.

"I think . . ." Tyla said thoughtfully, "that I can use magic for this."

"Gonna burn them all up?" Kelsey said hopefully.

"No . . . the vines and roots are wet and contain water. It would take a very strong spell to set them aflame, and I cannot cast strong spells as yet. But I *can* control plants, and keeping a plant still is only a weak spell."

"Give it a try," Anton suggested, stepping back from the tangle. Tyla stood closer and stared at the vines. At a signal that Aris couldn't see, Anton moved forward and slashed at a vine. This time it fell to the ground, severed without reacting.

"That will make things easier," Anton said. "We still have to watch out for vinelurkers and black maw writhers which move through gaps in the roots that we can't see. They'll slip by any scouts we put out and go straight for the back line."

"Hey, that's me!" Kelsey objected. "I'll be vulnerable!"

Anton looked at her with a flat, unblinking stare. "Yeah, you are pretty fragile," he said. "Maybe you should put on a helmet or something."

"Good plan!" Kelsey said. She pulled a round helmet out of nowhere and plonked it on her head. Everyone stared at her, but it was Zaphar who failed to resist the urge to ask the question.

"Why . . . why is it yellow?" he asked reluctantly.

"For safety!" Kelsey answered.

Anton took a deep breath. "Let's just get moving," he said. "Stay close, and stay alert."

Everyone nodded. Zaphar pulled out another light-stone. Arranged in a new formation, they set off to conquer the fourth floor.

CHAPTER FORTY-THREE

Slave 2 the Rhythm

TYLA

Tyla didn't gain a level until the fifth floor. That floor was still choked with strangleweed and blisterbloom blossoms, but more monsters were added to the mix. Marluks were one such creature. It was a larger hunched quadruped with thick, chitinous plates covering its body like overlapping armor.

Tyla took it out with a shot through the creature's eye. It was an easier shot than it sounded—the eye was large and glowing.

"Not that it matters, but the eyes are the most valuable part," Lord Nos said from behind her. "They're an important alchemical ingredient, apparently."

Tyla didn't respond. Something else was occupying her attention.

You have reached Level 2.
Applying Benefits for Level 2
Toughness + 1
Dexterity + 1
Perception + 1
Willpower + 1
Charisma + 1
Please allocate free Ability point.

Tyla selected Perception without hesitation.

Please select a new Trait. Available Traits: Discern Enchantment, Identify Potion, Commune, Empower Alchemy

Tyla winced slightly. She had hoped for a trait that let her cast higher-level spells, but everyone had agreed that the first trait of a new class was almost always a perception one. The main exception here was *Empower Alchemy*, which was a holdover from her Apprentice class. And Commune, which Tyla was unfamiliar with.

"I've made a level," she announced. "Has anyone heard of the *Commune* trait?"

Everyone looked to Lord Nos, who shook his head. "Never heard of it," he said. "I know most of the common wizard ones, but . . ."

"If it's not common, then it's got to be related to the purpose of Tyla's class," Kelsey mused. "As a Dungeon Witch, it's got to be dungeon related."

"It lets me . . . commune with dungeons?" Tyla asked. "Should I take it, then? That is what we're here for, after all."

"That might not be it," Kelsey cautioned. "It might only work with the dungeon you've got strapped to you."

"That would be good as well," Tyla said. "I feel there is . . . something there, but I cannot reach it."

"It's your decision," Lord Nos reminded her. "I know you revere Kelsey, but her advice can be questionable."

"Hey, no *questioning* my advice!" Kelsey retorted. "You can recognize that it's good or you can fear where following it may take you, but which it is, is never in *question*."

"Fair point," Lord Nos said. "Kelsey's advice is always terrible."

Tyla chuckled at the byplay. "I will take Commune," she said. "And see where it leads me."

She selected the trait. She didn't feel any different, but traits did not always make themselves known. She looked at her status page.

Tyla Greenwalker of the Padascar Tribe, Dungeon Witch (Level 2)
Overall Level: 14
Paths: Padascar Hunter (Broken)/Doxy (Broken)/Apprentice Dungeon Witch/Dungeon Witch
Strength: 12
Toughness: 8
Agility: 12
Dex: 19
Perception: 22
Will: 16
Charisma: 11
Traits:
Persistent Tracker
Silent Shot

Danger Sense
Sense Magic
Cast Lesser Charm (10)
Commune

"Try touching the wall of the dungeon and . . . *opening your mind*," Kelsey said dramatically.

Tyla went to try it but found herself stymied. The roots and vines covered everything; there was no wall that she could touch.

"Oops!" Kelsey said when she realized what the problem was. "Time for violence, Anton! Time to realize your old dream of being a woodcutter."

"No need," Tyla said. "I can fix this with a spell."

She laid her hands on the plants and reached for the magic that was hers. Plants weren't meant to move. Well, some of *these* could, but not in the way Tyla wanted. Magic could change that. Tyla concentrated on the mana of Control and Plants and let it flow through her. It wasn't much, but it was enough to move the roots aside. Not far, just a hole big enough to put her arm through.

A vinelurker jumped out of the hole with a squeal. Tyla jerked backward, too startled to do anything but dodge. She fell to the vine-covered floor while Zaphar took care of her attacker.

"Are—are you all right?" he asked, once the vinelurker had been skewered on his daggers. "You need to take more care."

"Thank you." Tyla glared at the hole, but no more monsters came out. The vinelurker had . . . lurked . . . underneath the roots. There were spaces there that a monster could crawl through while she was concentrating on her *Commune* trait.

She could fix that with another spell, though. Tyla focused on her Plant magic again, twisting the roots around the hole to cut off any access from the wider area.

Now it was safe to use.

"I'm going to try it," she announced. Without waiting for a response, she put her hand on the cavern wall and . . . opened her mind.

Or, she tried to. What exactly Kelsey had meant by the phrase was not clear to Tyla, but she thought it might mean something like how a hunter stills themselves to better perceive the world around them. Only, instead of senses, she must have meant magic.

Tyla could sense magic now. She knew the cavern walls were filled with it. Not part of a spell, just raw magic like the magic that flowed through her. *Her* magic, she could control. This magic wasn't hers, but she reached out for it anyway, letting her magic *touch* it. It was right there, she was . . . she *wasn't* there.

She wasn't in a root-filled cavern, dripping with moisture. She was in a grey void, limitless in extent, and yet only just large enough to hold three people. There were three people there. Herself and two others.

One of them was staring at her. They looked like a human-sized sligg, without the hardened growth that served as armor on the larger ones. Just a slimy-skinned humanoid. They were naked, but Tyla couldn't tell if they were male or female.

The other one was flying agitatedly around the first. It was a winged humanoid with blue skin. It was much smaller than the other figure, less than a foot tall. Blue light flickered around its wings as it furiously fluttered them. As Tyla watched, the winged figure flew at her.

"You're not supposed to be here!" she . . . squeaked. It was probably supposed to be a yell. Flying towards Tyla was probably supposed to be a threat, but Tyla was still too startled to move. The little winged creature halted itself a few inches from Tyla's face and glared at her.

"Well? What do you have to say for yourself!" she demanded.

Tyla blinked. "A good day to you," she said. "I am Tyla Greenwalker of the Padascar Tribe and I am very pleased to meet you."

"You think we don't know that!" the little creature yelled. "We know *everything*. We know you're level fourteen, we know you're a—a Dungeon Witch!"

The large sligg held up its hand. "I told her," it announced. "Sorry if I wasn't meant to."

"That is fine," Tyla said absently. She pointed at the sligg. "You—you're the dungeon, aren't you?"

"Don't answer that!" the little creature shouted.

"And Kelsey talked about her dungeon fairy, Mel. Is that what you are?" Tyla asked.

"I'm not Mel!" the tiny humanoid yelled.

"I meant, are you a dungeon fairy, like Mel is?" Tyla clarified.

"Oh." The little person looked a little lost for a second. Then she rallied. "I'm not going to answer that!"

"You're right about both things," the sligg confided. "This is Aelisinne."

"Don't *tell* her things!" the fairy protested.

"It's only fair," the numen replied evenly. "We know things about her, she should know things about us."

"Do you have a name?" Tyla asked the numen.

"Yes! It is The Hungry Depths," the sligg said proudly. "Lots of people know this name."

"I meant—but I suppose you *are* the numen, aren't you? I meant how Kelsey has a different name from what people call her dungeon."

"It is Kelsey who is strange, not me. There is something wrong with the way her name is written. Names should not be in quotes."

"That doesn't surprise me," Tyla admitted. "Kelsey is a very strange numen."

"She is a dungeon, then?" The Hungry Depths frowned. "She is a dead city. Has she come to kill me?"

"She hasn't," Tyla said. "We have only come to talk to you."

"As if!" Aelisinne objected. "Humans always come here to kill us."

"I'm not a human," Tyla replied. "Nor is Kelsey."

"But the others are! And you—" The fairy's voice choked off, and she flew behind The Hungry Depths.

"You carry the corpse," The Hungry Depths said. "You have killed before."

"Not numina!" Tyla protested. "Kelsey killed wizards and gave me their cores. She said that I would make better use of them than they would."

The sligg stared at her. "Perhaps I see more clearly now. She *uses* dead things, that is why she is a city of the dead."

"Would you like . . . do you want me to hand them over to you?" Tyla asked.

The Hungry Depths cocked its head as it looked at her. "You would do such a thing?" it asked.

"I was raised to honor the numina," Tyla said. "I don't know . . . what the respectful thing to do is in this situation. Kelsey said I should take it, and I am of use to her, with my magic. But if you say that I should not, then Kelsey will understand."

Tyla had her doubts that Kelsey would understand, or agree. She fully expected the avatar to get into a huge argument with The Hungry Depths on the matter. But, in the end, she thought that Kelsey would honor Tyla's wishes.

The Hungry Depths narrowed its eyes as it looked at her. "Elves," it said. It looked over its shoulder at Aelisinne. "Sin, you said things about elves?"

"Elves are all right," Aelisinne muttered. Tyla had the impression she wasn't supposed to hear that admission, but there was no distance here. "When they're not carrying corpses."

"All right," the numen repeated. "High praise, from Sin."

It thought some more and then frowned. "Kelsey is right. You should keep it," it said. "If it stays here, it will go back to the wizards."

Tyla bowed. Or not. Now that she was trying to do a physical movement, she had the distinct impression that she didn't have a physical body. But the *intent* of the bow was communicated, so it was all right.

"Will you speak with Kelsey, numen?" Tyla asked.

"Speak? I cannot. And Sin is afraid of her."

"I am not!"

"She doesn't like dead things," The Hungry Depths confided. "But we are speaking now, yes? Why does another dungeon seek to talk to me? What interests do we have in common when we cannot move or act outside ourselves?"

"Kelsey can," Tyla stated. "She has established communications with the humans that live above her. She is starting to take a role in society."

"That's forbidden!" Aelisinne hissed. She flew up to Tyla, to make her displeasure known. "Dungeons aren't supposed to do that!"

"Which part?" The Hungry Depths asked wryly.

"All of it!" Aelisinne insisted. "This Kelsey has gone rogue and is sure to be punished."

The Hungry Depths blinked slowly. "Perhaps she will," it agreed. "But there is no rule against talking to her, is there?"

"There should be!"

"But there is not," The Hungry Depths concluded. "What, then, does Kelsey want?"

"She wants to know about the King, Ranon Kalond the Fourth. Or perhaps he is not the King. His class and his path are the main things she wants to know."

The Hungry Depths stared at Tyla, its face unreadable. "Ranon Kalond has not delved in four years, ten months, and fifteen days," it said.

"That is fine," Tyla said. "We don't need the information to be recent."

"And what do you offer in return?"

"Before we start trading, I should ask if you want the corpses of your monsters back. Kelsey took them, but she's ready to give them back if taking them offends you."

The sligg waved its webbed hand. "My garden is green, good for growing things. You have not damaged it enough for it not to grow back."

Tyla bowed again. "We are grateful for your gifts. I will have to talk with Kelsey again to find out what she offers, but I'm sure she would offer you mana, monsters, or weapons if you desire them. What is it that you want?"

"If you were really an elf, you would give her what she needs without a bargain!" Aelisinne declared.

The numen cocked her head at the fairy. "Is this true?" it—she—asked.

"It is the way of my people to support the numina in any way that we can," Tyla agreed. "If there is something you need that is within my power to grant, I will give it freely."

The Hungry Depths narrowed her eyes again. "You are a wizard, but not a strong one," she said.

"I hope to grow stronger."

"I see. You are not dead, but she uses you. This is what talking can do." She glanced at the fuming Aelisinne. "Tell me of Anton Nos. His class."

"Lord Nos? He is a hero . . ."

"A Heroic Liberator," The Hungry Depths corrected. "What does this mean?"

"It's . . . a *type* of hero? One that specializes in freeing people from slavery?"

"I see. And he aids The Kelsey?"

"We're all working together, yes."

"Then tell The Kelsey this. She will have her answer when Anton Nos frees me."

CHAPTER FORTY-FOUR

The Evil That Men Do

Tyla gasped and fell to the floor.

"Tyla! Are you all right?" Aris dashed forward and raised the elf into a sitting position.

"I am . . . fine," Tyla said. "It is just very disorientating."

"But it worked, right?" Kelsey asked eagerly. "Did you get anything?"

"It—she said that she would tell you once L—Anton had freed her." Tyla rose to her feet and shook her head to clear it.

"Freed her from what?" Anton asked.

"She didn't say, but . . ."

"Isn't it obvious?" Kelsey exclaimed. "It's the wizards! They must have cast spells on her core. That's why she's giving out so much treasure."

"Is—is that a bad thing, though?" Zaphar asked. He quickly backed away when Kelsey glared at him. "I mean for us—for humans! More treasure is more treasure, right?"

"Delir thought that the reduced death rates and increased treasure were due to the understanding that the guild had developed with the dungeon," Aris said. "But it was forced to do that?"

"Maybe one of those things," Kelsey mused. "If the wizards *wanted* the dungeon to stop killing people, they could have made it stop entirely. Just an endless all-you-can-eat treasure buffet."

"Why *don't* they do that?" Zaphar said. He held up his hands when Kelsey glared at him. "I—I mean, if they turned the dungeon into a—a treasure buffet, they wouldn't need to hide it. Everyone would love it!"

"Part of it might be that they just don't care if adventurers die," Kelsey said. "But I bet a big part of it is that they need the dungeon to grow."

"What do you mean?" Anton asked.

"Dungeons need deaths to grow." Kelsey shrugged. "I mean, *technically*, we just have to test delvers to the *edge* of death, but that involves more than a few fatalities."

"Why is that?" Anton asked, glowering.

"It's not an edge if people don't fall off," Kelsey said lightly. "And there need to be stakes or you lot don't get experience."

"You're saying that *you* need to grow so you can defend against *us*, but that makes *us* grow and so *you* need to grow some more?" Anton's head was spinning.

"There's a term for it," Kelsey said. "A Red Queen's Race, where you have to run as fast as you can, just to avoid falling behind."

"Who was the Red Queen?" Aris asked.

"She wasn't real," Kelsey replied. "She was probably red because of all the blood involved in that kind of race."

"Getting back to the game we are hunting," Tyla said. "The wizards want the nu—the dungeon to grow?"

"The more it grows, the more they get of whatever it is they're getting," Kelsey explained.

"Whatever?" Zaphar asked. "Aren't—aren't they getting treasure?"

"No," Kelsey said. "The *delvers* are getting treasure. The crown might be getting a piece of that, but the wizards are getting something else."

"What?" Aris asked.

"Magic, I'd guess," Kelsey said thoughtfully. "That's what dungeons make, and that's what wizards want, so that's my guess."

"But wizards already have magic," Anton objected.

"Doesn't mean they don't want more," Kelsey told him.

"Whatever the desires of the wizards, we should free the dungeon, should we not?" Tyla asked.

"Of course!" Kelsey replied. "Solidarity for our enslaved sister!"

"Hang on," Anton said. "We're just supposed to go along with this? We don't know why the dungeon was enslaved, or who by, or even if it is actually enslaved! We're just speculating around what it told Tyla."

"I don't think she was lying," Tyla said. She glowered at him. "Numina don't lie."

"*Kelsey* can lie," Anton retorted. "She's proud of it."

"Well, not exactly *proud*, I mean anyone can do it," Kelsey said. "I guess I *enjoy* it more than most?"

"Even so," Tyla insisted. "Kelsey is special."

"Wait. Special in a good way, right? Right?"

Tyla paused for a long beat, thinking about it. "Yes," she finally said. "In a good way."

"Whew! Come on Anton, why would she lie about something like this?"

"I don't know!" Anton said, "Maybe she was restrained because she was killing too many people!"

Kelsey gasped in what Anton was pretty sure was mock shock. "Anton!" she said, looking at him with wide eyes. "Do you think *I* should be locked up for killing people?"

"At least you stopped!"

"Paused." Kelsey stopped her eyes shifting. "Oh, this is a little awkward—wait, I already told you about the Stormguard."

"Ah, right."

"I murdered those guys *good*," Kelsey said with a grin. "Except for the one that got away."

"They were trying to kill you, though," Anton objected. "It was self-defense, not murder."

"That doesn't change the fact that I was put on this world to murder," Kelsey said. "Oh, sorry, I meant dragged screaming into this world and stuffed into a Pokéball to murder."

Anton stared at Kelsey, waiting for the strangeness of that sentence to fade. He didn't try and process it, just waited it out.

"Fine," he said. "Dungeons are *supposed* to kill. Even so, how is it enslaved? What am I supposed to do to free it?"

"I think," Tyla replied, "that she may have been waiting for a commitment before she explained further. If we are going ahead with the deal, I can try and get more details."

"Don't bother," Kelsey said. "I already know this one. We have to get to the deepest level and see the cruel and malevolent spell for ourselves. Only then can we break the curse and free the fair maiden."

Anton stared at her. "I have so many problems with that, I don't have the time to worry about how you came up with it."

"Problems? Oh, ye of little faith. Speak! So that I might address your petty concerns!"

Anton shook his head. "Fine. Not counting you, I'm the highest leveled here, and I'm only level twenty. The dungeon is level thirty-six."

"Not a problem! We can punch well above our weight and our levels will be much higher all around by the time we get to level twenty."

"Can't the dungeon make things easier for us to get down there?" Aris asked.

"Maybe . . . but we shouldn't ask. If it goes easy on us, we won't get those levels—and we need them."

"That's . . . true in the long run, but we don't have the time to keep delving and gaining levels. If we don't get to the bottom today, it will be three weeks before another slot opens." Anton sighed in frustration. "Gaining that many levels in one delve . . ."

"You're forgetting about the bonuses," Kelsey said. She pointed at Aris. "One. Shooting stuff with guns. Every kill is double experience."

She pointed at Anton. "You'll be on a quest to free a dungeon, which has got to be a pretty rare occurrence, if not unique. Bam! Extra experience."

She pointed at Tyla. "She's a Dungeon Witch, and this quest involves gaining the trust of the dungeon. Bam! Class-related, extra experience."

"What—what about me?" Zaphar asked when Kelsey stopped. She winced.

"Sorry kid, you're out of luck. But *your* growth is your patron's problem, not mine. He's pretty resourceful, though. I imagine at some point you'll be seducing someone down here. Maybe the dungeon!"

"I do not think you would enjoy that," Tyla said, straight-faced. "She appears as a human-sized sligg."

"A challenge like that is nothing to a Fae-Touched Rogue!" Kelsey declared.

"Wait, wait, I never said I was going to do it!" Zaphar protested.

"Even if *any* of that was right," Anton cut in, "what am I supposed to do with a spell?"

"You're kidding, right?" Kelsey exclaimed incredulously. "You're going to be getting levels, you're going to be getting traits. You've got a quest that needs you to break a spell—you're *certain* to get a trait that breaks spells."

"Are classes really that convenient?" Anton asked doubtfully.

"For heroes, they are," Kelsey said. "Other classes as well, but heroes most of all. Normally it bases what it offers on what you've done in the past. But if you're *on* a quest that is *going* to require something from you, your class will step up to the plate."

"I'm not sure what that means," Anton muttered. "And I'm not sure I like the idea of my quest choosing my traits for me."

"You always get a choice," Kelsey said, shrugging. "Nothing is stopping you from picking another trait and solving the quest another way, or failing the quest. The choice is still yours."

"Will I have a choice?" Anton wondered. "If I agree to this, won't I be bound by a geas?"

"Nah, that's a me thing, not a dungeon thing," Kelsey said. "It's because I'm an Outsider, and as far as I know, all the other dungeons are home-grown."

"That's something, at least," Anton said. "I still want Tyla to get more details from the dungeon, though."

"Fine, fine." Kelsey waved dismissively at Tyla. "Get it over with. Wait! Find out the dungeon fairy's name!"

"It's Aelisinne," Tyla said.

Kelsey paused, and she made a thoughtful face.

"I don't think Mel likes Aelisinne," she said. "At least, not enough to overcome the whole 'dungeons shouldn't talk to each other' thing."

Tyla cocked her head and stared at Kelsey, unsure of how to respond. Kelsey waved her off. "Go on, get that confirmation."

Tyla nodded. "Very well," she said and placed her hand on the wall again.

It went just like before, only this time Aris was there to catch her before she fell. It still took a moment for her to report.

"She says that Kelsey is right."

"About everything? Including the seduction?" Kelsey said gleefully.

"She wasn't that specific." Tyla frowned. "She can hear everything we say, of course, and she just told me that you were correct."

"It's nice to be recognized," Kelsey said. "Shall we press on? Onward to glory and all that?"

"Fine, fine," Zaphar said. "But I am not seducing a lizard!"

"Pretty sure sliggs are amphibians," Kelsey said. "Which might, admittedly, make the sex difficult. What you need to do is find a pond—"

"Let's get moving," Anton said.

Zaphar got his level on the sixth floor. He didn't want to talk about the trait he got, just that it would be useful outside of the dungeon. Kelsey took that to mean that it was a seduction trait and wouldn't be told otherwise. She also bullied him until he put his free point into Strength. He was still the weakest person in the party, weaker even than Suliel, but his Agility and Dexterity were higher than Anton's so he did okay in a fight.

The sixth floor did away with tunnels entirely, leaving them to clamber through a seemingly endless three-dimensional maze of roots and vines. Progress was slow, and would have been even slower without Tyla to identify which vines could be climbed on.

Fortunately, half the party could sense mana. The subtle gradient of magic was an unerring guide through the maze. They could avoid dead ends, and pass through what *looked* like dead ends, where the way forward was blocked by a few sturdy-looking but actually fragile vines.

As they moved deeper into the maze, the monsters grew more numerous. Zaphar and Tyla grew hard-pressed, dealing with the tangle-stalkers, the chitterwraiths, and the creeping maws that crawled out of the darkness through the tiniest gaps in the roots around them.

The attacks became so relentless that Aris was finally called on. It helped that the organic surroundings absorbed the echoes of her gunfire. They established a routine where Kelsey would identify a threat that was in danger of getting through and light it up with her torch.

Sometimes that was enough. The bright light would cause a chitterwraith to drop off its vine and fall . . . perhaps to its death, but at the least, out of the fight. Some monsters could hang on to their perch, shield their eyes, and press on.

Those monsters caught a bullet in their center of mass.

"Finally," Aris said. "It feels like I'm getting somewhere."

CHAPTER FORTY-FIVE

Closer to Fine

The monsters of the sixth floor weren't worth much in the way of experience. Aris felt she was getting about a tenth as much from each one as she had received from killing the archer on Suliel's estate.

There were a lot more than ten of them, though. Despite taking the most direct route possible and having her only kill the ones that threatened to slip through the cracks of their defense, she could feel the experience adding up. She could feel the next level getting closer as they descended.

It was almost a disappointment when they got to a rock wall and Anton announced that they were about to enter the boss chamber.

"Shouldn't we . . . clear out the rest first?" she asked. She gestured back to the darkness-covered vines.

"Maybe when we get to the eighth or ninth floor," Anton said. "The experience gain is still too low for us here—even for you two."

"Easy challenges are *easy*," Kelsey said. "But if there's no risk, there's hardly any reward."

Aris pursed her lips. It was true that she hadn't been challenged so far, *and* that she hadn't gained a level.

"So this boss won't be a challenge either?" she asked.

"It will out-level the two of you," Anton said. "But Zaphar should even that out. Honestly, though, your guns should be more than enough to finish it."

"Oh, oh! That is very fine. All I have to do is hold off the biting so that she can kill it," Zaphar said. "But how can I dodge if I must protect her?"

"Front-line fighter is more suited to someone with more strength than you,"

Anton agreed. "But you've got this. Just keep it distracted. Once Aris lands a few shots, it won't be in any position to attack."

Zaphar looked doubtful, but he nodded. "Then we go. Go in, yes?"

"Yes," Aris said, hefting one of her guns. She needed the other hand to steady herself on the uneven footing.

"I am ready," Tyla said.

This floor had featured more than a few snakes. Anton had named them as they appeared, using his *Delver's Discernment.* Stranglefang vipers had dangled from above, waiting for an unwary delver. Veincoil serpents had twisted around existing vines, looking just like harmless plants until they struck. The hollowroot adder had hidden in the crevices between the roots, waiting for the right moment to strike.

The boss of this floor, Anton had told them, was known as a Stranglefang King. Looking into the darkness of the crevice in front of them, Aris wondered how bad it would be.

Tyla sent a light into the darkness. They had a few options, but her lights were the best for this. Kelsey could shine a light ahead of them, as long as they didn't block her line of sight. That made a dazzling circle, which was perfect for lighting up a target, but less useful for inspecting the entire area. Light-stones needed to be carried, here, lest they fall down through a gap in the vines and be lost forever.

That left Tyla's floating ball of light as the best way to see what was ahead of them. The light revealed a circular, possibly spherical chamber. It was lined with vines, leaving an open space in the center. There was no sign of the monster.

Tyla hissed in dismay. "I see it . . ." she said. "But where is the head?"

"Where?" Aris demanded. Tyla pointed at an area of the wall, but there was nothing there but vines. Vines coiled around roots around . . .

Underneath a vine, something moved. It was only a glimpse, but there was something there.

Aris cursed. "I don't have a good shot," she admitted. "I'll try—stand clear!"

Her gun rang out. She couldn't use *Sure Shot* for this as there was no center of mass for her to aim for, but she had become quite practiced at aiming. The shot hit more or less what she was aiming for, but there were only vines there.

"The head must be behind the entrance," Tyla speculated. "So it can attack whomever comes in."

Zaphar looked at her sourly. "Just—just distract it, she said. So easy."

"Anton can do it," Aris offered. "He's got a trait for dodging."

"No," Zaphar sighed. "No. I must fill my role. Gain levels. Get ready. Do not shoot me."

The last two commands were directed at Aris, who nodded as Zaphar braced himself. Then he dashed into the chamber.

The snake struck as soon as he entered, dropping a part of itself down to sink its fangs into Zaphar's neck. He didn't wait for it to arrive, however. As soon as he was far enough into the cave to be attacked, he dived to one side. Thanks to his Agility, he moved faster than the snake could track.

That left the head of the snake hanging right in front of Aris. Before it could turn or withdraw, she took the shot that had been set up for her. She couldn't use *Sure Shot* for this, she needed something fancier.

"*Trick Shot*," she called as she squeezed the trigger. Anton would tease her later about speaking her traits, but it did make it easier to use.

The snake twisted around as she spoke. Faster than she could believe, its jaws gaped wide and rushed at her, but she was already pulling the trigger.

Hitting its head was too pedestrian a target for *Trick Shot*. Aris shot it in the brain.

You have reached Level 9.
Applying Benefits for Level 9
Toughness + 1
Agility + 1
Dexterity + 1
Perception + 1
Willpower + 1
Please allocate free Ability points.

Aris held off on selecting her ability points because, well . . .

"It's still alive!" she screamed. It was true. Even though its head had been shattered, even though she had received the experience, the snake was still moving, thrashing about like . . . well, like it had lost its head.

Zaphar rushed in and stabbed it. His blade went right through its neck. Or body. Whichever it was, the action did not help. The snake continued to thrash, tearing the dagger right out of Zaphar's hand. He dived out of the way before the snake's coils could entangle him.

"Oh no, now it's armed!" Kelsey said with amusement from behind them. She wasn't wrong. The end of the snake was even more dangerous, now that it was thrashing about with a sharp blade on its end.

"Is it some kind of zombie?" Aris asked.

"Nah, it's just twitching. You got your experience, right?"

"I got a level," Aris admitted. "But it's still alive . . ."

"Nah." Kelsey looked thoughtfully at the writhing dagger-headed snake. "If you got your level, there shouldn't be any experience for me to steal . . . unless one of you is nursing a Snake-Butcher class."

"What would that even be?" Aris asked. Kelsey ignored her, stepping up to the snake. Her hand lashed out, grabbing the snake just below the dagger. The thrashing didn't stop, but the grabbed end was now perfectly still as if it had been trapped in a vice. Kelsey gave a pull, and the whole length of the snake came crashing down from the ceiling. It was the longest animal Aris had ever seen.

"What is going on?" Aris pleaded.

Kelsey pulled out the knife with her other hand and tossed it to Zaphar. The snake had started to wrap around her legs, but she didn't seem to care.

"Snakes are simple creatures," she said. "Brains are wasted on them, they barely need one to live."

Aris stared. "But it's their brain! How can they live without it?"

"They have a second one, farther down," Kelsey said. "This one's so long, it might have a third. The secondary brain can keep it moving, keep the heart going . . . which is alive *enough* that I can't just send it home."

She glowered at the snake.

"It'll run out of blood eventually, but . . . Tyla! Can you hear this guy's heartbeat?"

"If it is not moving, perhaps. And if everyone was quiet."

Holding it in place required that Anton join in to grab the other end. He and Kelsey stretched it between them, allowing Tyla to walk the length of the snake, listening intently.

Stretched out, Aris got a fresh impression of how large the thing was. About fifteen yards from head to tail, which was . . . huge.

"It has two hearts," Tyla announced. "That are beating, anyway."

"Just stab them," Kelsey said. "We don't have all day to wait for it to die."

Tyla nodded and made two precise cuts, slipping her dagger between the scales and pushing through the flesh underneath. The snake shuddered with each wound, but it didn't stop twitching.

"That should be enough," Kelsey said. "Let go, Anton."

Anton looked at her doubtfully but did as she said. As soon as he did, the body started lashing randomly about, but a moment later it disappeared.

"That was way more trouble than it was worth," Kelsey said. "Though I might get some nice snakeskin out of it. Do you need to finish up, Aris?"

"Huh? Oh yeah."

Her class was still waiting for her to assign her free points. It didn't take much consideration before she assigned them to Agility and Dexterity. She was, she had to admit, jealous of the way that Zaphar moved. Not that her current Abilities in those areas were anything to sneeze at, but she wanted more. She looked over her status with a sense of disbelief at how far she'd come.

Aris Lucina, Original Gunslinger (Level 9)
Overall Level: 14

Paths: Scullion/(Broken), Original Gunslinger
Strength: 9
Toughness: 12
Agility: 17
Dex: 17
Perception: 22
Will: 20
Charisma: 12
Traits:
Eye for Freshness
Heat Resistance
Sonic Resistance
Sure Shot
Trick Shot
Camouflaged Lurker

There was no trait for this level, but soon she would reach level ten of Gunslinger. That meant a capstone trait and after that . . . her Tier Three class.

"If you're done staring at your numbers," Anton teased her, "you killed the boss, so you get to open the chest."

Oh, right, the reward. Aris had become used to Kelsey providing for her every need. At the same time, she was not yet accustomed to the lifestyle that a lord's wife was entitled to. Tyla and Zaphar had been dutifully collecting the rewards, but Aris suspected it was only out of habit. Most of it ended up in Kelsey's bottomless storage.

On the boss's death, a part of the wall had rotated, revealing a passage beyond. Anton had to cut away some vines to gain access, but he'd done that while Aris was still looking at her status. The chest was supported on a pillar in the middle of the tunnel, at about chest height.

Aris opened the chest and took out a thin, flat, wooden box.

"Is this an item?" she asked.

"Open it," Anton said.

Inside was an elaborately crafted quill. Silver wire wound around a goose feather, ending in a carved silver tip.

"What on earth?" Aris wondered, picking the thing up. "I thought it would be—oh!"

The quill had trembled in her hand.

"It's magical," Anton said. "It's weak, but it's definitely enchanted."

"Here," Kelsey said, holding out a piece of paper backed by a thick wooden panel.

"Should I just—oh! Hold this over—oh!" Aris gasped as the quill jumped out of her hand and started writing her words on the paper. Ink was flowing out of the tip and her words, stumbling and confused as they were, were being transcribed.

"Does it work with anyone?" Kelsey said. The quill stayed still. She picked it up and said "Testing, testing."

The pen jumped up and wrote that.

"Right, so it works with whoever used it last," Kelsey said, watching her words get transcribed. "I wonder . . . Anton, did the records mention any magical quills coming out of this dungeon?"

"No," Anton said thoughtfully. "Armor and weapons, mostly. I couldn't say if there's never been a magical quill, but it's not common."

"Huh," Kelsey said. "I think we may have already affected the dungeon. I think she's trying to work out how to communicate."

"She did say something about how you used words to get people to help you," Tyla offered. "I suppose that she never had to think about that before?"

"Huh," Kelsey said. "Well, I could have told her that wouldn't work. *Aelisinne* might be able to get one of these to work, but a dungeon can't."

"Is that a solution, then?" Anton asked.

Kelsey shook her head. "Then you run into the problem where your fairy *won't* communicate."

She stared in a direction that no one happened to be. "That's when you learn that your fairy is there to *stop* you from communicating. To keep you silent. She may have raised you, but she's your jailor as much as she's anything else."

"I thought you liked Mel," Aris said.

Kelsey shook her head. "My relationship with Mel is too complex to fit into a word," she said. "Or an afternoon's dissertation. We've come up with an arrangement that lets us work together. We're like an old married couple in that way."

She shook her head again. "Anyway, this might make a nice gift for Suliel. Let's move on."

CHAPTER FORTY-SIX

Straight Out the Jungle

The first thing Anton noticed, when they entered the seventh floor, was the cold. The first few floors of the dungeon had been wet, ranging from water dripping down the walls to ponds from which sliggs could spring ambushes. As they got deeper, the caverns got warmer and the air became more humid. The tangle of vines and roots they'd been struggling through weren't exactly like a jungle—there were no leaves to catch the sunlight—but they were similar in many ways.

Now, they stood on a cliff's edge, with an icy wind blowing in their faces. The illumination of Aris's light-stone didn't go far enough for them to see anything other than darkness.

"Kelsey?" Anton asked.

Without saying a word, Kelsey flicked her device to a wider beam and shone it around. It was quite a sight.

This floor was a wide open cavern again, stretching further than Kelsey's light could reach. The ceiling was covered with roots, perhaps from the plants on the floor above. The floor was also draped with a carpet of thick vegetation. It was difficult to tell how thick it was.

Rising out of the jungle were several flat-topped buttes. They could see three from where they were, but Anton knew from reports that there were seven in total. They also featured thorny bushes and vines, but the coverage was much sparser than it was below.

"There's a key on top of each pillar," he told the others. "We have to collect all seven keys to open the boss chamber."

"A fetch quest, I hate it already," Kelsey said.

"Now that we're here . . ." Anton ran his gaze over the view. "I wonder if it might be best to split up."

Kelsey raised an eyebrow. "Is that considered best practice?" she asked.

"For Tier Three parties, yeah," Anton replied. "If each party member can take a mini-boss on their own, you can save a lot of time."

"We're *not* a Tier Three party, though," Aris said.

"Yeah, what I had in mind was a little different," Anton said. "You see, the quickest way to get to the keys is . . ."

He got Kelsey to shine her light on the cliff face below them. Eventually, he found it: a cluster of vines growing out of the cliff about five yards down that stretched towards the nearest plateau. Kelsey traced its path as far as she could, making it clear that it went all the way across.

You could consider the vines a bridge. To Anton it looked more like a death trap that you had to volunteer for, but the notes said that the vines would hold. Safety was an entirely different matter.

"There are bridges like that connecting all the pillars," he said. "They're not easy to cross, though, so I was thinking that Zaphar and I would take care of all the keys while the rest of you made your way through the jungle and met us at the center—where the boss chamber is."

"Did you say something about mini-bosses?" Zaphar said warily.

"They're only level fifteen, you should be able to take them," Anton said. "If you can't, that's why I'm coming."

"I don't much like the idea of climbing along that," Aris said.

"It's trickier than it looks," Anton agreed. "There are ice patches and a few other dangers."

"Are you gonna be all right on your own?" Kelsey asked.

"I'll be fine," Anton said. "*Unwavering* has dealt with worse. You won't even be that far away. Given that you'll be lit up, I might be able to keep you in sight most of the time."

"Fair enough," Kelsey said. She turned to the other two. "You up for a girls' only dungeon crawl?"

"I suppose," Aris said.

Anton kept his fears to himself as he watched the girls make their way down the cliff. It was steep, and tall, but there were plenty of handholds, and Kelsey had gone down first to catch them. Catch Aris, really—Tyla had swarmed down the rock face as though she did it every day.

There were dangers down there, but nothing that they couldn't handle. It was mostly the same monsters, with some ice-based variants. Nothing that needed a solution more elaborate than "shoot it." The real dangers were on the upper levels.

"You said there was ice? Ice patches?" Zaphar said, gingerly making his way down the cliff. Like Anton, he had *Spider Climb*, so his feet and hands simply stuck to any surface whenever he wanted to. It still looked as if he was climbing, but only because walking down the sheer face would have been awkward.

"Yeah. It shouldn't be any problem for us, though," Anton said. He started making his own way down. "It's slippery and can chill your hands if you're holding on, but we should be fine. Oh, but keep an eye out for snakes."

They made it to the top without any issues, passing easily through the one ice trap on the way. They were as sudden and mysterious as the notes had described, a small patch of lower temperature, cold enough to put a layer of ice on the vine, existing for no reason that Anton could see.

Magic, he decided. The dungeon didn't need a reason, other than dislodging unwary trespassers.

The top of the pillar was sparsely covered by thorny bushes. They would have lacerated the skin of anyone without armor, but even the flexible sligg-skin pants that Zaphar was wearing were enough to protect him. Now that they were here, they could see that the top was shaped like a huge bowl. Cold air wafted up from further down.

Anton let Zaphar lead the way. They encountered just one monster on the way in, a frozen vinelurker with blue skin that burst out of a bush only to be skewered on Zaphar's dagger.

Zaphar cursed when they got to the center. The ground dipped more steeply, culminating in a vertical drop of about a yard, ending in a pool of icy water. Out of the middle of the pool, a thin column of rock rose, supporting a stone chest.

Above the pool, bridging the gap between the edge of the drop and the column, was a latticework of ice.

"That isn't strong enough to hold me," Zaphar stated.

"The notes say that it is," Anton replied. "As long as you're careful, and don't make any sudden moves."

Zaphar stared at him. "Why would I make sudden moves?" he asked suspiciously.

"Because you'll be fighting a Frostbite Reaver," Anton said. His attention was on the pond, looking for signs of where the thing was.

"One of those big sliggs?" Zaphar asked. He grimaced. "It's in the pond, isn't it?"

"Maybe," Anton said. "I don't see it. Maybe you can sneak across while it's hidden."

Zaphar studied the ice lattice and pool beneath it. "No such luck," he stated, pointing out a figure climbing out of the water below.

Anton would have whistled, but you didn't do things like that when you were delving. The sligg that climbed out of the pool was larger than any they'd seen so far, and its blue-white, translucent skin was excellent camouflage against the ice.

"You might be better at this than you think," he told Zaphar. "Dodging seems like it would be the way to go. You need firm footing to parry."

"You—you need sound footing to dodge!" Zaphar retorted.

"You out-level it," Anton said. He tried to maintain a tone of reasonableness. "You're faster than it is. You may not be stronger, but you've got daggers."

"It can go in the water with—without issue," Zaphar spat. "*I* can't."

"If you fall in, I'll kill it and pull you out," Anton promised. He patted the coil of rope at his side. An adventurer was always prepared. "Don't fall in, though."

"Like I want to," Zaphar muttered. He drew his knives and crept forward.

Anton had seen Zaphar practicing with his daggers, but he'd never really had the chance to evaluate the man when he was fighting for real. On the previous floors, Anton had been too busy looking out for Aris to pay close attention to how Zaphar fought.

To put it bluntly, he wasn't very good. Daggers were not Anton's chosen weapon, but he'd been drilled in their use. His parents had wanted him to know the strengths and weaknesses of each weapon and had pointed out that you never knew what weapon you would be forced to take up in an emergency.

Zaphar had not been drilled. He'd picked up a few tricks on the streets; he was at least holding it correctly. But his line was off, he was dropping the point too much, and he wasn't able to put his weight behind his thrusts.

He was *really* good at dodging, though. Anton didn't think he could match him, not without using *Uncanny Dodge*. Even on the treacherous footing of the ice lattice, Zaphar wove about, avoiding the sligg's claws easily.

But then, that was *why* Anton had *Uncanny Dodge*. That was Zaphar's problem—he didn't have any good attack traits. Anton thought he saw *Feint* being used, but that wasn't strong on its own. It almost guaranteed a hit for your next strike, but it needed to be chained to a decently strong attack.

Anton resolved to get Zaphar a rapier at the next opportunity.

For now, though, Zaphar was doing all right. The Reaver wasn't attacking with any great skill and was already sporting some small cuts from Zaphar's glancing attacks. However, Zaphar was getting tired and the monster wouldn't . . .

Anton blinked. He was too used to fighting undead. The monsters here *did* get tired. He could see it happening in front of him.

Well, I guess it remains even then, he thought. Zaphar *Feinted* again, and came in for a slash. The Reaver was off balance, but he . . .

Breathed out a cloud of freezing mist. Zaphar aborted his attack and dived out of the way. The ice cracked where he landed, but he kept moving, sliding forward onto safer ground.

The Reaver didn't follow him onto the weakened ice, but howled furiously. Anton could see flakes of ice falling off Zaphar's arm. The icy breath had instantly covered it with a thin layer of ice. Anton could only imagine how cold Zaphar must be feeling.

Standing on the edge of the battle, Anton felt a little extra chill. The cold was spreading, and it was more intense where Zaphar was standing. Anton could see his breath beginning to mist up.

Zaphar wasn't going to retreat. As he stood on the edge, he was mapping out a route across the ice, gauging the strength and soundness of the way forward. The Reaver bellowed a challenge, but kept its position between Zaphar and the prize.

This time, Zaphar didn't move cautiously. He dashed across the ice, his feet firmly placed exactly where he wanted them. He didn't move in a straight line, but it made little difference to the Reaver, who stoically met his charge. At the last second, as Zaphar's dagger was rising to strike, the Reaver breathed again—and Zaphar dropped to the ground.

Anton hadn't noticed, but the Reaver had chosen to stand on a flat patch of ice. Anton wasn't sure why—the Reaver moved as easily on the ice as Zaphar did—but level ground was the easiest to fight on. Now, Zaphar used that against it, as he dived under the icy breath and let himself slide right past the confused sligg. But that wasn't all.

As he slid past, Zaphar's dagger flashed, and the Reaver howled in pain. Even as it whirled around to strike him, its leg collapsed from under it. Zaphar had hamstrung the brute. It roared its outrage and pounded on the ice.

Anton thought it was just frustration, but it was an attack just as deadly as its breath. The ice splintered under its fist, cracks spreading as the entire lattice started to collapse.

Zaphar must have heard the cracking, but he hadn't looked back since tumbling to his feet. Even as the Reaver's fists pounded the ice, Zaphar was running for the pillar. It was the right move. He reached the chest, just as half of the lattice collapsed with a splintering crash, sending the Reaver into the pond.

For just a moment, it felt as if everything was still and quiet. It wasn't—the waters beneath roiled with the impact of all the ice, and Zaphar was breathing heavily as he held on to the chest. Then he opened it, taking out a handful of gold and a small, strangely shaped black stone.

Stowing his reward in a pouch, Zaphar carefully walked across the remains of the lattice and around the edge to where Anton waited.

Anton looked down at the pool. "You know, you won't get the full experience reward unless you finish it off," he said.

Zaphar glared at him, and then at the pond. "I'm fine with missing out," he said.

CHAPTER FORTY-SEVEN

On and On

ARIS

Aris's heart surged with relief when Anton and Zaphar staggered out of the darkness and into the ring of illumination from her light-stone. Well, Anton was moving normally, but Zaphar was staggering enough for the both of them.

"You're back!" she exclaimed.

"I *told* you," Kelsey said. "There's nothing on this floor that can threaten Anton."

"Anyone can die on any level of a dungeon, if they don't stay alert," Anton said. He embraced Aris and she leaned into his warmth.

"Also! Also, I am right here and *I am not Anton*!" Zaphar complained, glaring at Kelsey. "There is so, so, much that can threaten *me*!"

"You did fine, Zaphar," Anton said, his voice rumbling through Aris. "I didn't have to step in once."

"I wish you had, you monster! I begged you to!" Zaphar railed. "It hurt so much!"

"You look fine, though?" Aris said questioningly. While there were some holes in Zaphar's armor, she couldn't see any blood.

"He needed to take a healing potion," Anton confided. Aris winced.

"It hurt, so, so much," Zaphar whined.

But you're here now!" Kelsey declared. "You did collect all the keys, right? Are you ready for the floor boss?"

Zaphar groaned. "I've *been* fighting bosses. Nothing but bosses. And still no level."

"They were all under your level," Anton told him. "You got more than I would have, but not that much."

"The next floor . . ." Aris said. Anton nodded.

"The next floor you'll be fighting at-level or above," he said. "We'll clear it out for the maximum gain. That's where it will get tough."

He held out a handful of oddly shaped pieces. "Did you want to do the honors?"

Aris shook her head. "It sounds like Zaphar did the work collecting them," she said.

"I don't want to see, touch, hear, or feel them again," Zaphar groaned.

"I would be honored," Tyla said. "Is it some kind of puzzle?"

"They're keys," Anton said. "They go in a lock."

He jerked his thumb back in the direction he had come. "We actually ran into it on the way here," he said. Of course, there was nothing but darkness in that direction.

"The hill?" Kelsey asked. "We ran into that when we were clearing the area."

"Did we?" Aris asked. "I don't remember a hill."

"We didn't climb it, but it was there," Kelsey assured her. "I should have known it was significant by the lack of monsters near it."

"There should be a stone slab clear of the vines," Anton said. "If you didn't see it, we'll need to search."

They did search, but it wasn't hard to find. At least it wasn't for those who could see in the dark. For Aris, stumbling over roots with her light, the first sign of it was when they had already stopped.

The slab of stone was there, with seven indentations. Anton gestured for Tyla to place the key stones. It took her a few moments of fumbling to find which stone went in which hole, but she soon worked out where each of them had to go. When she pressed the final key into place, there was a moment where nothing happened. Then—

A rumble rolled through the cavern, deep and resonant, like the growl of some great beast waking from its slumber. Aris stiffened, fingers tightening around her light-stone. The warm, steady glow barely pushed back the darkness, illuminating only a five-meter bubble around her—just enough to see the rough stone beneath her boots and the creeping roots that slithered over its surface.

"Well, that did something," she muttered, stepping back as a tremor shook the ground. "What's happening?"

To her left, Anton adjusted his grip on his sword, eyes scanning the darkness beyond her light. "The whole hill is shifting. There's something . . . peeling away."

Kelsey made an irritated noise. "Oh, fantastic. Collapsing floor? Rising walls? Someone please tell me it's not a pit of writhing horrors."

A sharp crack echoed from beneath them, and suddenly, light burst from the altar—not warm like her light-stone, but cold, eerie, and wrong. Pale blue lines, like veins of trapped lightning, crawled across the rock, tracing out long-dead symbols.

Then came the *crack* of rock splitting.

The rock around them tore open with the slow, grinding protest of stone giving way to some unseen force. Aris caught glimpses—jagged cracks widening into yawning fissures, roots snapping like tendons, something massive shifting in the unseen depths.

Zaphar's voice came from beyond the light. "The walls—the walls are moving!"

Aris exhaled sharply, willing her heart to slow. "Someone please explain what is happening!"

A new sound joined the shifting stone—a wet, organic slither. The sensation of something uncoiling in the dark, vast and ancient, sent an unwelcome shiver down her spine.

Anton let out a quiet breath. "The cavern is opening up. There's a platform inside . . . a big one. There's something sitting on it."

Aris swallowed, gripping her revolver. The light-stone in her palm felt pitifully small against the crushing weight of the unknown pressing in. She couldn't see it—not yet. But she could hear it.

And worse, she could feel it watching her.

Kelsey's voice carried a grim edge. "There sure is. Let's light it up."

She clicked her torch on and a beam of light shone out, illuminating the boss of the floor.

Aris had grown up in a port town. She'd seen the tentacled horrors that kabimen would bring in from the depths. This was like those, only larger and more plant-like. Aris wasn't sure if it *was* a plant.

It did not move like one. Long, thick tentacles branched out from a central trunk, covered with thorns, and *writhing*.

"I don't know if this is going to be a good match-up for Aris," Kelsey said thoughtfully. "Bullets aren't *great* against plants."

"Give it a try," Anton suggested. Aris shrugged and brought her pistol up. The range was a bit long, but it was a big target. *Sure Shot* aligned her pistol to target the center of the writhing mass.

The gun boomed. Aris couldn't see a visible effect, but there was an immediate change.

The monster *screamed*. Loud enough to cause damage. It didn't affect three of the group, but Zaphar and Tyla curled up, pressing the mundane hearing protection that Kelsey had provided closer to their ears.

"I don't think it *liked* it," Kelsey said once the screaming had stopped. "But it doesn't seem unduly affected."

"That—that was loud," Zaphar stammered. "Much louder than the gunfire."

"Oh!" Tyla said. "I just realized I can use magic to make myself not hear. That seems like a good idea."

"That's fine, honey," Kelsey said. "Just wait until we've worked out a plan before you do."

"I can shoot it some more?" Aris said doubtfully. "It seems safe, aside from the noise, and Kelsey isn't going to run out of bullets."

"I feel that you're abusing the revolutionary industrial paradigm I'm bringing to the table here," Kelsey complained. "But sure, fill the thing full of lead."

"I might have a better way," Tyla said. "Destroying plants is easier than destroying . . . most things. I can kill it with a spell. But . . . I will have to touch it."

"That sounds like a terrible idea," Aris said. "Those tentacles look *dangerous*."

"Invisibility doesn't work on it, and it's very accurate with those tentacles," Anton said. "That was in the notes."

"If it's a plant, it won't have eyes," Kelsey mused. "It must be targeting based on vibrations in the ground."

"Like a spider on its web?" Tyla asked. "I can step lightly, but not lightly enough. We could throw rocks to distract it, or . . ."

She paused in thought. "Lady Aris, if you could shoot the ground, away from my approach, I believe that would cover the vibrations of my movement."

"Um, I guess I can do that," Aris agreed.

"Hold on, what about me?" Zaphar asked.

Tyla frowned. "I don't think your daggers are the optimal weapon in this case," she said.

"No, no, I mean when you start hurting it, it's gonna scream, right? You've got your spell, all I got is these weird earmuffs."

"You don't have to use them if you don't want to," Kelsey huffed. "I won't get *offended*."

Zaphar glared at her. "You're not, not even resistant to the sound, are you?" he asked. "You just don't *feel pain*."

"Guilty!" Kelsey said. "And yeah, I suppose these things are for preventing hearing loss from long-term exposure, *not* for preventing damage from magical plant beasts."

"I can cast the spell on you as well," Tyla said. "It will not last long, only a few minutes."

"You had better move—move fast, then," Zaphar said. "'Cause I don't think it will die easy."

Tyla nodded and put her hand on the man's forehead.

"How will I—oh. Can the rest of you hear me?" Zaphar asked.

Aris nodded, as Tyla didn't wait for a response. She turned and moved silently towards the boss, coming in at an angle to avoid Kelsey's light beam and also, Aris belatedly realized, the covering fire that she was supposed to be providing.

She quickly raised her gun and took a shot at the ground near the monster's trunk. The tentacles snapped in close, defending the body. Aris took another shot farther away.

She kept firing at a slow, steady pace as Tyla drew near. Kelsey provided reloading services, taking the gun off her when it was empty and replacing it with a full one. Soon, Tyla was within reach of the monster.

With just a touch, one of the tentacles started crumbling into dust.

The monster screamed again and lashed out with its remaining limbs, but Tyla had already jumped back. Aris put another shot on the other side of the boss. Two tentacles slammed down where the shot had hit, and Tyla jumped in for another touch.

With two tentacles gone, the screaming was unending, and the monster no longer reacted to her shots. It just flailed around wildly in all directions. Aris considered attacking the center, but before she could, Tyla dashed in for another attack.

She reached out again. This time, though, the thorny tentacle was moving, striking out at anything that might be within reach. It died even as it touched her, but Aris could see the impact fling Tyla's arm out to the side. Something dark glittered in the air. Two more limbs swung in to attack. Tyla dodged, but not well enough.

One of the tentacles hit her, sending her sprawling away from the monster. That limb died, too, but the damage had been done.

"Tyla!" Aris yelled, but the elf couldn't hear her. Anton ran forward to see if she was okay, while the three remaining tentacles lashed and whirled about.

Aris could see the monster's mouth now. Not that a plant should have a mouth, but it was there, flesh-like lips drawn back to reveal jagged teeth. It seemed as good a target as any.

Anton was keeping out of her line of fire, so she poured all six shots into the creature's mouth. There was something vital in there. It had already been screaming, but now the pitch rose, before the scream was choked off as it lost control of whatever it was that Aris was shooting.

She changed guns again and moved forward, seeking a better shot. Anton was feeding Tyla a healing potion. The creature was just hissing now, its limbs limp. It was still making noise, though, so Aris shot it some more, walking the fire down the trunk from its mouth.

Finally, *finally*, it died. Aris might have doubted the death if the chest hadn't risen from the platform.

"Nice work!" Kelsey said from behind her. "Time to loot!"

The chest was quite large, the stone lid too heavy for Aris to lift until Kelsey gave her a hand. The reason it was so big was the sword it contained. The small pile of gold that accompanied it looked lost in the massive container.

Kelsey examined the rapier that Aris pulled out. Her eye caught on the green leather wrapped around the hilt.

"I think this one's for Zaphar," she said.

"I was just thinking we should get him a rapier," Anton said. He was helping Tyla walk as she shook off the effects of the potion. Everyone turned to look at Zaphar.

"What? What?" Zaphar said. Tyla waved her hand in his direction.

"Oh! I can hear again. Why are you all looking at me?"

"We were just thinking that you should upgrade to a rapier," Kelsey said.

Zaphar frowned. "Why? Why? Daggers are great, you can hide them."

"You can keep the daggers," Kelsey assured him. "But a rapier is the weapon of a gentleman, and that's the direction you're headed."

Zaphar scowled, but he didn't contradict her. "Is it magical?" he asked.

"It is," Anton answered. "Tier Two, I can tell that much."

"What does it do?" Zaphar asked.

"I'm not sure," Kelsey admitted. "Destroys . . . magic, but it's too weak to break spells . . . let me try something."

She took the sword off Aris and made it disappear.

"Huh," she said a moment later. "It's *slightly* more effective at killing skeletons—it can slice through the magic that holds them together. That can't be its main purpose, though. Hang on."

There was another pause as they all stood around awkwardly.

"Ah." Kelsey made the rapier appear again and handed it to Zaphar. "It cuts ghosts. It cuts other things as well, of course, but cutting ghosts is what makes it special."

"Ghosts?" Zaphar said, looking skeptically at the sword. "Do . . . do we fight ghosts?"

"*I've* got some," Kelsey said. "They don't seem like this place's *thing*, admittedly. But I've got a feeling that it will come in handy."

"For ghosts?" Zaphar repeated.

"Maaaybee," Kelsey said. "I can't test it, but I think it could cut *any* magically immaterial being. Useful against shadow-walking assassins . . . and other things."

CHAPTER FORTY-EIGHT

It's Catching Up

Aris didn't get a level from the floor boss, but they hadn't been on the eighth floor for very long when she made a pleased sound after shooting a Frigid Stalker.

"I did it!" she crowed. "The peak of second tier!"

Anton gave her a moment to assign her abilities.

"What's the capstone trait?" he asked. He used *Delver's Discernment* to see her stats.

Aris Lucina, Level 15, Human, Original Gunslinger, Scullion/(Broken), Original Gunslinger, S: 9 T: 13 A: 19 D: 19 P: 23 W: 21 C: 12

That was . . . impressive. At the rate her Agility and Dexterity were shooting up, she'd overtake Zaphar in no time. Although that did depend on her next class . . .

She frowned. "I'm not sure what to make of all these. I've got *Instant Reload, Ice Shot, Last Word,* and *Deadly Shot* to choose from. The first of those seems simple enough, but the rest . . . Why would I need *Deadly Shot?* Aren't my bullets deadly enough already?"

"Not against high tiers," Anton told her. "*Deadly Shot* sounds like *Deadly Strike,* the trait that Kelsey is expecting me to get. It's more likely to kill tougher people and it burns through traits like the one that kept al-Kadir alive before."

"Yeah! Get that one, teach that guy a lesson next time," Kelsey said.

"*Ice Shot* sounds like it imbues your bullets with magical energy," Anton continued. "In this case, ice. You don't normally get traits like that until Tier Three."

"Is that because of . . . where we are?" Aris asked, looking around at the ice-lined walls. On this floor, the overgrown caverns had been replaced by icy tunnels. The walls were made of a blue-white translucent stone, which made it hard to tell where they started and the ice began.

"Maybe," Anton said. "Or it could be because our time in Elitra was so hot. It's based on your entire experience, not just the last level."

"What about *Last Word?*" Kelsey asked. "It sounds ominous. In a good way."

Anton frowned. "If it were *Last Shot*, I'd think it was something like *Final Strike*, which I wouldn't recommend. I don't want you to trade your life for anything."

"But it's last *word,* which . . . the class doesn't seem to be about talking," Aris said.

"Intimidation is a *form* of talking," Kelsey pointed out.

"Try thinking about it," Anton said. "Your class is a part of you, and you can often get some clues about the intention if you imagine using the skill."

Aris looked at him doubtfully, but furrowed her brow in concentration.

"I think . . ." she said after a while. "I *feel* that it's about when the conversation stops. Or stopping the conversation. The last word said is . . . something."

"I think I get it," Kelsey said. "The conversation stops when the shooting starts, so the last word is the first *shot.*"

"So it's about firing faster?" Anton asked. "I don't know if that's good enough to be a capstone trait."

"Not *just* faster—first," Kelsey said. Her gaze drifted away, looking at something only she could see. "It's part of the legend of the gunfighter, you know? Facing his enemy at high noon, telling him to draw first . . . and only when the guy's gun clears his holster does the gunfighter pull his own gun out and fire . . . but he still fires first."

"That still just sounds like a fast-drawing skill," Anton said.

"It's got to be more than that, with a name like *Last Word,*" Kelsey countered. "But I think you should take *Deadly Shot.*"

"We've had exactly one enemy who needed that trait," Anton said. "*Instant Reload* is a lot more useful."

"We *have* had more than the one time where we've faced more than twelve enemies," Kelsey admitted. "But, going forward, I think we'll be facing a lot more al-Kadirs than scrubs."

Aris stared at them both with a glum expression on her face. "But which one should I take?" she asked.

Anton and Kelsey looked at each other. They were about to continue the argument when Kelsey sighed and held up a hand.

"We can advise, Aris, but the decision has to be yours. Think about what calls to you, what you need, and something should just *click*."

Aris thought about it. "I do feel something . . ." she said. "Maybe it's just because I felt for it before, but I feel . . . a connection with *Last Word*."

"Go for it," Kelsey said. Aris looked at Anton, who shrugged.

"It's probably more than just a fast-draw skill," he said. "Capstones are normally pretty good, regardless."

"All right," Aris said. There was a short pause as she selected it.

"Can you feel what it does?" Kelsey asked.

"I feel . . . that it's *available*," Aris said slowly. "It's like . . . having the confidence to know that if something bad happens, I can stop it."

"Something bad . . ." Kelsey mused. "Zaphar! We need you to take the next hit, see if Aris can stop it."

"Let's not do that," Anton said quickly, before Zaphar could protest. "An appropriate situation is bound to come up at some point. No need to rush it."

"Oh, all right," Kelsey grumbled. "Let's get going then."

This floor was a little less claustrophobic than the previous floors. The ground—or ice—was smooth underneath their feet, if a little slippery. Anton was glad that *Spider Climb* kept his footing stable. Kelsey and Aris had a little trouble with the floors, but neither of them needed to move quickly. Tyla was the most disadvantaged, at least until she switched back to her bow.

That left Zaphar alone at the front, with Anton right behind him in case he got into trouble. They still left the fighting to Aris and Tyla, which meant Zaphar was constantly jogging back to get himself out of the line of fire when he found a new monster.

On this floor, the tunnels were straighter and not at all clogged with writhing plant life, so it was easier to attack at range. The light was better as well. The tunnel walls seemed to catch the illumination of Aris's light-stone and reflect it far ahead of them. Everywhere that Kelsey shone her torch glittered as if it were made of diamonds.

The first sign that this floor held more than Frigid Stalkers came when Anton felt something wrap around his leg. Looking down, he saw a gleaming white vine extending out of—and *through*—the ice. Wicked-looking thorns suggested it didn't intend to stay gleaming, but its fangs were no match for Anton's armor.

"Watch out for vines!" he called, bringing his sword down and severing the frosty tendril with one blow. He moved quickly to protect Aris, but Kelsey had already grabbed the two vines that came out near them. They had wrapped around her hands and arms, the thorns piercing her skin, but she seemed unbothered, taking the time to look closely at the plants she captured.

Then she closed her hands and crushed the life out of them.

"Interesting," she said. "I had no idea there was this much variety in ice-themed plants."

"Sorry! Sorry!" Zaphar called back. He was having more trouble with his attackers. His dagger was an appropriate weapon to use against them, but he wasn't strong enough to slice through in one cut. "I couldn't stop them, they move through the ice!"

Nothing but dust remained of the ones that had attacked Tyla. Now, she moved to assist Zaphar. Moving as gracefully as someone could over ice, she slid over to him and laid her hand on the vine that was wrapped around his leg. It disintegrated into dust.

"Ah! I gained a level!" she exclaimed.

They paused to let her choose her abilities. Since this was an odd level for her, she didn't get to choose a trait. Anton spared a glance at her when she was done.

Tyla of the Padascar Tribe, Level 15, Elf, Dungeon Witch, Padascar Hunter (Broken)/Doxy (Broken)/Apprentice Dungeon Witch/ Dungeon Witch, S: 12 T: 9 A: 14 D: 20 P: 22 W: 17 C: 12

Even though she was the same level as Aris, Tyla had taken a much more winding path to get there. While Aris was finishing her second class, Tyla was just starting on her *fourth*.

Before they moved on, Anton checked on Kelsey. "Are you all right?" he asked. "Those vines looked like they hurt you badly."

"It's fine," Kelsey said, holding her arms up to show him. They were unmarked. "They did some damage, but nothing I couldn't heal."

"All right then," Anton said, and they moved on.

After a few fights, they came to the first chasm. Sheer cliffs descended into the darkness and rose up just as high. Aside from climbing to the bottom, there was just one way across—a narrow ice bridge extending from under their feet to a black cave on the other side.

"This should be easy enough," Anton said. "We're a good match for this bit."

"What are you talking about?" Aris asked shrilly. "That's a big problem!" she exclaimed, pointing at the bridge. "It's so narrow and it's *made of ice*!"

"We'll get to that, but first things first," Anton assured her. "Zaphar, are you ready to go out on the bridge and play bait?"

"Wait, wait, what what? I am most definitely not! Why would I?"

Anton pointed to the empty air above the bridge. "We can get across it, but first we have to take care of the ice drakes. On this floor, they're quite small, but they'll be swooping on us from all directions. You'll go out and attract their attention while the girls finish them off with ranged attacks. Don't worry, I'll tether us together with a rope, so if you dodge off the bridge you won't fall far."

Zaphar looked dubiously over the edge. "Not far might be quite far enough," he said. "But you have *Spider Climb* as well. Why do you not do it?"

"Two reasons," Anton said. "This is contributing to the fight, so you should get some experience. It'll be reduced, but only by a half or a quarter. For me, it will be reduced by much more."

"One sixteenth or one thirty-second," Kelsey put in.

"And the second reason," Anton continued, "is that if you fall, I can support your weight. Can you support mine?"

Zaphar looked at Anton. He looked over the cliff again. He looked at the rope. His face screwed up into a grimace.

"Fine, fine," he said. "Tie me up."

Kelsey thought the ice drakes were pretty. Anton supposed that there was a certain grace to how they swooped through the air. They weren't made of ice, but their blue-white scales glittered like ice would. Graceful or not, Anton preferred it when their swooping arcs ended with a bullet from Aris or an arrow from Tyla. Zaphar had also made his preferences known.

"Oh gods, can't you shoot it? Shoot it now, it's right there!" he called. Every now and then one got through the barrage and Zaphar was forced to dodge until it was taken care of. Stabbing one himself would have risked being knocked off the bridge.

Eventually, the attacks stopped and it was time to cross the bridge. Anton explained the plan.

"Won't it crack, if we're all on it?" Aris asked.

"It's strong enough, even if we all jumped on it," Kelsey said. "It looks like ice but there's dungeon stone underneath."

"It's never broken in all the accounts," Anton agreed. "Zaphar and I will be fixed points, we'll stretch the rope tight between us, and you'll all hold onto the rope."

"I'm not sure . . ." Aris said. She looked down into the darkness below.

"You can hold on to me, then," Anton offered. Aris perked up.

"That sounds much . . . safer," she said.

Without any drakes divebombing them, they made it across the bridge safely.

"Thank the gods that is over," Zaphar said.

"Oh," Anton said. "Do you want the bad news now?"

"What? What bad news?" Zaphar asked suspiciously.

"We'll need to cross three more chasms on this floor," Anton told him. "Four if we get lost."

CHAPTER FORTY-NINE

The Safety Dance

TYLA

You should have this."

The words broke Tyla's concentration and she looked away from the body of the Frostwyrm. The corpse was now *warming*, which seemed an odd thing to say about a corpse. It was odd, too, to think of this room as warm. It wasn't, but the Frostwyrm had been colder still. Cold enough for Tyla to feel it past the potion they had all taken to ward off the chill of these levels.

Looking at the source of the words, Tyla saw that Kelsey was offering her a blue and silver cloak. Tyla reached out to grasp it. Just before she did, her fingers felt a brief chill, which evaporated as soon as she grasped the fabric. Magic, of course. The cloak must be the reward for clearing this floor.

"Why me?" Tyla asked. She looked closely at the cloak with her *Sense Magic*. She didn't have the trait that let her identify enchantments, but she could tell what types of magic it held: Control, Fire, and Water.

"Anton identified it as having a *Frozen Step* effect," Kelsey said. "We tested it, and it stops you slipping on ice."

"That *is* useful . . ." Tyla said. She glanced at Aris, the person in the party most prone to slipping.

"Oh, Aris can *use* it," Kelsey agreed. "But you can *learn* from it. I know you're having trouble with a spell to do the same thing."

"Ah, I see," Tyla agreed. Trouble was one way to say it. Another was that she hadn't the faintest clue about how to go about it. Ice was a little tricky when it came to magic. It was frozen water, so Water mana applied to it, but it was also cold, which meant Fire mana also applied. Knowing *which* applied *when* was tricky, especially when she was operating almost entirely on instinct.

Not wanting to delay the revelation, she put the cloak on and took a step. The floor of the boss chamber was mostly flat, aside from the parts that had been torn up by the Frostwyrm, but it was still ice, still slippery.

Her step was firmly planted, though, as was the next. It was as if she was walking on rock. Tyla watched what it was doing. Control and Fire mana suffused her entire body—that must explain the warmth she was feeling. The cloak itself was also imbued with water, which must be a third, weaker magical effect. Tyla suspected that it was the same as the one on her bow, which protected it from damp.

On her feet, though, was Water mana. Tyla took another step. It was . . . *freezing* the ice underfoot? Not freezing, exactly, since no heat was involved. The magic was simply turning water into ice.

Tyla hadn't known that Control could change water into ice. She had thought that would come under Change—and she didn't have any ability with Change. But a bigger question was . . .

"What water?" she said aloud.

"Hmm?" Kelsey asked.

"It's turning water into ice, but what water?" Tyla asked. "Numen," she added belatedly, remembering her manners. Kelsey didn't seem to mind, or even notice, but she needed to show her respect for the being that had saved her.

"Oh, is that what's happening?" Kelsey cocked her head to the side, thinking. "Ice isn't something I've worked with much, but I remember that it's always covered by a thin layer of semi-water."

"Semi . . . water?" Tyla repeated.

"It's sort of in-between," Kelsey explained. "That's why ice is slippery and the pressure and heat of your foot melts a little more and makes it *more* slippery!"

"So by freezing that thin layer . . ." Tyla mused.

"You solve your slipping problem!"

"Then I just have to . . . can you give me some water?"

The numen handed Tyla a cup of water without comment. She had been carrying all their nonessential supplies for this delve, so it wasn't the first time a request like that had been made. Tyla looked at the water. It was cold enough that it would soon freeze on its own, but she could . . .

With a flex of Control Water magic, she changed its state. With another, she changed it back again.

That's not enough, she thought. *I need to wrap it around the subject's feet, include a duration . . .*

"May I test it on you, numen?" she asked.

"The name's Kelsey, but sure," the numen said and held out her hand. Magic could be done at range, but it was easier if you were touching the target. Tyla drew on the mana of the Core she carried and wove it how she thought she needed to. The weave snapped into place, and Kelsey tried a few exploratory steps.

"It works!" she said with a grin. "How long will it last?"

"I'm not sure," Tyla admitted. "A while . . . perhaps six hours?"

"We'll time it, get some numbers for you," Kelsey promised. She called over to the rest of the team. "Hey, we've got something for the slip and slide!"

"A spell for Aris?" Lord Anton asked. He was indeed wise if he could get that from the strange phrase Kelsey had used. "That's great! The next floor was going to be difficult without it."

"It's not more chasm bridges, is it?" Zapahar asked. "I don't, I *don't* want to go over any more rickety ice death traps."

"Well . . ." Lord Anton temporized. "We don't have to *cross* any ice chasms."

They stared into the howling void. An icy wind tore past their faces. It was *probably* not strong enough to rip them off their feet and pull them into the darkness. Probably.

Kelsey shone her torch directly ahead of them. It illuminated some mist and small particles of ice, driven past them by the wind, but it couldn't reach the wall on the other side.

"This is crazy! Madness!" Zaphar shouted.

"This is actually one of the more popular floors!" Lord Anton yelled back. "We have to go down the cliff! We get out at the bottom!"

Kelsey braved the winds and stuck her head out of the tunnel.

"There's a path!" she reported loudly. "Looks like a death trap!"

She gestured for them to go back down the tunnel. About ten yards back, it became possible to hear one another without shouting.

"What's the plan?" she asked Lord Anton.

"About the same as before," Anton said, pulling out his rope. "The difference is we tie ourselves together with the rope. We'll all be fighting and we won't be able to hold on to it."

"I can't—I can't dodge when I'm tied to a rope."

"I'm surprised you think you can dodge when you're clinging to an ice ledge," Kelsey said. "Surprised and impressed!"

Zaphar glared at her. "*Why*? Why is it one of the most popular floors?"

"It's lucrative," Anton explained. "Most of the cliff face is covered in frost-silk. That's the stuff Tyla's new cloak is made of, and it's pretty popular for high-tier nobles' clothing."

Zaphar's eyes narrowed. "What makes frost-silk?"

Anton shrugged. "Ice-spiders. Frostbite Crawlers, Shardfang Weavers, Chillfang Broodguards . . . some others. They're all over the cliff face."

"I bet they're pretty big if they're Tier Three!" Kelsey said enthusiastically.

"Dog sized or bigger," Anton agreed.

"Poisonous?" Kelsey asked.

"Frostbite. Ices up your blood," Anton said. "Our antivenom potions will work on it, but get one down as soon as possible because the more time it has to work, the worse the damage. Too long and you'll need to take a potion."

Zaphar groaned. "Why is this my life?" he asked rhetorically. Anton clapped him on the shoulder.

"Cheer up!" he said. "You're finally going up against monsters a higher level than you. You'll finally be getting decent experience!"

The experience *was* far greater than before. That just meant the challenge was more severe. They had reached the point where it would be almost impossible to continue without magical aid. Potions negated the cold, and her spell glued them to the wall, reducing the difficulty of the climb and rendering the howling wind impotent.

There were still dangers. Collapsing ice ledges, either underfoot or above them. Sticky threads of frost-silk, indistinguishable from ice until you became entangled in them. And the monsters, of course.

This was the first level where Lord Anton fought as many monsters as they did. Not because they were finally providing him with "decent experience," but because the spiders attacked from every direction. From the front, behind, above or below, it made no difference to the gelid arachnids.

The crack of Lady Aris's weapon marked the demise of another spider. Tyla heard the corpse tumble down behind her, along with some ice fragments. She didn't look, not least because the flash of the gun would spoil her night vision. She kept an alert vigil on the cliff face below them.

A spider crawled into her line of sight. White-furred, it was almost invisible against the ice. Almost.

Her arrow slammed into it with barely a thought. It wasn't enough, though. It twitched, and Tyla thought it would have screamed if it had a voice, but it didn't even lose its grip on the frozen wall. Another arrow sent it to the bottom.

Ten arrows left, Tyla counted, and took another step. When she got to four, she would ask for another load from Kelsey, if the numen had not already noticed.

Two of them this time—no, *three*—"Ware!" she called, even as she put an arrow in the lead spider. One of them lit up, brilliantly glittering as Kelsey shone her torch down. That spider exploded from one of Lady Aris's bullets. The light flew away and Aris's gun sounded again as spiders from above tried to take advantage. Tyla put an arrow in the remaining uninjured spider, and another in the first one.

Six arrows left, Tyla counted. She shot another spider and took another step.

"Order up!" Kelsey shouted. "Twenty arrows, fresh off the lathe!"

She always said that. Tyla wasn't sure how she knew there were twenty arrows but there always were. Tyla's quiver could hold twenty-five arrows easily—thirty in a pinch—so this was exactly the right number for her. She shot another spider.

Twenty-four arrows left, she counted, readying a second shot. It died. *Twenty-three arrows left*, she counted. She took another step.

You have reached Level 4.
Applying Benefits for Level 4
Dexterity + 1
Perception + 2
Willpower + 1
Charisma + 1
Please allocate free Ability point.

"Level!" she called out. It would only distract her for a moment, but that moment could be deadly.

"I gotcha!" Kelsey called back. The group stopped moving while they waited for her.

Agility, she chose.

Please select a new Trait. Available Traits: Cast Standard Charm, Enchant Item, Create Potion

Tyla thought about it. Kelsey had made her promise to think about what her choice meant for her future. Looked at from a long-term perspective, Cast Standard Charm would only be a small immediate power boost, while Enchant Item and Create Potion were the foundations for two different careers. She could use her magic to make items that would sell, without risking her life in a dungeon. Even if she lost her core, she could still enchant and make potions using monster cores.

That just wasn't her, though. She was a hunter, not a shopkeeper. While Dungeon Witch wasn't either of those, it was a lot closer to hunter. And as a Dungeon Witch, she needed to be in a dungeon.

Cast Standard Charm, she selected.

"Ready!" she called out.

"Get anything good?" Kelsey asked as they started moving forward.

"I took the best one," Tyla said, smiling. Another spider showed its head and Tyla put an arrow into it. This time, though, she set the arrowhead aflame while she was aiming. The fire-arrow punched into the spider with disproportionate effect, lodging deep inside. This time, she killed it with one shot.

"Nice!" Kelsey yelled over the wind. Tyla nodded.

Twenty-two arrows left, she counted. She took another step.

"Oh, thank all the gods, I can see the bottom!" Zaphar called.

CHAPTER FIFTY

Blow at High Dough

ARIS

The wind stopped when they got to the bottom.

"Smart," Kelsey opined. "Maintaining a wind like that is expensive; there's no point in doing it if there's no one on the walls."

"And it makes drake attacks possible," Anton said. His sword was in his hand and his gaze was directed . . . not at the sky, but above them.

"At least we left the spiders behind," Aris said. She hadn't liked them. The best thing about her guns was that they killed at a distance, and one of the best things about Anton was that he kept them away from her. She shuddered, thinking back to her first experience in a dungeon. Life would be a lot less pleasant if Kelsey had found some kind of melee weapon for her.

"The smaller ones," Anton agreed. "We'll still have to face larger ones."

Zaphar groaned, and Aris had to agree. Larger spiders? *Ugh.*

"Incoming," Kelsey stated plainly. She pointed with her torch. The drakes were bigger this time. This one was sporting a wingspan of at least three yards. It's scales glittered in the bright light of Kelsey's torch as it swooped towards them.

Aris's gun boomed. She used *Trick Shot* this time. It took a little longer, but it let her aim right into its gaping mouth. A geyser of blood and blue scales burst from the back of its head and a corpse crashed to the ground.

It was the first time Aris had fired since the wind stopped, and she was surprised by how loud it was. The drake had glided in silently, and the sound of her gun was still echoing more loudly than the crash of its body.

From far away, out in the darkness, screeches of rage started to sound out.

"I—I don't like the sound of that," Zaphar muttered.

Kelsey was looking out into the darkness. "I think we're getting a rush," she said. "Your notes mention anything about that?" she asked Anton.

"No, but I don't think anyone came down with a weapon as *loud* as that," Anton replied. "Everyone bunch up and get close to the wall."

The group obeyed as best they could. "Sorry," Aris said.

"It's fine," Anton said. His sword was drawn and he was looking tensely out into the darkness. "It just means we'll get past this floor quicker. *And* we'll have something to add to the records."

There were a few more moments of waiting, and then something about the screeching changed.

"They're coming," Kelsey said. Aris raised her gun, her aim following where Kelsey's light was pointing. Then blue scales loomed into the light.

Aris fired, and kept firing. The fight descended into madness as a dozen drakes descended on them. Scales, teeth, and ice-cold claws were everywhere. Zaphar was slashing away with his rapier; Anton was calmly lopping off limbs. Drakes were dropping on them from above and biting at them from the ground.

Aris couldn't look away, couldn't spare a moment, until she'd emptied her first gun. When it clicked empty, she looked for Kelsey for a reload even as she raised her other gun to continue fighting.

Out of the corner of her eye, she saw Tyla, about to lose her life. Glittering teeth were swooping out of the darkness, aimed directly at the elf girl. Aris stared. She tried to react in time but her gun on that side was empty. She started to shout a warning but there was no way Tyla was going to be able to act in time.

Time stopped.

Tyla, the drake, the entire fight around them, and most especially Aris, all stopped moving. Or nearly so. They still kept moving at a snail's pace, a single moment drawn out into an impossible hour. Whatever this was, it didn't help. Aris could see the moment of Tyla's death approaching ever more clearly, but she was trapped in the moment as much as anyone.

Except she somehow knew that she wasn't.

Last Word, Aris thought. Suddenly she was free to act. Her gun came around to bear at the target. *Trick Shot* aimed it right at the roof of the monster's gaping mouth. She pulled the trigger and—

At the moment of the explosion, everything returned to normal. Her arm felt sore, the sound of her shot was ringing in her ears, and Tyla was alive.

"What the hell was that?" Kelsey yelled at her, taking Aris's empty gun.

Aris shook her head. "*Last Word*," was all the explanation that she had time for.

You have completed Level 10! Please select a new class to continue your progression.

She didn't have time for that either. She shot another drake and accepted her reloaded gun back.

When the fight had finished, everyone but Anton and Kelsey crashed to the ground. Anton stood over them while they recovered, staring out into the darkness in case there was a second wave. Kelsey looked them over, handing Zaphar a potion. Then she moved out into the circle of corpses they'd created, sending them back to her dungeon one at a time.

"This is some good stuff!" she crowed. "Maybe we'll outfit all of Suliel's soldiers in dragonscale, what do you say?"

"Sure," Anton agreed. He looked at Aris. "Are you all right?" he asked.

"Yes, I finished my level," Aris answered. "I have to pick a new class."

"I got a new—a new level as well." Zaphar said, wincing. He was looking suspiciously at the potion Kelsey had given him. His armor had been torn by a nasty gash on his arm.

"Just take it," Aris advised. "It hurts, but you've got to be hurting already."

"True, true." Zaphar winced again, but he drained the potion bottle. Then he hissed, screwing his eyes shut. "Hurts . . . so much much more . . ."

With Anton keeping watch over her, Aris felt safe taking the time to select her new Class. She started reviewing the options, skipping over the ordinary ones. There were a few that were anything but.

There was one that looked like the continuation of Gunslinger:

Original Gunfighter (Tier 3, Unique)
Requisites: Complete Gunslinger
Ability Improvement: 8 points per level. STADPWC (1 Free)

But there were some others . . .

Black Powder Widowmaker (Tier 3, Epic)
Requisites: Complete Gunslinger, more than 50 human kills
Ability Improvement: 9 points per level. STAADDPC (1 Free)

Gun Saint (Tier 3, Unique)
Requisites: Complete Gunslinger, save 50 entities
Ability Improvement: 8 points per level. STADPWWC

Deadeye Harbinger (Tier 3, Epic)
Requisites: Complete Gunslinger, Last Word Trait

Ability Improvement: 9 points per level. [S|T]AADDPPC (1 Free)

"I have Epic classes," she squeaked. She didn't mean to say anything, it just slipped out of her.

"Congratulations," Anton said. "Do you know what you want to take?"

Aris didn't know. She looked at the options again. It would be a waste to take a class that was merely Unique, right?

Merely Unique. Hard to imagine thinking that. But that left just two classes, and . . . choosing between those two was fairly easy. Black Powder Widowmaker was all about death. Deadeye Harbinger was just as ominous a name, but the requisites were the *Last Word* trait, which she had just used to *save* a life.

That criteria made Gun Saint more attractive, but it was only Unique, so . . . *I choose Deadeye Harbinger*, she thought.

Applying Benefits for Level 1
Strength + 1
Agility + 2
Dexterity + 2
Perception + 2
Charisma + 1
Assign free point.

Feeling giddy, she assigned the free point to Perception. *My Perception went up by three!*

She quickly went over her status to see the changes.

Aris Lucina, Deadeye Harbinger (Level 1)
Overall Level: 16
Paths: Scullion/(Broken), Original Gunslinger/Deadeye Harbinger
Strength: 10
Toughness: 13
Agility: 21
Dex: 21
Perception: 26
Will: 21
Charisma: 13
Traits:
Eye for Freshness
Heat Resistance
Sonic Resistance
Sure Shot

Trick Shot
Camouflaged Lurker
Last Word

"I'm ready," she stated, getting back on her feet.

"We'll be a bit longer yet," Kelsey said. The drakes had all been cleared away, but Zaphar was still writhing on the ground under the influence of his potion. "You want a bite to eat?"

Aris and Tyla gratefully accepted some kind of meat in a bun from Kelsey's kitchen and a bottle of water. They both watched Zaphar slowly recover from his potion. Kelsey—Aris assumed it was Kelsey—had put a pillow under his head so that he would be more comfortable.

Eventually, the potion ran its course. Zaphar never lost consciousness, but he would have been hard pressed to defend himself.

"Why does everything have to hurt so much?" he complained, rolling to his feet.

"Life *is* pain, Highness," Kelsey said. "Anyone who tells you differently is selling something."

"Easy for you to say," Anton countered, "when your body doesn't feel pain."

"That is true," Kelsey admitted. "But I have to feel the pain of no one getting my movie references, which is a bitter, bitter pill."

Clearing out all the drakes meant that the passage across the chasm floor was relatively uneventful. They still had to fight territorial spiders along the way, but they came in small groups and weren't much of a threat. Anton explained that normally you'd have to defend against a swooping drake at all times, which made the spiders more difficult to deal with.

"Is the final boss a big drake?" Kelsey asked as they neared the far side of the chasm.

"No, that's farther down," Anton said grimly. "The boss of this floor is a spider."

"A boss spider?" Aris asked with dismay.

"I'm afraid so. It's big and lives in a cave on its own," Anton said.

Soon enough—or rather far too soon for Aris's liking—they were standing in front of the cave. It was dark inside, even Kelsey's torch having trouble penetrating the thick silk shrouding the interior.

"We're supposed to go into that?" Aris asked.

"I'm afraid so," Anton said. "It will hide in the silk, which is sticky. We have to clear it out bit by bit before we can engage with it on equal terms."

"We could burn it out?" Kelsey suggested. "I bet the silk has some sort of fire retardant, but I've got some accelerants that could deal with that."

"But then we wouldn't get to collect the valuable silk," Anton pointed out.

"Oh . . ." Kelsey said. "Yeah, you should definitely risk your lives for my profits."

"I think I may be able to help," Tyla said, stepping forward. She reached out to touch the silk at the entrance.

"Careful," Anton said. "It's *really* sticky. We've got some washes to get it off, but if it sticks to you in a fight, it's there for the duration."

"I should be fine," Tyla promised. The silk shivered under her touch, a shiver that ran through the silk nearby. The webs started twisting, tearing themselves free from the walls, wrapping themselves into a cord of fine silk.

The cord itself lashed about, finding more silk in the cave to wrap around itself. It cleared away all the silk that Aris could see, extending into the darkness of the cave. Then it twisted back, curling up on its own length, coiling into a compact package.

Tyla turned to Kelsey. "This is what you wanted, yes?" she asked.

"Hell yeah," Kelsey said, taking and vanishing the rough coil of silk. "How much did you get?"

"The range of the spell is limited," Tyla said. "I will have to enter the cave to clear the rest, but the entrance should be clear enough."

Unable to hide, the spider boss did not last long. For once, its level was high enough for Anton to join in the fray. He chopped off its legs one by one, while Tyla and Aris shot out its eyes. That left the final blow for Zaphar, who plunged his rapier deep in the ugly mottled carapace until it died.

"You know," Kelsey said, holding up one of the legs prior to disappearing it. "I hear that giant spider flesh tastes a lot like lobster."

Aris ignored her, choosing to focus on the floor reward. Anton had already opened the chest. He frowned in surprise.

"It's called Widow's Mercy," he said, drawing . . . something out of the chest. It looked like a loose net made out of frost-silk. Anton found the right way to hold it, and it became clear that it was a vest, only made entirely out of thin bands of silk.

"Is it a sex thing?" Kelsey asked. "Tell me it's a sex thing."

"The main ability is *Spider's Descent*," Anton said. "It looks like it's designed to be worn?"

He turned to Aris. "You're due for the next item," he said. "Do you want it?"

"Um, sure, I guess?" Aris said, taking the light garment. "Are items ever dangerous?"

"Not normally," Anton said.

Aris shrugged and pulled it on over her armor. It felt awkward at first, but once everything was tightened up, it felt as if it had always been a part of her armor.

"It has a warming effect," she reported. "But as for the descent thingy . . ."

Anton pointed at a nearby ledge. "Try jumping off of there."

Aris did so, finding that her fall was much slower than it should be. Repeating the jump, she found that she could slow herself more, or speed it up.

"Not bad," Anton said. "No need to worry about falling any more."

CHAPTER FIFTY-ONE

Bust a Move

Anton joined in the fighting on the tenth floor. It wasn't long after that he got his next level. Fighting the mercenaries had gotten him most of the way there, and the second Ice Gorger he fought put him over the line.

You have reached Level 6.
Applying Benefits for Level 6
Strength + 1
Toughness + 1
Agility + 1
Dexterity + 1
Perception + 1
Willpower + 1
Charisma + 1
Please allocate free Ability points.

Anton put both his free points into Strength and felt his power surge. It still didn't match the overwhelming force that al-Kadir had wielded, but he *would* get there.

Please select a new Trait.
Available Traits: Inspiring Speech, Draw Focus, Chainbreaker

Anton felt a surge of annoyance that Kelsey had been right. He'd never seen

Chainbreaker on any of the lists in the guild, but he *knew* it was what he needed right now. Not that the other two were useless. *Draw Focus was* one that he'd seen before. It would let him protect his party by drawing enemies to him. And *Inspiring Speech* would relieve one of his main worries about his new role as a noble.

But a choice between what he needed and what he wanted was no choice at all. He selected *Chainbreaker.*

"Did'ja get it?" Kelsey asked eagerly.

"Yes." Like most traits, knowledge of how to use it was seeping into him. Like a well-trained muscle memory, he just *knew.*

"How does it work? Is it a spell?"

"It takes a blow," he said slowly, feeling out the ramifications. It wasn't clear to him how he could hit something insubstantial like a spell, but he knew that he *could.* "Maybe we should test it."

"On what?" Kelsey asked. Anton looked at her.

"There's a chain between us, isn't there?"

Kelsey's unnaturally pale face went even whiter. "I prefer to think of it as a bond. An *unbreakable* bond. Of friendship and love!"

"Do you even know what those words mean?" Anton snorted. "And it's not so unbreakable, not anymore."

"Hey, hey, can you really say you regret the times we've had together?" Kelsey asked. "You and me—and the others—against the world!"

"If we're such good buddies, then we hardly need a geas keeping us together, do we?" Anton asked. "You're still the dungeon in the land that I'm in charge of; we're not going to go our separate ways. This chain is just getting in the way of our *friendship.*"

"Come on, this is just *ungrateful.* I've saved your life so many times—"

"Risked it just as many."

"I got both your wives Epic classes—"

"You may have pointed them on the way, but they *earned* those classes. You set Suliel against her mother, and you broke Aris's bones!"

"She got better? And there was a lot going on with Suliel already, I just gave her an opportunity."

"I'm not ungrateful." Anton paused, wanting to be sure how he felt. "Just not *so* grateful that I want to be a slave."

He raised his sword. A silver light gathered along its edge.

"There's more to it than that!" Kelsey yelled.

Anton stopped, but he kept his sword in the air. "What more?"

"I need you," Kelsey said. "I need you to take me where I need to go."

"Where is that?" Anton asked.

Kelsey shrugged. "If I knew that, I wouldn't need you."

"*I* don't know, so how am I supposed to take you there?"

"You will," Kelsey said. "It's part of being a hero. You'll go there, and I need you to take me with you."

"Can't you just . . . follow me?"

"Nah, man." Kelsey shook her head. "There are forces. I've set myself up against at least one god. They don't throw lightning bolts, but they work with certain ineluctable forces to get what they want. I *need* the geas to keep us together. They can't fight that, it works off their own power."

"But why?" Anton asked. "Why do you need to be . . . wherever it is?"

"I can't tell you that," Kelsey insisted. "They're *listening*. They've already worked out the part I'm telling you, but the rest . . . I can't tell them my plans."

"What if I don't like your plans—most of them involve killing at lot of people!"

"You'll be there," Kelsey said. "In the fullness of time, at the climax of it all, you'll be there. You have to be. If you don't like what I'm doing, you can stop me."

"I suppose that's true," Anton said, lowering his sword. "I'll think about it some more."

"Whew! Don't scare me like that, okay? Come on, Tier Four isn't going to reach itself!"

Floor ten was a labyrinth of ice corridors. Some of the ice was clear, some was opaque, and some was as reflective as any mirror that Anton had seen. Finding their way, even with the guidance of previous expeditions, was a wearying chore.

Zaphar got to test his rapier on the insubstantial Glacial Phantoms. Anton winced to see the lack of skill he displayed with the weapon after the one lesson Anton had given him. Rapiers were said to be the most difficult weapon to learn, and while that wasn't wrong, it really only applied against human opponents.

Against an animal, you didn't need the elaborate parries, disengages, and ripostes that dueling required. All you needed to do was keep the point aimed at your target and either lunge or wait for them to impale themselves. Zaphar's Agility and Dexterity were more than enough to handle that. Complicated techniques could be learned with time.

That said, Anton was glad to hear that Zaphar's next level featured attacking traits.

"What do you have?" he asked, looking the man over.

Zaphar Alpashan, Level 19, Human, Fae-Touched Rogue, Thief/Burglar/ Fae-Touched Rogue, S: 6 T: 17 A: 30 D: 33 P: 20 W: 13 C: 10

Thanks to the free ability point of Zaphar's class, his Strength was going up slowly.

"Precision Attack, Acrobatic Attack, and Flèche," Zaphar said.

"*Precision Attack* is like the *Sneak Attack* you already have, but it doesn't require the target to be unaware," Anton told him. "It might absorb the older trait; if it does, it will do more damage than another person's version of the trait. *Flèche* is something you normally find in duelist classes—it lets you move and attack. *Acrobatic Attack . . .*"

Anton racked his memory. "I've never seen it before, but it probably lets you do acrobatics before or after an attack? That could be pretty good, like my *Leaping Attack*."

Anton remained happy with *Leaping Attack*; it was the kind of basic trait that just kept getting better as his Strength and Tier increased. Was *Acrobatic Attack* an advanced version that let you do tumbles and cartwheels as well as jumps?

Zaphar didn't seem too pleased with the idea.

"I need—I need more damage," he said, and Anton couldn't disagree. Even with the rapier, he was only just beating out Tyla—before she used magic.

Zaphar nodded as he made his decision. "Precision Attack." He stated his choice aloud, which wasn't something you had to do.

"Good work," Anton said. "Let's keep going."

Tyla and Aris both made their next levels before they cleared the floor. They were taking their time now, clearing out every single monster, rather than pressing deeper.

Tyla's level was just ability points.

Tyla of the Padascar Tribe, Level 17, Elf, Dungeon Witch, Padascar Hunter (Broken)/Doxy (Broken)/Apprentice Dungeon Witch/ Dungeon Witch, S: 12 T: 9 A: 16 D: 22 P: 27 W: 20 C: 14

But Aris got to pick a trait.

Aris Lucina, Level 17, Human, Deadeye Harbinger, Scullion/(Broken), Original Gunslinger/Deadeye Harbinger, S: 10 T: 15 A: 23 D: 23 P: 28 W: 21 C: 14

Double progression on three stats was costing her a balanced build, but her abilities were shooting up.

"The first trait for a Tier Three class is generally a perception one," he told her. There were exceptions, like Zaphar's class. "What did you get offered?"

"Sense Intent, Identify Target, and Longsight," Aris said.

"*Sense Intent* seems fairly obvious, though I don't think I've ever seen that one," Anton mused. "Or *Identify Target*, but that sounds like an identification trait, like *Delver's Discernment* or *Nobility's Privilege*."

"What about *Longsight*?" Aris asked.

"That's pretty common in archer classes," Anton said. You can make faraway things seem close. As a third-tier trait, it should be . . . five times closer? Though you're an Epic class, so maybe six or seven."

"*Sense Intent* will probably give you a warning when someone wants to kill you," Kelsey put in. "Like *Danger Sense*, but only for people."

"It won't tell me if someone is lying?" Aris asked.

"It might." Kelsey shrugged. "The . . . idiom I think it's chasing is two gunfighters standing each other off . . . are they gonna shoot? Though gunfighters are often supposed to have a keen eye for human nature, so it could work that way."

"I don't think I need an identification trait, what with both Anton and Suliel having one," Aris mused. "And Longsight must be for long-range shooting, which I don't want to focus on."

"You don't?" Anton asked, surprised. "It's safer than fighting at close range."

"But it means fighting far away from you, so it doesn't *feel* safer," Aris replied. "So I think I'll take *Sense Intent*."

They continued on. With Anton fighting, the floor boss was fairly easy to deal with. Another spider, fifteen feet in height, the Frostfang Weaver fought with poison and illusions. But it couldn't penetrate Anton's defenses, and its illusions depended on reflections from panes of ice that were easily destroyed by Aris's shooting.

The floor reward was a pair of gauntlets that both protected from the cold and added a considerable freezing effect to any damage they did. No one fought with their fists, so they packed it away in Kelsey's vaults.

The eleventh floor was an endless howling blizzard. Tyla had spells that could blunt the cold, but she didn't have the right mana type to do anything about the relentless gale. Kelsey provided some jackets made of some thin, slippery substance that somehow blocked most of the wind. They linked themselves together with Anton's handy rope and fought their way across the icy plain.

The monsters here were too much for most second-tier adventurers to fight. Even without the winds and the ice and mist that whipped past, too thick to see through, they would have been too much. Tyla's fire-arrows were extinguished as soon as they were fired, the arrows caught by the wind and sent flying.

Zaphar's unnatural reflexes stood him in good stead, but he was having a hard time keeping on his feet. He would have gone tumbling into the darkness if it wasn't for the rope keeping him down.

It was Anton and Aris who did most of the fighting. The first monsters they saw were Blizzard Striders, according to *Delver's Discernment*. Wolf-like creatures, three feet high at the shoulder, they swept out of the darkness without a sound to give away their approach. A single shot, punching right through the chest of the leading monster, scared them away. They scattered in all directions with high-pitched yips.

They didn't stay scared for long. The second attack came from all directions. Rather than charge in, they swept past, never staying in the light for long, looking for a vulnerability. The party formed a ring, back-to-back with Kelsey and Aris in the center. Aris picked off striders whenever they were unlucky enough to fall under her sights while Zaphar and Tyla did their best to fend off attacks. Setting her sword on fire made the beasts wary enough of her that she didn't have to test how effective the spell was in combat.

Anton punished any strider that came close enough to his side of the ring. *Quick Attack* lashed out again and again, disabusing any strider that thought attacking him from two sides would force a gap in his guard.

When the attacks finally stopped, they all held in place, wondering if it was over or if this was just a lull. Eventually, Anton was convinced they had seen them off.

"The pelts of these monsters are pretty rare," he told Kelsey, who was gleefully gathering them up. "This floor doesn't lend itself to taking the time to skin them, so if you want a pelt, you pretty much have to cart the whole corpse out."

"I'll take good care of them," Kelsey promised. "Better care than *you*, mister chop-them-all-up."

Anton just shrugged and they moved on. The darkness and the blizzard made it hard for them to tell where they needed to go, but this was another floor that Anton wanted to clear out. He was finally getting decent experience for his kills, and Aris was racing to her next level with all these higher-level monster deaths to her name.

Zaphar's progress had slowed, but the appearance of some Frost Wraiths that were vulnerable to the rogue's special blade helped his progress. Tyla, too, was having trouble making kills. But she was casting spells and contributing to the party, so she was making some progress.

Then she gained her next level and the game changed.

CHAPTER FIFTY-TWO

I'm on Fire

TYLA

Aris was drawing ahead of her. It wasn't something that Tyla should have been worried about. There was no competition between them. They had entirely different classes, so there was no real way to compare them. In fact, to one way of thinking, the gap between them was already insurmountable. Their overall levels might have been comparable, but Aris was Tier Three and Tyla was still in the middle of Tier Two. That gap was more significant than a few levels.

Back home, Tyla would have to bow her head and call Aris *vaer*. Things were a little less formal among rangers, but still. The point was that she was drawing further away. The weapons that the numina had provided let her fight higher tiers on an even footing, and now that she was a higher tier, she was unstoppable.

Tyla wondered if she should have accepted a gun of her own, but the thought repelled her. They were loud, they stank of something worse than fire, and they hurt to use. She greatly preferred her new bow, even if she had to accept that it was a dead end for her. She had magic now.

She needed more of it.

As she was now, her magic could *help*, but it was starkly limited in scope. She needed more powerful spells, spells that could *compare* at least to the devastating damage that Aris's guns could do. At least until Aris started adding magical damage to her attacks.

That was why it hurt to hear Aris call out "Level" for the *second* time on this floor. It was only to be expected. The monsters here were at a higher level than them, and she was killing *so many* of them. It only helped them as a party for Aris to grow stronger. It just hurt to get left behind.

She was getting there. She was casting spells, helping the team. She even managed the occasional kill. Zaphar might have the only weapon that could hurt Frost Wraiths, but they died with fire as well.

It was another monster, equally insubstantial, that put her over the edge. Anton had never gotten a look at them to identify them, but they were airborne fragments of pure cold. They flew with the wind, trying to latch on to a warm body to feed. They were repelled by the spells she had woven around her party members, but that didn't stop them from trying. When they came near her, she gave them more warmth than they could handle.

You have reached Level 6.
Applying Benefits for Level 6
Strength + 1
Dexterity + 1
Perception + 1
Willpower + 1
Charisma + 1
Please allocate free Ability point.

"Level!" Tyla called out, but she knew she wouldn't need long to choose. In a moment of weakness, Tyla selected Toughness. Even through the spells, she still felt the cold.

Please select a new Trait. Available Traits: Intimidating Glare, Core Heal, Cast Greater Charm

Tyla barely looked at the list before selecting *Cast Greater Charm*. This, *this*, was the power that she needed. There were more powerful spells, she knew. She could feel them waiting for her. But the number of times she had tried for a spell only to feel it *just* out of reach . . . she could cast those spells now.

Even as she returned her attention to the world, she felt herself get dragged out of the way by Kelsey. A monster was rising out of the ice beneath their feet. They had seen this one before. Rime-serpent, Anton had called it. That time, she'd been unable to contribute. It was too dangerous for her to approach into hand-to-hand range.

This time . . . Tyla announced her level with a torrent of fire. It speared out from her outstretched hand, slamming into the monster and carving a jagged scar six inches deep in its ice-rimed flesh.

The monster screamed. It hadn't done that last time.

The fights went a little better after that. It was still hard, but in the end, ice gave way to fire. When they finished the final boss, Tyla slumped to the ground, exhausted.

The boss of this floor had been a frozen wraith encased in a body of ice. Its giant, four-armed form gave it a strength that could only be matched by Anton, and its immaterial nature meant that it could only be harmed by Zaphar's sword. Tyla was able to melt the ice enough that the rapier could penetrate, but it kept re-freezing.

Zaphar slumped down next to her. It had been a hard fight.

"We can take a break here," Anton said. He opened the chest and pulled out a crystalline shield. He and Zaphar started discussing who should use it. Tyla let the words wash over her. The boss arena was surrounded by rough, jagged walls of ice that had the welcome effect of blocking out the winds. For the first time in a while, she thought she might be able to rest.

Her thoughts wouldn't let her rest, though. And the dungeon was right there . . . pulling off her glove, she laid her palm against the ground.

Commune.

The Hungry Depths was the same sligg that she'd seen before, looking at her with an expression she couldn't read.

"What is it now?" it asked. Tyla couldn't tell if it was annoyed or not.

"We're not going to make it," she said. "It's only the eleventh floor and we're exhausted."

"Only two of you are," the sligg said. "The Kelsey, Anton, and Aris are still energetic."

"But for how long?" Tyla asked. "This is the first floor that out-leveled Anton, and it only gets harder from here. The rest of us are already out of our depth."

The Hungry Depths cocked its head to one side. "So, return to the surface, rest, and try again. Is that not what delvers do?"

Tyla shook her head. "We need to go back to Lord Anton's hometown, but we need to find out about the King before we do. So Anton will keep pushing."

"That is acceptable."

"It won't be if he dies!" Tyla exclaimed. "If he dies, he won't get to use *Chainbreaker* on you."

The Hungry Depths started to say something, then stopped. It looked at something Tyla couldn't see.

"This is more of the words that bind without binding," the dungeon said. "You seek to bind me to your cause, bind me to defeat myself."

"If we work together, we both get what we want," Tyla said. "If you don't help us, we won't be able to help you."

"I *have* been helping you," The Hungry Depths replied. "Have my treasures not been useful?"

"They have," Tyla admitted. "But it's not enough. Not to get to the lowest level."

The sligg frowned, the only expression that Tyla was able to read.

"That remains to be seen," she said. "The Kelsey believes you can make it. I wish to see what she sees."

The vision ended, and Tyla was returned to her tired and weary body. A wave of exhaustion swept over her. She hadn't realized it was gone until it came back.

"Any luck?" Kelsey asked. Tyla shook her head.

Floor twelve was a nightmare of shifting ice. A labyrinth of cracks that opened and closed, seemingly at random. The shield proved critical here. Its bearer was able to create an ice wall, of whatever configuration desired. Placed high enough that they could walk under it, it would hold the clashing chasms open long enough for them to dash through safely.

The monsters were tougher, and Tyla was glad that her fire worked on all of them. Anton had his hands full with the Chillborn Revenants, which Kelsey had declared inferior variants of her own monsters. They also had to face Frost Wraiths, which only Zaphar's sword and her fire could touch. That left the Glacial Spinners, giant spiders that clung to the higher reaches and tried to draw the unwary up with frost-silk strands that were stronger than steel. Aris dealt with them. They were big enough that they were a real danger when they fell, but at least they hunted alone.

Anton wanted to farm this level as well, but the evershifting maze prevented them from moving deliberately. You could dash forward when a passage opened up, or not. You didn't get to choose *which* passage opened up.

Previous expeditions had not mastered the maze, or if they had, they had kept it a secret. When they finally found the boss arena, there were still monsters available, but they were too tired to try and find them. Instead, they elected to proceed.

At least everyone made a level on this floor.

Tyla Greenwalker of the Padascar Tribe, Dungeon Witch (Level 7)
Overall Level: 18
Paths: Padascar Hunter (Broken)/Doxy (Broken)/Apprentice Dungeon
Witch/Dungeon Witch
Strength: 13
Toughness: 12
Agility: 16
Dex: 24
Perception: 29
Will: 22
Charisma: 16

Traits:
Persistent Tracker, Silent Shot
Danger Sense
Sense Magic, Cast Lesser Charm
Commune, Cast Standard Charm, Cast Greater Charm

The boss arena was a massive frozen amphitheater. They started at the top row of seats and made their way down cautiously. The main arena was a frozen lake, the ice clear enough to see the cold water underneath. According to the expedition notes, it was more than deep enough to drown in.

"Not another battle over water," Zaphar groaned.

"Stay on the seating for now," Anton said. "Tyla, can you walk an illusion out on the ice?"

Tyla nodded. Before, she wouldn't have been able to extend her magic so far, but now it was no problem. An image of Anton strode boldly out on the ice. It reached the center and turned around, waving at them.

There was only the briefest warning: a dark flicker under the ice. Then, a huge form burst out from underneath. The illusion was dispersed instantly—a real Anton might not have lasted longer.

A colossal, elemental beast had formed from the lake itself, a towering, four-legged monster of living ice and enchanted permafrost. It looked a little like a lion, with a jagged icicle mane, a serpentine tail of swirling frost, and blue eyes burning deep within its crystalline skull.

The flat, frozen surface of the lake had turned into a nightmare of spikes and craggy cliffs of ice. The water had gone, but so had any hint of a flat surface.

"No complaints, right?" Kelsey said brightly. "No more water."

Zaphar glowered at her. "No, this is better," he admitted. "It looks nasty, but it gives me more surfaces to jump off."

"Me too," Anton added. "Just remember that that thing, the Heartfrost Tyrant, can merge with the ice. If we start winning, it will retreat back into it."

"You're gonna be smashing a lot of Tier Three ice with that sword," Kelsey said. "You sure your sword is up to it?"

"It'll be fine," Anton said. "It's enchanted for damage and durability, after all."

"Well, sure," Kelsey agreed. "But who needs magic when you have a big hammer?"

She held out the biggest war hammer that Tyla had ever seen. If it was a hammer. One of the ends was pointed, which Tyla thought might change its name. Heavy weapons were not an elven specialty.

Tyla doubted she could even lift the weapon, but Anton hefted it in one hand easily. "Tier Two, but not magical?" he asked.

"I'm saving my mana," Kelsey said. "I might need it later. This is a product of the Skeletarm Armaments Factory."

"Fine," Anton said. "Thanks. Zaphar, you're with me. I don't think you'll be able to hurt it with a rapier or knives, but you might be able to with the right opportunity. Just try and attract its attention. Tyla and Aris, stay on the risers and pelt it from a distance. It might not care about arrows, but I'm betting fire and bullets will hurt it."

They all nodded grimly. They'd done this a few times now, they all knew what was expected of them. Anton nodded back.

"Right," Anton said. "Let's clear this level."

CHAPTER FIFTY-THREE

Masochism World

The fifteenth floor was too much. They were lucky to find a small, secure cavern when they did, as Anton couldn't go much farther. He called a rest break—everyone collapsed where they stood.

"I'll just keep watch then, shall I?" Kelsey asked. She handed out some hot meat wrapped in bread and then posted herself at the entrance. Out of all of them, she was the only one not at the end of her endurance. She hadn't been doing any of the fighting, and she was immune to the cold, but she had been forced to clamber over the same icy cliffs and caverns that the rest of them had.

"Floor" was an ironic term for this part of the dungeon; it was missing one. The maze of cracks and fissures had gone three-dimensional, and they were reduced to picking their way through an endless series of dead ends. The monsters they'd fought so far, the Shardborn and the Frozen Wretches, moved through the environment as if they were a part of it. In the case of the Shardborn—made from ice—they actually *were*.

Anton looked over at all his party members. All of them had come so far. Zaphar was collapsed against a wall right now, but when he was moving, he moved with a grace that Anton could only dream of.

Zaphar Alpashan, Level 21, Human, Fae-Touched Rogue, Thief/Burglar/ Fae-Touched Rogue, S: 8 T: 17 A: 34 D: 37 P: 22 W: 15 C: 12

He had picked up *Uncanny Evasion* on his last level; it was odd how their traits seemed to be lining up. His strength was still too low, though. He was finding it harder to damage anything, and his role was often reduced to a mere distraction. Unable to make kills, he was falling behind, only gaining one level on the past two floors.

Aris was also becoming supernaturally graceful. For her, though, that just meant that she was able to keep her footing on the fractured and shifting ice and whirl around quickly to meet new threats. Anton thought that, given some training, she could quickly learn to dodge while firing, making her a threat even at close range. For now, she relied on his protection.

Aris Lucina, Level 22, Human, Deadeye Harbinger, Scullion/(Broken), Original Gunslinger/Deadeye Harbinger, S: 13 T: 20 A: 33 D: 33 P: 37 W: 21 C: 19

Her damage was still keeping up with the higher-leveled monsters. Her *Deadly Shot* was just that, even if it was a little slower than her other attacks. She'd been a little embarrassed that her latest trait hadn't been combat-related, but no class was *entirely* focused on combat. Deadeye Harbinger seemed to have a social component, judging by the traits she was offered at level six. *Commanding Speech*, *Aura of Fear*, and *Erase Presence* were all good, but they suggested a role of delivering dark pronouncements of doom.

She'd taken *Erase Presence* in the hope that it would work on monsters, but as far as they could tell, it didn't.

It was Tyla, perhaps, that had seen the greatest improvement.

Tyla of the Padascar Tribe, Level 21, Elf, Dungeon Witch, Padascar Hunter (Broken)/Doxy (Broken)/Apprentice Dungeon Witch/ Dungeon Witch, S: 13 T: 14 A: 17 D: 26 P: 32 W: 24 C: 18

Tyla couldn't keep up with Aris's kills, or Anton's for that matter, but she was gaining experience from casting spells *and* killing monsters. She was keeping up. Her spells had saved them countless times, from thawing or shattering ice with fire, to levitating the falling and even breaking through the illusions this dungeon made with ice reflections. Her core seemed to be an inexhaustible source of mana, but there was a cost to casting spells, one that they hadn't been aware of until she started casting more powerful ones.

Each spell caused an amount of mental fatigue. Easily recovered from, but the bigger spells cost more and required more recovery time. Tyla hadn't even noticed with the lesser spells, but now she had to ration out her spellcasting, giving her enough time to avoid a lengthy period of exhaustion.

For her level eight trait, she had elected to forego more powerful spells in favor of *Enduring Caster*. It seemed to be making a difference. If nothing else, they should be able to rest here long enough for Tyla to fully recover.

Then there was Anton.

Anton Nos, Heroic Liberator, Level 9
Overall Level: 24
Paths: Delver/Adventurer/Heroic Liberator
Class: Heroic Liberator
Strength: 38
Toughness: 36
Agility: 28
Dex: 28
Perception: 25
Will: 22
Charisma: 19
Traits:
Delvers Discernment, Leaping Attack
Stone Skin, Uncanny Evasion, Sense Mana, Spider Climb, Unwavering
Sense Destiny, Quick Attack, Chainbreaker, Aegis

It was better, but it wasn't enough.

"It's too dangerous to keep going," he told Kelsey.

"We can't stop now, we've only got three floors left!" she protested. "We're so close!"

"Three *Tier Four* floors," Anton countered. "They'll be beyond anything we've faced so far."

"You fought up-tier before," Kelsey argued. "Back when you were Tier Two. You've got all those bonuses from your Epic and Unique classes. You can take them."

"It's just . . . we're going to lose somebody," Anton said softly. "I can protect Aris, *maybe*, but stuff gets through. And I can't be everywhere at once."

"We have survived so far," Tyla put in from her position on the floor. "We have healing now, and your Aegis helps as well."

Anton stared at her. Tyla's healing was only good for flesh wounds at the moment, but it was far less painful than a potion. Her other spells were more powerful, too, but not strong enough.

"Risking your life like this goes against the principles of the Adventurers Guild," he said. "It's always better to fall back and try again."

"But we do not have that option, do we?" Tyla asked. "We cannot save the dungeon if we retreat. We go back to Kirido after this, whether we succeed or fail."

She pulled herself into a sitting position. "Both Kelsey and The Hungry Depths think we can succeed. I don't want to give up while they have faith in us."

"Are you sure they won't be just as happy to see us dead?" Anton asked, glaring at Kelsey, who affected an innocent demeanor.

"It's possible," Tyla admitted. "The Hungry Depths has no love for humankind. She might have a soft spot for elves, though."

"And I'm shocked that you'd think I'd risk your life needlessly," Kelsey said. "You have reserves you haven't tapped yet. You can do this."

Anton groaned. "I wish someone had informed me about these reserves, because I'm sure not feeling them."

"Uh," Kelsey said. "Might be time to start tapping them, because something's coming up."

Anton could hear it as soon as she finished speaking. His own perception was quite high these days. What he was hearing was voices. His own, and Kelsey's.

" . . . going to lose . . ."

" . . . stop now . . ."

"Whisperhounds," Anton said, grimacing. He climbed to his feet and stood at the entrance. Kelsey moved aside to let him. The passageway sloped down at a steep angle, but that wasn't a problem for him. At the edge of the light, he could see shadows moving.

"Everyone, get ready. Whisperhounds can ice-jump," he told them. He activated *Aegis*, letting the aura of protection surround his friends.

"That is the thing where they move through the ice, yes?" Zaphar asked, getting to his feet.

Anton was watching the hounds creep forward. They looked a little like wolves with blue, ice-rimed fur. Their jaws were bigger, and their claws were three inches long, digging into the ice for grip.

"No," he said shortly. One of the hounds jumped into a nearby wall. Anton whirled around and slashed as hard as he could at the monster emerging from the wall behind him. "It's a teleport."

Then the monsters were running at him and there was no time for talking. Holding the entrance was futile; they could jump right past him. Instead, he charged in, attracting the attention of the pack.

To his dismay, they scattered, jumping into the walls. One of the four remaining launched an attack on his back, but the others disappeared. The sound of gunfire and the feeling of his Aegis shattering told him where they went. Against monsters of this level, his new shield was only good for a single hit. One of his party members was now vulnerable.

Anton quickly finished off the only Whisperhound brave enough to attack him and rushed back to the ice cave. Aris had stopped shooting, which could be a good or a bad sign . . .

When he got back, he stopped, startled. There was another person in the room. A tall woman with pale skin, wearing a dress like the one Suliel had been wearing lately. She was holding some sort of chain weapon, which she'd used to strangle one of the wolves. The other two were dead, one burned, one shot.

Anton looked back at the woman, just as she turned around to look at him, giving him a wide smile that showed her pointed teeth.

Not a person, Anton realized. Not a human. A monster.

"You must be Anton," the monster said. "I've heard *so* much about you."

Kelsey cleared her throat. "Uh, this is Sheryl. I figured you could use some reinforcements on the front line. Keep in mind that she's under orders as long as she's in my sight."

"Orders that specifically forbid me from drinking blood from any of you," the Vampire Queen pouted. "It seems a shame. You can't spare just a few drops for little old me?"

Anton stared at the monster. "No," he said flatly. "We can't."

It did work, as much as Anton didn't want it to. With two frontline fighters, they could cover the ranged fighters much more effectively. Zaphar was relegated to covering the back. He still saw plenty of action, but the confusing labyrinth made flanking maneuvers easy for the monsters. He just had to delay them long enough for Anton or . . . Sheryl to make their way back.

When they reached the end of the maze, Anton held them back, right before the crack opened up into a large ice cavern. "This is going to be tough," he told them. "This will be our first Tier Four monster."

"Did you forget al-Kadir that easily?" Kelsey joked.

"Not a monster, no matter how scary he was," Anton shot back. "It has flight and it's a wide cavern so it will have the advantage there. We'll need to shoot it with guns and fire until it comes close to attack."

"We're ready," Aris assured him. The others nodded grimly, except for Sheryl, who gave him a sardonic smile. Anton shook his head and led them into the cavern.

It was just as the notes described. A huge chamber with jagged ice covering the floor and a high, high, ceiling. They didn't have to wait long for the boss to descend. It was easily the biggest monster Anton had ever seen, and it roared a challenge as it descended. Anton made sure he got a glance.

Ice Dragon, Level 32, Dragon, Ice-Aspected, Vulnerable to Lightning

Aris fired her rifle at it. Anton guessed she was using *Deadly Shot*, but the dragon slipped to the side with terrifying speed. It screamed, but he couldn't tell if it was anger or pain.

"It's vulnerable to lightning!" he called out. He would have thought it would be weak against fire, but the notes did say that its weakness changed between visits.

Tyla hissed. "I can't do lightning at long range," she admitted. "It doesn't travel far enough."

"Don't worry about it," Kelsey said. Anton glanced over at her, to see that she had her hands on Sheryl. As he watched, she made the vampire disappear.

"You guys haven't seen this one," she said. "I was saving it for when I got my new floor. But I figure that the best way to fight a dragon . . . is with one of your own."

It grew out of her hand with startling speed. Only the size of it let him see that it was growing and not appearing all at once. It only took a moment before a second titanic lizard spread its wings and hissed a challenge at the ceiling.

Dracolisk, Level 29, Undead, Lightning-Aspected, Vulnerable to Holy

"You can—" Anton started before he was cut off by the blast of wind as the Dracolisk took to the air.

"Yeah," Kelsey said. "I might not be able to match the level, but I figure the aspect will make up for that. Should be a good fight."

CHAPTER FIFTY-FOUR

Gigantic

Anton picked his way down the pile of bodies. Normally, he wouldn't say two bodies could make a pile, but the corpses of the Dracolisk and the Ice Dragon were so huge and so entangled, that was the only word for it.

You have reached Level 10.
Applying Benefits for Level 10
Strength +1
Toughness + 1
Agility + 1
Dexterity + 1
Perception + 1
Willpower + 1
Charisma + 1
Assign 2 free points.

Anton put his free points into Dexterity and Agility, bringing the pair of stats up to an even thirty.

"I can't believe you got a level, when I did all the work!" Kelsey called up to him. He scowled at her. The statement was . . . inaccurate. Even if he accepted that the Dracolisk's actions were hers, Anton had still done his fair share.

"It was a Tier Four!" he called back. Really, that was all that needed to be said. He focused on his new level.

Please select a new Trait. Traits available: Banner of Freedom, Voice of Rebellion, Iron Mercy

Huh. Anton had never seen *any* of those traits before. He wondered if he should ask Kelsey's advice.

No. Kelsey had been insufferable since she'd started helping them—or carrying them, as she put it. Giving her more opportunities to lord it over him was out of the question.

Iron Mercy felt like a combat trait . . . with some kind of twist. The other two . . . well, they were obviously leadership traits. That wasn't going to help him here, but Anton knew he needed to think beyond his current situation. Leadership was something he would need in the future. He wondered if *Voice of Rebellion* was a sign that he was going to be on the side of the rebels.

Probably not, he thought. Freeing slaves and rebellion went hand in hand, but if Anton did rebel against the King, it wasn't going to be over slaves he wasn't keeping. Still . . . *Banner of Freedom* sounded like something passive. *Voice of Rebellion* would surely help with public speaking. Anton selected it.

Nothing changed. That meant that the trait could only be used under certain conditions, which were not currently met. When the time came, Anton would know what to do.

Anton joined the others on the ground. Just by looking at them, he could tell that the girls had gotten to their next levels, while Zaphar's disappointed look spoke volumes. The rogue had been pretty much shut out of the fight. He must have received some experience, just not enough. Anton clapped him on the back.

"Better luck next time," he said.

"Sorry, sorry," Zaphar said. "I just couldn't . . ."

"Your build's not suited for it," Anton said reassuringly. "It happens."

When the Dracolisk had brought the Ice Dragon crashing to the ground, Anton had been able to jump into the twisting pile of limbs and teeth. It had taken both Agility and Strength to do that—Zaphar would have been crushed in the writhing mass.

Aris and Tyla had been able to pour in fire from a distance—literally, in Tyla's case. That contribution had gotten them their levels.

Anton looked them over.

Aris Lucina, Level 23, Human, Deadeye Harbinger, Scullion/(Broken), Original Gunslinger/Deadeye Harbinger, S: 13 T: 21 A: 35 D: 35 P: 39 W: 22 C: 20

Tyla of the Padascar Tribe, Level 22, Elf, Dungeon Witch, Padascar

Hunter (Broken)/Doxy (Broken)/Apprentice Dungeon Witch/ Dungeon Witch, S: 13 T: 14 A: 18 D: 27 P: 33 W: 26 C: 19

Tyla's grin was particularly smug.

"Capstone?" Anton asked. Tyla nodded.

"Cast Minor Spell," she said proudly.

"Doesn't sound like much of a capstone, to be honest," he teased. She shook her head.

"Spells are more powerful than charms, and Minor is not at the bottom of that ladder," she said. "I can use more mana, now, than my core can supply."

"Looking for another upgrade, are we?" Kelsey said.

Tyla bowed. "I wouldn't presume," she said. "But I would be more useful."

Kelsey looked away. "I've been hanging on to this latest one in case the King makes Anton give it back. I'm still not sure where we are on that."

Tyla nodded. "I understand," she said earnestly.

"Right, well . . ." Kelsey said. She paused awkwardly. "Get yourselves some rest. This dragon is so big, I'll have to chop it up to take it out."

"I don't think anyone's ever hauled out the entire dragon," Anton said thoughtfully. "Most of the notes only mention prices for small parts."

"I'm sure there's some good stuff in there," Kelsey said. "The reward chest is over there, by the way."

Anton nodded and went to grab the reward. Inside the chest was . . . a sword.

Stormfang, Weapon, Tier 3,
Wrath of the Thunderlord, Echo of the Tempest

Anton blinked in surprise. *I guess The Hungry Depths thinks I contributed my share*, he thought. Taking it out of the chest, he drew the sword from the scabbard.

He could feel the winds pick up around him. It was subtle. It wasn't a breeze, just the feeling that the air was moving around him, just out of his reach.

"New sword?" Aris asked.

"I think so," Anton replied. "Can you see what it can do, Tyla?"

Tyla studied him and the sword intently. "There is a shield around you," she said. "Not like the Aegis . . . something else."

Anton frowned and reached out to touch Aris. There was nothing in between them.

"Now it is around you both," Tyla reported. "As for the sword itself, I see lightning."

Anton raised an eyebrow and used his own *Sense Mana*. Sure enough, there was a shifting current of mana flowing around Aris and himself. It seemed too weak to keep anybody out, though. Whatever it was, it must be the *Echo of the Tempest* power. Lightning in the sword sounded like *Wrath of the Thunderlord*.

It might be released when he hit something, or he might be able to . . . Anton took a few steps away from the group and pointed his sword at an ordinary chunk of ice. He forced his will into the sword . . . sometimes it helped to think the name of the ability . . . no matter how cheesy it sounded.

Wrath of the Thunderlord.

There was a flash, a *crack*, and the ice exploded. Anton blinked the lights out of his eyes. That was going to take some getting used to.

The sound attracted Kelsey's attention from a little way away. She paused in her butchery and waved at him.

"Nice!" she called out.

Anton nodded and waved back. "I think I like it," he told the others as he returned.

"It seems powerful," Aris agreed. She looked over at Kelsey as sounds of swearing came from the dragon's corpse. "Should we go help?"

"Nah," Anton said, sitting down on the ice. "I think she's having fun. Let's rest up while we can."

The transition between the root jungle of Tier Two and the ice waste of Tier Three had been gradual, the ice taking hold of the plants over one or two floors. The transition to Tier Four was anything but. It started with the exit gate, a blank pane of darkly translucent material. At first, Anton thought it was black ice, but it was warm to the touch and its edges were sharper than knives. Anton identified it, just to be sure.

Brimstone Obsidian, Material, Tier 3, Shatter-Prone, Sharp

It couldn't slice Anton's Stone Skin, but Zaphar had to touch for himself. Just the lightest of touches on the gate's edge sliced his finger open, requiring a spell from Tyla.

"Masks on," Anton said. "This stuff is tough, but the monsters are tougher. Some of their misses will pulverize part of the walls into dust. Breathe it in and it will slice your lungs up."

"I should be able to heal such tiny cuts," Tyla said thoughtfully, "But I don't have the right mana to do anything about the shards themselves, so they will just cut you again."

"You can use water to wash them out!" Kelsey said brightly. "It will feel like you're drowning, but only temporarily."

"Oh great, you mean this dungeon has found something *worse* than biting cold and endless chasms?" Zaphar said bitterly, his voice muffled by the mask he was tying tightly around his face.

"We're almost done," Kelsey said reassuringly. "And remember, bigger monsters cost more, so there will be less of them!"

Anton didn't say anything; he just made sure that everyone was ready before he pushed the wall panel aside.

It was dark inside, of course. Kelsey shone her light ahead of them, and Aris came forward with her light-stone. The light revealed walls that were carved with forgotten scripts and images of unknown saints or kings. A passageway—ten feet wide and twenty feet tall—stretched out ahead of them, opening out into a wider section. The passageway continued past the open area.

Anton led the group forward. The notes made no mention of traps in this section. He expected his footsteps to echo in the empty space, but they were muffled, silenced by the air.

As they got closer, they could see that the wider section contained two statues, carved from obsidian, about nine feet tall.

"Those . . . those things are going to come to life, aren't they?" Zaphar whispered.

"Yeah, they're Graven Sentinels," Anton answered. To his surprise, his voice came out quieter than he'd intended. "Do you want to try something?"

"What?" Zaphar asked warily.

"Sentinels aren't *slow*," Anton said, "But they're slower than you. If it was just you in the room, I doubt they'd be able to hit you."

"Sure, sure, but I can't hurt *them*," Zaphar pointed out. "My blade can't cut through obsidian—I doubt yours can."

"Probably not," Anton agreed. "But two big monsters and one little guy they can't hit . . ."

"Oh no," Zaphar said. "No, no, no. That is worse than being bait."

"You'd be soloing them," Anton said. "Think of the experience."

"We gotta have some other way," Zaphar pleaded.

"Sure. Aris can shoot them from here with a rifle. It might take a few shots, but obsidian will shatter. I just thought you might want a chance to catch up."

Zaphar winced. "They've got ten levels on me," he said.

"Yep."

"And there's two of them."

"Might be more where we can't see," Anton cautioned. "But honestly, that would make it easier for you."

Zaphar took a deep breath and screwed his eyes shut. "I hate it that you're right," he said. "Hate it."

Anton clapped him on the back. "I'll make sure Aris is ready to back you up."

Zaphar muttered some words that Anton couldn't hear. Then he dashed forward.

Rushing in was the best plan. If there had been Sentinels hiding at the entrance, he could have swept past them before they could react. As it happened, they weren't there, but the ones they could see wasted no time in coming to life and swinging at him. Their obsidian blades swept forward, one high, one low.

Zaphar lazily dived between them. He landed on his hands and pushed himself into a flip. He was strong enough, now, to do things like that. He paused, midway between the two Sentinels, giving them a chance to reorient.

Just getting between them wouldn't work; their training or magical programming had them move apart far enough not to endanger themselves. Zaphar had to move in close to one of them, slipping behind the clumsy Sentinel. A few swings, a few misses, and it was plain that he was in too close for the statue to use its sword effectively. Its partner needed to come in and help.

It didn't come in swinging. It waited for its chance, observing Zaphar's movement, judging its moment. It chose well, picking a time when he was off balance, with no way to avoid the blow.

Anton winced as Zaphar's body *twisted* in ways it shouldn't be able to.

Is that how it looks when I do it?

However it looked, it was effective. The Sentinel's sword swung into the side of its partner, carving a deep wound into the body of the statue. It made no sound as it fell, no scream of rage, but the slash it sent back at its former companion showed that it wasn't happy. It only managed a glancing blow, but it was enough to make the upright Sentinel back off.

Zaphar flitted around the downed Sentinel with impunity. It swung at him, but it couldn't aim properly from the ground. He examined it closely for weaknesses. The upright Sentinel kept its distance, giving Zaphar all the time in the world.

Once he decided, Zaphar moved swiftly. A quick reposition, a lunge, and then his sword was buried deep in the statue's head.

The second Sentinel rushed at him, but Zaphar twisted out of the way.

"Okay, yes, I have got the level," he called. "You can be shooting him in the head now."

CHAPTER FIFTY-FIVE

Keep On Movin'

The silence grew oppressive as they continued down the obsidian tunnels. Not because of any reticence on their part; some magic—probably coming from the carvings on the wall—deadened all sounds. The effect grew stronger as they progressed. At first, they noticed the sounds of their footsteps diminished into silence. Then, speech became harder. Anton had to shout to make himself heard at all.

It did make Aris's guns less loud, so it wasn't all bad. Anton wasn't sure if it helped monsters sneak up on them. Most of the ones that tried seemed preternaturally silent anyway.

The fights were all hard, harder than anything they'd faced so far. There were more of the Sentinels, of course. Zaphar managed to trick two more of them into attacking each other, but when they appeared alone, Anton and Sheryl had to hold them back while Aris slowly smashed them to pieces.

Ashborn Wretches were Anton's first experience with Tier Four undead. They were almost impossible to damage. They seemed to be made of ash, and normal weapons passed right through them. Their clawed hands slipped right through Anton's guard and drew fiery lines across his *Stone Skin*.

Even Zaphar's rapier only hurt them a little. In the end, it was only the discovery that they were vulnerable to Tyla's magic that saved them.

Zaphar was of more use against the shadowy creatures that came out of the walls without warning. They came and went too quickly for Anton to get a read on them. Previous adventurers had reported the same problem; they were only known in the notes as ghosts. Zaphar had a weapon that could hurt them, but it would have been useless without his speed and perception. He could spot a flicker of shadow and lunge at it before Anton knew it was there. Once his sword lashed out at one, it invariably retreated into the rock; Anton never knew if Zaphar managed to kill one, but they stopped bothering them after a time.

That might have been because they had entered the territory of the Forgotten Choir, a group of spectres that made the only sound they heard on this level. Aris, Zaphar, and Tyla were all instantly enthralled as soon as they heard the singing. Anton and the monsters were unaffected, so he had the two of them hold the humans back while he stalked forward with Zaphar's sword.

In some ways, it was the easiest fight on the floor, but the ease at which Aris had been mesmerized spooked him.

The silence intensified as they got to the final room. Anton found that he couldn't make himself heard. Aris pointed back the way they came, asking if he wanted to go back to give them their final briefing, but he shook his head. They'd use the standard formation for this one.

The doors swung open silently. Massive as they were, the figure before them would have had to crawl to get through them. It was kneeling now, in the center of the arena, but as Anton and Sheryl entered the chamber, it slowly stood to face them.

Anton looked around, but it was just as the notes had said. An arena of packed sand, with a single row of elevated seats—all empty.

The obsidian statue rose gracefully to its feet. It was twelve feet tall, carved to resemble a knight. Its armor was carved on, but a cloak of obsidian plates hung from its back. Its head was a blank helmet split with a vertical arcane sigil.

Despite its increased size, the notes warned that it was just a little faster than the smaller Graven Sentinels. Anton used *Discernment*.

Stone Oathbound, Level 34, Golem, Runic Defense, Vulnerable to Sonic

It gestured gracefully with its sword, welcoming their approach.

Aris's rifle shot smashed into its face.

Anton knew that Aris greatly preferred her pistols to the rifle. Its greater power and range just weren't worth its unwieldiness, in her opinion. Especially since most monsters went down with a single shot.

That wasn't true on this floor. And now, from just outside the arena, she had a perfect line of fire, clear over Anton's head. While he bore the brunt of the statue's attack, she got in some much-needed rifle practice.

The massive sword, seven feet long, swung down, and Anton grunted with the effort of parrying it. Normally he would have dodged, but a parry held up the blade for a little longer, opening up a gap for his partner.

By now, Anton had had plenty of chances to see Sheryl's weapon at work. It was a long flail, a heavy weight attached to a chain six or seven feet long. It would have been unwieldy, but there was some magic to it that let Sheryl twist the chain back and forth however she wanted. She could entangle smaller monsters quite effectively, but against the larger Oathbound, she just used its immense leverage to deliver a massive crushing blow.

The knight parried it with his cape, sweeping it around with one hand. The obsidian plate at the point of contact was destroyed, but its rune was activated, unleashing a fiery explosion.

The whole thing happened in eerie silence. Sheryl was flung back by the blast, and Anton let the flames wash over him. Between his armor, *Stone Skin*, and Toughness, an attack of this level could only singe him slightly.

As the Oathbound withdrew his sword from the bind, Anton triggered his lightning. As he'd expected, there was no visible effect on the giant, though it did distract it from Aris's next shot. More splinters of glass flew off the creature's head.

From then on, it was a battle of attrition. The statue started making a point of keeping its cloak raised against Aris's fire. That just opened it up to Sheryl's powerful attacks, and Kelsey joined in as well, providing a withering barrage of fire from her "automatics." The shots mostly impacted the runic plates, turning the obsidian cape into a loose patchwork of plates and causing the spells to discharge harmlessly.

Mostly harmlessly. Anton had to remain planted right between the knight and Aris to keep it from attacking its greatest threat. The discharges weren't directed at him, but some of the magic managed to reach him. Anton was scoured by scourging sands, shocked by lightning, and burned by fire. It wasn't anything his Toughness couldn't handle, but he was feeling quite worn by the time a final shot shattered the statue's head.

> You have reached Level 11.
> Applying Benefits for Level 11
> Strength +1
> Toughness + 1
> Agility + 1
> Dexterity + 1
> Perception + 1
> Willpower + 1
> Charisma + 1
> Assign 2 free points.

Anton put the two points into Toughness, just to recognize how he'd depended on it in the last fight. He sighed and sank to the ground, belatedly realizing that he made a sound doing so. The oppressive silence was gone.

"Nice fight," Kelsey said, clapping. "Levels all round!"

Zaphar trailed along behind her. "Sorry, sorry I couldn't be of much use."

Anton shook his head. "Not much you could have done, and those blasts would have finished you."

"I don't seem to detect any concern for *my* well-being," Sheryl sniffed. "My dress is absolutely *ruined*."

The vampire had lost more than a dress. She was burned all over from fire blasts and was missing an arm from a lucky swing. She didn't seem to care, though.

"Yeah," Kelsey said, drawing air in between her teeth. "Why don't you head back and we'll get you fixed up."

"Feh!" the Queen snorted. "I was hoping for a feast, but I'll I've had so far is dry ash, glass, and shadows. Must I go back without even a drop of blood?"

"Yep," Kelsey said, holding out her hand. The vampire scowled, but took it and disappeared.

"There's still some fresh blood in that Ice Dragon," Kelsey said to no one in particular. "I think I'll decant some of it and see if she likes it."

"May I heal you, Lord Anton?" Tyla said, approaching him.

"Please," Anton said. "And please . . . leave off the Lord."

The elf blushed. "I'll try," she promised. She laid a hand on his shoulder, and Anton felt her magic running through him. "You are very durable, L—Anton. More than your armor, even."

Anton winced. "I'll need a new set after this."

"Dragonscale leather! Ice Ice version!" Kelsey called over.

In the meantime, Aris had opened the reward chest. She brought the contents back to the group.

"Look at it!" she said. "It's beautiful."

Kelsey glanced at it. "It's for Zaphar," she said.

"What? Why?" Aris asked, swirling the cloak around. It looked as though it was made of silk, shimmering between green and blue. Anton used *Delver's Discernment*.

Mantle of the Esoteric Entente, Clothing, Tier 4, Skybound, Trackless

"It lets you fly?" he guessed. "Why does that make it for Zaphar?"

"The name," Kelsey said. She was picking through the shards of shattered obsidian with a stick. "I doubt Zaphar's sligg girlfriend even knows what Esoteric Entente means."

"I'm not sure I do," Anton confessed.

"Secret Pact," Kelsey told him, not looking up from her scavenging. She kept on muttering to herself. "Tier Three obsidian isn't *nothing*, but I don't think I can even process it . . ."

"Flying sounds nice," Zaphar said cautiously. "As long as it isn't too high."

Aris pouted and passed it to him. "I doubt I'm allowed to wear it, anyway," she said. "It doesn't suit my *idiom*."

"What—what does that mean?" Zaphar asked, taking the mantle.

Aris shrugged. "It means I can't wear pretty clothes?" she said.

"You're beautiful the way you are," Anton said automatically. "But there are lots of pretty dresses waiting for you back in Suliel's—our—mansion."

Aris smiled at him, and Anton felt energy flowing back into his body.

"Let's get going," he said. "Kelsey, take that junk or leave it. We're pushing on . . . to the Tomb of Shattered Crowns."

The entrance to the seventeenth floor was a long staircase.

"Everyone take a stone potion," Anton said as they descended. Kelsey handed them out, and he swigged his down. It tasted of cold and grit, with a bitter metallic tang.

"What do these do? Zaphar asked.

"They stop you from turning into stone. There are basilisks down here, and they breathe a gas that turns you into stone." He didn't mention that the potions cost five gold each and they might need more than one. Apparently, his lordly finances could handle it.

Zaphar chugged his potion down.

"It lasts for one hour," Anton continued, "Or until you get a dose of the gas. So grab another one to have ready."

"Why does the next floor have a name?" Tyla asked.

"All of them have names," Anton said. "This one just stuck with me. It's called that because there are seven tombs—eight if you count the boss chamber. Each tomb is supposed to hold an ancient king, lost to history."

Kelsey snorted. "Made up," she said. "Those kings are from the catalogue, same as the rest."

"If you say so," Anton said non-committedly. "We don't have to go through every chamber, and each one will be a hard fight. The minimum path is five chambers, which is what I think we should take."

"What other monsters are there?" Aris asked.

"The kings will have servants, undead or ghosts," Anton said. "There are also monsters that roam between the crypts—the basilisks, but also animated chains. They wrap around you and force you to serve one of the kings."

Zaphar shuddered. "You—you got a potion for that?" he asked.

"Sorry, no," Anton said. "I've got *Chainbreaker*, though. I don't know how it works, so try not to make me test it."

"Stairs are leveling out," Kelsey reported. "Actually . . . Aris, can you put your light out?"

Aris did so with a shrug. In the resulting darkness, they could see a dim light ahead.

"First time for everything," Kelsey said. "But . . . it looks too dim to be of any use, so I guess we're still on light duty."

"Standard formation, everybody," Anton commanded. He looked at Kelsey. "Are we getting Sheryl back?"

Kelsey winced. "Ah, turns out that while Ice Dragon blood *is* tasty and *does* let a vampire heal, it also . . . freezes their insides. She'd going to need a little while to defrost. I can give you one of her lieutenants."

Anton grimaced as a lithe, dark-clad form appeared beside him. This wasn't the time to go in with a sub. Still, it was just a body to place between Aris and danger, so he supposed it was fine.

"Stay with me," he told the pale-skinned male figure.

"Yessss . . . I will stay . . . closssssse," the vampire whispered.

They came to the end of the stairs and entered what had once been an elaborately decorated hall. Now it was ruined. Tattered banners hung from the ceiling, tiled walls had been defaced, and some of the black marble slabs that made up the floor had been shattered. There was light that came from stained glass windows on the ceiling. They were intact but were blackened with dirt or smoke.

At the far end of the hall sat what Anton assumed was the dead King.

"Kneel, my servants," the dead King commanded. Anton felt a flash of magic go over the entire party.

Aris, Zaphar, and Tyla all knelt.

"Yes, my King," they all said in unison.

"Kill yourselves for my greater glory," the King commanded.

"Oh, come *on*!" Kelsey complained.

CHAPTER FIFTY-SIX

Master of Puppets

There wasn't a second to lose. Anton wrested the gun out of Aris's hand, just before she could hold it to her head. Kelsey pinned Tyla in some sort of complicated tangle of limbs, and the vampire grabbed Zaphar's wrists, preventing him from using his daggers.

Zaphar struggled in the vampire's grip, which only served to amuse it.

"How ironic!" it hissed. "You *want* to die, and I am forced to save you! Surely, if you begged enough, I might be able to disobey my orders and grant you death's sweet embrace."

"Oi! Enough of that," Kelsey ordered.

"Wretches!" the dead King shouted. "You think to defy me in front of my very throne! You will die horribly, traitors!"

Around the room, dead things stirred. Corpses started crawling out of alcoves. Insubstantial wights, glowing faintly green, started coming out of the walls.

Something stirred within Anton. His new trait was telling him that now was the time to use it. He opened his mouth and words came out.

"They *won't* die," he stated. His voice rang with conviction. "They *won't* serve you. Not my friends, not anyone that comes to this dry and dusty tomb."

Anton felt his words light a fire in his friends's hearts. They stopped struggling and looked at him. *Voice of Rebellion* didn't free them, but it strengthened them, bolstered their wills. That was enough. When it came down to it, the authority of a dead king was a thin, fragile, thing.

"Your rule is over!" he yelled, his voice ringing off the walls. Anton could feel his friends shrugging off the control, but his trait was not yet done.

"You are conquered, defeated, and long dead," he declared. "You won't stop us. No tyrant, no crown of bone, no curse carved in shadow will ever be enough to break us. We are free!"

As he spoke his final words, Anton felt the fire in his friends spread beyond them, filling the room with the spirit of rebellion. There was a short, silent pause.

Then a glowing, transparent wight launched itself at the King. A zombie tried to stop it, but it flowed right through the animated corpse, screaming its defiance.

Kelsey released Tyla and looked over the chaos that was filling the hall. "I don't know what I'm seeing, but I like it!" she declared.

It wasn't enough to win the fight for them. Even if all the undead thralls had managed to free themselves, they would have been no match for the King. Nor could the delvers take the side of the freed monsters; they were still monsters and all too eager to attack their liberators if given a chance.

In the end, they were just a distraction. However, distractions were lethal with Aris on the team. The delvers hung back from the chaos and let Aris pump *Deadly Shot* after *Deadly Shot* into the dead King. The few thralls that came their way were dealt with by the front line of Anton and the Vampire, with Zaphar and Tyla as backup for the insubstantial ones.

In his last moments, the King set off a pulse of dark magic that swirled around him. It had no effect on the few remaining thralls, and the delvers were far away.

"Death magic," Kelsey said. "Good thing we're nowhere near him."

She looked over at Anton. "Didja miss that bit about the mind control?"

Anton frowned. "It was mentioned that he—all of the Crypt Lords—try to command parties, but never that they succeeded."

"It might only work on third-tiers or below?" Aris suggested.

"That's probably right," Kelsey agreed. "There must not have been any delvers crazy enough to try this floor at Tier Three."

Anton gave her a sour look. "Or they didn't survive," he said.

"That, too!" she replied brightly.

"Did anyone level?" Anton asked and looked them over.

Aris Lucina, Level 24, Human, Deadeye Harbinger, Scullion/(Broken),
    Original Gunslinger/Deadeye Harbinger, S: 13 T: 23 A: 37 D: 37
    P: 41 W: 22 C: 21

Tyla of the Padascar Tribe, Level 23, Elf, Dungeon Wife, Padascar Hunter
    (Broken)/Doxy (Broken)/Apprentice Dungeon Witch/Dungeon
    Witch/Dungeon Wife, S: 13 T: 14 A: 18 D: 27 P: 33 W: 26 C: 19

Tyla had been a little embarrassed by her new class, but it was the next one on her path. Anton wondered what sort of traits she'd get.

Zaphar Alpashan, Level 23, Human, Fae-Touched Rogue, Thief/Burglar/ Fae-Touched Rogue, S: 11 T: 17 A: 38 D: 41 P: 24 W: 17 C: 14

Zaphar had picked up another trait that wouldn't be useful in the dungeon. *Vanish in the Crowd* needed . . . well, crowds, before it would become useful.

"So we have five more fights like that?" Zaphar asked. "I—I don't want to start every fight by stabbing myself. *Or* wrestling with a vampire."

"I think the effects of my speech are still on you guys?" Anton said hesitantly. It felt that way, at least. "We can see how long it lasts, and I'll use it again when it fades."

"Oh you should definitely use that speech thing at the start of all these tombs," Kelsey said gleefully. "The chaos was *delicious.*"

It wasn't that easy. For a start, there were the basilisks to get past in the tunnels between the tombs. The wandering chains made an appearance as well. Anton's *Chainbreaker* felt positively *gleeful* as he used it to shatter them. The chance to shatter enslavement magic *and* break a literal chain was right at the pinnacle of what that trait was supposed to do.

They managed to handle the other tombs in much the same way. Each king had a different form of magic, in addition to its command spell, which made things a little different. For the most part, smashing it from a distance while the servants were engaged in rebellion was effective. The one with Plant magic was a little more problematic until Tyla stepped up with her Fire magic.

They stopped for a break at the elaborately carved doors that led to the final chamber. Kelsey handed out food and drinks.

"Thanks for these," Anton said. "Not having to carry our own supplies has been a game changer."

"And no dried rations or trail bread," Kelsey said smugly. "All of it fresh from my kitchens."

They took a little time, but not too long. The end was so close, they could taste it. Soon enough, Anton started pushing on the great doors.

Beyond them was a short flight of stairs, leading down to a throne room of epic scale. A vaulted ceiling was held up with obsidian arches over a floor of black marble with silver veins running through it. Three shattered pillars lined each side of the room, glowing softly with a magical light. An identical pillar stood behind the throne which sat at the far end of the room. It was a misshapen thing, which looked to have been formed from fusing . . . some great number of things.

The boss was seated on the throne.

Obsidian Autarch, Level 36, Lich, Spellcaster, Vulnerable to Divine

It was hard to tell when he was seated, but Anton made him out to be at least nine feet tall. He wore a robe that looked as if it was formed out of volcanic glass. Above his head floated a crown with seven points.

He spoke, his voice resounding like the clanging of rusted chains and forgotten anthems.

"You come before me, mortals, to the center of my kingdom," he boomed. "Have you tired of life that you desire to stand beside me as one of my eternal servants?"

"No," Anton said, *Voice of Rebellion* springing to life as he stepped forward. "We've come to end your tyranny, to shatter the chains by which you have bound a nation."

It was a little embarrassing. Anton *knew* that that kingdom he was speaking of wasn't real, not even in the sense that it had existed. Its legend had been created out of whole cloth, along with the kings. But his trait seemed to relish the lore. It made him speak the words as if he was really facing an ancient king.

The rest of the frontline followed him down into the main section of the great hall. The Autarch was unimpressed.

"Another fool. Do you not know that even kings bow down before me? If you have not the wit to learn, then burn," he grated. A ball of fire flickered into life in his hand and he tossed it towards them with a dismissive sneer.

Tyla extinguished it with a wave of her hand and a grunt of effort. It was time—they were close enough. Anton dashed to the side.

Leaping Attack.

He flew through the air. He had the strength, now, to make truly spectacular leaps.

Chainbreaker.

His sword sank into the basalt column as though it were made of flesh. The Obsidian Autarch screamed.

"What have you done!" he yelled. Anton didn't answer; he was too busy making another *Leaping Attack.*

It had been a guess, but he thought this might work. The notes had explained that the Autarch could summon each of the Crypt Lords from the other tombs to fight for him. He didn't do this all at once, but as the fight progressed, if he was losing, he'd call for reinforcements.

There were seven tombs. Seven Crypt Lords. And seven pillars in the chamber. No one had ever worked out what the magic they held did—at least, not that was recorded in the notes.

Now he was rocketing across the hall, headed for another pillar. The Autarch snarled and threw lightning at him, but Tyla unraveled the spell before it reached him. The vampire and Zaphar were racing forward, hoping to prove a distraction to the spellcasting lich. Zaphar moved like quicksilver now. He was still lacking in offensive capability, but his dodging was insane.

Anton saw the flare of magic in the pillar was approaching and smiled. The dead kings were always summoned in the same order, and Anton had suspected they were each chained to a different pillar. That meant that the pillars had to be triggered in order. Before this one could finish its summon, Anton's sword cleaved a deep gash and *Chainbreaker* shattered the enchantment contained within.

The Autarch screamed again. Causing him pain was an unexpected bonus and might prove distraction enough . . .

The thunder of Aris's rifle was a sign that she felt the same way. The plan was for her to hold back until she had cover from the frontline, but the lich was in no condition to return her fire.

Anton leapt again, moving forward this time. The one he wanted would be one of the second row, so he had a fifty-fifty chance . . . there it was. Another flare.

Chainbreaker. Leaping Attack.

He had the pattern now. This was going to be easy.

Chainbreaker. Leaping—

Something smashed him out of the air like a bug.

"Impudent fool!" The Autarch yelled. A bullet smashed into his face.

Recovering quickly, Anton glanced over to where Tyla was. She was slumped to the ground, still alive but exhausted. Countering the Autarch's spells had taken it out of her, and he seemed to have an inexhaustible supply of mana. It must have been one of his spells that knocked Anton down.

Looking forward, Anton saw that Zaphar and the vampire had engaged the Autarch, dancing around the lich, their blades looking for an opening. They didn't find one. As Anton struggled to get his legs back under him, the vampire seemed to tire of using his blades. He darted in close, his fangs reaching for the lich's neck.

Do liches even have blood? Anton wondered. He didn't find out. A hand grabbed ahold of the vampire's face—and *squeezed.*

Anton looked away even as he heard Aris fire off another *Deadly Shot*, punishing the lich for his inattention.

Distraction, he thought. *I have a job to do.*

Leaping Attack.

He launched himself at the next pillar, keeping as low as possible. The magic was flaring on this one, but he still had time.

Chainbreaker. Another scream from the Autarch. Anton thought they might sound weaker now.

He leapt again, keeping an eye out for spells this time. The lich didn't disappoint, sending another fireball his way. Uncanny Evasion twisted him out of its path, but the lich snarled and detonated his spell.

Flames washed over him, but it wasn't a direct hit. It couldn't stop him.
Chainbreaker.

There was only one pillar left. Magic and flickering light started to surround it.

"No," the Autarch growled. His skull had been broken open, revealing a sickly green light inside. Half of his jaw was missing, but he didn't seem to need it to talk. "You cannot defeat me."

The lich was standing between Anton and the pillar, backed up against it, in fact. Anton couldn't leap towards it, so he just darted forward, as quickly as he could, while staying ready to dodge.

The Autarch held up a hand to protect him against Aris's next shot. It worked, but the hand was shattered into dust.

"I will defeat you," the lich grated. The flickering form of the final King started to gather itself, but a darting slash from Zaphar disrupted the ghostly figure.

The lich snarled as Anton drew closer. Green light gathered around his remaining hand, but then it faded. Anton glanced behind him to see that Tyla was back on her feet, clutching her core.

Anton swallowed. Part of him—his Heroic class, his *Voice of Rebellion,* maybe—wanted him to make a speech. Even though there was no need. This wasn't a real battle, against an evil king. It was just a construct.

This was just a stepping stone.

Leaping Attack.

To cover the move, he released the lightning from Stormfang. The lich screamed as the bolt smashed into him. Anton was already flinging himself forward, his sword thrusting ahead of him.

Chainbreaker.

Still under the effect of his lightning, the Obsidian Autarch *shattered,* along with the pillar behind him. Anton and Zaphar were flung back by the explosion.

The moment of silence was spoiled by the sound of basalt fragments clinking off the ceiling and walls. Anton let himself stay on the ground for a moment.

You have reached Level 12.
Applying Benefits for Level 12
Strength + 1
Toughness + 1
Agility + 1
Dexterity + 1
Perception + 1
Willpower + 1
Charisma + 1
Please assign 2 free points.

CHAPTER FIFTY-SEVEN

Push It

"**D**id you miss me?"

"No," Anton said flatly. He turned away from the Vampire Queen and went back to contemplating his available traits.

Available Traits: Iron March, Second Wind, Inescapable Grip

Anton had heard of two of them. *Inescapable* Grip was a generally useful trait for anyone who needed to hold a weapon. It wasn't as good as *Second Wind*, though. A surge of vitality just when you needed it the most was game-changing for a hero. However, between Tyla's healing and Kelsey's inexhaustible supplies, he didn't need it as much as most people would.

Anton thought about Iron March, and what the name implied. He thought about what they'd be facing on the next floor. He selected *Iron March*.

Sadly, Sheryl was not done pestering him. "I cannot believe that you would prefer his inferior skill and power to my own overpowering greatness."

Anton rolled his eyes. "You're only one level above him."

Only one level above me now, he realized. The Vampire Queen had been the definition of power for most of his life, and now he had almost surpassed her. Or had already, he supposed. He was faster, stronger, and tougher. She had tricks, but so did he . . .

The realization made him feel warm inside. It made him feel a little generous towards the monster that, for whatever reason, wanted his approval.

"Fine," he said. "You are a little less creepy than he was."

"*Well*," Sheryl said, smiling. "We all know why *that* is."

Anton blinked. "No," he said flatly. "A thousand times no."

"You're not fooling anybody," the vampire crooned. "You feel it, don't you? The lure of the forbidden, the excitement of mastering a dangerous monster. And all quite safe as long as you let my mistress *watch*."

"Kelsey," Anton grated.

"I don't kink-shame, Anton," Kelsey said with a chuckle. "However and with whomever people want to have sex is fine with me."

"Make it shut up," Anton insisted.

"Oh, fine," Kelsey said. "I suppose that's enough teasing. Are we ready for the final floor?"

Anton looked over at the others, who were nodding in agreement. He gave them one final check with *Delver's Discernment.*

Tyla of the Padascar Tribe, Level 24, Elf, Dungeon Wife, Padascar Hunter (Broken)/Doxy (Broken)/Apprentice Dungeon Witch/Dungeon Witch/Dungeon Wife, S: 14 T: 16 A: 21 D: 29 P: 35 W: 29 C: 21

Zaphar Alpashan, Level 24, Human, Fae-Touched Rogue, Thief/Burglar/ Fae-Touched Rogue, S: 11 T: 17 A: 40 D: 43 P: 25 W: 18 C: 15

Aris Lucina, Level 25, Human, Deadeye Harbinger, Scullion/(Broken), Original Gunslinger/Deadeye Harbinger, S: 14 T: 23 A: 39 D: 39 P: 43 W: 23 C: 22

He hoped Zaphar would be okay.

"All right," he told them. "The first thing you need to know is that this floor *does* come with a warning about mind control."

"So it's stronger than the Crypt Lords?" Aris asked in dismay.

"Maybe not," Kelsey said. "If this magic can affect fourth-tiers, then it might have some other disadvantage."

"Maybe," Anton agreed. "The notes didn't describe it as inescapable, so we should be able to resist it. I'll be using *Voice of Rebellion* as we go in, of course."

Sheryl laughed mockingly. "And us monsters will be able to save any frail humans that need rescuing from themselves."

"Right," Anton agreed. He paused, thinking of what to say next. "Moving on, the final floor is one big boss arena."

"Someone hasn't finished their final floor," Kelsey sang. Anton shrugged.

"It's a big cavern, and the Pale King sits on his throne at the far end," he said. "I hardly need to say that the entire cavern is shrouded in darkness, and there are lots of traps and chasms in the floor. There is a route through, but it means walking ten times the distance as you go back and forth."

"Is there another way?" Zaphar asked.

"For you, maybe," Anton said. "Your mantle lets you fly, so you can go over the obstacles. The notes say that works, but . . . the Pale King has a presence."

"What does that mean?" Aris asked.

"The notes say that it's a physical force that pushes you back and grinds you down," Anton said grimly. "The closer you get, the stronger it gets until it's all you can do to crawl forward. *That's* when the mind control strikes."

"So you need strength as well as willpower to approach him," Kelsey mused. "Well, Sheryl and I should be fine . . ."

Everyone looked at Zaphar.

"Yes, yes, I am the weakest in both these things," he said testily. "Perhaps I should stay behind?"

"Not unless it does become a problem," Anton declared. "I have some ideas . . . but we'll have to see what it's like in there before we try them. The only other warning I have is to stay as far away from the chasms as possible. Some of them will spawn monsters, others will try and drag you in."

"Charming," Kelsey commented. "Well, let's get this show on the road, shall we?"

Not every floor in this dungeon featured a large cavern with no light sources, but enough did that the moment felt familiar. Standing at the entrance, a short flight of three steps led down to a black marble floor that extended to the farthest range of their light source. It was only three steps, but each one dropped double the normal distance. Annoying, but not impassable.

"Kelsey, how far can your light reach?" Anton asked.

Not all the way across the cavern was the answer. Kelsey was able to pick up some of the hazards that lay ahead of them. There were signs of damage all across the floor. Broken flagstones and piles of rubble concealed traps, according to Anton's note, and some jagged scars of darkness must have been the chasms.

"It should go farther than that," Kelsey stated. "Something's blocking the light."

Anton nodded, noting the clear path that twisted through all the obstacles.

"It looks like . . . a hundred yards," he estimated. "The notes say the chamber is a hundred and fifty, so it gets two-thirds of the way. That shouldn't be too bad."

"Whatever you say, boss," Kelsey agreed. "Lead the way?"

Anton felt the weight as soon as he took the first step. He was unprepared for it and his foot came down much harder than he meant it to.

"Careful!" he exclaimed, "It hits right away."

He took the next steps, feeling the weight increase with each one, and then turned, ready to catch anyone who was taken unaware. Everyone made it down safely, though Zaphar grunted with the effort.

"This is just the start?" he asked. "At least it's flat all the way."

"I'm not sure that's the case," Anton said. It *looked* flat, but from what the notes had said . . .

Sure enough, it wasn't that easy. The pressure wasn't just a weight, it was a force pushing them back from the unseen Pale King. Even Kelsey and the vampire felt it, though from how Kelsey described it, there was a component that was passing them by.

Anton didn't feel it either, but Zaphar could feel the beginnings of an unreasoning fear. It wasn't strong enough to hold him back . . . yet, but this was only the first step of their journey.

Anton activated *Iron March* and was pleased to see that the trait lived up to expectations. *Unwavering* didn't do anything about the physical force he felt, but when he activated his new trait, he felt the weight on him lift.

"We can do this," he declared, refreshing *Voice of Rebellion*. We've made it this far and we're not going to stop. Not for anything. Stay close and call out if you get overwhelmed."

He pushed forward. Indomitable. Unrelenting. The others followed. If need be, he'd drag them behind him on a rope, but it hadn't come to that yet.

The first few traps were nothing to worry about. All you had to do was stay away from them. As they rounded the first turn and started to tack back across the hallway, they discovered the hidden danger from the unrelenting pressure.

Zaphar was the first to succumb. Anton was making constant checks behind him and caught the rogue drifting off course.

"Watch out!" he cautioned, grabbing the man. "We need to thread the needle here."

"Sorry, sorry," Zaphar apologized. "It's just . . . hard." He wasn't staggering just yet, and *Voice of Rebellion* was helping with the fear, but the grace was gone from his step.

"Not much farther," Anton said. "Just around the next corner, and there's something we can try.

It wasn't far, really. Just sixty, seventy yards. It wasn't a problem, but for everyone else, it might as well have been a mile uphill. Not impossible, but stressful nonetheless.

They rounded the corner, and the pressure intensified. Zaphar groaned.

"Buck up," Anton told him. "Kelsey, we're closer now. Can your light reach the back?"

Kelsey shone her light out without a word. There was some rubble blocking the line of sight, but she held the torch up high and angled it a bit. The Pale King was sitting on a throne on a dais about twenty feet higher than them. Anton knew this because he could see the pale giant sitting there. Kelsey's light was so dim at this distance that if the King hadn't been so pale, if his skin had been anything less than porcelain white, they wouldn't have been able to make him out.

It was enough. "Aris," Anton commanded.

"*Mark of Doom*," she said softly. It was her new trait. In the distance, the King gleamed just a hair brighter.

"I get it," Kelsey said. "You want to start things off from here."

"The King doesn't start throwing things at you until you get halfway," Anton replied. "Arrows fall short, even if you can see him at long distance. Guns, though . . ."

Kelsey nodded. "You'll want to aim high," she told Aris. "Use *Trick Shot* until you get the feel of it. And . . ."

She conjured a chair for Aris to sit on and a table for her to rest her rifle.

"Looks like we're taking it easy this run," Kelsey joked. "I'll get some sofas for the rest of you in a bit.

Aris didn't laugh. She was under too much strain. She sat down gratefully and took careful aim.

The *crack* of the gun was immediately followed by a deep roar of outrage. Aris probably wasn't doing too much damage yet, not if she was using *Trick Shot*. Although that might not be true with *Mark of Doom*. From what they'd managed to gather, the trait allowed Aris to mark one target for extra damage.

Aris must have switched to *Deadly Shot* for the second round, because the cry that came from the King was much more pained. He still didn't move from this throne, though. Kelsey kept the light fixed firmly on his unmoving form.

Another *crack*, another scream. Aris kept firing, pouring death onto the far-away dead King. Some critical point must have been passed, because on the fifth shot, the King stood up.

Normally, this wouldn't happen until you'd run the gauntlet and reached melee range. The reports Anton had read spoke of fighting past the traps, the pressure, and the King's overpowering will, only to be flung back with a swing of his giant crystal sword. He was coming for them now, charging into the light.

But at least for the moment, all that did was make him easier to hit. Aris fired again, shattering the hand that was held up in front of his face. He stepped into one of the chasms. For a human, that would have meant a short plummet to their deaths. For him, it was like tripping over a rabbit hole.

Still. Even easier to hit. Aris's shot slammed into his head and upper body as he struggled to free himself.

Kelsey switched out Aris's rifle with a loaded one.

The Pale King staggered back, free from his own trap. He fell and started crawling back to his throne. Aris had no mercy and shot him in the back.

He screamed this time, a scream full of rage and hate. Anton grabbed Zaphar and Tyla as they staggered back, their hands over their ears. The scream was so loud that it destabilized the ceiling above the King. Or maybe it had been rigged to fall. A thousand tons of rock fell, crashing down on the King and all around him. A hundred yards away, Anton *felt* the sound of it crashing through him.

Anton felt the pressure lift off him, the first sign that it was over. When the reverberations faded away and the dust settled, there was a huge pile of rock where the throne had been. Kelsey's light was stronger now, allowing them to pick up more details.

There was no sign of the King. Behind the throne, a dark hole gaped.

"I'm pretty sure that was cheating," Kelsey said. "I hope we don't get dinged by the referee."

CHAPTER FIFTY-EIGHT

No Way Back

TYLA

Tyla didn't think the dungeon was upset about the cheating. She didn't *look* upset.

"I got a level!" Aris exclaimed. She seemed surprised. Tyla couldn't imagine why. She'd just destroyed a monster more than ten levels higher than her, on her own. Tyla didn't have the context to judge just how impressive a feat that was, but she suspected it was extremely improbable.

But that was how the stories went—legends about Epic or Legendary class holders triumphing over impossible odds or achieving unimaginably difficult tasks. Tyla had never thought they were real, but now she found herself carried along in one.

She looked over at The Hungry Depths, watching the numen observe the party. The first trait of Tyla's new class was a perception one. *Dungeon Sight* let her . . . see as the dungeon saw, she supposed. There had been other options, but they hadn't resonated. Tyla had no need to track dungeons, or inspect them.

"That was amazing," Anton said, congratulating his wife. Tyla could hear the relief that flowed through his voice. They had won, and all that remained was to claim their reward and settle their deal.

The party picked their way through the ruined remains of the throne room. There were still traps and hazards to avoid, but it was so much easier without the terrible pressure that had borne down on them. The Hungry Depths kept an eye on them. Sometimes the human-sized sligg would walk or float to follow them; at other times, she just faded away and appeared farther ahead.

Tyla was fairly sure that the dungeon had noticed her staring, but the numen hadn't reacted in any way. Tyla was eager to ask about it, but they didn't have time for her to zone out with *Commune*.

The rubble had seemed to fall naturally from the ceiling with the Pale King's death, but it had been at least partially engineered. A pile of broken stone led up to the hole in the wall. Tyla didn't need to be told that the hole was where the core was. She felt a pull on her soul, leading her forward. The others didn't feel the same pull, but they could follow an obvious cue.

"Shouldn't there be a treasure chest?" Zaphar asked.

Anton shrugged. "Maybe it's under all the rubble," he said.

"It's ahead of us," Tyla stated. "I can feel it."

Anton gave her a searching look. Tyla wasn't sure what he saw, but he nodded. "Let's go then."

The climb was trivially easy, for most of them. Aris would have had the most trouble, but Anton just swept her off her feet and carried her up. His physical prowess was incredible. He could jump twenty feet while carrying Aris in his arms, and his landing was solid and sure-footed. Tyla couldn't replicate *that*, but she could scramble up a cliff face faster than some could run.

She only saw the chains when she got to the top. They flickered into being as she drew near the hole. Six silvery chains, as thick as her arm, stretched taunt, coming out of the hole and ascending into the darkness above her. She followed them with her eyes and then looked back at the numen.

For the first time, The Hungry Depths was looking back at her.

"Does everyone else see this?" Zaphar asked. "There's a light in there."

Tyla tore her gaze away to look into the hole. There was a light, and it was growing brighter.

"Come on," Anton said. He gently released Aris and let her lead them into the final chamber.

The light ahead of them grew to match the light-stone that Aris carried. It was a short tunnel, easily traversed since the others couldn't feel or see the chains that ran down the center. Tyla walked to the side, avoiding them. She thought about trying to touch them but balked at the idea. They felt cold and forbidding.

The tunnel opened up into a cubical room where every edge and corner was rounded. In the center of the room was a narrow plinth, and floating above it was the core.

Or so it must appear to the others. To Tyla, it was apparent that the core wasn't floating. It was wrapped so tightly and so completely with chains that it rested six inches off the plinth.

"Now what?" Aris asked, looking around the plain room.

The sligg avatar drifted ahead of them, placing herself so that her belly was superimposed over the core. She looked down on them all, her face expressionless. Or, at least, not an expression that Tyla could read.

Anton was looking at the core. "I can see magic around it," he said. "But I can't tell if that's just the core, a controlling enchantment, or just the spell that holds it up."

"Heck if I know," Kelsey said, peering at the core as well. "You normally use *Chainbreaker* by hitting the thing with your sword, right? I'm gonna suggest you *don't* give the core a chop."

"The chains are there," Tyla said, pointing. "They run from the core through the tunnel—right through Zaphar."

Zaphar gaped at her and then stepped to one side. "Why didn't you tell me I had magic running through me?" he complained.

Anton looked at where she indicated. "I see magic," he admitted, "But it looks pretty much the same as the rest of the magic that's strung about the place."

"That is the chain," Tyla insisted.

"It feels weird, slicing at empty air," Anton grumbled.

"It's not like you've got charges on it," Kelsey said. "And it's better than stabbing a core. Nine out of ten dentists *do not* recommend."

Anton shook his head with bemusement and drew his sword. He glanced around the room, making sure no one was going to stumble into his strike.

"*Chainbreaker,*" he said softly. The word still carried. It echoed in Tyla's ears as he struck the blow.

As Tyla saw it, the sword embedded itself in the chains. To the others, it must have seemed that it halted in midair. For a moment, Tyla thought that the trait had failed, that it wasn't enough to sever the chains that bound the numen.

Then fire started to spread from the point of contact. Blue and yellow flames spluttered to life along the links.

Exclamations from the other onlookers told her that the rest of her party was seeing at least some of this.

"What do you see?" she asked.

"The light," Aris answered. "It flickers like flames and it goes all the way outside."

"The chains are burning," Tyla told her. "They—" She cut off when she saw that the flames had reached the other end of the chains. They now engulfed the core. The numen stayed where she was, the fire licking at the chains within her belly, making it look as if she was being consumed.

She didn't seem bothered, though. The fire continued to burn until the chains were gone. Anton's sword was released from whatever held it, almost knocking him off balance as it swung free.

There was a grinding sound as a chest rose into view.

"Was that . . . it?" Anton asked.

"The chains are gone," Tyla confirmed.

"What's in the chest?" Kelsey asked. "Aris should open it; she did all the hard work."

"Sure," Aris said and went over. Opening it and looking in, she frowned. "This seems a little inappropriate?" she said uncertainly. "Anton is only a baron."

"What is it?" Anton asked.

Aris shrugged and pulled the item out. It was . . .

Anton made a strangled sound, choked up on his own words.

"A crown?" Kelsey asked. "Seems impractical. And what—"

She frowned. "*False* Crown? Powers are . . . *Layers of Deceit* and *False Identification*? What *is* this?"

Anton managed to get his words back.

"It's the same as the crown the King wears," he managed to say.

Kelsey looked at him, and then back at the crown. "Ooooh," she said slowly. "Did you get a chance to use *Discernment* on the one on his head?"

Anton shook his head. "No, but I'd wager that it can disguise its own identification when it's being worn."

"True," Kelsey admitted. "I guess we have our answer."

"Do—do you think we can use that as evidence?" Zaphar asked. "Or is it just a death sentence if we're caught with it?"

"What?" Aris said, looking down at the crown in alarm. "A death sentence? Why?"

"A king isn't going to like us having a copy of his crown," Zaphar told her. "Even without the whole fake king thing. If someone puts it on, are they a king?"

"No," Anton said. "It's just symbolic . . . I think. You'd need a lot more to pretend to the throne."

"Suliel agrees," Kelsey said. "And she says that while it's not an automatic death sentence, anyone in a position of authority is going to have some very pointed questions if they find out about it."

She held out her hand. "I can take care of it," she said. "We're going to have to be very careful who we show this to."

Aris nodded and handed it over then looked at Anton. "So this is it?" she asked. "We got what we came for?"

Anton nodded slowly. "The levels and items are nothing to sneeze at," he argued, "but this is why we're here."

"Don't forget the mundane resources!" Kelsey put in. "Why, this expedition has finally put Operation Fund Anton's Crazy Adventures in the black!"

Anton glared at her. "You say that as if you weren't the instigator for nearly all of this."

"Hey, I was a willing investor, sure. But every investor looks forward to the point at which we start making a profit."

"I think he's referring to the Crazy part," Zaphar put in.

"What? Crazy is good! Don't object to that—own it!"

Kelsey grinned wildly. Then she dropped the expression, changing moods in an instant.

"Anyway, we may have gotten what we came for, but we're not done. Not by a long shot. We have to get out, get out of town, and contact the Rose Circle. Muggins here—"

She pointed at the core so they all knew who she was talking about.

"—might be free, but somewhere upstairs a member of the Wizards Guild is wondering why his spell broke. They're gonna come for you, kid."

For the first time, an expression appeared on the sligg avatar's face. A frown. Unaware, Kelsey ploughed on.

"Tyla, you need to go under and get a verbal confirmation of what this—" She waved the crown before making it disappear. "—means. While you're there, get her to open up the secret passage that takes us back to the top."

"How do you know there's a secret passage?" Anton asked.

"Pstbh! As if High Wizard Muckity Muck is gonna go through this gauntlet every time he wants to visit."

"I guess," Anton turned to Tyla. "Let her know that we consider her our ally in this."

"She can hear what you say," Tyla pointed out. Anton nodded.

"Just make sure she understands. We're going to be out of the city for months, at least, so there won't be much aid we can give her. If there's something she needs from us, she should let us know, now."

"Is that all?" Tyla asked.

"I think so," Anton said. Tyla walked up to the plinth. It felt audacious, bordering on disrespectful to *Commune* with the core itself, but Tyla was feeling bold. At least the avatar made no move to dissuade her.

Going into the formless void was jarring this time, mainly because the numen had been right in front of her and was now five paces away.

"The passage needs to be destroyed," the numen said.

"Can it be destroyed after we use it?" Tyla asked.

The Hungry Depths frowned. "I suppose so. Verbal confirmation means that you want me to tell you what you already know."

"I suppose so, yes."

"Then. Your Ranon Kalond came here, many times. At first, he was a Prince, then a False King. Then Teleran Vaust made me give him that crown."

Tyla made a note of the name. She was sure he was a prominent guild member, but she'd have to ask Anton or Suliel.

"Thank you for clarifying," she said.

"As for what your man said, speaking words that bind without binding, there is nothing I need. I am aware that the wizards will come. I will fight them."

"Um," Tyla said, blushing. "Lord Anton is not my man."

"Is he not?" The numen cocked her head. "He does not breed you?"

"He does not," Tyla managed to say. "He is married to Lady Aris."

The Hungry Depths stepped closer, observing her. "You do what he says, though. He binds you with words that do not bind."

"I follow him, yes, but not *that* way!"

"He is strong . . ." the numen said consideringly. "If he desired to breed you, you could not resist. But would you?"

Tyla was blushing furiously now. "He . . . would not do such a thing. The laws of his people and mine prevent it."

"But would you? Prevent it?"

Tyla didn't answer. The Hungry Depths stepped back.

"Interesting. You can go now."

The world faded back in around her, and she repeated to the others what she'd been told. All the *relevant* parts, anyway.

"So where's the exit?" Kelsey asked.

The avatar pointed and a spell circle lit up at the back of the room.

"Perfect," Kelsey said. "Now, let's run like we stole something."

About the Author

Christopher Hall, also known as Maxlex, is the author of the Phantasm series. Hall started writing his first novel while sailing the Tyrrhenian Sea one summer, the salty night air flavoring and enriching his worldbuilding. Since then, he has continued to hone his craft while holding down diverse jobs in metalworking, marketing, perfume sales, and briefly, modeling. In addition to writing, Hall's interests include illuminated lettering and artisanal brewing. He endeavors to convey a sense of l'esprit in all his creative pursuits.

RESPAWN YOUR CURIOSITY

follow us on our socials

 podiumentertainment.com

 @podiumentertainment

 /podiumentertainment

 @podium_ent

 @podiumentertainment